LADY CONNIE

A Novel

Mary A. Ward

DOVER PUBLICATIONS
Garden City, New York

This Dover edition, first published in 2025, is an unabridged republication of the work, first published by Hearst's International Library Co., New York, in 1916.

Library of Congress Cataloging-in-Publication Data

Names: Ward, Humphry, Mrs., 1851–1920 author
Title: Lady Connie : a novel / Mary A. Ward.
Description: Dover edition. | Garden City, New York : Dover Publications, 2025. | Series: Dover romance | "This Dover edition, first published in 2025, is an unabridged republication of the work, first published by Hearst's International Library Co., New York, in 1916."—Title page verso. | Summary: "Lady Constance Bledlow, recently orphaned, moves to Oxford to live with her aunt and uncle. Wealthy and privileged yet naïve, she navigates class distinctions and gender dynamics and challenges societal norms while seeking independence. Amid romance and self-discovery, she confronts her past to define her desires"—Provided by publisher.
Identifiers: LCCN 2025012329 | ISBN 9780486855684 trade paperback
Subjects: LCGFT: Fiction | Novels
Classification: LCC PR5714 .L33 2025 | DDC 823/.8—dc23/eng/20250528
LC record available at https://lccn.loc.gov/2025012329

Publisher: Betina Cochran
Acquisitions Editor: Allyson D'Antonio
Managing Editorial Supervisor: Susan Rattiner
Senior Production Editor: Michael Croland
Cover Designer: Peter Donahue
Creative Manager: Marie Zaczkiewicz
Production: Pam Weston, Tammi McKenna, Ayse Yilmaz

Printed in India
85568601 2025
www.doverpublications.com

PART I

I

"WELL, NOW we've done all we can, and all I mean to do," said Alice Hooper, with a pettish accent of fatigue. "Everything's perfectly comfortable, and if she doesn't like it, we can't help it. I don't know why we make such a fuss."

The speaker threw herself with a gesture of fatigue into a dilapidated basket-chair that offered itself. It was a spring day, and the windows of the old schoolroom in which she and her sister were sitting were open to a back garden, untidily kept, but full of fruit-trees just coming into blossom. Through their twinkling buds and interlacing branches could be seen grey college walls—part of the famous garden front of St. Cyprian's College, Oxford. There seemed to be a slight bluish mist over the garden and the building, a mist starred with patches of white and dazzlingly green leaf. And, above all, there was an evening sky, peaceful and luminous, from which a light wind blew towards the two girls sitting by the open window. One, the elder, had a face like a Watteau sketch, with black velvety eyes, hair drawn back from a white forehead, delicate little mouth, with sharp indentations at the corners, and a small chin. The other was much more solidly built—a girl of seventeen, in a plump phase, which however an intelligent eye would have read as not likely to last; a complexion of red and brown tanned by exercise; an expression in her clear eyes which was alternately frank and ironic; and an inconvenient mass of golden brown hair.

"We make a fuss, my dear," said the younger sister, "because we're bound to make a fuss. Connie, I understand, is to pay us a good round sum for her board and lodging, so it's only honest she should have a decent room."

"Yes, but you don't know what she'll call decent," said the other rather sulkily. "She's probably been used to all sorts of silly luxuries."

"Why of course, considering Uncle Risborough was supposed to have twenty-odd thousand a year. We're paupers, and she's got to put up with us. But we couldn't take her money and do nothing in return."

Nora Hooper looked rather sharply at her sister. It fell to her in the family to be constantly upholding the small daily traditions of honesty and fair play. It was she who championed the servants, or insisted, young as she was, on bills being paid, when it would have been more agreeable to buy frocks and go to London for a theatre. She was a great power in the house, and both her languid, incompetent mother, and her pretty sister were often afraid of her. Nora was a "Home Student," and had just begun to work seriously for English Literature Honours. Alice on the other hand was the domestic and social daughter. She helped her mother in the house, had a head full of undergraduates, and regarded the "Eights" week and Commemoration as the shining events of the year.

Both girls were however at one in the uneasy or excited anticipation with which they were looking forward that evening to the arrival of a newcomer, who was, it seemed, to make part of the household for some time. Their father, Dr. Ewen Hooper, the holder of a recently founded classical readership, had once possessed a younger sister of considerable beauty, who, in the course of an independent and adventurous career, had captured—by no ignoble arts—a widower, who happened to be also an earl and a rich man. It happened while they were both wintering at Florence, the girl working at paleography, in the Ambrosian Library, while Lord Risborough, occupying a villa in the neighbourhood of the Torre San Gallo, was giving himself to the artistic researches and the cosmopolitan society which suited his health and his tastes. He was a dilettante of the old sort, incurably in love with living, in spite of the loss of his wife, and his only son; in spite also of an impaired heart—in the physical sense—and various other drawbacks. He came across the bright girl student, discovered that she could talk very creditably about manuscripts and illuminations, gave her leave to work in his own library, where he possessed a few priceless things, and presently found her company, her soft voice, and her eager, confiding eyes quite indispensable. His elderly sister, Lady Winifred, who kept house for him, frowned on the business in vain; and finally departed in a huff to join another maiden sister, Lady Marcia, in an English country *ménage,* where for some years she did little but lament the flesh-pots of Italy—Florence. The married sister, Lady Langmoor, wrote reams of plaintive remonstrances which remained unanswered. Lord Risborough married the girl student, Ella Hooper, and never regretted it. They had one daughter, to whom they devoted themselves—preposterously, their friends thought; but for twenty years, they were three happy people together. Then virulent influenza, complicated with pneumonia, carried off the mother during a spring visit to Rome, and six weeks later Lord Risborough died of the damaged heart which had held out so long.

The daughter, Lady Constance Bledlow, had been herself attacked by the influenza epidemic which had killed her mother, and the double blow of her parents' deaths, coming on a neurasthenic condition, had hit her youth rather hard. Some old friends in Rome, with the full consent of her guardian, the Oxford Reader, had carried her off, first to Switzerland, and then to the Riviera for the winter, and now in May, about a year after the death of her parents, she was coming for the first time to make acquaintance with the Hooper family, with whom, according to her father's will, she was to make her home till she was twenty-one. None of them had ever seen her, except on two occasions; once, at a hotel in London; and once, some ten years before this date, when Lord Risborough had been D.C.L-ed at the Encænia, as a reward for some valuable gifts which he had made to the Bodleian, and he, his wife, and his little girl, after they had duly appeared at the All Souls' luncheon, and the official fête in St. John's Gardens, had found their way to the house in Holywell, and taken tea with the Hoopers.

Nora's mind, as she and her sister sat waiting for the fly in which Mrs. Hooper had gone to meet her husband's niece at the station, ran persistently on her own childish recollections of this visit. She sat in the window-sill, with her hand behind her, chattering to her sister.

"I remember thinking when Connie came in here to tea with us—'What a stuck-up thing you are!' And I despised her, because she couldn't climb the mulberry in the garden, and because she hadn't begun Latin. But all the time, I envied her horribly, and I expect you did too, Alice. Can't you see her black silk stockings—and her new hat with those awfully pretty flowers, made of feathers? She had a silk frock too—white, very skimp, and short; and enormously long black legs, as thin as sticks; and her hair in plaits. I felt a thick lump beside her. And I didn't like her at all. What horrid toads children are! She didn't talk to us much, but her eyes seemed to be always laughing at us, and when she talked Italian to her mother, I thought she was showing off, and I wanted to pinch her for being affected."

"Why, of course she talked Italian," said Alice, who was not much interested in her sister's recollections.

"Naturally. But that didn't somehow occur to me. After all I was only seven."

"I wonder if she's really good-looking," said Alice slowly, glancing, as she spoke, at the reflection of herself in an old dilapidated mirror, which hung on the schoolroom wall.

"The photos are," said Nora decidedly. "Goodness, I wish she'd come and get it over. I want to get back to my work—and till she comes, I can't settle to anything."

"Well, they'll be here directly. I wonder what on earth she'll do with all her money. Father says she may spend it, if she wants to. He's trustee, but Uncle Risborough's letter to him said she was to have the income if she wished—*now*. Only she's not to touch the capital till she's twenty-five."

"It's a good lot, isn't it?" said Nora, walking about. "I wonder how many people in Oxford have two thousand a year? A girl too. It's really rather exciting."

"It won't be very nice for us—she'll be so different." Alice's tone was a little sulky and depressed. The advent of this girl cousin, with her title, her good looks, her money, and her unfair advantages in the way of talking French and Italian, was only moderately pleasant to the eldest Miss Hooper.

"What—you think she'll snuff us out?" laughed Nora. "Not she! Oxford's not like London. People are not such snobs."

"What a silly thing to say, Nora! As if it wasn't an enormous pull everywhere to have a handle to your name, and lots of money!"

"Well, I really think it'll matter less here than anywhere. Oxford, my dear—or some of it—pursues 'the good and the beautiful' "—said Nora, taking a flying leap on to the window-sill again, and beginning to poke up some tadpoles in a jar, which stood on the window-ledge.

Alice did not think it worth while to continue the conversation. She had little or nothing of Nora's belief in the other-worldliness of Oxford. At this period, some thirty odd years ago, the invasion of Oxford on the north by whole new tribes of citizens had already begun. The old days of University exclusiveness in a ring fence were long done with; the days of much learning and simple ways, when there were only two carriages in Oxford that were not doctors' carriages, when the wives of professors and tutors went out to dinner in "chairs" drawn by men, and no person within the magic circle of the University knew anybody—to speak of—in the town outside. The University indeed, at this later moment, still more than held its own, socially, amid the waves of new population that threatened to submerge it; and the occasional spectacle of retired generals and colonels, the growing number of broughams and victorias in the streets, or the rumours of persons with "smart" or "county" connections to be found among the rows of new villas spreading up the Banbury Road were still not sufficiently marked to disturb the essential character of the old and beautiful place. But new ways and new manners were creeping in, and the young were sensitively aware of them, like birds that feel the signs of coming weather.

Alice fell into a brown study. She was thinking about a recent dance given at a house in the Parks, where some of her particular friends had been present, and where, on the whole, she had enjoyed herself greatly. Nothing is ever perfect, and she would have liked it better if Herbert Pryce's sister had not—past all denying—had more partners and a greater success than herself, and if Herbert Pryce himself had not been—just a little—casual and inattentive. But after all they had had two or three glorious supper dances, and he certainly would have kissed her hand, while they were sitting out in the garden, if she had not made haste to put it out of his reach. "You never did anything of the kind till you were sure he did not mean to kiss it!" said conscience. "I did not give myself away in the least!"—was vanity's angry reply. "I was perfectly dignified."

Herbert Pryce was a young fellow and tutor—a mathematical fellow; and therefore, Alice's father, for whom Greek was the only study worth the brains of a rational being, could not be got to take the smallest interest in him. But he was certainly very clever, and it was said he was going to get a post at Cambridge—or something at the Treasury—which would enable him to marry. Alice suddenly had a vague vision of her own wedding; the beautiful central figure—she would certainly look beautiful in her wedding dress!—bowing so gracefully; the bridesmaids behind, in her favourite colours, white and pale green; and the tall man beside her. But Herbert Pryce was not really tall, and not particularly good-looking, though he had a rather distinguished hatchet face, with a good forehead. Suppose Herbert and Vernon and all her other friends, were to give up being "nice" to her as soon as Connie Bledlow appeared? Suppose she was going to be altogether cut out and put in the background? Alice had a kind of uneasy foreboding that Herbert Pryce would think a title "interesting."

Meanwhile Nora, having looked through an essay on "Piers Plowman," which she was to take to her English Literature tutor on the following day, went aimlessly upstairs and put her head into Connie's room. The old house was panelled, and its guestroom, though small and shabby, had yet absorbed from its oaken walls, and its outlook on the garden and St. Cyprian's, a certain measure of the Oxford charm. The furniture was extremely simple—a large hanging cupboard made by curtaining one of the panelled recesses of the wall, a chest of drawers, a bed, a small dressing-table and glass, a carpet that was the remains of one which had originally covered the drawing-room for many years, an armchair, a writing-table, and curtains which having once been blue had now been dyed a serviceable though ugly dark red. In Nora's eyes it was all comfortable and nice. She herself had insisted on having the carpet and curtains redipped, so that they really looked almost new, and the one mattress on the bed "made over"; she had brought up the armchair, and she had gathered the cherry-blossoms, which stood on the mantelpiece shining against the darkness of the walls. She had also hung above it a photograph of Watts's "Love and Death." Nora looked at the picture and the flowers with a throb of pleasure. Alice never noticed such things.

And now what about the maid? Fancy bringing a maid! Nora's sentiments on the subject were extremely scornful. However Connie had simply taken it for granted, and she had been housed somehow. Nora climbed up an attic stair and looked into a room which had a dormer window in the roof, two strips of carpet on the boards, a bed, a washing-stand, a painted chest of drawers, a table, with an old looking-glass, and two chairs. "Well, that's all I have!" thought Nora defiantly. But a certain hospitable or democratic instinct made her go downstairs again and bring up a small vase of flowers like those in Connie's room, and put it on the maid's table. The maid was English, but she had lived a long time abroad with the Risboroughs.

Sounds! Yes, that was the fly stopping at the front door! Nora flew downstairs, in a flush of excitement. Alice too had come out into the hall, looking shy and uncomfortable. Dr. Hooper emerged from his study. He was a big, loosely built man, with a shock of grizzled hair, spectacles, and a cheerful expression.

A tall, slim girl, in a grey dust-cloak and a large hat, entered the dark panelled hall, looking round her. "Welcome, my dear Connie!" said Dr. Hooper, cordially, taking her hand and kissing her. "Your train must have been a little late."

"Twenty minutes!" said Mrs. Hooper, who had followed her niece into the hall. "And the draughts in the station, Ewen, were something appalling."

The tone was fretful. It had even a touch of indignation as though the speaker charged her husband with the draughts. Mrs. Hooper was a woman between forty and fifty, small and plain, except for a pair of rather fine eyes, which, in her youth, while her cheeks were still pink, and the obstinate lines of her thin slit mouth and prominent chin were less marked, had beguiled several lovers, Ewen Hooper at their head.

Dr. Hooper took no notice of her complaints. He was saying to his niece—"This is Alice, Constance—and Nora! You'll hardly remember each other again, after all these years."

"Oh, yes, I remember quite well," said a clear, high-pitched voice. "How do you do?—how do you do?"

And the girl held a hand out to each cousin in turn. She did not offer to kiss either Alice or Nora. But she looked at them steadily, and suddenly Nora was aware of that expression of which she had so vivid although so childish a recollection—as though a satiric spirit sat hidden and laughing in the eyes, while the rest of the face was quite grave.

"Come in and have some tea. It's quite ready," said Alice, throwing open the drawing-room door. Her face had cleared suddenly. It did not seem to her, at least in the shadows of the hall, that her cousin Constance was anything of a beauty.

"I'm afraid I must look after Annette first. She's much more important than I am!"

And the girl ran back to where a woman in a blue serge coat and skirt was superintending the carrying in of the luggage. There was a great deal of luggage, and Annette, who wore a rather cross, flushed air, turned round every now and then to look frowningly at the old gabled house into which it was being carried, as though she were more than doubtful whether the building would hold the boxes. Yet as houses went, in the older parts of Oxford, Medburn House, Holywell, was roomy.

"Annette, don't do any unpacking till after tea!" cried Lady Constance. "Just get the boxes carried up, and rest a bit. I'll come and help you later."

The maid said nothing. Her lips seemed tightly compressed. She stepped into the hall, and spoke peremptorily to the white-capped parlourmaid who stood bewildered among the trunks.

"Have those boxes——" she pointed to four—two large American Saratogas, and two smaller trunks—"carried up to her ladyship's room. The other two can go into mine."

"Miss!" whispered the agitated maid in Nora's ear, "we'll never get any of those boxes up the top-stairs. And if we put them four into her ladyship's room, she'll not be able to move."

"I'll come and see to it," said Nora, snatching up a bag. "They've got to go somewhere!"

Mrs. Hooper repeated that Nora would manage it, and languidly waved her niece towards the drawing-room. The girl hesitated, laughed, and finally yielded, seeing that Nora was really in charge. Dr. Hooper led her in, placed an armchair for her beside the tea-table, and stood closely observing her.

"You're like your mother," he said, at last, in a low voice; "at least in some points." The girl turned away abruptly, as though what he said jarred, and addressed herself to Alice.

"Poor Annette was very sick. It was a vile crossing."

"Oh, the servants will look after her," said Alice indifferently.

"Everybody has to look after Annette!—or she'll know the reason why," laughed Lady Constance, removing her black gloves from a very small and slender hand. She was dressed in deep mourning with crape still upon her hat and dress, though it was more than a year since her mother's death. Such mourning was not customary in Oxford, and Alice Hooper thought it affected.

Mrs. Hooper then made the tea. But the newcomer paid little attention to the cup placed beside her. Her eyes wandered round the group at the tea-table, her uncle, a man of originally strong physique, marred now by the student's stoop, and by weak eyes, tried by years of Greek and German type; her aunt—

"What a very odd woman Aunt Ellen is!" thought Constance.

For, all the way from the station, Mrs. Hooper had talked about scarcely anything but her own ailments, and the Oxford climate. "She told us all about her rheumatisms—and the east winds—and how she ought to go to Buxton every year—only Uncle Hooper wouldn't take things seriously. And she never asked us anything at all about our passage, or our night journey! And there was Annette—as yellow as an egg—and as *cross*——"

However Dr. Hooper was soon engaged in making up for his wife's shortcomings. He put his niece through many questions as to the year which had elapsed since her parent's death; her summer in the high Alps, and her winter at Cannes.

"I never met your friends—Colonel and Mrs. King. We are not military in Oxford. But they seem—to judge from their letters—to be very nice people," said the Professor, his tone, quite unconsciously, suggesting the slightest shade of patronage.

"Oh, they're dears," said the girl warmly. "They were awfully good to me."

"Cannes was very gay, I suppose?"

"We saw a great many people in the afternoons. The Kings knew everybody. But I didn't go out in the evenings."

"You weren't strong enough?"

"I was in mourning," said the girl, looking at him with her large and brilliant eyes.

"Yes, yes, of course!" murmured the Reader, not quite understanding why he felt himself a trifle snubbed. He asked a few more questions, and his niece, who seemed to have no shyness, gave a rapid description, as she sipped her tea, of the villa at Cannes in which she had passed the winter months, and of the half dozen families, with whom she and her friends had been mostly thrown. Alice Hooper was secretly thrilled by some of the names which dropped out casually. She always read the accounts in the *Queen*, or the *Sketch*, of "smart society" on the Riviera, and it was plain to her that Constance had been dreadfully "in it." It would not apparently have been possible to be more "in it." She was again conscious of a hot envy of her cousin which made her unhappy. Also Connie's good looks were becoming more evident. She had taken off her hat, and all the distinction of her small head, her slender neck and sloping shoulders, was more visible; her self-possession, too, the ease and vivacity of her gestures. Her manner was that of one accustomed to a large and varied world, who took all things without surprise, as they came. Dr. Hooper had felt some emotion, and betrayed some, in this meeting with his sister's motherless child; but the girl's only betrayal of feeling had lain in the sharpness with which she had turned away from her uncle's threatened effusion. "And how she looks at us!" thought Alice. "She looks at us through and through. Yet she doesn't stare."

But at that moment Alice heard the word "prince," and her attention was instantly arrested.

"We had some Russian neighbours," the newcomer was saying; "Prince and Princess Jaroslav; and they had an English party at Christmas. It was great fun. They used to take us out riding into the mountains, or into Italy." She paused a moment, and then said carelessly—as though to keep up the conversation—"There was a Mr. Falloden with them—an under-graduate at Marmion College, I think. Do you know him, Aunt Ellen?" She turned towards her aunt.

But Mrs. Hooper only looked blank. She was just thinking anxiously that she had forgotten to take her tabloids after lunch, because Ewen had hustled her off so much too soon to the station.

"I don't think we know him," she said vaguely, turning towards Alice.

"We know all about him. He was introduced to me once."

The tone of the eldest Miss Hooper could scarcely have been colder. The eyes of the girl opposite suddenly sparkled into laughter.

"You didn't like him?"

"Nobody does. He gives himself such ridiculous airs."

"Does he?" said Constance. The information seemed to be of no interest to her. She asked for another cup of tea.

"Oh, Falloden of Marmion?" said Dr. Hooper. "I know him quite well. One of the best pupils I have. But I understand he's the heir to his old uncle, Lord Dagnall, and is going to be enormously rich. His father's a millionaire already. So of course he'll soon forget his Greek. A horrid waste!"

"He's detested in college!" Alice's small face lit up vindictively. "There's a whole set of them. Other people call them 'the bloods.' The dons would like to send them all down."

"They won't send Falloden down, my dear, before he gets his First in Greats, which he will do this summer. But this is his last term. I never knew any one write better Greek iambics than that fellow," said the Reader, pausing in the middle of his cup of tea to murmur certain Greek lines to himself. They were part of the brilliant copy of verses by which Douglas Falloden of Marmion, in a fiercely contested year, had finally won the Ireland, Ewen Hooper being one of the examiners.

"That's what's so abominable," said Alice, setting her small mouth. "You don't expect reading men to drink, and get into rows."

"Drink?" said Constance Bledlow, raising her eyebrows.

Alice went into details. The dons of Marmion, she said, were really frightened by the spread of drinking in college, all caused by the bad example of the Falloden set. She talked fast and angrily, and her cousin listened, half scornfully, but still attentively.

"Why don't they keep him in order?" she said at last. "We did!" And she made a little gesture with her hand, impatient and masterful, as though dismissing the subject.

And at that moment Nora came into the room, flushed either with physical exertion, or the consciousness of her own virtue. She found a place at the tea-table, and panting a little demanded to be fed.

"It's hungry work, carrying up trunks!"

"You didn't!" exclaimed Constance, in large-eyed astonishment. "I say, I am sorry! Why did you? I'm sure they were too heavy. Why didn't Annette get a man?"

And sitting up, she bent across the table, all charm suddenly, and soft distress.

"We did get one, but he was a wretched thing. I was worth two of him," said Nora triumphantly. "You should feel my biceps. There!"

And slipping up her loose sleeve, she showed an arm, at which Constance Bledlow laughed. And her laugh touched her face with something audacious—something wild—which transformed it.

"I shall take care how I offend you!"

Nora nodded over her tea.

"Your maid was shocked. She said I might as well have been a man."

"It's quite true," sighed Mrs. Hooper. "You always were such a tomboy, Nora."

"Not at all! But I wish to develop my muscles. That's why I do Swedish exercises every morning. It's ridiculous how flabby girls are. There isn't a girl in my lecture I can't put down. If you like, I'll teach you my exercises," said Nora, her mouth full of tea-cake, and her expression half friendly, half patronising.

Connie Bledlow did not immediately reply. She seemed to be quietly examining Nora, as she had already examined Alice, and that odd gleam in the eyes under depths appeared again. But at last she said, smiling—

"Thank you. But my muscles are quite strong enough for the only exercise I want. You said I might have a horse, Uncle Ewen, didn't you?" She turned eagerly to the master of the house.

Dr. Hooper looked at his wife with some embarrassment. "I want you to have anything you wish for—in reason—my dear Connie; but your aunt is rather exercised about the proprieties."

The small dried-up woman behind the tea-urn said sharply:

"A girl can't ride alone in Oxford—she'd be talked about at once!"

Lady Connie flushed mutinously.

"I could take a groom, Aunt Ellen!"

"Well, I don't approve of it," said Mrs. Hooper, in the half plaintive tone of one who must speak although no one listens. "But of course your uncle must decide."

"We'll talk it over, my dear Connie, we'll talk it over," said Dr. Hooper cheerfully. "Now wouldn't you like Nora to show you to your room?"

The girls went upstairs together, Nora leading the way.

"It's an awful squash in your room," said Nora abruptly. "I don't know how you'll manage."

"My fault, I suppose, for bringing so many things! But where else could I put them?"

Nora nodded gravely, as though considering the excuse. The newcomer suddenly felt herself criticised by this odd schoolgirl and resented it.

The door of the spare-room was open, and the girls entered upon a scene of chaos. Annette rose from her knees, showing a brick-red countenance of wrath that strove in vain for any sort of dignity. And again that look of distant laughter came into Lady Connie's eyes.

"My dear Annette, why aren't you having a rest, as I told you! I can do with anything to-night."

"Well, my lady, if you'll tell me how you'll get into bed, unless I put some of these things away, I should be obliged!" said Annette, with a dark look at Nora. "I've asked for a wardrobe for you, and this young lady says there isn't one. There's that hanging cupboard"—she pointed witheringly to the curtained recess—"your dresses will be ruined there in a fortnight. And there's that chest of drawers. Your things will have to stay in the trunks, as far as I can see, and then you might as well sleep on them. It would give you more room!"

With which stroke of sarcasm, Annette returned to the angry unpacking of her mistress's bag.

"I must buy a wardrobe," said Connie, looking round her in perplexity. "Never mind, Annette, I can easily buy one."

It was now Nora's turn to colour.

"You mustn't do that," she said firmly. "Father wouldn't like it. We'll find something. But do you want such a lot of things?"

She looked at the floor heaped with every variety of delicate mourning, black dresses, thick and thin, for morning and afternoon; and black and white, or pure white, for the evening. And what had happened to the bed? It was already divested of the twilled cotton sheets and marcella quilt which were all the Hoopers ever allowed either to themselves or their guests. They had been replaced by sheets of the finest and smoothest linen, embroidered with a crest and monogram in the corners, and by a coverlet of old Italian lace lined with pale blue silk; while the down pillows at the head with their embroidered and lace-trimmed slips completed the transformation of what had been a bed, and was now almost a work of art.

And the dressing-table! Nora went up to it in amazement. It too was spread with lace lined with silk, and covered with a toilet-set of mother-of-pearl and silver. Every brush and bottle was crested and initialled. The humble looking-glass, which Nora, who was something of a carpenter, had herself mended before her cousin's arrival, was standing on the floor in a corner, and a folding mirror framed in embossed silver had taken its place.

"I say, do you always travel with these things?" The girl stood open-mouthed, half astonished, half contemptuous.

"What things?"

Nora pointed to the toilet-table and the bed.

Connie's expression showed an answering astonishment.

"I have had them all my life," she said stiffly. "We always took our own linen to hotels, and made our rooms nice."

"I should think you'd be afraid of their being stolen!" Nora took up one of the costly brushes, and examined it in wonder.

"Why should I be? They're nothing. They're just like other people's!" With a slight but haughty change of manner, the girl turned away, and began to talk Italian to her maid.

"I never saw anything like them!" said Nora stoutly.

Constance Bledlow took no notice. She and Annette were chattering fast, and Nora could not understand a word. She stood by awkward and superfluous, feeling certain that the maid who was gesticulating, now towards the ceiling, and now towards the floor, was complaining both of her own room and of the kitchen accommodation. Her mistress listened carelessly, occasionally trying to soothe her, and in the middle of the stream of talk, Nora slipped away.

"It's horrid!—spending all that money on yourself," thought the girl of seventeen indignantly. "And in Oxford too!—as if anybody wanted such things here."

Meanwhile, she was no sooner gone than her cousin sank down on the armchair, and broke into a slightly hysterical fit of laughter.

"Can we stand it, Annette? We've got to try. Of course you can leave me if you choose."

"And I should like to know how you'd get on then!" said Annette, grimly, beginning again upon the boxes.

"Well, of course, I shouldn't get on at all. But really we might give away a lot of these clothes! I shall never want them."

The speaker looked frowning at the stacks of dresses and lingerie. Annette made no reply; but went on busily with her unpacking. If the clothes were to be got rid of, they were her perquisites. She was devoted to Constance, but she stood on her rights.

Presently a little space was cleared on the floor, and Constance, seeing that it was nearly seven o'clock, and the Hoopers supped at half past, took off her black dress with its crape, and put on a white one, high to the throat and long-sleeved; a French demi-toilette, plain, and even severe in make, but cut by the best dressmaker in Nice. She looked extraordinarily tall and slim in it and very foreign. Her maid clasped a long string of opals, which was her only ornament, about her neck. She gave one look at herself in the glass, holding herself proudly, one might have said arrogantly. But as she turned away, and so that Annette could not see her, she raised the opals, and held them a moment softly to her lips. Her mother had habitually worn them. Then she moved to the window, and looked out over the Hoopers' private garden, to the spreading college lawns, and the grey front beyond.

"Am I really going to stay here a whole year—nearly?" she asked herself, half laughing, half rebellious.

Then her eye fell upon a medley of photographs; snaps from her own camera, which had tumbled out of her bag in unpacking. The topmost one represented a group of young men and maidens standing under a group of stone pines in a Riviera landscape. She herself was in front, with a tall youth beside her. She bent down to look at it.

"I shall come across him I suppose—before long."

And raising herself, she stood awhile, thinking; her face alive with an excitement that was half expectation, and half angry recollection.

II

"MY DEAR Ellen, I beg you will not interfere any more with Connie's riding. I have given leave, and that really must settle it. She tells me that her father always allowed her to ride alone—with a groom—in London and the Campagna; she will of course pay all the expenses of it out of her own income, and I see no object whatever in thwarting her. She is sure to find our life dull enough anyway, after the life she has been living."

"I don't know why you should call Oxford dull, Ewen!" said Mrs. Hooper resentfully. "I consider the society here much better than anything Connie was likely to see on the Riviera—much more respectable anyway. Well, of course, everybody will call her fast—but that's your affair. I can see already she won't be easily restrained. She's got an uncommonly strong will of her own."

"Well, don't try and restrain her, dear, too much," laughed her husband. "After all she's twenty, she'll be twenty-one directly. She may not be more than a twelvemonth with us. She need not be, as far as my functions are concerned. Let's make friends with her and make her happy."

"I don't want my girls talked about, thank you, Ewen!" His wife gave an angry dig to the word "my." "Everybody says what a nice ladylike girl Alice is. But Nora often gives me a deal of trouble—and if she takes to imitating Connie, and wanting to go about without a chaperon, I don't know what I shall do. My dear Ewen, do you know what I discovered last night?"

Mrs. Hooper rose and stood over her husband impressively.

"Well—what?"

"You remember Connie went to bed early. Well, when I came up, and passed her door, I noticed something—somebody in that room was—smoking! I could not be mistaken. And this morning I questioned the housemaid. 'Yes, ma'am,' she said, 'her ladyship smoked two cigarettes last night, and Mrs. Tinkler'—that's the maid—'says she always smokes two before she goes to bed.' Then I spoke to Tinkler—whose manner to me, I consider, is not at all what it should be—and she said that Connie smoked three cigarettes a day always—that Lady Risborough smoked—that all the ladies in Rome smoked—that Connie began it before her mother died—and her mother didn't mind——"

"Well then, my dear, you needn't mind," exclaimed Dr. Hooper.

"I always thought Ella Risborough went to pieces—rather—in that dreadful foreign life," said Mrs. Hooper firmly. "Everybody does—you can't help it."

"I don't know what you mean by going 'to pieces,' " said Ewen Hooper warmly. "I only know that when they came here ten years ago, I thought her one of the most attractive—one of the most charming women I had ever seen."

From where he stood, on the hearth-rug of his study, smoking an after-breakfast pipe, he looked down—frowning—upon his wife, and Mrs. Hooper felt that she had perhaps gone too far. Never had she forgotten, never had she ceased to resent her own sense of inferiority and disadvantage, beside her brilliant sister-in-law on the occasion of that long past visit. She could still see Ella Risborough at the All Souls' luncheon given to the newly made D.C.Ls, sitting on the right of the Vice-Chancellor, and holding a kind of court afterwards in the library; a hat that was little more than a wreath of forget-me-nots on her dark hair, and a long, lace cloak draping the still young and graceful figure. She remembered vividly the soft, responsive eyes and smile, and the court of male worshippers about them. Professors, tutors young and old, undergraduates and heads of houses, had crowded round the mother and the longlegged, distinguished-looking child, who clung so closely to her side; and if only she could have given Oxford a few more days, the whole place would have been at Ella Risborough's feet. "So intelligent too!" said the enthusiastic—"so learned even!" A member of the Roman "Accademia dei Lincei," with only one other woman to keep her company in that august band; and yet so modest, so unpretending, so full of laughter, and life, and sex! Mrs. Hooper, who generally found herself at these official luncheons in a place which her small egotism resented, had watched her sister-in-law from a distance, envying her dress, her title, her wealth, bitterly angry that Ewen's sister should have a place in the world that Ewen's wife could never hope to touch, and irrevocably deciding that Ella Risborough was "fast" and gave herself airs. Nor did the afternoon visit, when the Risboroughs, with great difficulty, had made time for the family call on the Hoopers, supply any more agreeable memories. Ella Risborough had been so rapturously glad to see her brother, and in spite of a real effort to be friendly had had so little attention to spare for his wife! It was true she had made much of the Hooper children, and had brought them all presents from Italy. But Mrs. Hooper had chosen to think the laughing sympathy and evident desire to please "affectation," or patronage, and had been vexed in her silent corner to see how little her own two girls could hold their own beside Constance.

As for Lord Risborough, he had frankly found it difficult to remember Mrs. Hooper's identity, while on the other hand he fell at once into keen discussion of some recent finds in the Greek islands with Ewen Hooper, to whom in the course of half an hour it was evident that he took a warm liking. He put up his eye-glass to look at the Hooper children; he said vaguely, "I hope that some day you and Mrs. Hooper will descend upon us in Rome"; and then he hurried his wife away with the audible remark—"We really must get to Blenheim, Ellie, in good time. You promised the Duchess——"

So ill-bred—so snobbish—to talk of your great acquaintances in public! And as for Lady Risborough's answer—"I don't care twopence about the Duchess, Hugh! and I haven't seen Ewen for six years,"—it had been merely humbug, for she had obediently followed her husband, all the same.

Recollections of this kind went trickling through Mrs. Hooper's mind, roused by Ewen's angry defence of his sister. It was all very well, but now the longlegged child had grown up, and was going to put her—Ellen Hooper's—daughters in the shade, to make them feel their inferiority, just as the mother had done with herself. Of course the money was welcome. Constance was to contribute three hundred a year, which was a substantial addition to an income which, when all supplemental earnings—exams, journalism, lectures—were counted, rarely reached seven hundred. But they would be "led into expenses"—the maid was evidently a most exacting woman; and meanwhile, Alice, who was just out, and was really quite a pretty girl, would be entirely put in the background by this young woman with her forward manner, and her title, and the way she had as though the world belonged to her. Mrs. Hooper felt no kinship with her whatever. She was Ewen's blood—not hers; and the mother's jealous nature was all up in arms for her own brood—especially for Alice. Nora could look after herself, and invariably did. Besides Nora was so tiresome! She was always ready to give the family case away—to give everything away, preposterously. And, apropos, Mrs. Hooper expressed her annoyance with some silly notions Nora had just expressed to her.

"I do hope, Ewen, you won't humour and spoil Constance too much! Nora says now she's dissatisfied with her room and wants to buy some furniture. Well, let her, I say. She has plenty of money, and we haven't. We have given her a great deal more than we give our own daughters——"

"She pays us, my dear!"

Mrs. Hooper straightened her thin shoulders.

"Well, and you give her the advantage of your name and your reputation here. It is not as though you were a young don, a nobody. You've made your position. Everybody asks us to all the official things—and Connie, of course, will be asked, too."

A smile crept round Dr. Hooper's weak and pleasant mouth.

"Don't flatter yourself, Ellen, that Connie will find Oxford society very amusing after Rome and the Riviera."

"That will be her misfortune," said Mrs. Hooper, stoutly. "Anyway, she will have all the advantages we have. We take her with us, for instance, to the Vice-Chancellor's to-night?"

"Do we?" Dr. Hooper groaned. "By the way, can't you let me off, Ellen? I've got such a heap of work to do."

"Certainly not! People who shut themselves up never get on, Ewen. I've just finished mending your gown, on purpose. How you tear it as you do, I can't think! But I was speaking of Connie. We shall take her, of course——"

"Have you asked her?"

"I told her we were all going—and to meet Lord Glaramara. She didn't say anything."

Dr. Hooper laughed.

"You'll find her, I expect, a very independent young woman——"

But at that moment his daughter Nora, after a hurried and perfunctory knock, opened the study door vehemently, and put in a flushed face.

"Father, I want to speak to you!"

"Come in, my dear child. But I can't spare more than five minutes."

And the Reader glanced despairingly at a clock, the hands of which were pointing to half past ten a.m. How it was that, after an eight o'clock breakfast, it always took so long for a man to settle himself to his work he really could not explain. Not that his conscience did not sometimes suggest the answer, pointing to a certain slackness and softness in himself—the primal shrinking from work, the primal instinct to sit and dream—that had every day to be met and conquered afresh, before the student actually found himself in his chair, or lecturing from his desk with all his brains alert. Anyway, the Reader, when there was no college or university engagement to pin him down, would stand often—"spilling the morning in recreation"; in other words, gossiping with his wife and children, or loitering over the newspapers, till the inner monitor turned upon him. Then he would work furiously for hours; and the work when done was good. For there would be in it a kind of passion, a warmth born of the very effort and friction of the will which had been necessary to get it done at all.

Nora, however, had not come in to gossip. She was in a white heat.

"Father!—we ought not to let Connie furnish her own rooms!"

"But, my dear, who thinks of her doing any such thing? What do you mean?" And Dr. Hooper took his pipe out of his mouth, and stood protesting.

"She's gone out, she and Annette. They slipped out just now when mother came in to you; and I'm certain they've gone to B's"—the excited girl named a well-known Oxford furniture shop—"to buy all sorts of things."

"Well, after all, it's my house!" said the Reader, smiling. "Connie will have to ask my leave first."

"Oh, she'll persuade you!" cried Nora, standing before her father with her hands behind her. "She'll make us all do what she wants. She'll be like a cuckoo in the nest. She'll be too strong for us."

Ewen Hooper put out a soothing hand, and patted his youngest daughter on the shoulder.

"Wait a bit, my dear. And when Connie comes back just ask her to step in here a moment. And now will you both please be gone—at once?—quick march!"

And taking his wife and daughter by the shoulders, he turned them both forcibly out, and sat down to make his final preparations for a lecture that afternoon on the "feminism" of Euripides.

Meanwhile Connie Bledlow and her maid were walking quickly down the Broad towards the busy Cornmarket with its shops. It was a brilliant morning—one of those east wind days when all clouds are swept from the air, and every colour of the spring burns and flashes in the sun. Every outline was clear; every new-leafed tree stood radiant in the bright air. The grey or black college walls had lost all the grimness of winter, they were there merely to bring out the blue of the sky, the yellow gold, the laburnum, the tossing white of the chestnuts. The figures, even, passing in the streets, seemed to glitter with the trees and the buildings. The white in the women's dresses; the short black gowns and square caps of the undergraduates; the gay colours in the children's frocks; the overhanging masses of hawthorn and lilac that here and there thrust themselves, effervescent and rebellious, through and over college walls:—everything shimmered and shone in the May sunlight. The air too was tonic and gay, a rare thing for Oxford; and Connie, refreshed by sleep, walked with such a buoyant and swinging step that her stout maid could hardly keep up with her. Many a passer-by observed her. Men on their way to lecture, with battered caps and gowns slung round their necks, threw sharp glances at the tall girl in black, with the small pale face, so delicately alive, and the dark eyes that laughed—aloof and unabashed—at all they saw.

"What boys they are!" said Constance presently, making a contemptuous lip. "They ought to be still in the nursery."

"What—the young men in the caps, my lady?"

"Those are the undergraduates, Annette—the boys who live in the colleges."

"They don't stare like the Italian young gentlemen," said Annette, shrugging her shoulders. "Many a time I wanted to box their ears for the way they looked at you in the street."

Connie laughed. "I liked it! They were better-looking than these boys. Annette, do you remember that day two years ago when I took you to that riding competition—what did they call it?—that gymkhana—in the Villa Borghese—and we saw all those young officers and their horses? What glorious fellows they were, most of them! and how they rode!"

Her cheek flushed to the recollection. For a moment the Oxford street passed out of sight. She saw the grassy slopes, the stone pines, the white walls, the classic stadium of the Villa Borghese, with the hot June sun stabbing the open spaces, and the deep shadows under the ilexes; and in front of the picture, the crowd of jostling horses, with their riders, bearing the historic names of Rome—Colonnas, Orsinis, Gaetanis, Odescalchis, and the rest. A young and splendid brood, all arrogant life and gaiety, as high-mettled as their English and Irish horses. And in front a tall, long-limbed cavalry officer in the Queen's household, bowing to Constance Bledlow, as he comes back, breathless and radiant from the race he has just won, his hand tight upon the reins, his athlete's body swaying to each motion of his horse, his black eyes laughing into hers. Why, she had imagined herself in love with him for a whole week!

Then, suddenly, she perceived that in her absence of mind she was running straight into a trio of undergraduates who were hurriedly stepping off the path to avoid her. They looked at her, and she at them. They seemed to her all undersized, plain and sallow. They carried books, and two wore glasses. "Those are what *he* used to call 'smugs'!" she thought contemptuously, her imagination still full of the laughing Italian youths on their glistening horses. And she began to make disparaging remarks about English young men to Annette. If this intermittent stream of youths represented them, the English *gioventù* was not much to boast of.

Next a furniture shop appeared, with wide windows, and a tempting array of wares, and in they went. Constance had soon bought a wardrobe and a cheval-glass for herself, an armchair, a carpet, and a smaller wardrobe for Annette, and seeing a few trifles, like a French screen, a small sofa, and an inlaid writing-table in her path, she threw them in. Then it occurred to her that Uncle Ewen might have something to say to these transactions, and she hastily told the shopman not to send the things to Medburn House till she gave the order.

Out they went, this time into the crowded Cornmarket, where there were no colleges, and where the town that was famous long before the University began, seemed to be living its own vigorous life, untrammelled by the men in gowns. Only in seeming, however, for in truth every single shop in the street depended upon the University.

They walked on into the town, looking into various colleges, sitting in Broad Walk, and loitering over shops, till one o'clock struck from Oxford's many towers.

"Heavens!" said Constance—"and lunch is at 1:15!"

They turned and walked rapidly along the "Corn," which was once more full of men hurrying back to their own colleges from the lecture rooms of Balliol and St. John's. Now, it seemed to Constance that the men they passed were of a finer race. She noticed plenty of tall fellows, with broad shoulders, and the look of keen-bitten health.

"Look at that pair coming!" she said to Annette. "That's better!"

The next moment, she stopped, confused, eyes wide, lips parted. For the taller of the two had taken off his cap, and stood towering and smiling in her path. A young man, of about six foot three, magnificently made, thin with the leanness of an athlete in training,—health, power, self-confidence, breathing from his joyous looks and movements—was surveying her. His lifted cap showed a fine head covered with thick brown curls. The face was long, yet not narrow; the cheek-bones rather high, the chin conspicuous. The eyes—very dark and heavily lidded—were set forward under strongly marked eyebrows; and both they, the straight nose with its close nostrils, and the red mouth, seemed to be drawn in firm yet subtle strokes on the sunburnt skin, as certain Dutch and Italian painters define the features of their sitters in a containing outline as delicate as it is unfaltering. The aspect of this striking person was that of a young king of men, careless, audacious, good-humoured; and Constance Bledlow's expression, as she held out her hand to him, betrayed, much against her will, that she was not indifferent to the sight of him.

"Well met, indeed!" said the young man, the gaiety in his look, a gaiety full of meaning, measuring itself against the momentary confusion in hers. "I have been hoping to hear of you—for a long time!—Lady Constance. Are you with the—the Hoopers—is it?"

"I am staying with my uncle and aunt. I only arrived yesterday." The girl's manner had become, in a few seconds, little less than repellent.

"Well, Oxford's lively. You'll find lots going on. The Eights begin the day after to-morrow, and I've got my people coming up. I hope you'll let Mrs. Hooper bring you to tea to meet them? Oh, by the way, do you know Meyrick? I think you must have met him." He turned to his companion, a fair-haired giant, evidently his junior. "Lord Meyrick—Lady Constance Bledlow. Will you come, Lady Connie?"

"I don't know what my aunt's engagements are," said Constance stiffly.

The trio had withdrawn into the shade of a wide doorway belonging to an old Oxford inn. Annette was looking at the windows of the milliner's shop next door.

"My mother shall do everything that is polite—everything in the world! And when may I come to call? You have no faith in my manners, I know!" laughed the young man. "How you did sit upon me at Cannes!" And again his brilliant eyes, fixed upon her, seemed to be saying all sorts of unspoken things.

"How has he been behaving lately?" said Constance drily, turning to Lord Meyrick, who stood grinning.

"Just as usual! He's generally mad. Don't depend on him for anything. But I hope you'll let me do anything I can for you! I should be only too happy."

The girl perceived the eager admiration with which the young fellow was regarding her, and her face relaxed.

"Thank you very much. Of course I know all about Mr. Falloden! At Cannes, we made a league to keep him in order."

Falloden protested vehemently that he had been a persecuted victim at Cannes, the butt of Lady Connie and all her friends.

Constance, however, cut the speech short by a careless nod and good-bye, beckoned to Annette and was moving away, when he placed himself before her.

"But I hope we shall meet this very night—shan't we?—at the Vice-Chancellor's party?"

"I don't know."

"Oh, but of course you will be there! The Hoopers are quite sure to bring you. It's at St. Hubert's. Some old swell is coming down. The gardens are terribly romantic—and there'll be a moon. One can get away from all the stuffy people. Do come!"

He gave her a daring look.

"Good-bye," said Constance again, with a slight decided gesture, which made him move out of her way.

In a few moments, she and her maid were lost to sight on the crowded pavement.

Falloden threw back his head and laughed, as he and Lord Meyrick pursued the opposite direction. But he said nothing. Meyrick, his junior by two years, who was now his most intimate friend in the Varsity, ventured at last on the remark—

"Very good-looking! But she was certainly not very civil to you, Duggy!"

Falloden flushed hotly.

"You think she dislikes me? I'll bet you anything you please she'll be at the party to-night."

Constance and her maid hurried home along the Broad. The girl perceived little or nothing on the way; but her face was crossed by a multitude of expressions, which meant a very active brain. Perhaps sarcasm or scorn prevailed, yet mingled sometimes with distress or perplexity.

The sight of the low gabled front of Medburn House recalled her thoughts. She remembered her purchases and Nora's disapproving eyes. It would be better to go and beard her uncle at once. But just as she approached the house, she became aware of a slenderly built man in flannels coming out of the gates of St. Cyprian's, the college of which the gate and outer court stood next door to the Hoopers.

He saw her, stopped with a start of pleasure, and came eagerly towards her.

"Lady Constance! Where have you sprung from? Oh, I know—you are with the Hoopers! Have you been here long?"

They shook hands, and Constance obediently answered the newcomer's questions. She seemed indeed to like answering them, and nothing could have been more courteous and kind than his manner of asking them. He was clearly a senior man, a don, who, after a strenuous morning of lecturing, was hurrying—in the festal Eights week—to meet some friends on the river. His face was one of singular charm, the features regular, the skin a pale olive, the hair and eyes intensely black. Whereas Falloden's features seemed to lie, so to speak, on the surface, the mouth and eyes scarcely disturbing the general level of the face mask—no indentation in the chin, and no perceptible hollow under the brow,—this man's eyes were deeply sunk, and every outline of the face—cheeks, chin and temples—chiselled and fined away into an almost classical perfection. The man's aspect indeed was Greek, and ought only to have expressed the Greek blitheness, the Greek joy in life. But, in truth, it was a very modern and complex soul that breathed from both face and form.

Constance had addressed him as "Mr. Sorell." He turned to walk with her to her door, talking eagerly. He was asking her about various friends in whose company they had last met—apparently at Rome; and he made various references to "your mother," which Constance accepted gently, as though they pleased her.

They paused at the Hoopers' door.

"But when can I see you?" he asked. "Has Mrs. Hooper a day at home? Will you come to lunch with me soon? I should like to show you my rooms. I have some of those nice things we bought at Syracuse—your father and I—do you remember? And I have a jolly look out over the garden. When will you come?"

"When you like. But chaperons seem to be necessary!"

"Oh, I can provide one—any number! Some of the wives of our married fellows are great friends of mine. I should like you to know them. But wouldn't Mrs. Hooper bring you?"

"Will you write to her?"

He looked a little confused.

"Of course I know your uncle very well. He and I work together in many things. May I come and call?"

"Of course you may!" She laughed again, with that wilful sound in the laugh which he remembered. He wondered how she was going to get on at the Hoopers. Mrs. Hooper's idiosyncrasies were very generally known. He himself had always given both Mrs. Hooper and her eldest daughter a wide berth in the social gatherings of Oxford. He frankly thought Mrs. Hooper odious, and had long since classed Miss Alice as a stupid little thing with a mild talent for flirtation.

Then, as he held out his hand to say good-bye, he suddenly remembered the Vice-Chancellor's party.

"By the way, there's a big function to-night. You're going, of course? Oh, yes—make them take you! I hadn't meant to go—but now I shall—on the chance!"

He grasped her hand, holding it a little. Then he was gone, and the Hoopers' front door swung suddenly wide, opened by some one invisible.

Connie, a little flushed and excited, stepped into the hall, and there perceived Mrs. Hooper behind the door.

"You are rather late, Constance," said that lady coldly. "But, of course, it doesn't matter. The servants are at their dinner still, so I opened the door. So you know Mr. Sorell?"

From which Constance perceived that her aunt had observed her approach to the house, in Mr. Sorell's company, through the little side window of the hall. She straightened her shoulders impatiently.

"My father and mother knew him in Rome, Aunt Ellen. He used to come to our apartment. Is Uncle Ewen in the study? I want to speak to him."

She knocked and went in. Standing with her back to the door she said abruptly—

"I hope you won't mind, Uncle Ewen, but I've been buying a few things we want, for my room and Annette's. When I go, of course they can be turned out. But may I tell the shop now to send them in?"

The Reader turned in some embarrassment, his spectacles on his nose.

"My dear girl, anything to make you comfortable! But I wish you had consulted me. Of course, we would have got anything you really wanted."

"Oh, that would have been dreadfully unfair!" laughed Constance. "It's my fault, you see. I've got far too many dresses. One seemed not to be able to do without them at Cannes."

"Well, you won't want so many here," said Dr. Ewen cheerfully, as he rose from his table crowded with books. "We're all pretty simple at Oxford. We ought to be of course—even our guests. It's a place of training." He dropped a Greek word absently, putting away his papers the while, and thinking of the subject with which he had just been busy. Constance opened the door again to make her escape, but the sound recalled Dr. Ewen's thoughts.

"My dear—has your aunt asked you? We hope you'll come with us to the Vice-Chancellor's party to-night. I think it would interest you. After all, Oxford's not like other places. I think you said last night you knew some undergraduates——"

"I know Mr. Falloden of Mannion," said Constance, "and Mr. Sorell."

The Reader's countenance broke into smiles.

"Sorell? The dearest fellow in the world! He and I help each other a good deal, though of course we differ—and fight—sometimes. But that's the salt of life. Yes, I remember, your mother used to mention Sorell in her letters. Well, with those two and ourselves, you'll have plenty of starting-points. Ah, luncheon!" For the bell rang, and sent Constance hurrying upstairs to take off her things.

As she washed her hands, her thoughts were very busy with the incidents of her morning's walk. The colours had suddenly freshened in the Oxford world. No doubt she had expected them to freshen; but hardly so soon. A tide of life welled up in her—a tide of pleasure. And as she stood a moment beside the open window of her room before going down, looking at the old Oxford garden just beneath her, and the stately college front beyond, Oxford itself began to capture her, touching her magically, insensibly, as it had touched the countless generations before her. She was the child of two scholars, and she had been brought up in a society both learned and cosmopolitan, traversed by all the main currents and personalities of European politics, but passionate all the same for the latest find in the Forum, the newest guesses in criticism, for any fresh light that the present could shed upon the past. And when she looked back upon the moments of those Roman years which had made the sharpest mark upon her, she saw three figures stand out—her gracious and graceful mother; her father, student and aristocrat, so eagerly occupied with life that he had scarcely found the time to die; and Mr. Sorell, her mother's friend, and then her own.

Together—all four—they had gone to visit the Etruscan tombs about Viterbo, they had explored Norba and Ninfa, and had spent a marvellous month at Syracuse.

"And I have never seen him since papa's death!—and I have only heard from him twice. I wonder why?" She pondered it resentfully. And yet what cause of offence had she? At Cannes, had she thought much about him? In that scene, so troubled and feverish, compared with the old Roman days, there had been for her, as she well knew, quite another dominating figure.

"Just the same!" she thought angrily. "Just as domineering—and provoking. Boggling about Uncle Ewen's name, as if it was not worth his remembering! I shall compel him to be civil to my relations, just because it will annoy him so much."

At lunch Constance declared prettily that she would be delighted to go to the Vice-Chancellor's party. Nora sat silent through the meal.

After lunch, Connie went to talk to her aunt about the incoming furniture. Mrs. Hooper made no difficulties at all. The house had long wanted these additions, only there had been no money to buy them with. Now Mrs. Hooper felt secretly certain that Constance, when she left them, would not want to take the things with her, so that she looked on Connie's purchases of the morning as her own prospective property.

A furniture van appeared early in the afternoon with the things. Nora hovered about the hall, severely dumb, while they were being carried upstairs. Annette gave all the directions.

But when later on Connie was sitting at her new writing-table contemplating her transformed room with a childish satisfaction, Nora knocked and came in.

She walked up to Connie, and stood looking down upon her. She was very red, and her eyes sparkled.

"I want to tell you that I am disappointed in you—dreadfully disappointed in you!" said the girl fiercely.

"What do you mean?" Constance rose in amazement.

"Why didn't you insist on my father's buying these things? You ought to have insisted. You pay us a large sum, and you had a right.

Instead, you have humiliated us—because you are rich, and we are poor! It was mean—and purse-proud."

"How dare you say such things?" cried Connie. "You mustn't come into my room at all, if you are going to behave like this. You know very well I didn't do it unkindly. It is you who are unkind! But of course it doesn't matter. You don't understand. You are only a child!" Her voice shook.

"I am not a child!" said Nora indignantly. "And I believe I know a great deal more about money than you do—because you have never been poor. I have to keep all the accounts here, and make mother and Alice pay their debts. Father, of course, is always too busy to think of such things. Your money is dreadfully useful to us. I wish it wasn't. But I wanted to do what was honest—if you had only given me time. Then you slipped out and did it!"

Constance stared in bewilderment.

"Are you the mistress in this house?" she said.

Nora nodded. Her colour had all faded away, and her breath was coming quick. "I practically am," she said stoutly.

"At seventeen?" asked Connie, ironically.

Nora nodded again.

Connie turned away, and walked to the window. She was enraged with Nora, whose attack upon her seemed quite inexplicable and incredible. Then, all in a moment, a bitter forlornness overcame her. Nora, standing by the table, and already pierced with remorse, saw her cousin's large eyes fill with tears. Connie sat down with her face averted. But Nora—trembling all over—perceived that she was crying. The next moment, the newcomer found Nora kneeling beside her, in the depths of humiliation and repentance.

"I am a beast!—a horrid beast! I always am. Oh, please, please don't cry!"

"You forget"—said Connie, with difficulty—"how I—how I miss my mother!"

And she broke into a fit of weeping. Nora, beside herself with self-disgust, held her cousin embraced, and tried to comfort her. And presently, after an agitated half-hour, each girl seemed to herself to have found a friend. Reserve had broken; they had poured out confidences to each other; and after the thunder and the shower came the rainbow of peace.

Before Nora departed, she looked respectfully at the beautiful dress of white satin, draped with black, which Annette had laid out upon the bed in readiness for the Vice-Chancellor's party.

"It will suit you perfectly!" she said, still eager to make up. Then—eyeing Constance—

"You know, of course, that you are good-looking?"

"I am not hideous—I know that," said Constance, laughing. "You odd girl!"

"We have heard often how you were admired in Rome. I wonder—don't be offended!"—said Nora, bluntly—"have you ever been in love?"

"Never!" The reply was passionately prompt.

Nora looked thoughtful.

"Perhaps you don't know whether you were or not. Girls get so dreadfully mixed up. But I am sure people—men—have been in love with you."

"Well, of course!" said Connie, with the same emphatic gaiety.

Nora opened her eyes.

"'Of course?' But I know heaps of girls with whom nobody has ever been in love!"

As soon as she was alone, Connie locked her door, and walked restlessly up and down her room, till by sheer movement she had tamed a certain wild spirit within her let loose by Nora's question. And as she walked, the grey Oxford walls, the Oxford lilacs and laburnums, vanished from perception. She was in another scene. Hot sun—gleaming orange-gardens and blue sea—bare-footed, black-eyed children—and a man beside her, on whom she has been showering epithets that would have shamed—surely!—any other human being in the world. Tears of excitement are in her eyes; in his a laughing triumph mixed with astonishment.

"But, now—" she thinks, drawing herself up, erect and tense, her hands behind her head; "now, I am ready for him. Let him try such ways again—if he dare!"

III

THE PARTY given at St. Hubert's on this evening in the Eights week was given in honour of a famous guest—the Lord Chancellor of the day, one of the strongest members of a strong Government, of whom St. Hubert's, which had nurtured him through his four academic years, was quite inordinately proud. It was very seldom that their great nursling was able or willing to revisit the old nest. But the head of the college, who had been in the same class-list and rowed in the same boat with the politician, was now Vice-Chancellor of the University; and the greater luminary had come to shine upon the lesser, by way of heightening the dignity of both. For the man who has outsoared his fellows likes to remind himself by contrast of his callow days, before the hungry and fighting impulses had driven him down—a young eaglet—upon the sheepfolds of law and politics; while to the majority of mankind, even to-day, hero-worship, when it is not too exacting, is agreeable.

So all Oxford had been bidden. The great hall of St. Hubert's, with its stately portraits and its emblazoned roof, had been adorned with flowers and royally lit up. From the hills round Oxford the "line of festal light" made by its Tudor windows, in which gleamed the escutcheons of three centuries, could have been plainly seen. The High Street was full of carriages, and on the immaculate grass of the great quadrangle, groups of the guests, the men in academic costume, the women in the airiest and gayest of summer dresses, stood to watch the arrivals. The evening was clear and balmy; moonrise and dying day disputed the sky; and against its pale blue still scratched over with pale pink shreds and wisps of cloud, the grey college walls, battlemented and flecked with black, rose warmed and transfigured by that infused and golden summer in which all Oxford lay bathed. Through open gateways there were visions of green gardens, girdled with lilacs and chestnuts; and above the quadrangle towered the crocketed spire of St. Mary's, ethereally wrought, it seemed, in ebony and silver, the broad May moon behind it. Within the hall, the guests were gathering fast. The dais of the high table was lit by the famous candelabra bequeathed to the college under Queen Anne; a piano stood ready, and a space had been left for the college choir who were to entertain the party. In front of the dais in academic dress stood the Vice-Chancellor, a thin, silver-haired man, with a determined mouth, such as befitted the champion of a hundred orthodoxies; and beside him his widowed sister, a nervous and rather featureless lady who was helping him to receive. The guest of the evening had not yet appeared.

Mr. Sorell, in a master's gown, stood talking with a man, also in a master's gown, but much older than himself, a man with a singular head—both flat and wide—scanty reddish hair, touched with grey, a massive forehead, pale blue eyes, and a long pointed chin. Among the bright colours of so many of the gowns around him—the yellow and red of the doctors of law, the red and black of the divines, the red and white of the musicians—this man's plain black was conspicuous. Every one who knew Oxford knew why this eminent scholar and theologian had never become a doctor of divinity. The University imposes one of her few remaining tests on her D.D's; Mr. Wenlock, Master of Beaumont, had never been willing to satisfy it, so he remained undoctored. When he preached the University sermon he preached in the black gown; while every ambitious cleric who could put a thesis together could flaunt his red and black in the Vice-Chancellor's procession on Sundays in the University church. The face was one of mingled irony and melancholy, and there came from it sometimes the strangest cackling laugh.

"Well, you must show me this phoenix," he was saying in a nasal voice to Sorell, who had been talking eagerly. "Young women of the right sort are rare just now."

"What do you call the right sort, Master?"

"Oh, my judgment doesn't count. I only ask to be entertained."

"Well, talk to her of Rome, and see if you are not pleased."

The Master shrugged his shoulders.

"They can all do it—the clever sort. They know too much about the Forum. They make me wish sometimes that Lanciani had never been born."

Sorell laughed.

"This girl is not a pedant."

"I take your word. And of course I remember her father. No pedantry there. And all the scholarship that could be possibly expected from an earl. Ah, is this she?"

For in the now crowded hall, filled with the chatter of many voices, a group was making its way from the doorway, on one member of which many curious eyes had been already turned. In front came Mrs. Hooper, spectacled, her small nose in air, the corners of her mouth sharply drawn down. Then Dr. Ewen, grey-haired, tall and stooping; then Alice, pretty, self-conscious, provincial, and spoilt by what seemed an inherited poke; and finally a slim and stately young person in white satin, who carried her head and her long throat with a remarkable freedom and self-confidence. The head was finely shaped, and the eyes brilliant; but in the rest of the face the features were so delicate, the mouth, especially, so small and subtle, as to give a first impression of insignificance. The girl seemed all eyes and neck, and the coils of brown hair wreathed round the head were disproportionately rich and heavy. The Master observing her said to himself—"No beauty!" Then she smiled—at Sorell apparently, who was making his way towards her—and the onlooker hurriedly suspended judgment. He noticed also that no one who looked at her could help looking again; and that the nervous expression natural to a young girl, who realises that she is admired but that policy and manners forbid her to show any pleasure in the fact, was entirely absent.

"She is so used to all her advantages that she forgets them," thought the Master, adding with an inward smile—"but if we forgot them—perhaps that would be another matter! Yes—she is like her mother—but taller."

For on that day ten years earlier, when Ella Risborough had taken Oxford by storm, she and Lord Risborough had found time to look in on the Master for twenty minutes, he and Lord Risborough having been frequent correspondents on matters of scholarship for some years. And Lady Risborough had chattered and smiled her way through the Master's lonely house—he had only just been appointed head of his college and was then unmarried—leaving a deep impression.

"I must make friends with her," he thought, following Ella Risborough's daughter with his eyes. "There are some gaps to fill up."

He meant in the circle of his girl protégées. For the Master had a curious history, well known in Oxford. He had married a cousin of his own, much younger than himself; and after five years they had separated, for reasons undeclared. She was now dead, and in his troubled blue eyes there were buried secrets no one would ever know. But under what appeared to a stranger to be a harsh, pedantic exterior the Master carried a very soft heart and an invincible liking for the society of young women. Oxford about this time was steadily filling with girl students, who were then a new feature in its life. The Master was a kind of queer patron saint among them, and to a chosen three or four, an intimate mentor and lasting friend. His sixty odd years, and the streaks of grey in his red straggling locks, his European reputation as a scholar and thinker, his old sister, and his quiet house, forbade the slightest breath of scandal in connection with these girl-friendships. Yet the girls to whom the Master devoted himself, whose essays he read, whose blunders he corrected, whose schools he watched over, and in whose subsequent love affairs he took the liveliest interest, were rarely or never plain to look upon. He chose them for their wits, but also for their faces. His men friends observed it with amusement. The little notes he wrote them, the birthday presents he sent them—generally some small worn copy of a French or Latin classic—his coveted invitations, or congratulations, were all marked by a note of gallantry, stately and old-fashioned like the furniture of his drawing-room, but quite different from anything he ever bestowed upon the men students of his college.

Of late he had lost two of his chief favourites. One, a delicious creature, with a head of auburn hair and a real talent for writing verse, had left Oxford suddenly to make a marriage so foolish that he really could not forgive her or put up with her intolerable husband; and the other, a muse, with the brow of one and the slenderest hand and foot, whom he and others were hopefully piloting towards a second class at least—possibly a first—in the Honour Classical School, had broken down in health, so that her mother and a fussy doctor had hurried her away to a rest-cure in Switzerland, and thereby slit her academic life and all her chances of fame. Both had been used to come—independently—for the Master was in his own way far too great a social epicure to mix his pleasures—to tea on Sundays; to sit on one side of a blazing fire, while the Master sat on the other, a Persian cat playing chaperon on the rug between, and the book-lined walls of the Master's most particular sanctum looking down upon them; while in the drawing-room beyond, Miss Wenlock, at the tea-table, sat patiently waiting till her domestic god should declare the seance over, allow her to make tea, and bring in the young and honoured guest. And now both charmers had vanished from the scene and had left no equals behind. The Master, who possessed the same sort of tact in training young women that Lord Melbourne showed in educating the girl-Queen, was left without his most engaging occupation.

Ah!—that good fellow, Sorell, was bringing her up to him.

"Master, Lady Constance would like to be introduced to you."

The Master was immensely flattered. Why should she wish to be introduced to such an old fogey? But there she was, smiling at him.

"You knew my father. I am sure you did!"

His elderly heart was touched, his taste captured at once. Sorell had engineered it all perfectly. His description of the girl had fired the Master; and his sketch of the Master in the girl's ear, as a kind of girlhood's arbiter, had amused and piqued her. "Yes, do introduce me! Will he ever ask me to tea? I should be so alarmed!"

It was all settled in a few minutes. Sunday was to see her introduction to the Master's inner circle, which met in summer, not between books and a blazing fire, but in the small college garden hidden amid the walls of Beaumont. Sorell was to bring her. The Master did not even go through the form of inviting either Mrs. Hooper or Miss Hooper. In all such matters he was a chartered libertine and did what he pleased.

Then he watched her in what seemed something of a triumphal progress through the crowded hall. He saw the looks of the girl students from the newly-organised women's colleges—as she passed—a little askance and chill; he watched a Scotch metaphysical professor, with a fiery face set in a mass of flaming hair and beard, which had won him the nickname from his philosophical pupils of "the devil in a mist," forcing an introduction to her; he saw the Vice-Chancellor graciously unbending, and man after man come up among the younger dons to ask Sorell to present them. She received it all with a smiling and nonchalant grace, perfectly at her ease, it seemed, and ready to say the right thing to young and old. "It's the training they get—the young women of her sort—that does it," thought the Master. "They are in society from their babyhood. Our poor, battered aristocracy—the Radicals have kicked away all its natural supports, and left it *dans l'air*; but it can still teach manners and the art to please. The undergraduates, however, seem shy of her."

For although among the groups of men, who stood huddled together mostly at the back of the room, many eyes were turned upon the newcomer, no one among them approached her. She held her court among the seniors, as no doubt, thought the Master, she had been accustomed to do from the days of her short frocks. He envisaged the apartment in the Palazzo Barberini whereof the fame had often reached Oxford, for the Risboroughs held open house there for the English scholar and professor on his travels. He himself had not been in Rome for fifteen years, and had never made the Risboroughs' acquaintance in Italy. But the kind of society which gathers round the English peer of old family who takes an apartment in Rome or Florence for the winter was quite familiar to him—the travelling English men and women of the same class, diplomats of all nations, high ecclesiastics, a cardinal or two, the heads of the great artistic or archæological schools, Americans, generals, senators, deputies—with just a sprinkling of young men. A girl of this girl's age and rank would have many opportunities, of course, of meeting young men, in the free and fascinating life of the Roman spring, but primarily her business in her mother's salon would have been to help her mother, to make herself agreeable to the older men, and to gather her education—in art, literature, and politics—as a coming woman of the world from their talk. The Master could see her smiling on a monsignore, carrying tea to a cardinal, or listening to the Garibaldian tales of some old veteran of the Risorgimento.

"It is an education—of its own kind," he thought. "Is it worth more or less than other kinds?"

And he looked round paternally on some of the young girl students then just penetrating Oxford; fresh, pleasant faces—little positive beauty—and on many the stamp, already prematurely visible, of the anxieties of life for those who must earn a livelihood. Not much taste in dress, which was often clumsy and unbecoming; hair, either untidy, or treated as an enemy, scraped back, held in, the sole object being to take as little time over it as possible; and, in general, the note upon them all of an educated and thrifty middle-class. His feelings, his sympathies, were all with them. But the old gallant in him was stirred by the tall figure in white satin, winding its graceful way through the room and conquering as it went.

"Ah—now that fellow, Herbert Pryce, has got hold of her, of course! If ever there was a climber!—But what does Miss Hooper say?"

And retreating to a safe corner the Master watched with amusement the flattering eagerness with which Mr. Pryce, who was a fellow of his own college, was laying siege to the newcomer. Pryce was rapidly making a great name for himself as a mathematician. "And is a second-rate fellow, all the same," thought the Master, contemptuously, being like Uncle Ewen a classic of the classics. But the face of little Alice Hooper, which he caught from time to time, watching—with a strained and furtive attention—the conversation between Pryce and her cousin, was really a tragedy; at least a tragi-comedy. Some girls are born to be supplanted!

But who was it Sorell was introducing to her now?—to the evident annoyance of Mr. Pryce, who must needs vacate the field. A striking figure of a youth! Golden hair, of a wonderful ruddy shade, and a clear pale face; powerfully though clumsily made; and with a shy and sensitive expression.

The Master turned to enquire of a Christ Church don who had come up to speak to him.

"Who is that young man with a halo like the 'Blessed Damosel'?"

"Talking to Lady Constance Bledlow? Oh, don't you know? He is Sorell's protege, Radowitz, a young musician—and poet!—so they say. Sorell discovered him in Paris, made great friends with him, and then persuaded him to come and take the Oxford musical degree. He is at Marmion, where the dons watch over him. But they say he has been abominably ragged by the rowdy set in college—led by that man Falloden. Do you know him?"

"The fellow who got the Ireland last year?"

The other nodded.

"As clever and as objectionable as they make 'em! Ah, here comes our great man!"

For amid a general stir, the Lord Chancellor had made his entrance, and was distributing greetings, as he passed up the hall, to his academic contemporaries and friends. He was a tall, burly man, with a strong black head and black eyes under bushy brows, combined with an infantile mouth and chin, long and happily caricatured in all the comic papers. But in his D.C.L. gown he made a very fine appearance; assembled Oxford was proud of him as one of the most successful of her sons; and his progress toward the dais was almost royal.

Suddenly, his voice—a famous *voix d'or*, well known in the courts' and in Parliament—was heard above the general buzz. It spoke in astonishment and delight.

"Lady Constance! where on earth have you sprung from? Well, this is a pleasure!"

And Oxford looked on amused while its distinguished guest shook a young lady in white by both hands, asking eagerly a score of questions, which he would hardly allow her to answer. The young lady too was evidently pleased by the meeting; her face had flushed and lit up; and the bystanders for the first time thought her not only graceful and picturesque, but positively handsome.

"Ewen!" said Mrs. Hooper angrily in her husband's ear, "why didn't Connie tell us she knew Lord Glaramara! She let me talk about him to her—and never said a word!—a single word!"

Ewen Hooper shrugged his shoulders.

"I'm sure I don't know, my dear."

Mrs. Hooper turned to her daughter who had been standing silent and neglected beside her, suffering, as her mother well knew, torments of wounded pride and feeling. For although Herbert Pryce had been long since dismissed by Connie, he had not yet returned to the side of the eldest Miss Hooper.

"I don't like such ways," said Mrs. Hooper, with sparkling eyes. "It was ill-bred and underhanded of Connie not to tell us at once—I shall certainly speak to her about it!"

"It makes us look such fools," said Alice, her mouth pursed and set. "I told Mr. Pryce that Connie knew no one to-night, except Mr. Sorell and Mr. Falloden."

The hall grew more crowded; the talk more furious. Lord Glaramara insisted, with the wilfulness of the man who can do as he pleases, that Constance Bledlow—whoever else came and went—should stay beside him.

"You can't think what I owed to her dear people in Rome three years ago!" he said to the Vice-Chancellor. "I adored her mother! And Constance is a charming child. She and I made great friends. Has she come to live in Oxford for a time? Lucky Oxford! What—with the Hoopers? Don't know 'em. I shall introduce her to some of my particular allies."

Which he did in profusion, so that Constance found herself bewildered by a constant stream of new acquaintances—fellows, professors, heads of colleges—of various ages and types, who looked at her with amused and kindly eyes, talked to her for a few pleasant minutes and departed, quite conscious that they had added a pebble to the girl's pile and delighted to do it.

"It is your cousin, not the Lord Chancellor, who is the guest of the evening!" laughed Herbert Pryce, who had made his way back at last to Alice Hooper. "I never saw such a success!"

Alice tossed her head in a petulant silence; and a madrigal by the college choir checked any further remarks from Mr. Pryce. After the madrigal came a general move for refreshments, which were set out in the college library and in the garden. The Lord Chancellor must needs offer his arm to his host's sister, and lead the way. The Warden followed, with the wife of the Dean of Christ Church, and the hall began to thin. Lord Glaramara looked back, smiling and beckoning to Constance, as though to say—"Don't altogether desert me!"

But a voice—a tall figure—interposed—

"Lady Constance, let me take you into the garden? It's much nicer than upstairs."

A slight shiver ran, unseen, through the girl's frame. She wished to say no; she tried to say no. And instead she looked up—haughty, but acquiescent.

"Very well."

And she followed Douglas Falloden through the panelled passage outside the hall leading to the garden. Sorell, who had hurried up to find her, arrived in time to see her disappearing through the lights and shadows of the moonlit lawn.

"We can do this sort of thing pretty well, can't we? It's banal because it happens every year, and because it's all mixed up with salmon mayonnaise, and cider-cup—and it isn't banal, because it's Oxford!"

Constance was sitting under the light shadow of a plane-tree, not yet fully out; Falloden was stretched on the grass at her feet. Before her ran a vast lawn which had taken generations to make; and all round it, masses of flowering trees, chestnuts, lilacs, laburnums, now advancing, now receding, made inlets or promontories of the grass, turned into silver by the moonlight. At the furthest edge, through the pushing pyramids of chestnut blossom and the dim drooping gold of the laburnums, could be seen the bastions and battlements of the old city wall, once a fighting reality, now tamed into the mere ornament and appendage of this quiet garden. Over the trees and over the walls rose the spires and towers of a wondrous city; while on the grass, or through the winding paths disappearing into bosky distances, flickered white dresses, and the slender forms of young men and maidens. A murmur of voices rose and fell on the warm night air; the sound of singing—the thin sweetness of boyish notes—came from the hall, whose decorated windows, brightly lit, shone out over the garden.

"It's Oxford—and it's Brahms," said Constance. "I seem to have known it all before in music: the trees—the lawn—the figures—appearing and disappearing—the distant singing——"

She spoke in a low, dreamy tone, her chin propped on her hand. Nothing could have been, apparently, quieter or more self-governed than her attitude. But her inner mind was full of tumult; resentful memory; uneasy joy; and a tremulous fear, both of herself and of the man at her feet. And the man knew it, or guessed it. He dragged himself a little nearer to her on the grass.

"Why didn't you tell me when you were coming?"

The tone was light and laughing.

"I owe you no account of my actions," said the girl quickly.

"We agreed to be friends."

"No! We are not friends." She spoke with suppressed violence, and breaking a twig from the tree overshadowing her, she threw it from her, as though the action were a relief.

He sat up, looking up into her face, his hands clasped round his knees.

"That means you haven't forgiven me?"

"It means that I judge and despise you," she said passionately; "and that it was not an attraction to me to find you here—quite the reverse!"

"Yet here you are—sitting with me in this garden—and you are looking delicious! That dress becomes you so—you are so graceful—so exquisitely graceful. And you never found a more perfect setting than this place—these lawns and trees—and the old college walls. Oxford was waiting for you, and you for Oxford. Are you laughing at me?"

"Naturally!"

"I could rave on by the hour if you would listen to me."

"We have both something better to do—thank goodness! May I ask if you are doing any work?"

He laughed.

"Ten hours a day. This is my first evening out since March. I came to meet you."

Constance bowed ironically. Then for the first time, since their conversation began, it might have been seen that she had annoyed him.

"Friends are not allowed to doubt each other's statements!" he said with animation. "You see I still persist that you allowed me that name, when—you refused me a better. As to my work, ask any of my friends. Talk to Meyrick. He is a dear boy, and will tell you anything you like. He and I 'dig' together in Beaumont Street. My schools are now only three weeks off. I work four hours in the morning. Then I play till six—and get in another six hours between then and 1 a.m."

"Wonderful!" said Constance coolly. "Your ways at Cannes were different. It's a mercy there's no Monte Carlo within reach."

"I play when I play, and work when I work!" he said with emphasis. "The only thing to hate and shun always—is moderation."

"And yet you call yourself a classic! Well, you seem to be sure of your First. At least Uncle Ewen says so."

"Ewen Hooper? He is a splendid fellow—a real Hellenist. He and I get on capitally. About your aunt—I am not so sure."

"Nobody obliges you to know her," was the tranquil reply.

"Ah!—but if she has the keeping of you! Are you coming to tea with me and my people? I have got a man in college to lend me his rooms. My mother and sister will be up for two nights. Very inconsiderate of them—with my schools coming on—but they would do it. Thursday?—before the Eights? Won't my mother be chaperon enough?"

"Certainly. But it only puts off the evil day."

"When I must grovel to Mrs. Hooper?—if I am to see anything of you? Splendid! You are trying to discipline me again—as you did at Cannes!"

In the semidarkness she could see the amusement in his eyes. Her own feeling, in its mingled weakness and antagonism, was that of the feebler wrestler just holding his ground, and fearing every moment to be worsted by some unexpected trick of the game. She gave no signs of it, however.

"I tried, and I succeeded!" she said, as she rose. "You found out that rudeness to my friends didn't answer! Shall we go and get some lemonade? Wasn't that why you brought me here? I think I see the tent."

They walked on together. She seemed to see—exultantly—that she had both angered and excited him.

"I am never rude," he declared. "I am only honest! Only nobody, in this mealy-mouthed world, allows you to be honest; to say and do exactly what represents you. But I shall not be rude to anybody under your wing. Promise me to come to tea, and I will appear to call on your aunt and behave like any sucking dove."

Constance considered it.

"Lady Laura must write to Aunt Ellen."

"Of course. Any other commands?"

"Not at present."

"Then let me offer some humble counsels in return. I beg you not to make friends with that redhaired *poseur* I saw you talking to in the hall."

"Mr. Radowitz!—the musician? I thought him delightful! He is coming to play to me to-morrow."

"Ah, I thought so!" said Falloden wrathfully. "He is an impossible person. He wears a frilled shirt, scents himself, and recites his own poems when he hasn't been asked. And he curries favour—abominably—with the dons. He is a smug—of the first water. There is a movement going on in college to suppress him. I warn you I may not be able to keep out of it."

"He is an artist!" cried Constance. "You have only to look at him, to talk to him, to see it. And artists are always persecuted by stupid people. But you are not stupid!"

"Yes, I am, where *poseurs* are concerned," said Falloden coldly. "I prefer to be. Never mind. We won't excite ourselves. He is not worth it. Perhaps he'll improve—in time. But there is another man I warn you against—Mr. Herbert Pryce."

"A great friend of my cousins'," said Constance mockingly.

"I know. He is always flirting with the eldest girl. It is a shame; for he will never marry her. He wants money and position, and he is so clever he will get them. He is not a gentleman, and he rarely tells the truth. But he is sure to make up to you. I thought I had better tell you beforehand."

"My best thanks! You breathe charity!"

"No—only prudence. And after my schools I throw my books to the dogs, and I shall have a fortnight more of term with nothing to do except—are you going to ride?" he asked her abruptly. "You said at Cannes that you meant to ride when you came to Oxford."

"My aunt doesn't approve."

"As if that would stop you! I can tell you where you can get a horse—a mare that would just suit you. I know all the stables in Oxford. Wait till we meet on Thursday. Would you care to ride in Lathom Woods? (He named a famous estate near Oxford.) I have a permit, and could get you one. They are relations of mine."

Constance excused herself, but scarcely with decision. Her plans, she said, must depend upon her cousins. Falloden smiled and dropped the subject for the moment. Then, as they moved on together through the sinuous ways of the garden, flooded with the scent of hawthorns and lilacs, towards the open tent crowded with folk at the farther end, there leapt in both the same intoxicating sense of youth and strength, the same foreboding of passion, half restlessness, and half enchantment . . .

"I looked for you everywhere," said Sorell, as he made his way to Constance through the crowd of departing guests in the college gateway. "Where did you hide yourself? The Lord Chancellor was sad not to say good-bye to you."

Constance summoned an answering tone of regret.

"How good of him! I was only exploring the garden—with Mr. Falloden."

At the name, there was a quick and stiffening change in Sorell's face.

"You knew him before? Yes—he told me. A queer fellow—very able. They say he'll get his First. Well—we shall meet at the Eights and then we'll make plans. Good night."

He smiled on her, and went his way, ruminating uncomfortably as he walked back to his college along the empty midnight streets. Falloden? It was to be hoped there was nothing in that! How Ella Risborough would have detested the type! But there was much that was not her mother in the daughter. He vowed to himself that he would do his small best to watch over Ella Risborough's child.

There was little or no conversation in the four-wheeler that bore the Hooper party home. Mrs. Hooper and Alice were stiffly silent, while the Reader chaffed Constance a little about her successes of the evening. But he, too, was sleepy and tired, and the talk dropped. As they lighted their bedroom candles in the hall, Mrs. Hooper said to her niece, in her thin, high tone, mincing and coldly polite:

"I think it would have been better, Constance, if you had told us you knew Lord Glaramara. I don't wish to find fault, but such—such concealments—are really very awkward!"

Constance opened her eyes. She could have defended herself easily. She had no idea that her aunt was unaware of the old friendship between her parents and Lord Glaramara, who was no more interesting to her personally than many others of their Roman *habitués*, of whom the world was full. But she was too preoccupied to spend any but the shortest words on such a silly thing.

"I'm sorry, Aunt Ellen. I really didn't understand."

And she went up to bed, thinking only of Falloden; while Alice followed her, her small face pinched and weary, her girlish mind full of pain.

IV

ON THE day after the Vice-Chancellor's party, Falloden, after a somewhat slack morning's work, lunched in college with Meyrick. After hall, the quadrangle was filled with strolling men, hatless and smoking, discussing the chances of the Eights, the last debate at the Union, and the prospects of individual men in the schools.

Presently the sound of a piano was heard from the open windows of a room on the first floor.

"Great Scott!" said Falloden irritably to Meyrick, with whom he was walking arm in arm, "what a noise that fellow Radowitz makes! Why should we have to listen to him? He behaves as though the whole college belonged to him. We can't hear ourselves speak."

"Treat him like a barrel-organ and remove him!" said Meyrick, laughing. He was a light-hearted, easygoing youth, a "fresher" in his first summer term, devoted to Falloden, whose physical and intellectual powers seemed to him amazing.

"Bombard him first!" said Falloden. "Who's got some soda-water bottles?" And he beckoned imperiously to a neighbouring group of men,—"bloods"—always ready to follow him in a "rag," and heroes together with him of a couple of famous bonfires, in Falloden's first year.

They came up, eager for any mischief, the summer weather in their veins like wine. They stood round Falloden laughing and chaffing, till finally three of them disappeared at his bidding. They came rushing back, from various staircases, laden with soda-water bottles.

Then Falloden, with two henchmen, placed himself under Radowitz's windows, and summoned the offender in a stentorian voice:

"Radowitz! stop that noise!"

No answer—except that Radowitz in discoursing some "music of the future," and quite unaware of the shout from below, pounded and tormented the piano more than ever. The waves of crashing sound seemed to fill the quadrangle.

"We'll summon him thrice!" said Falloden. "Then—fire!"

But Radowitz remained deaf, and the assailant below gave the order. Three strong right arms below discharged three soda-water bottles, which went through the open window.

"My goody!" said Meyrick, "I hope he's well out of the way!" There was a sound of breaking glass. Then Radowitz, furious, appeared at his window, his golden hair more halolike than ever in the bright sun.

"What are you doing, you idiots?"

"Stop that noise, Radowitz!" shouted Falloden. "It annoys us!"

"Can't help it. It pleases me," said Radowitz shortly, proceeding to close the window. But he had scarcely done so, when Falloden launched another bottle, which went smash through the window and broke it. The glass fell out into the quadrangle, raising all the echoes. The rioters below held their laughing breaths.

"I say, what about the dons?" said one.

"Keep a lookout!" said another.

But meanwhile Radowitz had thrown up the injured window, and crimson with rage he leaned far out and flung half a broken bottle at the group below. All heads ducked, but the ragged missile only just missed Meyrick's curly poll.

"Not pretty that!—not pretty at all!" said Falloden coolly. "Might really have done some mischief. We'll avenge you, Meyrick. Follow me, you fellows!"

And in one solid phalanx, they charged, six or seven strong, up Radowitz's staircase. But he was ready for them. The oak was sported, and they could hear him dragging some heavy chairs against it. Meanwhile, from the watchers left in the quad, came a loud cough.

"Dons!—by Jove! Scatter!" And they rushed further up the staircase, taking refuge in the rooms of two of the "raggers." The lookout in the quadrangle turned to walk quietly towards the porter's lodge. The Senior Tutor—a spare tall man with a Jove-like brow—emerged from the library, and stood on the steps surveying the broken glass.

"All run to cover, of course!" was his reflection, half scornful, half disgusted. "But I am certain I heard Falloden's voice. What a puppy stage it is! They would be much better employed worrying old boots!"

But philosopher or no, he got no clue. The quadrangle was absolutely quiet and deserted, save for the cheeping of the swallows flitting across it, and the whistling of a lad in the porter's lodge. The Senior Tutor returned to the library, where he was unpacking a box of new books.

The rioters emerged at discreet intervals, and rejoined each other in the broad street outside the college.

"Vengeance is still due!"—said Falloden, towering among them, always with the faithful and grinning Meyrick at his side—"and we will repay. But now, to our tents! Ta, ta!" And dismissing them all, including Meyrick, he walked off alone in the direction of Holywell. He was going to look out a horse for Constance Bledlow.

As he walked, he said to himself that he was heartily sick of this Oxford life, ragging and all. It was a good thing it was so nearly done. He meant to get his First, because he didn't choose, having wasted so much time over it, not to get it. But it wouldn't give him any particular pleasure to get it. The only thing that really mattered was that Constance Bledlow was in Oxford, and that when his schools were over, he would have nothing to do but to stay on two or three weeks and force the running with her. He felt himself immeasurably older than his companions with whom he had just been rioting. His mind was set upon a man's interests and aims—marriage, travel, Parliament; they were still boys, without a mind among them. None the less, there was an underplot running through his consciousness all the time as to how best to punish Radowitz—both for his throw, and his impertinence in monopolising a certain lady for at least a quarter of an hour on the preceding evening.

At the well-known livery-stables in Holywell, he found a certain animation. Horses were in demand, as there were manœuvres going on in Blenheim Park, and the minds of both dons and undergraduates were drawn thither. But Falloden succeeded in getting hold of the manager and absorbing his services at once.

"Show you something really good, fit for a lady?"

The manager took him through the stables, and Falloden in the end picked out precisely the beautiful brown mare of which he had spoken to Constance.

"Nobody else is to ride her, please, till the lady I am acting for has tried her," he said peremptorily to Fox. "I shall try her myself to-morrow. And what about a groom?—a decent fellow, mind, with a decent livery."

He saw a possible man and another horse, reserving both provisionally. Then he walked hurriedly to his lodgings to see if by any chance there were a note for him there. He had wired to his mother the day before, telling her to write to Constance Bledlow and Mrs. Hooper by the evening's post, suggesting that, on Thursday before the Eights, Lady Laura should pick her up at Medburn House, take her to tea at Falloden's lodgings and then on to the Eights. Lady Laura was to ask for an answer addressed to the lodgings.

He found one—a little note with a crest and monogram he knew well.

Medburn House.

"Dear Mr. Falloden,—I am very sorry I can not come to tea to-morrow. But my aunt and cousins seem to have made an engagement for me. No doubt I shall see Lady Laura at the boats. My aunt thanks her for her kind letter.

"Yours very truly,

"Constance Bledlow."

Falloden bit his lip. He had reckoned on an acceptance, having done everything that had been prescribed to him; and he felt injured. He walked on, fuming and meditating, to Vincent's Club, and wrote a reply.

"DEAR LADY CONSTANCE,—A thousand regrets! I hope for better luck next time. Meanwhile, as you say, we shall meet to-morrow at the Eights. I have spent much time to-day in trying to find you a horse, as we agreed. The mare I told you of is really a beauty. I am going to try her to-morrow, and will report when we meet. I admire your nepticular (I believe *neptis* is the Latin for niece) docility!

"Yours sincerely,
"DOUGLAS FALLODEN."

"Will that offend her?" he thought. "But a pinprick is owed. I was distinctly given to understand that if the proprieties were observed, she would come."

In reality, however, he was stimulated by her refusal, as he was by all forms of conflict, which, for him, made the zest of life.

He shut himself up that evening and the following morning with his Greats work. Then he and Meyrick rushed up to the racket courts in the Parks for an hour's hard exercise, after which, in the highest physical spirits, a splendid figure in his white flannels, with the dark blue cap and sash of the Harrow Eleven—(he had quarrelled with the captain of the Varsity Eleven very early in his Oxford career, and by an heroic sacrifice to what he conceived to be his dignity had refused to let himself be tried for it)—he went off to meet his mother and sister at the railway station.

It was, of course, extremely inconsiderate of his mother to be coming at all in these critical weeks before the schools. She ought to have kept away. And yet he would be very glad to see her—and Nelly. He was fond of his home people, and they of him. They were his belongings—and they were Fallodens. Therefore his strong family pride accepted them, and made the most of them.

But his countenance fell when, as the train slowed into the railway station, he perceived beckoning to him from the windows, not two Fallodens, but four!

"What has mother been about?" He stood aghast. For there were not only Lady Laura and Nelly, but Trix, a child of eleven, and Roger, the Winchester boy of fourteen, who was still at home after an attack of measles.

They beamed at him as they descended. The children were quite aware they were superfluous, and fell upon him with glee.

"You don't want us, Duggy, we know! But we made mother bring us."

"Mother, really you ought to have given me notice!" said her reproachful son. "What am I to do with these brats?"

But the brats hung upon him, and his mother, "fat, fair and forty," smiled propitiatingly.

"Oh, my dear Duggy, never mind. They amuse themselves. They've promised to be good. And they get into mischief in London, directly my back's turned. How nice you look in flannels, dear! Are you going to row this afternoon?"

"Well, considering you know that my schools are coming on in a fortnight——" said Falloden, exasperated.

"It's so annoying of them!" said Lady Laura, sighing. "I wanted to bring Nelly up for two or three weeks. We could have got a house. But your father wouldn't hear of it."

"I should rather think not! Mother, do you want me to get a decent degree, or do you not?"

"But of course you're sure to," said Lady Laura with provoking optimism, hanging on his arm. "And now give us some tea, for we're all ravenous! And what about that girl, Lady Constance?"

"She can't come. Her aunt has made another engagement for her. You'll meet her at the boats."

Lady Laura looked relieved.

"Well then, we can go straight to our tea. But of course I wrote. I always do what you tell me, Duggy. Come along, children!"

"Trix and I got a packet of Banbury cakes at Didcot," reported Roger, in triumph, showing a greasy paper. "But we've eat 'em all."

"Little pigs!" said Falloden, surveying them. "And now I suppose you're going to gorge again?"

"We shall disgrace you!" shouted both the children joyously—"we knew we should!"

But Falloden hunted them all into a capacious fly, and they drove off to Marmion, where a room had been borrowed for the tea-party. Falloden sat on the box with folded arms and a sombre countenance. Why on earth had his mother brought the children? It was revolting to have to appear on the barge with such a troop. And all his time would be taken up with looking after them—time which he wanted for quite other things.

However, he was in for it. At Marmion he led the party through two quads and innumerable passages, till he pointed to a dark staircase up which they climbed, each member of the family—except the guide—talking at the top of their voices. On the third floor, Falloden paused and herded them into the room of a shy second-year man, very glad to do such a "blood" as Falloden a kindness, and help entertain his relations.

"Well, thank God, I've got you in!" said Falloden gloomily, as he shut the door behind the last of them.

"How Duggy does hustle us! I've had nothing of a tea!" said Roger, looking resentfully, his mouth full of cake, at his elder brother, who was already beginning to take out his watch, to bid his mother and sisters resume their discarded jackets, and to send a scout for a four-wheeler.

But Falloden was inexorable. He tore his sister Nelly, a soft fluffy creature of seventeen, away from the shy attentions of the second-year man, scoffed in disgust at Trix's desire for chocolates after a Gargantuan meal, and declared that they would all be late for the Eights, if any more gorging was allowed. His mother rose obediently. To be seen with such a son in the crowded Oxford streets filled her with pride. She could have walked beside him for hours.

At the college gate, Trix pinched her brother's arm.

"Well, Duggy, say it!"

"Say what, you little scug?"

" 'Thank God, I've got you out!' " laughed the child, laying her cheek against his coat-sleeve. "That's what you're thinking. You know you are. I say, Duggy, you do look jolly in those colours!"

"Don't talk rot!" grumbled Falloden, but he winked at her in brotherly fashion, and Trix was more than happy. Like her mother, she believed that Douglas was simply the handsomest and cleverest fellow in the world. When he scolded it was better than other people's praise, and when he gave you a real private wink, it raised a sister to the skies. On such soil does male arrogance grow!

Soon they were in the stream of people crossing Christ Church river on their way to the boats. The May sunshine lay broad on the buttercup meadows, on the Christ Church elms, on the severe and blackened front of Corpus, on the long gabled line of Merton. The river glittered in the distance, and towards it the crowd of its worshippers—young girls in white, young men in flannels, elderly fathers and mothers from a distance, and young fathers and mothers from the rising tutorial homes of Oxford—made their merry way. Falloden looked in all directions for the Hooper party. A new anxiety and eagerness were stirring in him which he resented, which he tried to put down. He did not wish, he did not intend, if he could help it, to be too much in love with anybody. He was jealous of his own self-control, and intensely proud of his own strength of will, as he might have been of a musical or artistic gift. It was his particular gift, and he would not have it weakened. He had seen men do the most idiotic things for love. He did not intend to do such things. Love should be strictly subordinate to a man's career; women should be subordinate.

At the same time, from the second week of their acquaintance on the Riviera, he had wished to marry Constance Bledlow. He had proposed to her, only to be promptly refused, and on one mad afternoon, in the woods of the Esterels, he had snatched a kiss. What an amazing fuss she made about that kiss! He thought she would have cut him for ever. It was with the greatest difficulty, and only after a grovelling apology, that he had succeeded in making his peace. Yet all through the days of her wrath he had been quite certain that he would in the end appease her; which meant a triumphant confidence on his part that to a degree she did not herself admit or understand, he had captured her. Her resolute refusal to correspond with him, even after they had made it up and he was on the point of returning to Oxford, had piqued him indeed. But he was aware that she was due at Oxford, as her uncle's ward, some time in May; and meanwhile he had coolly impressed upon himself that in the interests of his work, it was infinitely better he should be without the excitement of her letters. By the time she arrived, he would have got through the rereading of his principal books, which a man must do in the last term before the schools, and could begin to "slack." And after the schools, he could devote himself.

But now that they had met again, he was aware of doubts and difficulties that had not yet assailed him. That she was not indifferent to him—that his presence still played upon her nerves and senses—so much he had verified. But during their conversation at the Vice-Chancellor's party he had become aware of something hard and resistant in her—in her whole attitude towards him—which had considerably astonished him. His arrogant self-confidence had reckoned upon the effect of absence, as making her softer and more yielding when they met again. The reverse seemed to be the case, and he pondered it with irritation. . . .

"Oh, Duggy, isn't it ripping?" cried Trix, leaping and sidling at his elbow like a young colt.

For they had reached the river, which lay a vivid blue, flashing under the afternoon sun and the fleecy clouds. Along it lay the barges, a curving many-tinted line, their tall flag-staffs flying the colours of the colleges to which they belonged, their decks crowded with spectators. Innumerable punts were crossing and recrossing the river—the towing-path opposite was alive with men. Everything danced and glittered, the white reflections in the river, the sun upon the oars, the row of extravagantly green poplars on the further bank. How strong and lusty was the May light!—the yellow green of the elms—the gold of the buttercupped meadow! Only the dying moon in the high blue suggested a different note; as of another world hidden behind the visible world, waiting patiently, mysteriously, to take its place—to see it fade.

"Oh, Duggy, there's somebody waving to you. Oh, it's Lord Meyrick. And who's that girl with him? She's bowing to you, too. She's got an awfully lovely frock! Oh, Duggy, do look at her!"

Falloden had long since looked at her. He turned carelessly to his mother. "There's Meyrick, mother, on that barge in front. You know you're dining with him to-night in Christ Church. And that's Constance Bledlow beside him, to whom I asked you to write."

"Oh, is it? A good-looking girl," said his mother approvingly. "And who is that man beside her, with the extraordinary hair? He looks like somebody in Lohengrin."

Falloden laughed, but not agreeably.

"You've about hit it! He's a Marmion man. A silly, affected creature—half a Pole. His music is an infernal nuisance in college. We shall suppress it and him some day."

"What barge is it, Duggy? Are we going there?"

Falloden replied impatiently that the barge they were nearing belonged to Christ Church, and they were bound for the Marmion barge, much further along.

Meanwhile he asked himself what could have taken the Hooper party to the Christ Church barge? Ewen Hooper was a Llandaff man, and Llandaff, a small and insignificant college, shared a barge with another small college some distance down the river.

As they approached the barge he saw that while Constance had Radowitz on her right, Sorell of St. Cyprian's stood on the other side of her. Ah, no doubt, that accounted for it. Sorell had been originally at "the House," was still a lecturer there, and very popular. He had probably invited the Hoopers with their niece. It was, of course, the best barge in the best position. Falloden remembered how at the Vice-Chancellor's party Sorell had hovered about Constance, assuming a kind of mild guardianship; until he himself had carried her off. Why? What on earth had she to do with Sorell? Well, he must find out. Meanwhile, she clearly did not intend to take any further notice of his neighbourhood. Sorell and Radowitz absorbed her. They were evidently explaining the races to her, and she stood between them, a docile and charming vision, turning her graceful head from side to side. Falloden and his party crossed her actual line of sight. But she took no further notice; and he heard her laugh at something Radowitz was saying.

"Oh, Mr. Falloden, is that you—and Lady Laura! This is a pleasure!"

He turned to see a lady whom he cordially detested—a head's wife, who happened to be an "Honourable," the daughter of a small peer, and terribly conscious of the fact. She might have reigned in Oxford; she preferred to be a much snubbed dependent of London, and the smart people whose invitations she took such infinite trouble to get. For she was possessed of two daughters, tall and handsome girls, who were an obsession to her, an irritation to other people, and a cause of blushing to themselves. Her instinct for all men of family or title to be found among the undergraduates was amazingly extensive and acute; and she had paid much court to Falloden, as the prospective heir to a marquisate. He had hitherto treated her with scant attention, but she was not easily abashed, and she fastened at once on Lady Laura, whom she had seen once at a London ball.

"Where are you going, Lady Laura? To Marmion? Oh, no! Come on to our barge, you will see so much better, and save yourself another dusty bit of walk. Here we are!"

And she waved her parasol gaily towards a barge immediately ahead, belonging to one of the more important colleges. Lady Laura looked doubtfully at her son.

Falloden suddenly accepted, and with the utmost cordiality.

"That's really very good of you, Mrs. Manson! I shall certainly advise my mother to take advantage of your kind offer. But you can't do with all of us!" He pointed smiling to Trix and Roger.

"Of course I can! The more the merrier!" And the lively lady stooped, laid an affectionate hand on Roger's shoulder, and said in a stage aside—"Our ices are very good!"

Roger hastily retreated.

The starting-gun had boomed—communicating the usual thrill and sudden ripple of talk through the crowded barges.

"Now they're off!"

Lady Laura, Nelly, and "the babes" hung over the railing of the barge, looking excitedly for the first nose of a boat coming round the bend. Falloden, between the two fair-haired Miss Mansons, manœuvred them and himself into a position at the rear where he could both see and be seen by the party on the Christ Church barge, amid which a certain large white hat with waving feathers shone conspicuous. The two girls between whom he stood, who had never found him in the least accessible before, were proud to be seen with him, and delighted to try their smiles on him. They knew he was soon going down, and they had visions of dancing with him in London, of finding an acquaintance, perhaps even a friend, at last, in those chilly London drawing-rooms, before which, if their mother knew no such weakness, they often shivered.

Falloden looked down upon them with a half sarcastic, half benignant patronage, and made himself quite agreeable. From the barge next door, indeed, the Manson and Falloden parties appeared to be on the most intimate terms. Mrs. Manson, doing the honours of the college boat, flattering Lady Laura, gracious to the children, and glancing every now and then at her two girls and their handsome companion, was enjoying a crowded and successful moment.

But she too was aware of the tall girl in white on the neighbouring deck, and she turned enquiringly to Falloden.

"Do you know who she is?"

"The Risboroughs' daughter—Lady Constance Bledlow." Mrs. Manson's eyebrows went up.

"Indeed! Of course I knew her parents intimately! Where is she staying?"

Falloden briefly explained.

"But how very interesting! I must call upon her at once. But—I scarcely know the Hoopers!"

Falloden hung over the barge rail, and smiled unseen.

"Here they come!—here they come!" shouted the children, laying violent hands on Falloden that he might identify the boats for them.

Up rolled a mighty roar from the lower reaches of the river as the boats came in sight, "Univ" leading; and the crowd of running and shouting men came rushing along the towing-path. "Univ" was gallantly "bumped" in front of its own barge, and Magdalen went head of the river. A delirious twenty minutes followed. Bump crashed on bump. The river in all its visible length flashed with the rising and falling oars—the white bodies of the rowers strained back and forth. But it was soon over, and only the cheering for the victorious crews remained; and the ices—served to the visitors!—of which Roger was not slow to remind his hostess.

The barges emptied, and the crowd poured out again into the meadows. Just outside the Christ Church barge, Constance with Nora beside her, and escorted by Sorell and Lord Meyrick, lifted a pair of eyes to a tall fellow in immaculate flannels and a Harrow cap. She had been aware of his neighbourhood, and he of hers, long before it was possible to speak. Falloden introduced his mother. Then he resolutely took possession of Constance.

"I hope you approve what I have been doing about the mare?"

"I am of course most grateful. When am I to try her?"

"I shall take her out to-morrow afternoon. Then I'll report."

"It is extremely kind of you." The tone was strictly conventional.

He said nothing; and after a minute she could not help looking up. She met an expression which showed a wounded gentleman beside her.

"I hope you saw the races well?" he said coldly.

"Excellently. And Mr. Sorell explained everything."

"You knew him before?"

"But of course!" she said, laughing. "I have known him for years."

"You never mentioned him—at Cannes."

"One does not always catalogue one's acquaintance, does one?"

"He seems to be more than an acquaintance."

"Oh, yes. He is a great friend. Mamma was so fond of him. He went with us to Sicily once. And Uncle Ewen likes him immensely."

"He is of course a paragon," said Falloden.

Constance glanced mockingly at her companion.

"I don't see why he should be called anything so disagreeable. All we knew of him was—that he was delightful! So learned—and simple—and modest—the dearest person to travel with! When he left us at Palermo, the whole party seemed to go flat."

"You pile it on!"

"Not at all. You asked me if he were more than an acquaintance. I am giving you the facts."

"I don't enjoy them!" said Falloden abruptly.

She burst into her soft laugh.

"I'm so sorry. But I really can't alter them. Where has my party gone to?"

She looked ahead, and saw that by a little judicious holding back Falloden had dexterously isolated her both from his own group and hers. Mrs. Manson and Lady Laura were far ahead in the wide, moving crowd that filled the new-made walk across the Christ Church meadow; so were the Hoopers and the slender figure and dark head of Alexander Sorell.

"Don't distress yourself, please. We shall catch them up before we get to Merton Street. And this only pays the very smallest fraction of your debt! I understood that if my mother wrote——"

She coloured brightly.

"I didn't promise!" she said hastily. "And I found the Hoopers were counting on me."

"No doubt. Oh, I don't grumble. But when friends—suppose we take the old path under the wall? It is much less crowded."

And before she knew where she was, she had been whisked out of the stream of visitors and undergraduates, and found herself walking almost in solitude in the shadow of one of the oldest walls in Oxford, the Cathedral towering overhead, the crowd moving at some distance on their right.

"That's better," said Falloden coolly. "May I go on? I was saying that when one friend disappoints another—bitterly!—there is such a thing as making up!"

There were beautiful notes in Falloden's deep voice, when he chose to employ them. He employed them now, and the old thrill of something that was at once delight and fear ran through Constance. But she looked him in the face, apparently quite unmoved.

"Now it is you who are piling it on! You will use such tragic expressions for the most trivial things. Of course, I am sorry if——"

"Then make amends!"—he said quickly. "Promise me—if the mare turns out well—you will ride in Lathom Woods—on Saturday?"

His eyes shone upon her. The force of the man's personality seemed to envelope her, to beat down the resistance which, as soon as he was out of her sight, the wiser mind in her built up.

She hesitated—smiled. And again the smile—or was it the May sun and wind?—gave her that heightening, that touch of brilliance that a face so delicate must often miss.

Falloden's fastidious sense approved her wholly: the white dress; the hat that framed her brow; the slender gold chains which rose and fell on her gently rounded breast; her height and grace. Passion beat within him. He hung on her answer.

"Saturday—impossible! I am not free till Monday, at least. And what about the groom?" She looked up.

"I shall parade him to-morrow, livery, horse and all. I undertake he shall give satisfaction. The Lathom Woods just now are a dream!"

"It is all a dream!" she said, looking round her at the beauty of field and tree, of the May clouds, and the grey college walls—youth and youth's emotion speaking in the sudden softening of her eyes.

He saw—he felt her—yielding.

"You'll come?"

"I—I suppose I may as well ride in Lathom Woods as anywhere else. You have a key?"

"The groom will have it. I meet you there."

She flushed a bright pink.

"That might have been left vague!"

"How are you to find your way through those woods without a guide?" he protested.

She was silent a moment, then she said with decision:

"I must overtake my people."

"You shall. I want you to talk to my mother—and—you have still to introduce me to your aunt and cousins."

Mirth crept into her eyes. The process of taming him had begun.

Falloden on the way back to his lodgings handed over his family to the tender offices of Meyrick and a couple of other gilded youths, who had promised to look after them for the evening. They were to dine at the Randolph, and go to a college concert. Falloden washed his hands of them, and shut himself up for five or six hours' grind, broken only by a very hasty meal. The thought of Constance hovered about him—but his will banished it. Will and something else—those aptitudes of brain which determined his quick and serviceable intelligence.

When after his frugal dinner he gave himself in earnest to the article in a French magazine, on a new French philosopher, which had been recommended to him by his tutor as likely to be of use to him in his general philosophy paper, his mind soon took fire; Constance was forgotten, and he lost himself in the splendour shed by the original and creative thought of a great man, climbing, under his guidance, as the night wore on, from point to point, and height to height, amid the Oxford silence, broken only by the chiming bells, and a benighted footfall in the street outside, until he seemed to have reached the bounds of the phenomenal and to be close on that outer vastness whence stream the primal forces—*Die Mütter*—as Goethe called them—whose play is with the worlds.

Then by way of calming the brain before sleep, he fell upon some notes to be copied and revised, on the "Religious Aspects of Greek Drama," and finally amused himself with running through an ingenious "Memoria Technica" on the 6th Book of the Ethics which he had made for himself during the preceding winter.

Then work was done, and he threw it from him. with the same energy as that wherewith he had banished the remembrance of Constance some hours before. Now he could walk his room in the May dawn, and think of her, and only of her. With all the activity of his quickened mental state, he threw himself into the future—their rides together—their meetings, few and measured till the schools were done—then!—all the hours of life, and a man's most obstinate effort, spent in the winning of her. He knew well that she would be difficult to win.

But he meant to win her—and before others could seriously approach her. He was already nervously jealous of Sorell—and contemptuously jealous of Radowitz. And if they could torment him so, what would it be when Constance passed into that larger world of society to which sooner or later she was bound? No, she was to be wooed and married now. The Falloden custom was to marry early—and a good custom too. His father would approve, and money from the estate would of course be forthcoming. Constance was on her father's side extremely well-born; the Hooper blood would soon be lost sight of in a Risborough and Falloden descent. She was sufficiently endowed; and she had all the grace of person and mind that a Falloden had a right to look for in his wife.

Marriage, then, in the autumn, when he would be twenty-four—two years of travel—then Parliament—

On this dream he fell asleep. A brisk wind sprang up with the sunrise, and rustled round his lightly-darkened room. One might have heard in it the low laughter of Fortune on the watch.

V

"YOU DO have the oddest ways," said Nora, perched at the foot of her cousin's bed; "why do you stay in bed to breakfast?"

"Because I always have—and because it's the proper and reasonable thing to do," said Constance defiantly. "Your English custom of coming down at half past eight to eat poached eggs and bacon is perfectly detestable."

She waved her teaspoon in Nora's face, and Nora reflected—though her sunburnt countenance was still severe—that Connie was never so attractive as when, in the freshest of white dressing-gowns, propped among the lace and silk of her ridiculous pillows and bedspreads, she was toying with the coffee and roll which Annette brought her at eight o'clock, as she had been accustomed to bring it since Connie was a child. Mrs. Hooper had clearly expressed her disapproval of such habits, but neither Annette nor Connie had paid any attention. Annette had long since come to an understanding with the servants, and it was she who descended at half past seven, made the coffee herself, and brought up with it the nearest thing to the morning rolls of the Palazzo Barberini which Oxford could provide—with a copy of *The Times* specially ordered for Lady Constance. The household itself subsisted on a copy of the *Morning Post*, religiously reserved to Mrs. Hooper after Dr. Hooper had glanced through it—he, of course, saw *The Times* at the Union. But Connie regarded a newspaper at breakfast as a necessary part of life.

After her coffee, accordingly, she read *The Times*, and smoked a cigarette, proceedings which were a daily source of wonder to

Nora and reprobation in the minds of Mrs. Hooper and Alice. Then she generally wrote her letters, and was downstairs after all by half past ten, dressed and ready for the day. Mrs. Hooper declared to Dr. Ewen that she would be ashamed for any of their Oxford friends to know that a niece of his kept such hours, and that it was a shocking example for the servants. But the maids took it with smiles, and were always ready to run up and down stairs for Lady Connie; while as for Oxford, the invitations which had descended upon the Hooper family, even during the few days since Connie's arrival, had given Aunt Ellen some feverish pleasure, but perhaps more annoyance. So far from Ewen's "position" being of any advantage to Connie, it was Connie who seemed likely to bring the Hoopers into circles of Oxford society where they had till now possessed but the slenderest footing. An invitation to dinner from the Provost of Winton and Mrs. Manson, to "Dr. and Mrs. Hooper, Miss Hooper and Lady Constance Bledlow," to meet an archbishop, had fairly taken Mrs. Hooper's breath away. But she declaimed to Alice none the less in private on the innate snobbishness of people.

Nora, however, wished to understand.

"I can't imagine why you should read *The Times*," she said with emphasis, as Connie pushed her tray away, and looked for her cigarettes. "What have you to do with politics?"

"Why, *The Times* is all about people I know!" said Connie, opening amused eyes. "Look there!" And she pointed to the newspaper lying open amid the general litter of her morning's post, and to a paragraph among the foreign telegrams describing the excitement in Rome over a change of Ministry. "Fall of the Italian Cabinet. The King sends for the Marchese Bardinelli."

"And there's a letter from Elisa Bardinelli, telling me all about it!" She tossed some closely-written sheets to Nora, who took them up doubtfully.

"It is in Italian!" she said, as though she resented the fact.

"Well, of course! Did you think it would be in Russian? You really ought to learn Italian, Nora. Shall I teach you?"

"Well—it might be useful for my Literature," said Nora slowly. "There are all those fellows Chaucer borrowed from—and then Shakespeare. I wouldn't mind."

"Thank you!" said Connie, laughing. "And then look at the French news. That's thrilling! Sir Wilfrid's going to throw up the Embassy and retire. I stayed with them a night in Paris on my way through—and they never breathed. But I thought something was up. Sir Wilfrid's a queer temper. I expect he's had a row with the Foreign Office. They were years in Rome, and of course we knew them awfully well. Mamma adored her!"

And leaning back with her hands behind her head, Connie's sparkling look subsided for a moment into a dreamy sweetness.

"I suppose you think Oxford a duck-pond after all that!" said Nora pugnaciously.

Constance laughed.

"Why, it's new. It's experience. It's all to the good."

"Oh, you needn't suppose I am apologising for Oxford!" cried Nora. "I think, of course, it's the most interesting place in the world. It's ideas that matter, and ideas come from the universities!" And the child-student of seventeen drew herself up proudly, as though she bore the honour of all *academie* on her sturdy shoulders.

Constance went into a fit of laughter.

"And I think they come from the people who do things, and not only from the people who read and write about them when they're done. But goodness—what does it matter where they come from? Go away, Nora, and let me dress!"

"There are several things I want to know," said Nora deliberately, not budging. "Where did you get to know Mr. Falloden?"

The colour ran up inconveniently in Connie's cheeks.

"I told you," she said impatiently. "No!—I suppose you weren't there. I met him on the Riviera. He came out for the Christmas holidays. He was in the villa next to us, and we saw him every day."

"How you must have hated him!" said Nora, with energy, her hands round her knees, her dark brows frowning.

Constance laughed again, but rather angrily.

"Why should I hate him, please? He's extraordinarily clever——"

"Yes, but such a snob!" said Nora, setting her white teeth. Connie sprang up in bed.

"Nora, really, the way you talk of other people's friends. You should learn—indeed, you should—not to say rude and provoking things!"

"Why should it provoke you? I'm certain you don't care for him—you can't!" cried Nora. "He's the most hectoring, overbearing creature! The way he took possession of you the other day at the boats! Of course he didn't care, if he made everybody talk about you!"

Constance turned a little white.

"Why should anybody talk?" she said coldly. "But really, Nora, I must turn you out. I shall ring for Annette." She raised herself in bed.

"No, no!" Nora caught her hand as it stretched out towards the bell. "Oh, Connie, you shall not fall in love with Mr. Falloden! I should go mad if you did."

"You are mad already," said Constance, half laughing, half furious. "I tell you Mr. Falloden is a friend of mine—as other people are. He is very good company, and I won't have him abused—for nothing. His manners are abominable. I have told him so dozens of times. All the same, he amuses me—and interests me—and you are not to talk about him, Nora, if you can't talk civilly."

And looking rather formidably great-ladyish, Constance threw severe glances at her cousin.

Nora stood up, first on one foot, then on the other. She was bursting with things to say, and could not find words to say them in. At last she broke out—

"I'm not abusing him for nothing! If you only knew the horrid, rude things—mean things too—at dances and parties—he does to some of the girls I know here; just because they're not swells and not rich, and he doesn't care what they think about him. That's what I call a snob—judging people by whether they're rich and important—by whether it's worth while to know them. Hateful!"

"You foolish child!" cried Connie. "He's so rich and important himself, what can it matter to him? You talk as though he were a hanger-on—as though he had anything to gain by making up to people. You are absurd!"

"Oh, no—I know he's not like Herbert Pryce," said Nora, panting, but undaunted. "There, that was disgusting of me!—don't remember that I ever said that, Connie!—I know Mr. Falloden needn't be a snob, because he's got everything that snobs want—and he's clever besides. But it is snobbish all the same to be so proud and stand-off, to like to make other people feel small and miserable, just that you may feel big."

"Go away!" said Constance, and taking up one of her pillows, she threw it neatly at Nora, who dodged it with equal skill. Nora retreated to the other side of the door, then quickly put her head through again.

"Connie!—don't!"

"Go away!" repeated Connie, smiling, but determined.

Nora looked at her appealingly, then shut her lips firmly, turned and went away. Connie spent a few minutes in meditation. She resented the kind of quasi-guardianship that this clever *backfisch* assumed towards her, though she knew it meant that Nora had fallen in love with her. But it was inconvenient to be so fallen in love with—if it was to mean interference with her private affairs.

"As if I couldn't protect myself!"

The mere thought of Douglas Falloden was agitating enough, without the consciousness that a pair of hostile eyes, so close to her, were on the watch.

She sprang up, and went through her dressing, thinking all the time. "What do I really feel about him? I am going to ride with him on Monday—without telling anybody; I vowed I would never put myself in his power again. And I am deliberately doing it. I am in my guardian's house, and I am treating Uncle Ewen vilely."

And why?—why these lapses from good manners and good feeling? Was she after all in love with him? If he asked her to marry him again, as he had asked her to marry him before, would she now say yes, instead of no? Not at all! She was further—she declared—from saying yes now, than she had been under his first vehement attack.

And yet she was quite determined to ride with him. The thought of their rides in the radiant Christmas sunshine at Cannes came back upon her with a rush. They had been one continuous excitement, simply because it was Falloden who rode beside her—Falloden, who after their merry dismounted lunch under the pines, had swung her to her saddle again—her little foot in his strong hand—so easily and powerfully. It was Falloden who, when she and two or three others of the party found themselves by mistake on a dangerous bridle-path, on the very edge of a steep ravine in the Esterels, and her horse had become suddenly restive, had thrown himself off his own mount, and passing between her horse and the precipice, where any sudden movement of the frightened beast would have sent him to his death, had seized the bridle and led her into safety. And yet all the time, she had disliked him almost as much as she had been drawn to him. None of the many signs of his autocratic and imperious temper had escaped her, and the pride in her had clashed against the pride in him. To flirt with him was one thing. The cloud of grief and illness, which had fallen so heavily on her youth, was just lifting under the natural influences of time at the moment when she and Falloden first came across each other. It was a moment for her of strong reaction, of a welling-up and welling-back of life, after a kind of suspension. The strong young fellow, with his good looks, his masterful ways, and his ability—in spite of the barely disguised audacity which seemed inseparable from the homage it pleased him to pay to women—had made a deep and thrilling impression upon her youth and sex.

And yet she had never hesitated when he had asked her to marry him. Ride with him—laugh with him—quarrel with him, yes!—marry him, no! Something very deep in her recoiled. She refused him, and then had lain awake most of the night thinking of her mother and feeling ecstatically sure, while the tears came raining, that the dear ghost approved that part of the business at least, if no other.

And how could there be any compunction about it? Douglas Falloden, with his egotism, his pride in himself, his family, his wits, his boundless confidence in his own brilliant future, was surely fair game. Such men do not break their hearts for love. She had refused his request that he might write to her without a qualm; and mostly because she imagined so vividly what would have been his look of triumph had she granted it. Then she had spent the rest of the winter and early spring in thinking about him. And now she was going to do this reckless thing, out of sheer wilfulness, sheer thirst for adventure. She had always been a spoilt child, brought up with boundless indulgence, and accustomed to all the excitements of life. It looked as though Douglas Falloden were to be her excitement in Oxford. Girls like the two Miss Mansons might take possession of him in public, so long as she commanded those undiscovered rides and talks which revealed the real man. At the same time, he should never be able to feel secure that she would do his bidding, or keep appointments. As soon as Lady Laura's civil note arrived, she was determined to refuse it. He had counted on her coming; therefore she would not go. Her first move had been a deliberate check; her second should be a concession. In any case she would keep the upper hand.

Nevertheless there was an inner voice which mocked, through all the patting and curling and rolling applied by Annette's skilled hands to her mistress's brown hair. Had not Falloden himself arranged this whole adventure ahead?—found her a horse and groom, while she was still in the stage of thinking about them, and settled the place of rendezvous?

She could not deny it; but her obstinate confidence in her own powers and will was not thereby in the least affected. She was going because it amused her to go; not because he prescribed it.

The following day, Saturday, witnessed an unexpected stream of callers on Mrs. Hooper. She was supposed to be at home on Saturday afternoons to undergraduates; but the undergraduates who came were few and shy. They called out of respect for the Reader, whose lectures they attended and admired. But they seldom came a second time; for although Alice had her following of young men, it was more amusing to meet her anywhere else than under the eyes of her small, peevish mother, who seemed to be able to talk of nothing else than ailments and tabloids, and whether the Bath or the Buxton waters were the better for her own kind of rheumatism.

On this afternoon, however, the Hoopers' little drawing-room and the lawn outside were crowded with folk. Alexander Sorell arrived early, and found Constance in a white dress strolling up and down the lawn under a scarlet parasol and surrounded by a group of men with whom she had made acquaintance on the Christ Church barge. She received him with a pleasure, an effusion, which made a modest man blush.

"This is nice of you!—I wondered whether you'd come!"

"I thought you'd seen too much of me this week already!" he said, smiling—"but I wanted to arrange with you when I might take you to call on the Master of Beaumont. To-morrow?"

"I shall be plucked, you'll see! You'll be ashamed of me."

"I'll take my chance. To-morrow then, at four o'clock before chapel?"

Constance nodded—"Delighted!"—and was then torn from him by her uncle, who had fresh comers to introduce to her. But Sorell was quite content to watch her from a distance, or to sit talking in a corner with Nora, whom he regarded as a child,—"a jolly, clever, little thing!"—while his mind was full of Constance.

The mere sight of her—the slim willowy creature, with her distinguished head and her beautiful eyes—revived in him the memory of some of his happiest and most sacred hours. It was her mother who had produced upon his own early maturity one of those critical impressions, for good or evil, which men so sensitive and finely strung owe to women. The tenderness, the sympathy, the womanly insight of Ella Risborough had drawn him out of one of those fits of bitter despondency which are so apt to beset the scholar just emerging, strained and temporarily injured, from the first contests of life.

He had done brilliantly at Oxford—more than brilliantly—and he had paid for overwork by a long break-down. After getting his fellowship he had been ordered abroad for rest and travel. There was nobody to help him, nobody to think for him. His father and mother were dead; and of near relations he had only a brother, established in business at Liverpool, with whom he had little or nothing in common. At Rome he had fallen in with the Risboroughs, and had wandered with them during a whole spring through enchanted land of Sicily, where it gradually became bearable again to think of the too-many things he knew, and to apply them to his own pleasure and that of his companions. Ella Risborough was then forty-two, seventeen years older than himself, and her only daughter was a child of sixteen. He had loved them all—father, mother, and child—with the adoring gratitude of one physically and morally orphaned, to whom a new home and family has been temporarily given. For Ella and her husband had taken a warm affection to the refined and modest fellow, and could not do enough for him. His fellowship, and some small savings, gave him all the money he wanted, but he was starved of everything else that man's kindred can generally provide—sympathy, and understanding without words, and the little gaieties and kindnesses of every day. These the Risboroughs offered him without stint, and rejoiced to see him taking hold on life again under the sunshine they made for him. After six months he was quite restored to health, and he went back to Oxford to devote himself to his college work.

Twice afterwards he had gone to Rome on short visits to see the Risboroughs. Then had come the crash of Lady Risborough's sudden death followed by that of her husband. The bitterness of Sorell's grief was increased by the fact that he saw no means, at that time, of continuing his friendship with their orphan child. Indeed his fastidious and scrupulous temperament forbade him any claim of the kind. He shrank from being misunderstood. Constance, in the hands of Colonel King and his wife, was well cared for, and the shrewd and rather suspicious soldier would certainly have looked askance on the devotion of a man around thirty, without fortune or family, to a creature so attractive and so desirable as Constance Bledlow.

So he had held aloof, and as Constance resentfully remembered she had received but two letters from him since her father's death. Ewen Hooper, with whom he had an academic rather than a social acquaintance, had kept him generally informed about her, and he knew that she was expected in Oxford. But again he did not mean to put himself forward, or to remind her unnecessarily of his friendship with her parents. At the Vice-Chancellor's party, indeed, an old habit of looking after her had seized him again, and he had not been able to resist it. But it was her long disappearance with Falloden, her heightened colour, and preoccupied manner when they parted at the college gate, together with the incident at the boat-races of which he had been a witness, which had suddenly developed a new and fighting resolve in him. If there was one type in Oxford he feared and detested more than another it was the Falloden type. To him, a Hellene in temper and soul—if to be a Hellene means gentleness, reasonableness, lucidity, the absence of all selfish pretensions—men like Falloden were the true barbarians of the day, and the more able the more barbarian.

Thus, against his own will and foresight, he was on the way to become a frequenter of the Hoopers' house. He had called on Wednesday, taken the whole party to the boats on Thursday, and given them supper afterwards in his rooms. They had all met again at the boats on Friday, and here he was on Saturday, that he might make plans with Constance for Sunday and for several other days ahead. He was well aware that things could not go on at that pace; but he was determined to grasp the situation, and gauge the girl's character, if he could.

He saw plainly that her presence at the Hoopers was going to transform the household in various unexpected ways. On this Saturday afternoon Mrs. Hooper's stock of teacups entirely ran out; so did her garden chairs. Mrs. Manson called—and Lord Meyrick, under the wing of a young fellow of All Souls, smooth-faced and slim, one of the "mighty men" of the day, just taking wing for the bar and Parliament. Falloden, he understood, had put in an appearance earlier in the afternoon; Herbert Pryce, and Bobbie Vernon of Magdalen, a Blue of the first eminence, skirmished round and round the newcomer, taking possssion of her when they could. Mrs. Hooper, under the influence of so much social success, showed a red and flustered countenance, and her lace cap went awry. Alice helped her mother in the distribution of tea, but was curiously silent and self-effaced. It was dismally true that the men who usually paid attention to her were now entirely occupied with Constance. Bobbie

Vernon, who was artistic, was holding an ardent though intermittent discussion with Constance on the merits of old pictures and new. Pryce occasionally took part in it, but only, as Sorell soon perceived, for the sake of diverting a few of Connie's looks and gestures, a sally or a smile, now and then to himself.

In the middle of it she turned abruptly towards Sorell. Her eyes beckoned, and he carried her off to the further end of the garden, where they were momentarily alone. There she fell upon him.

"Why did you never write to me all last winter?"

He could not help a slight flush.

"You had so many friends without me," he said, stammeringly, at last.

"One hasn't so many old friends." The voice was reproachful. "I thought you must be offended with me."

"How could I be!"

"And you call me Lady Constance," she went on indignantly. "When did you ever do such a thing in Rome, or when we were travelling?"

His look betrayed his feeling.

"Ah, but you were a little girl then, and now——"

"Now"—she said impatiently—"I am just Constance Bledlow, as I was then—to you. But I don't give away my Christian name to everybody. I don't like, for instance, being forced to give it to Aunt Ellen!"

And she threw a half-laughing, half-imperious glance towards Mrs. Hooper in the distance.

Sorell smiled.

"I hope you're going to be happy here!" he said earnestly.

"I shall be happy enough—if I don't quarrel with Aunt Ellen!"

"Don't quarrel with anybody! Call me in, before you do. And do make friends with your uncle. He is delightful."

"Yes, but far too busy for the likes of me. Oh, I dare say I shall keep out of mischief."

But he thought he detected in her tone a restlessness, a forlornness, which pained him.

"Why not take up some study—some occupation? Learn something—go in for Honours!" he said, laughing.

She laughed too, but with a very decided shake of the head. Then she turned upon him suddenly.

"But there is something I should like to learn! Papa began to teach me. I should like to learn Greek."

"Bravo!" he said, with a throb of pleasure. "And take me for a teacher!"

"Do you really mean it?"

"Entirely." They strolled on, arranging times and seasons, Constance throwing herself into the scheme with a joyous and child-like zest.

"Mind you—I shall make you work!" he said firmly.

"Rather! May Nora come too?—if she wishes? I like Nora!"

"Does that mean——"

"Only that Alice doesn't like me!" she said with a frank smile. "But I agree—my uncle is a dear."

"And I hear you are going to ride?"

"Yes. Mr. Falloden has found me a horse and groom."

"When did you come to know Mr. Falloden? I don't remember anybody of that name at the Barberini."

She explained carelessly.

"You are going out alone?"

"In general. Sometimes, no doubt, I shall find a friend. I must ride!"—she shook her shoulders impatiently—"else I shall suffocate in this place. It's beautiful—Oxford!—but I don't understand it—it's not my friend yet. You remember that mare of mine in Rome—Angelica! I want a good gallop—God and the grass!"

She laughed and stretched her long and slender arms, clasping her hands above her head. He realised in her, with a disagreeable surprise, the note that was so unlike her mother—the note of recklessness, of vehement will. It was really ill-luck that some one else than Douglas Falloden could not have been found to look after her riding.

*

"I suppose you will be 'doing' the Eights all next week!" said Herbert Pryce to the eldest Miss Hooper.

Alice coldly replied that she supposed it was necessary to take Connie to all the festivities.

"What!—such a *blasé* young woman! She seems to have been everywhere and seen everything already. She will be able to give you and Miss Nora all sorts of hints," said the mathematical tutor, with a touch of that patronage which was rarely absent from his manner to Alice Hooper. He was well aware of her interest in him, and flattered by it; but, to do him justice, he had not gone out of his way to encourage it. She had been all very well, with her pretty little French face, before this striking creature, her cousin, appeared on the scene. And now of course she was jealous—that was inevitable. But it was well girls should learn to measure themselves against others—should find their proper place.

All the same, he was quite fond of her, the small kittenish thing. An old friend of his, and of the Hoopers, had once described her as a girl "with a real talent for flirtation and an engaging penury of mind." Pryce thought the description good. She could be really engaging sometimes, when she was happy and amused, and properly dressed. But ever since the appearance of Constance Bledlow she seemed to have suffered eclipse; to have grown plain and dull.

He stayed talking to her, however, a little while, seeing that Constance Bledlow had gone indoors; and then he departed. Alice ran upstairs, locked her door, and stood looking at herself in the glass. She hated her dress, her hat, the way she had done her hair. The image of Constance in her white silk hat with its drooping feathers, her delicately embroidered dress and the necklace on her shapely throat, tormented her. She was sick with envy—and with fear. For months she had clung to the belief that Herbert Pryce would ask her to marry him. And now all expectation of the magic words was beginning to fade from her mind. In one short week, as it seemed to her, she had been utterly eclipsed and thrown aside. Bob Vernon too, whose fancy for her, as shown in various winter dances, had made her immensely proud, he being then in that momentary limelight which flashes on the Blue, as he passes over the Oxford scene—Vernon had scarcely had a word for her. She never knew that he cared about pictures! And there was Connie—knowing everything about pictures!—able to talk about everything! As she had listened to Connie's talk, she had felt fairly bewildered. Of course it was no credit to Connie to be able to rattle off all those names and things. It was because she had lived in Italy. And no doubt a great deal of it was showing off.

All the same, poor miserable Alice felt a bitter envy of Connie's opportunities.

VI

"MY BROTHER will be here directly. He wants to show you his special books," said Miss Wenlock shyly.

The Master's sister was a small and withered lady, who had been something of a beauty, and was now the pink of gentle and middle-aged decorum. She was one of those women it is so easy to ignore till you live with them. Then you perceive that in their relations to their own world, the world they make and govern, they are of the stuff which holds a country together, without which a country can not exist. She might have come out of a Dutch picture—a Terburg or a Metsu—so exquisite was she in every detail—her small, white head, her regular features, the lace coif tied under her chin, the ruffles at her wrist, the black brocade gown, which never altered in its fashion and which she herself cut out, year after year, for her maid to make,—the chatelaine of old Normandy silver, given her by her brother years before, which hung at her waist.

Opposite her sat a very different person, yet of a type no less profitable to this mixed life of ours. Mrs. Mulholland was the widow of a former scientific professor, of great fame in Oxford for his wit and Liberalism. Whenever there was a contest on between science and clericalism in the good old fighting days, Mulholland's ample figure might have been seen swaying along the road from the Parks to Convocation, his short-sighted eyes blinking at every one he passed, his fair hair and beard streaming in the wind, a flag of battle to his own side, and an omen of defeat to the enemy. His *mots* still circulated, and something of his gift for them had remained with the formidable woman who now represented him. At a time when short dresses for women were coming in universally, she always wore hers long and ample, though they were looped up by various economical and thrifty devices; on the top of the dress—which might have covered a crinoline, but didn't—a shawl, long after every one else had ceased to wear shawls; and above the shawl a hat, of the large mushroom type and indecipherable age. And in the midst of this antique and generally untidy gear, the youngest and liveliest face imaginable, under snow-white hair: black eyes full of Irish fun, a pugnacious and humorous mouth, and the general look of one so steeped in the rich, earthy stuff of life that she might have stepped out of a novel of Fielding's or a page of "Lavengro."

When Constance entered, Mrs. Mulholland turned round suddenly to look at her. It was a glance full of good will, but penetrating also, and critical. It was as though the person from whom it came had more than a mere stranger's interest in the tall young lady in white, now advancing towards Miss Wenlock.

But she gave no immediate sign of it. She and Miss Wenlock had been discussing an Oxford acquaintance, the newly-married wife of one of the high officials of the University. Miss Wenlock, always amiable, had discreetly pronounced her "charming."

"Oh, so dreadfully charming!" said Mrs. Mulholland with a shrug, "and so sentimental that she hardens every heart. Mine becomes stone when I talk to her. She cried when I went to tea with her—a wedding visit if you please! I think it was because one of the kangaroos at Blenheim had just died in childbirth. I told her it was a mercy, considering that any of them would hug us to death if they got a chance. Are you a sentimentalist, Lady Constance?" Mrs. Mulholland turned gaily to the girl beside her, but still with the same touch of something coolly observant in her manner.

Constance laughed.

"I never can cry when I ought to," she said lightly.

"Then you should go to tea with Mrs. Crabbett. She could train anybody to cry—in time. She cultivates with care, and waters with tears, every sorrow that blows! Most of us run away from our troubles, don't we?"

Constance again smiled assent. But suddenly her face stiffened. It was like a flower closing, or a light blown out.

Mrs. Mulholland thought—"She has lost a father and a mother within a year, and I have reminded her. I am a cruel, clumsy wretch."

And thenceforward she roared so gently that Miss Wenlock, who never said a malicious thing herself, and was therefore entirely dependent on Sarah Mulholland's tongue for the salt of life, felt herself cheated of her usual Sunday entertainment. For there were few Sundays in term-time when Mrs. Mulholland did not "drop in" for tea and talk at Beaumont before going on to the Cathedral service.

But under the gentleness, Constance opened again, and expanded. Mrs. Mulholland seemed to watch her with increasing kindness. At last, she said abruptly—

"I have already heard of you from two charming young men."

Constance opened a pair of conscious eyes. It was as though she were always expecting to hear Falloden's name, and protecting herself against the shock of it. But the mistake was soon evident.

"Otto Radowitz told me you had been so kind to him! He is an enthusiastic boy, and a great friend of mine. He deals always in superlatives. That is so refreshing here in Oxford where we are all so clever that we are deadly afraid of each other, and everybody talks drab. And his music is divine! I hear they talk of him in Paris as another Chopin. He passed his first degree examination the other day magnificently! Come and hear him some evening at my house. Jim Meyrick, too, has told me all about you. His mother is a cousin of mine, and he condescends occasionally to come and see me. He is, I understand, a 'blood.' All I know is that he would be a nice youth, if he had a little more will of his own, and had nicer friends!" The small black eyes under the white hair flamed.

Constance started. Miss Wenlock put up a soothing hand—

"Dear Sarah, are you thinking of any one?"

"Of course I am!" said Mrs. Mulholland firmly. "There is a young gentleman at Mannion who thinks the world belongs to him. Oh, you know Mr. Falloden, Grace! He got the Newdigate last year, and the Greek Verse the other day. He got the Ireland, and he's going to get a First. He might have been in the Eleven, if he'd kept his temper, and they say he's going to be a magnificent tennis player. And a lot of other tiresome distinctions. I believe he speaks at the Union, and speaks well—bad luck to him!"

Constance laughed, fidgeted, and at last said, rather defiantly—

"It's sometimes a merit to be disliked, isn't it? It means that you're not exactly like other people. Aren't we all turned out by the gross!"

Mrs. Mulholland looked amused.

"Ah, but you see I know something about this young man at home. His mother doesn't count. She has her younger children, and they make her happy. And of course she is absurdly proud of Douglas. But the father and this son Douglas are of the same stuff. They have a deal more brains and education than their forbears ever wanted; but still, in soul, they remain our feudal lords and superiors, who have a right to the services of those beneath them. And everybody is beneath them—especially women; and foreigners—and artists—and people who don't shoot or hunt. Ask their neighbours—ask their cottagers. Whenever the revolution comes, their heads will be the first to go! At the same time they know—the clever ones—that they can't keep their place except by borrowing the weapons of the class they really fear—the professional class—the writers and thinkers—the lawyers and journalists. And so they take some trouble to sharpen their own brains. And the cleverer they are, the more tyrannous they are. And that, if you please, is Mr. Douglas Falloden!"

"I wonder why you are so angry with him, my dear Sarah," said Miss Wenlock mildly.

"Because he has been bullying my nice boy, Radowitz!" said Mrs. Mulholland vehemently. "I hear there has been a disgraceful amount of ragging in Mannion lately, and that Douglas Falloden—can you conceive it?—a man in his last term, whom the University imagines itself to be turning out as an educated specimen!—is one of the ring-leaders—the ring-leader. It appears that Otto wears a frilled dress shirt—why shouldn't he?—that, having been brought up in Paris till he was nineteen, he sometimes tucks his napkin under his chin—that he uses French words when he needn't—that he dances like a Frenchman—that he recites French poetry actually of his own making—that he plays too well for a gentleman—that he doesn't respect the customs of the college, et cetera. There is a sacred corner of the Junior Common Room, where no freshman is expected to sit after hall. Otto sat in it—quite innocently—knowing nothing—and, instead of apologising, made fun of Jim Meyrick and Douglas Falloden who turned him out. Then afterwards he composed a musical skit on 'the bloods,' which delighted every one in college, who wasn't a 'blood.' And now there is open war between him and them. Otto doesn't talk of it. I hear of it from other people. But he looks excited and pale—he is a very delicate creature!—and we, who are fond of him, live in dread of some violence. I never can understand why the dons are so indulgent to ragging. It is nothing but a continuation of school bullying. It ought to be put down with the strongest possible hand."

Miss Wenlock had listened in tremulous sympathy, nodding from time to time. Constance sat silent and rather pale—looking down. But her mind was angry. She said to herself that nobody ought to attack absent persons who can't defend themselves,—at least so violently. And as Mrs. Mulholland seemed to wait for some remark from her, she said at last, with a touch of impatience:

"I don't think Mr. Radowitz minds much. He came to us—to my uncle's—to play last night. He was as gay as possible."

"Radowitz would make jokes with the hangman!" said Mrs. Mulholland. "Ah, well, I think you know Douglas Falloden"—the tone was just lightly touched with significance—"and if you can lecture him—do!" Then she abruptly changed her subject:

"I suppose you have scarcely yet made acquaintance with your two aunts who live quite close to the Fallodens in Yorkshire?"

Constance looked up in astonishment.

"Do you know them?"

"Oh, quite well!" The strong wrinkled face flashed into laughter. But suddenly the speaker checked herself, and laid a worn hand gently on Constance's knee—"You won't mind if I tell you things?—you won't think me an impertinent old woman? I knew your father"—was there just an imperceptible pause on the words?—"when he was quite a boy; and my people were small squires under the shelter of the Risboroughs before your father sold the property and settled abroad. I was brought up with all your people—your Aunt Marcia, and your Aunt Winifred, and all the rest of them. I saw your mother once in Rome—and loved her, like everybody else. But—as probably you know—your Aunt Winifred—who was keeping house for your father—gathered up her silly skirts, and departed when your father announced his engagement. Then she and your Aunt Marcia settled together in an old prim Georgian house, about five miles from the Fallodens; and there they have been ever since. And now they are tremendously excited about you!"

"About me?" said Constance, astonished. "I don't know them. They never write to me. They never wrote to father!"

Mrs. Mulholland smiled.

"All the same you will have a letter from them soon. And of course you remember your father's married sister, Lady Langmoor?"

"No, I never even saw her. But she did sometimes write to father."

"Yes, she was not quite such a fool as the others. Well, she will certainly descend on you. She'll want you for some balls—for a drawing-room—and that kind of thing. I warn you!"

The girl's face showed her restive.

"Why should she want me?—when she never wanted me before—or any of us?"

"Ah, that's her affair! But it is your other aunts who delight me. Your Aunt Marcia, when I first knew her, was in an ascetic phase. People called it miserliness—but it wasn't; it was only a moral hatred of waste—in anything. We envied her abominably, when I was a girl in my early teens, much bothered with dressing, because she had invented a garment—the only one of any kind that she wore under her dress. She called it a 'Unipantaloonicoat'—you can imagine why! It included stockings. It was thin in summer and thick in winter. There was only one putting on—pouf!—and then the dress. I thought it a splendid idea, but my mother wouldn't let me copy it. Your Aunt Winifred had just the opposite mania—of piling on clothes—because she said there were 'always draughts.' If one petticoat fastened at the back, there must be another over that which fastened at the front—and another at the side—and so on, *ad infinitum*. But then, alack!—they suddenly dropped all their absurdities, and became quite ordinary people. Aunt Winifred took to religion; she befriends all the clergy for miles round. She is the mother of Mother Church. And Aunt Marcia, after having starved herself of clothes for years and collected nothing more agreeable than snails, now wears silks and satins, and gossips and goes out to tea, and collects blue china like anybody else. I connect it with the advent of a certain General who after all went off solitary to Malta, and died there. Poor Marcia! But you will certainly have to go and stay there."

"I don't know!" said Constance, her delicate mouth setting rather stiffly.

"Ah, well—they are getting old!"

Mrs. Mulholland's tone had softened again, and when it softened there was a wonderful kindness in it.

A door opened suddenly. The Master came in, followed by Alexander Sorell.

"My dear Edward!" said Miss Wenlock, "how late you are!"

"I was caught by a bore, dear, after chapel. Horace couldn't get rid of his, and I couldn't get rid of mine. But now all is well. How do you do, Lady Constance? Have you had enough tea, and will you come and see my books?"

He carried her off, Connie extremely nervous, and wondering into what bogs she was about to flounder.

But she was a scholar's daughter, and she had lived with books. She would have scorned to pretend, and her pose, if she had one, was a pose of ignorance—she claimed less than she might. But the Master soon discovered that she had many of her father's tastes, that she knew something of archæology—he bore it even when she shyly quoted Lanciani—that she read Latin, and was apparently passionately fond of some kinds of poetry. And all the time she pleased his tired eyes by her youth and freshness, and when as she grew at ease with him, and began to chatter to him about Rome, and how the learned there love one another, the Master's startling, discordant laugh rang out repeatedly.

The three in the other room heard it.

"She is amusing him," said Miss Wenlock, looking rather bewildered. "They are generally so afraid of him."

The Master put his head into the drawing-room.

"I am taking Lady Constance into the garden, my dear. Will you three follow when you like?"

He took her through the old house, with the dim faces of former masters and college worthies shining softly on its panelled walls, in the golden lights from the level sun outside, and presently they emerged upon the garden which lay like an emerald encased on three sides by surfaces of silver-grey stone, and overlooked by a delicate classical tower designed by the genius of Christopher Wren. Over one-half of the garden lay an exquisite shadow; the other was in vivid light. The air seemed to be full of bells—a murmurous voice—the voice of Oxford; as though the dead generations were perpetually whispering to the living—"We who built these walls, and laid this turf for you—we, who are dead, call to you who are living—carry on our task, continue our march:

"On to the bound of the waste—
On to the City of God!"

A silence fell upon Constance as she walked beside the Master. She was thinking involuntarily of that absent word dropped by her uncle—"*Oxford is a place of training*"—and there was a passionate and troubled revolt in her. Other ghostly wills seemed to be threatening her—wills that meant nothing to her. No!—her own will should shape her own life! As against the austere appeal that comes from the inner heart of Oxford, the young and restless blood in her sang defiance. "I will ride with him to-morrow—I will—I will!"

But the Master merely thought that she was feeling the perennial spell of the Oxford beauty.

"You are going to like Oxford, I hope?"

"Yes—" said Constance, a little reluctantly. "Oh, of course I shall like it. But it oppresses me—rather."

"I know!" he said eagerly—always trying to place himself in contact with the young mind and life, always seeking something from them in which he was constantly disappointed. "Yes, we all feel that! We who are alive must always fight the past, though we owe it all we have. Oxford has been to me often a witch—a dangerous—almost an evil witch. I seemed to see her—benumbing the young forces of the present. And the scientific and practical men, who would like to scrap her, have sometimes seemed to me right. And then one changes—one changes!"

His voice dropped. All that was slightly grotesque in his outer man, the broad flat head, the red hair, the sharp wedge-like chin, disappeared for Constance in the single impression of his eyes—pale blue, intensely melancholy, and most human.

"Take up some occupation—some study—" he said to her gently. "You won't be long here; but still, ask us for what we can give. In Oxford one must learn something—or teach something. If not, life here goes sour."

Constance repeated Sorell's promise to teach her Greek.

"Excellent!" said the Master. "You will be envied. Sorell is a capital fellow! And one of the ablest of our younger scholars—though of course"—the speaker drew himself up with a slight acerbity—"he and I belong to different schools of criticism. He was devoted to your mother."

Constance assented dumbly.

"And shows already"—thought the Master—"some dangerous signs of being devoted to you. Poor wretch!" Aloud he said—"Ah, here they come. I must get some more chairs."

The drawing-room party joined them, and the gathering lasted a little longer. Sorell walked up and down with Constance. She liked him increasingly—could not help liking him. And apart from his personal charm, he recalled all sorts of pleasant things and touching memories to her. But he was almost oppressively refined and scrupulous and high-minded. "He is too perfect!" she thought rebelliously. "One can't be as good as that. It isn't allowed."

As to Mrs. Mulholland, Constance felt herself taken possession of—mothered—by that lady. She could not understand why, but though rather puzzled and bewildered, she did not resist. There was something, indeed, in the generous dark eyes that every now and then touched the girl's feeling intolerably, as though it reminded her of a tenderness she had been long schooling herself to do without.

"Come and see me, my dear, whenever you like. I have a house in St. Giles, and all my husband's books. I do a lot of things—I am a guardian—I work at the schools—the town schools for the town children, et cetera. We all try to save our souls by committees nowadays. But my real business is to talk, and make other people talk. So I am always at home in the evenings after dinner, and a good many people come. Bring Nora sometimes. Alice doesn't like me. Your aunt will let you come—though we don't know each other very well. I am very respectable."

The laughing face looked into Constance's, which laughed back.

"That's all right!" said Mrs. Mulholland, as though some confidences had been exchanged between them. "You might find me useful. Consider me a friend of the family. I make rather a good umbrella-stand. People can lean against me if they like. I hold firm. Good-bye. That's the Cathedral bell."

But Constance and Sorell, followed discreetly by Annette, departed first. Mrs. Mulholland stayed for a final word to the Master, before obeying the silver voice from St. Frideswide's tower.

"To think of that girl being handed over to Ellen Hooper, just when all her love affairs will be coming on! A woman with the wisdom of a rabbit, and the feelings of a mule! And don't hold your finger up at me, Master! You know you can't suffer fools at all—either gladly—or sadly. Now let me go, Grace!—or I shan't be fit for church."

"A very pretty creature!" said Ewen Hooper admiringly—"and you look very well on her, Constance."

He addressed his niece, who had been just put into her saddle by the neat groom who had brought the horses.

Mrs. Hooper, Alice and Nora were standing on the steps of the old house. A knot of onlookers had collected on the pavement—mostly errand boys. The passing undergraduates tried not to look curious, and hurried by. Constance, in her dark blue riding-habit and a *tricorne* felt hat which she had been accustomed to wear in the Campagna, kept the mare fidgeting and pawing a little that her uncle might inspect both her and her rider, and then waved her hand in farewell.

"Where are you going, Connie?" cried Nora.

"Somewhere out there—beyond the railway," she said vaguely, pointing with her riding-whip. "I shall be back in good time."

And she went off followed by Joseph, the groom, a man of forty, lean and jockey-like, with a russet and wrinkled countenance which might mean anything or nothing.

"A ridiculous hat!" said Alice maliciously. "Nobody wears such a hat in England to ride in. Think of her appearing like that in the Row!"

"It becomes her." The voice was Nora's, sharp and impatient.

"It is theatrical, like everything Connie does," said Mrs. Hooper severely. "I beg that neither of you will copy her."

Nora walked to the door opening on the back garden, and stood there frowning and smiling unseen.

Meanwhile Joseph followed close at Connie's side, directing her, till they passed through various crowded streets, and left the railway behind. Then trotting under a sunny sky, on a broad vacant road, they made for a line of hills in the middle distance.

The country was early June at its best. The river meadows blazed with buttercups; the river itself, when Constance occasionally caught a glimpse of its windings, lay intensely blue under a wide azure sky, magnificently arched on a great cornice built of successive strata of white and purple cloud, which held the horizon. Over the Lathom Woods the cloud-line rose and fell in curves that took the line of the hill. The woods themselves lay in a haze of heat, the sunlight on the rounded crests of the trees, and the shadows cast by the westerly sun, all fused within the one shimmering veil of blue. The air was fresh and life-giving. Constance felt herself in love with life and the wide Oxford scene. The physical exercise delighted her, and the breathless sense of adventure.

But it was disagreeable to reflect, as she must do occasionally, that the sphinx-like groom knew perfectly well that she was going to the Lathom Woods, that he had the key of the nearest gate in his pocket, that he would be a witness of her meeting with Falloden, whatever they did with him afterwards, and that Falloden had in all probability paid him largely to hold his tongue. All that side of it was odious—degrading. But the thought of the green rides, and the man waiting for her, set all the blood in her wild veins dancing. Yet there was little or nothing in her feeling of a girl's yearning for a lover. She wanted to see Falloden—to talk with him and dispute with him. She could not be content for long without seeing him. He excited her—provoked her—haunted her. And to feel her power over him was delightful, if it had not been spoilt by a kind of recurrent fear—a panic fear of his power over her.

What did she know of him after all? She was quite aware that her friends, the Kings, had made some enquiries at Cannes before allowing her to see so much of him as she had done during his stay with the rich and hospitable Jaroslavs. She believed Colonel King had not liked him personally. But Douglas Falloden belonged to one of the oldest English families, settled on large estates in Yorkshire, with distinguished records in all the great services; he was heir presumptive to a marquisate, so long as his uncle, Lord Dagnall, now past seventy, did not take it into his head to marry; and there was his brilliant career at Oxford, his good looks and all the rest of it. Constance had a strong dash of the worldling in her mixed character. She had been brought up with Italian girl friends of the noble class, in whom the practical instincts of a practical race were closely interwoven with what the Englishman thinks of as Italian "romance" or "passion." She had discussed dowries and settlements since she was fifteen; and took the current values of wealth and birth for granted. She was quite aware of her own advantages, and was not at all minded to throw them away. A brilliant marriage was, perhaps, at the back of her mind, as it is at the back of the minds of so many beautiful creatures who look and breathe poetry, while they are aware, within a few pounds, of what can be done in London on five thousand—or ten thousand—a year. She inevitably thought of herself as quite different from the girls of poor or middle-class families, who must earn their living—Nora, for instance.

And yet there was really a gulf between her and the ordinary worldling. It consisted in little else than a double dose of personality—a richer supply of nerve and emotion. She could not imagine life without money, because she had always lived with rich people. But money was the mere substratum; what really mattered was the excitement of loving, and being loved. She had adored her parents with an absorbing affection. Then, as she grew up, everywhere in her Roman life, among her girl friends, or the handsome youths she remembered riding in the Villa Borghese gymkhana, she began to be aware of passion and sex; she caught the hints of them, as it were of a lightning playing through the web of life, flashing, and then gone—illuminating or destroying. Her mind was full of love stories. At twenty she had been the confidante of many, both from her married and her unmarried friends. It was all, so far, a great mystery to her. But there was in her a thrilled expectation. Not of a love, tranquil and serene, such as shone on her parents' lives, but of something overwhelming and tempestuous; into which she might fling her life as one flings a flower into the current of Niagara.

It was the suggestion of such a possibility that had drawn her first to Douglas Falloden. For three golden days she had imagined herself blissfully in love with him. Then had come disillusion and repulsion. What was violent and imperious in him had struck on what was violent and imperious in her. She had begun to hold him off—to resist him. And that resistance had been more exciting even than the docility of the first phase. It had ended in his proposal, the snatched kiss, and a breach. And now, she had little idea of what would happen;

and would say to herself, recklessly, that she did not care. Only she must see him—must go on exploring him. And as for allowing her intimacy with him to develop in any ordinary way—under the eyes of the Hoopers—or of Oxford—it was not to be thought of. Rather than be tamely handed over to him in a commonplace wooing, she would have broken off all connection with him; and that she had not the strength to do.

"Here is the gate, my lady."

The man produced a key from his pocket and got down to open it. Constance passed into a green world. Three "drives" converged in front of her, moss-carpeted, and close-roofed by oak-wood in its first rich leaf. After the hot sun on the straight and shadeless road outside, these cool avenues stretching away into a forest infinity, seemed to beckon a visitant towards some distant Elysian scene—some glade haunted of Pan.

Constance looked down them eagerly. Which was she to take?—suddenly, far down the right hand drive, a horseman—coming into view. He perceived her, gave a touch to his horse, and was quickly beside her.

Both were conscious of the groom, who had reined in a few yards behind, and sat impassive.

Falloden saluted her joyously. He rode a handsome Irish horse, nearly black, with a white mark on its forehead, a nervous and spirited creature, which its rider handled with the ease of one trained from his childhood to the hunting field. His riding dress, with its knee-breeches and leggings pleased the feminine eye; so did his strong curly head as he bared it, and the animation of his look.

"This is better, isn't it, than ''ammer, 'ammer, 'ammer on the 'ard 'igh road!' I particularly want to show you the bluebells—they're gorgeous! But they're quite on the other side—a long way off. And then you'll be tired—you'll want tea. I've arranged it."

"Joseph"—he turned to the groom—"you know the head keeper's cottage?"

"Yes, sir."

"Well, go off there and wait. Tell the keeper's wife that I shall bring a lady to tea there in about an hour. She knows." Joseph turned obediently, took the left hand road, and was soon out of sight.

The two riders paced side by side through the green shadows of the wood. Constance was flushed—but she looked happy and gracious. Falloden had not seen her so gracious since Oxford had brought them again across each other. They fell at once, for the first time since her arrival, into the easy talk of their early Riviera days; and he found himself doing his very best to please her. She asked him questions about his approaching schools; and it amused him, in the case of so quick a pupil, to frame a "chaffing" account of Oxford examinations and degrees; to describe the rush of an Honour man's first year before the mods' gate is leaped; the loitering and "slacking" of the second year and part of the third; and then the setting of teeth and girding of loins, when a man realises that some of the lost time is gone forever, and that the last struggle is upon him.

"What I am doing now is degrading!—getting 'tips' from the tutors—pinning up lists—beastly names and dates—in my rooms—learning hard bits by heart—cribbing and stealing all I can. And I have still some of my first year's work to go through again. I must cut Oxford for the last fortnight—and go into retreat."

Constance expressed her wonder that any one could ever do any work in the summer term—

"You are all so busy lunching each other's sisters and cousins and aunts! It is a great picnic—not a university," she said flippantly.

"Distracting, I admit—but——"

He paused.

"But—what?"

After a moment, he turned a glowing countenance towards her.

"That is not my chief cause of flight!"

She professed not to understand.

"It is persons distract me—not tea-parties. Persons I want to be seeing and talking to—persons I can not keep myself away from."

He looked straight before him. The horses ambled on together, the reins on their necks. In the distance a cuckoo called from the river meadows, and round the two young figures one might have fancied an attendant escort of birds, as wrens, tits, pippets, fled startled by their approach.

Constance laughed. The laugh, though very musical, was sarcastic.

"I don't see you as a shuttlecock!"

"Tossed by the winds of fate? You think I can always make myself do what I wish?"

"That's how I read you—at present."

"Hm—a charming character! Everything calculated—nothing spontaneous. That I think is what you mean?"

"No. But I doubt your being carried away."

He flushed hotly.

"Lady Connie!——"

He paused. Her colour rushed too. She saw what he was thinking of; she perceived her blunder.

"For what else did you castigate me at Cannes?" he said, in a low voice. And his black eyes looked passionately into hers. But she recovered herself quickly.

"At any rate, you have more will than most people," she said lightly. "Aren't you always boasting of it? But you are quite right to go away."

"I am not going for a week," he put in quickly. "There will be time for two more rides."

She made no reply, and they paced on. Suddenly the trees began to thin before them, and a splendid wave of colour swept across an open glade in full sunlight.

"Marvellous!" cried Constance."Oh, stop a moment!"

They pulled up on the brink of a sea of blue. All around them the bluebells lay glowing in the sunshine. The colour and sparkle of them was a physical delight; and with occasional lingering tufts of primroses among them and the young oak scrub pushing up through the blue in every shade of gold and bronze, they made an enchanted garden of the glade.

Falloden dismounted, tied up his horse, and gathered a bunch for his companion.

"I don't know—ought we?" she said regretfully. "They are not so beautiful when they are torn away. And in a week they will be gone—withered!"

She stooped over them, caressing them, as, taking a strap from the pocket of his own saddle, he tied the flowers to her pommel.

He looked up impetuously.

"Only to spring again!—in this same wood—in other woods—for us to see. Do you ever think how full the world is of sheer pleasure—small and great?" And his eyes told her plainly what his pleasure was at that moment.

Something jarred. She drew herself away, though with fluttering pulses. Falloden, with a strong effort, checked the tide of impulse in himself. He mounted again, and suggested a gallop, through a long stretch of green road on the further side of the glade. They let their horses go, and the flying hoof-beats woke the very heart of the wood.

"That was good!" cried Falloden, as they pulled up, drawing in deep draughts of the summer wind. Then he looked at her admiringly.

"How well you hold yourself! You are a perfect rider!"

Against her will Constance sparkled under his praise. Then they turned their horses towards the keeper's cottage, and the sun fell lower in the west.

"Mr. Falloden," said Constance presently, "I want you to promise me something."

"Ask me," he said eagerly.

"I want you to give up ragging Otto Radowitz!"

His countenance changed.

"Who has been talking to you?"

"That doesn't matter. It is unworthy of you. Give it up."

Falloden laughed with good humour.

"I assure you it does him a world of good!"

She argued hotly; astonished, in her young inexperience, that his will could so soon reassert itself against hers; sharply offended, indeed, that after she had given him the boon of this rendezvous, he could hesitate for a moment as to the boon she asked in return—had humbled herself to ask. For had she not often vowed to herself that she would never, never ask the smallest favour of him; while on her side a diet of refusals and rebuffs was the only means to keep him in check?

But that diet was now gaily administered to herself.

Falloden argued with energy that a man who has never been to a public school has got to be "disciplined" at the university; that Otto Radowitz, being an artist, was specially in need of discipline; that no harm had been done him, or would be done him. But he must be made to understand that certain liberties and impertinences would not be tolerated by the older men.

"He never means them!" cried Constance. "He doesn't understand. He is a foreigner."

"No! He is an Englishman here—and must behave as such. Don't spoil him, Lady Connie!"

He looked at her imperiously—half smiling, half frowning.

"Remember!—he is my friend!"

"I do remember," he said drily. "I am not likely to forget." Constance flushed, and proudly dropped the subject. He saw that he had wounded her, but he quietly accepted it. There was something in the little incident that made her more aware of his overbearing character than ever.

"If I married him," she thought, "I should be his slave!"

Tea had been daintily spread for them under a birch-tree near the keeper's lodge. The keeper's wife served them with smiles and curtsies, and then discreetly disappeared. Falloden waited on Constance as a squire on his princess; and all round them lay the green encircling rampart of the wood. In the man's every action, there was the homage of one who only keeps silence because the woman he loves imposes it. But Constance again felt that recurrent fear creeping over her. She had been a fool—a fool!

He escorted her to the gate of the wood where Joseph was waiting.

"And now for our next merry meeting?" he said, as he got down to tighten her stirrup which had stretched a little.

Constance hurriedly said she could not promise—there were so many engagements.

Falloden did not press her. But he held her hand when she gave it him.

"Are you angry with me?" he said, in a low voice, while his eyes mocked a little.

"No—only disappointed!"

"Isn't that unkind? Haven't we had a golden time?" His tone smote her a little.

"It was heavenly," she said, "till——"

"Till I behaved like a brute?"

She laughed excitedly, and waved farewell.

Falloden, smiling, watched her go, standing beside his horse—a Siegfried parting from Brunhilde.

When she and the groom had disappeared, he mounted and rode off towards another exit.

"I must be off to-morrow!" he said to himself with decision—"or my schools will go to the dogs!"

VII

"THREE MORE invitations!—since lunch," said Mrs. Hooper, as she came into the schoolroom, where her elder daughter sat by the window renovating a garden hat.

Her mother dropped the envelopes on a small table beside Alice, and sitting down on the other side of it, she waited for her daughter's comments.

Alice threw down her work, and hastily opened the notes. She flushed an angry pink as she read them.

"I might as well not exist!" she said shortly, as she pushed them away again.

For two of the notes requested the pleasure of Dr. and Mrs. Hooper's and Lady Constance Bledlow's company at dinner, and the third, from a very great lady, begged "dear Mrs. Hooper" to bring Lady Constance to a small party in Wolsey College Gardens, to meet the Chancellor of the University, a famous Tory peer, who was coming down to a public meeting. In none of the three was there any mention of the elder Miss Hooper.

Mrs. Hooper looked worried. It was to her credit that her maternal feeling, which was her only passion, was more irritated by this sudden stream of invitations than her vanity was tickled.

What was there indeed to tickle anybody's vanity in the situation? It was all Constance—Constance—Constance! Mrs. Hooper was sometimes sick of the very name "Lady Constance Bledlow." It had begun to get on her nerves. The only defence against any sort of "superiority," as some one has said, is to love it. But Mrs. Hooper did not love her husband's niece. She was often inclined to wish, as she caught sight of Alice's pinched face, that the household had never seen her. And yet without Connie's three hundred a year, where would the household be!

Mrs. Hooper was painfully, one might have said, guiltily aware of that side of the business. She was an incompetent, muddling woman, who had never learnt to practise the simple and dignified thrift so common in the academic households of the University. For nowhere, really, was plain living gayer or more attractive than in the new Oxford of this date. The young mothers who wheeled their own perambulators in the Parks, who bathed and dressed and taught their children, whose house-books showed a spirited and inventive economy of which they were inordinately proud, who made their own gowns of Liberty stuff in scorn of the fashion, were at the same time excellent hostesses, keeping open house on Sundays for their husbands' undergraduate pupils, and gallantly entertaining their own friends and equals at small flowery dinner-parties in Morris-papered rooms, where the food and wine mattered little, and good talk and happy comradeship were the real fare. Meanwhile the same young mothers were going to lectures on the Angevins, or reading Goethe or Dante in the evenings—a few friends together, gathering at each other's houses; then were discussing politics and social reform; and generally doing their best—unconsciously—to silence the croakers and misogynists who maintained that when all the girl babies in the perambulators were grown up, and Oxford was flooded with womenkind like all other towns, Oxford would have gone to "Death and damnation."

But Mrs. Hooper, poor lady, was not of this young and wholesome generation. She was the daughter of a small Midland manufacturer, who had rushed into sudden wealth, for a few years, had spent it all in riotous living, over a period just sufficient to spoil his children, and had then died leaving them penniless. Ewen Hooper had come across her when he was lecturing at a northern university, immediately after his own appointment at Oxford. He had passed a harassed and penurious youth, was pining for a home. In ten days he was engaged to this girl whom he met at the house of a Manchester professor. She took but little wooing, was indeed so enchanted to be wooed that Ewen Hooper soon imagined himself in love with her; and all was done.

Nor indeed had it answered so badly for him—for a time. She had given him children, and a home, though an uncomfortable one. Greek scholarship and Greek beauty were the real idols of his heart and imagination. They did not fail him. But his wife did him one conspicuous ill turn. From the first days of their marriage, she ran her husband badly into debt; and things had got slowly worse with the years. Mrs. Hooper was the most wasteful of managers; servants came and went interminably; and while money oozed away, there was neither comfort nor luxury to show for it. As the girls grew up, they learnt to dread the sound of the front doorbell, which so often meant an angry tradesman; and Ewen Hooper, now that he was turning grey, lived amid a perpetual series of mean annoyances with which he was never meant to cope, and which he was now beginning to hand over, helplessly, to his younger daughter Nora, the one member of the family who showed some power to deal with them.

The situation had been almost acute, when Lord Risborough died. But there was a legacy in his will for Ewen Hooper which had given a breathing space; and Connie had readily consented to pay a year's maintenance in advance. Yet still the drawer of bills, on which Nora kept anxious watch, was painfully full; and of late the perennial difficulty of ready money had reappeared.

Mrs. Hooper declared she must have a new dress, if these invitations were to be accepted.

"I don't want anything extravagant," she said fretfully. "But really it's too bad of Nora to say that I could have my old blue one done up. She never seems to care how her mother looks. If all this fuss is going to be made about Constance and I am to take her out, I must be decent!"

The small underhung mouth shut obstinately. These musts of her mother's and Alice's were Nora's terror. They always meant a new bill.

Alice said—"Of course! And especially when Constance dresses so extravagantly!" she added bitterly. "One can't look like her scullery-maid!"

Mrs. Hooper sighed. She glanced round her to see that the door was shut.

"That silly child, Nora, had quite a scene with Connie this morning, because Connie offered to give her that pretty white dress in Brandon's window. She told me Connie had insulted her. Such nonsense! Why shouldn't Connie give her a dress—and you too? She has more money than she knows how to spend."

Alice did not reply. She, too, wanted new dresses; she could hardly endure the grace and costliness of Connie's garments, when she compared them with her own; but there was something in her sad little soul also that would not let her be beholden to Connie. Not without a struggle, anyway.

"I don't want Connie to give me things either," she said sulkily. "She's never been the least nice to me. She makes a pet of Nora, and the rest of us might be doormats for all the notice she takes of us."

"Well, I don't know—she's quite civil," said Mrs. Hooper reflectively. She added, after a minute—"It's extraordinary how the servants will do anything for her!"

"Why, of course, she tips them!" cried Alice, indignantly. Mrs. Hooper shrugged her shoulders. It was quite indifferent to her whether Connie tipped them or not, so long as she gained by the result. And there was no denying the fact that the house had never gone so smoothly as since Connie's arrival. At the same time her conscience reminded her that there was probably something else than "tipping" in the matter. For instance—both Constance and Annette were now intimately acquainted with each of Mrs. Hooper's three maids, and all their family histories; whereas Mrs. Hooper always found it impossible to remember their surnames. A few days before this date, Susan the housemaid had received a telegram telling her of the sudden death of a brother in South Africa. In Mrs. Hooper's view it was providential that the death had occurred in South Africa, as there could be no inconvenient question of going to the funeral. But

Connie had pleaded that the girl might go home for two days to see her mother; Annette had done the housework during her absence; and both maid and mistress had since been eagerly interested in the girl's mourning, which had been largely supplied out of Connie's wardrobe. Naturally the opinion of the kitchen was that "her ladyship is sweet!"

Alice, however, had not found any sweetness in Connie. Was it because Mr. Herbert Pryce seemed to take a mysterious pleasure in pointing out her charms to Alice? Alice supposed he meant it well. There was a didactic element in him which was always leading him to try and improve other people. But it filled her with a silent fury.

"Is everybody coming to the picnic to-morrow?" asked Mrs. Hooper presently.

"Everybody." Alice pointed indifferently to a pile of notes lying on her desk.

"You asked Connie if we should invite Mr. Falloden?"

"Of course I did, mother. He is away till next week."

"I wonder if she cares for him?" said Mrs. Hooper vaguely.

Alice laughed.

"If she does, she consoles herself pretty well, when he's not here."

"You mean with Mr. Sorell?"

Alice nodded.

"Such a ridiculous pretence, those Greek lessons!" she said, her small face flaming. "Nora says, after they have done a few lines, Constance begins to talk, and Mr. Sorell throws himself back in his chair, and they chatter about the places they've seen together, and the people they remember, till there's no more time left. Nora says it's a farce."

"I say, who's taking my name in vain?" said Nora, who had just opened the schoolroom door and overheard the last sentence.

"Come in and shut the door;" said Alice, "we were talking about your Greek lessons."

"Jolly fun they are!" said Nora, balancing herself, as usual, on the window-sill. "We don't do much Greek, but that don't matter! What are these notes, mother?"

Mrs. Hooper handed them over. Alice threw a mocking look at her sister.

"Who said that Oxford didn't care about titles? When did any of those people ever take any notice of us?"

"It isn't titles—it's Connie!" said Nora stoutly. "It's because she's handsome and clever—and yet she isn't conceited; she's always interested in other people. And she's an orphan—and people were very fond of her mother. And she talks scrumptiously about Italy. And she's new—and there's a bit of romance in it—and—well, there it is!"

And Nora pulled off a twig from the banksia rose outside, and began to chew it energetically with her firm white teeth, by way of assisting her thoughts.

"Isn't conceited!" repeated Alice with contempt. "Connie is as proud as Lucifer."

"I didn't say she wasn't. But she isn't vain."

Alice laughed.

"Can't you see the difference?" said Nora impatiently. "'Proud' means 'Don't be such a fool as to imagine that I'm thinking of you!'—'Vain' means 'I wonder dreadfully what you're thinking of me?'"

"Well then, Connie is both proud and vain," said Alice with decision.

"I don't mean she doesn't know she's rich, and good-looking and run after," said Nora, beginning to flounder. "But half the time, anyway, she forgets it."

"Except when she is talking to men," said Alice vindictively, to which Mrs. Hooper added with her little obstinate air—

"Any girl who likes admiration as much as Connie does must be vain. Of course, I don't blame her."

"Likes admiration? Hm," said Nora, still chewing at her twig. "Yes, I suppose she does. But she's good at snubbing, too." And she threw a glance at her sister. She was thinking of a small evening party the night before, at which, it seemed to her, Connie had several times snubbed Herbert Pryce rather severely. Alice said nothing. She knew what Nora meant. But that Connie should despise what she had filched away only made things worse.

Mrs. Hooper sighed again—loudly.

"The point is—is she carrying on with that man, Mr. Falloden?"

Nora looked up indignantly. Her mother's vulgarity tormented her.

"How can she be 'carrying on,' mother? He won't be in Oxford again till his schools."

"Oh, you never know," said Mrs. Hooper vaguely. "Well, I must go and answer these notes."

She went away. Nora descended gloomily from the window-sill.

"Mother wants a new dress. If we don't all look out, we shall be in Queer Street again."

"You're always so dismal," said Alice impatiently. "Things are a great deal better than they were."

"Well, goodness knows what would have happened to us if they weren't!" cried Nora. "Besides they're not nearly so much better as you think. And the only reason why they're better is that Uncle Risborough left us some money, and Connie's come to live here. And you and mother do nothing but say horrid things about her, behind her back!"

She looked at her sister with accusing eyes. But Alice tossed her head, and declared she wasn't going to be lectured by her younger sister. "You yourself told mother this morning that Connie had insulted you."

"Yes, and I was a beast to say so!" cried the girl. "She meant it awfully well. Only I thought she thought I had been trying to sponge on her; because I said something about having no dresses for the Commem. balls, even if I wanted to 'come out' then—which I don't!—and she straightaway offered to give me that dress in Brandon's. And I was cross, and behaved like a fiend. And afterwards Connie said she was awfully sorry if she'd hurt my feelings."

And suddenly Nora's brown eyes filled with tears.

"Well, you get on with her," said Alice, with fresh impatience—"and I don't. That's all there is to it. Now do go away and let me get on with the hat."

That night, after Connie had finished her toilet for the night and was safely in bed, with a new novel of Fogazzaro before her and a reading lamp beside her, she suddenly put out her arms, and took Annette's apple-red countenance—as the maid stooped over her to straighten the bed-clothes—between her two small hands.

"Netta, I've had a real bad day!"

"And why, please, my lady?" said Annette rather severely, as she released herself.

"First I had a quarrel with Nora—then some boring people came to lunch—then I had a tiresome ride—and now Aunt Ellen has been pointing out to me that it's all my fault she has to get a new dress, because people will ask me to dinner-parties. I don't want to go to dinner-parties!"

And Connie fell back on her pillows, with a great stretch, her black brows drawn over eyes that still smiled beneath them.

"It's very ungrateful of you to talk of a tiresome ride—when that gentleman took such pains to get you a nice horse," said Annette, still tidying and folding as she moved about the room. Constance watched her, her eyes shining absently as the thoughts passed through them. At last she said:

"Do come here, Annette!"

Annette came, rather unwillingly. She sat down on the end of Constance's bed, and took out some knitting from her pocket. She foresaw a conversation in which she would need her wits about her, and some mechanical employment steadied the mind.

"Annette, you know," said Constance slowly, "I've got to be married some time."

"I've heard you say that before." Annette began to count some stitches.

"Oh, it's all very well," said Constance, with amusement—"you think you know all about me, but you don't. You don't know, for instance, that I went to ride over a week ago with a young man, without telling you, or Aunt Ellen, or Uncle Ewen, or anybody!" She waited to see the effect of her announcement. Annette did appear rather startled.

"I suppose you met him on the road?"

"I didn't! I made an appointment with him. We went to a big wood, some miles out of Oxford, belonging to some people he knows, where there are beautiful grass rides. He has the key of the gates—we sent away the groom—and I was an hour alone with him—quite! There!"

There was a defiant accent on the last word. Annette shook her head. She had been fifteen years in the Risboroughs' service, and remembered Connie when she was almost a baby.

"Whatever were you so silly for? You know your mamma wouldn't have let you."

"Well, I've not got my mamma," said Connie slowly. "And I'm not going to be managed by Aunt Ellen, Netta. I intend to run my own show."

"Who is it?" said Annette, knitting busily.

Connie laughed.

"Do you think I'm going to tell you?"

"You needn't. I've got eyes in my head. It's that gentleman you met in France."

Connie swung herself round and laid violent hands on Annette's knitting.

"You shan't knit. Look at me! You can't say he's not good-looking?"

"Which he knows—a deal sight more than is good for him," said Annette, setting her mouth a little grimly.

"Everybody knows when they're good-looking, you dear silly! Of course, he's most suitable—dreadfully so. And I can't make up my mind whether I care for him a bit!"

She folded her arms in front of her, her little chin fell forward on her white wrappings, and she stared rather sombrely into vacancy.

"What's wrong with him?" said Annette after a pause—adopting a tone in which she might have discussed a new hat.

"Oh, I don't know," said Connie dreamily.

She was thinking of Falloden's sudden departure from Oxford, after his own proposal of two more rides. His note, "crying off" till after the schools, had seemed to her not quite as regretful as it might have been; his epistolary style lacked charm. And it was impertinent of him to suggest Lord Meyrick as a substitute. She had given the Lathom Woods a wide berth ever since her first adventure there; and she hoped that Lord Meyrick had spent some disappointed hours in those mossy rides.

All the same it looked as though she were going to see a good deal of Douglas Falloden. She raised her eyes suddenly.

"Annette, I didn't tell you I'd heard from two of my aunts to-day!"

"You did!" Annette dropped her knitting of her own accord this time, and sat open-mouthed.

"Two long letters. Funny, isn't it? Well, Aunt Langmoor wants me to go to her directly—in time anyway for a ball at Tamworth House—horribly smart—Prince and Princess coming—everybody begging for tickets. She's actually got an invitation for me—I suppose by asking for it!—rather calm of her. She calls me 'Dearest Connie.' And I never saw her! But papa used to be fond of her, and she was never rude to mamma. What shall I say?"

"Well, I think you'd much better go," said Annette decidedly. "You've never worn that dress you got at Nice, and it'll be a dish-cloth if you keep it much longer. The way we have to crush things in this place!"

And she looked angrily even at the capacious new wardrobe which took up one whole side of the room.

"All right!" laughed Constance. "Then I'll accept Aunt Langmoor, because you can't find any room for my best frock. It's a toss up. That settles it. Well, but now for Aunt Marcia——"

She drew a letter from the pages of her French book, and opened it.

"My dear Constance"—so it ran—"I should like to make your acquaintance, and I hear that you are at Oxford with your uncle. I would come and see you but that I never leave home. Oxford, too, depresses me dreadfully. Why should people learn such a lot of useless things? We are being ruined by all this education. However, what I meant to say was that Winifred and I would be glad to see you here if you care to come. Winifred, by the way, is quite aware that she behaved like a fool twenty-two years ago. But as you weren't born then, we suggest it shouldn't matter. We have all done foolish things. I, for instance, invented a dress—a kind of bloomer thing—only it wasn't a bloomer. I took a shop for it in Bond Street, and it nearly ruined me. But I muddled through—that's our English way, isn't it?—and somehow things come right. Now, I am very political, and Winifred's very churchy—it doesn't really matter what you take up. So do come. You can bring your maid and have a sitting-room. Nobody would interfere with you. But, of course, we should introduce you to some nice people. If you are a sensible girl—and I expect you are, for your father was a very clever man—you must know that you ought to marry as soon as possible. There aren't many young men about here. What becomes of all the young men in England, I'm sure I don't know. But there are a few—and quite possible. There are the Kenbarrows, about four miles off—a large family—*nouveaux riches*—the father made buttons, or something of the kind. But the children are all most presentable, and enormously rich. And, of course, there are the Fallodens—quite near—Mr. and Lady Laura, Douglas, the eldest son, a girl of seventeen, and two children. You'll probably see Douglas at Oxford. Oh, I believe Sir Arthur Falloden, *père,* told me the other day you had already met him somewhere. Winifred and I don't like Douglas. But that's neither here nor there. He's a magnificent creature, who can't be bothered with old ladies. He'll no doubt make himself agreeable to you—*cela va sans dire.* I don't altogether like what I hear sometimes about the Fallodens. Of course Sir Arthur's very rich, but they say he's been speculating enormously, and that he's been losing a good deal of money lately. However, I don't suppose it matters. Their place, Flood Castle, is really splendid—old to begin with, and done up! They have copied the Americans and given every room a bathroom. Absurd extravagance! And think of the plumbing! It was that kind of thing gave the Prince of Wales typhoid. I hate drains!

"Well, anyway, do come and see us. Sophia Langmoor tells me she has written to you, and if you go to her, you might come on here afterwards. Winifred who has just read this letter says it will 'put you off.' I don't see why it should. I certainly don't want it to. I'm downright,

I know, but I'm not hypocritical. The world's just run on white lies nowadays—and I can't stand it. I don't tell any—if I can help.

"Oh, and there is Penfold Rectory not very far off—and a very nice man there, though too 'broad' for Winifred. He tells me he's going to have some people staying with him—a Mr. Sorell, and a young musician with a Polish name—I can't remember it. Mr. Sorell's going to coach the young man, or something. They're to be paying guests, for a month at least. Mr. Powell was Mr. Sorell's college tutor—and Mr. Powell's dreadfully poor—so I'm glad. No wife, mercifully!

"Anyway, you see, there are plenty of people about. Do come.

"I am, dear Constance,
"Your affectionate aunt,
"MARCIA RISBOROUGH."

"Now what on earth am I going to do about that?" said Constance, tossing the letter over to Annette.

"Well, Mr. and Mrs. Hooper are going, cook says, to the Isle of Wight, and Miss Alice is going with them," said Annette, "and Miss Nora's going to join them after a bit in Scotland."

"I know all that," said Constance impatiently. "The question is—do you see me sitting in lodgings at Ryde with Aunt Ellen for five or six weeks, doing a little fancy-work, and walking out with Aunt Ellen and Alice on the pier?"

Annette laughed discreetly over her knitting, but said nothing.

"No," said Connie decidedly. "That can't be done. I shall have to sample Aunt Marcia. I must speak to Uncle Ewen to-morrow. Now put the light out, please, Annette; I'm going to sleep."

But it was some time before she went to sleep. The night was hot and thunderous, and her windows were wide open. Drifting in came the ever-recurring bells of Oxford, from the boom of the Christ Church "Tom," far away, through every variety of nearer tone. Connie lay and sleepily listened to them. To her they were always voices, half alive, half human, to which the dreaming mind put words that varied with the mood of the dreamer.

Presently, she breathed a soft good night into the darkness—"Mummy—mummy darling! good night!" It was generally her last waking thought. But suddenly another—which brought with it a rush of excitement—interposed between her and sleep.

"Tuesday," she murmured—"Mr. Sorell says the schools will be over by Tuesday. I wonder!——"

And again the bluebell carpet seemed to be all round her—the light and fragrance and colour of the wood. And the man on the black horse beside her was bending towards her, all his harsh strength subdued, for the moment, to the one end of pleasing her. She saw the smile in his dark eyes; and the touch of sarcastic *brusquerie* in the smile, that could rouse her own fighting spirit, as the touch of her whip roused the brown mare.

"Am I really so late?" said Connie, in distress, running downstairs the following afternoon to find the family and various guests waiting for her in the hall.

"Well, I hope we shan't miss everybody," said Alice sharply. "How late are we?"

She turned to Herbert Pryce.

The young don smiled and evaded the question.

"Nearly half an hour!" said Alice. "Of course they'll think we're not coming."

"They" were another section of the party who were taking a couple of boats round from the lower river, and were to meet the walkers coming across the Parks, at the Cherwell.

"Dreadfully sorry!" said Connie, who had opened her eyes, however, as though Alice's tone astonished her. "But my watch has gone quite mad."

"It does it every afternoon!" murmured Alice to a girl friend of Nora's who was going with the party. It was an aside, but plainly heard by Constance—whose cheeks flushed.

She turned appealingly to Herbert Pryce.

"Please carry my waterproof, while I button my gloves." Pryce was enchanted. As the party left the house, he and Constance walked on together, ahead of the others. She put on her most charming manners, and the young man was more than flattered.

What was it, he asked himself, complacently, that gave her such a delicate distinction? Her grey dress, and soft grey hat, were, he supposed, perfect of their kind. But Oxford in the summer term was full of pretty dresses. No, it must be her ease, her sureness of herself that banished any awkward self-consciousness both in herself and her companions, and allowed a man to do himself justice.

He forgot her recent snubs and went off at score about his own affairs, his college, his prospects of winning a famous mathematical prize given by the Berlin Academy, his own experience of German Universities, and the shortcomings of Oxford. On these last he became scornfully voluble. He was inclined to think he should soon cut it, and go in for public life. These university towns were really very narrowing!

"Certainly," said Constance amiably. Was he thinking of Parliament?

Well, no, not at once. But journalism was always open to a man with brains, and through journalism one got into the House, when the chance came along. The House of Commons was dangerously in want of new blood.

"I am certain I could speak," he said ardently. "I have made several attempts here, and I may say they have always come off."

Constance threw him a shy glance. She was thinking of a dictum of Uncle Ewen's which he had delivered to her on a walk some days previously. "What is it makes the mathematicians such fools? They never seem to grow up. They tell us they're splendid fellows, and of course we must believe them. But who's to know?"

Meanwhile, Alice and Sorell followed them at some distance behind, while Mrs. Hooper and three or four other members of the party brought up the rear. Sorell's look was a little clouded. He had heard what passed in the hall, and he found himself glancing uncomfortably from the girl beside him to the pair forging so gaily ahead. Alice Hooper's expression seemed to him that of something weak and tortured. All through the winter, in the small world of Oxford, the flirtation between Pryce of Beaumont and Ewen Hooper's eldest girl had been a conspicuous thing, even for those who had little or no personal knowledge of the Hoopers. It was noticed with amusement that Pryce had at last found some one to whom he might talk as long and egotistically as he pleased about himself and his career; and kindly mothers had said to each other that it would be a comfort to the Hoopers to have one of the daughters settled, though in a modest way.

"It is pleasant to see that your cousin enjoys Oxford so much," said Sorell, as they neared the museum, and saw Pryce and Connie disappearing through the gate of the park.

"Yes. She seems to like it," said Alice coldly.

Sorell began to talk of his first acquaintance with the Risboroughs, and of Connie's mother. There was no hint in what he said of his own passionate affection for his dead friends. He was not a profaner of shrines. But what he said brought out the vastness of Connie's loss in the death of her mother; and he repeated something of what he had heard from others of her utter physical and mental collapse after the double tragedy of the year before.

"Of course you'll know more about it than I do. But one of the English doctors in Rome, who is a friend of mine, told me that they thought at one time they couldn't pull her through. She seemed to have nothing else to live for."

"Oh, I don't think it was as bad as that," said Alice drily. "Anyway, she's quite well and strong now."

"She's found a home again. That's a great comfort to all her mother's old friends."

Sorell smiled upon his companion; the sensitive kindness in his own nature appealing to the natural pity in hers.

But Alice made no reply; and he dropped the subject.

They walked across the park, under a wide summer sky, towards the winding river, and the low blue hills beyond it. At the Cherwell boat-house they found the two boats, with four or five men, and Nora, as usual, taking charge of everything, at least till Herbert Pryce should appear.

Connie was just stepping into the foremost boat, assisted by Herbert Pryce, who was in his shirtsleeves, while Lord Meyrick and another Marmion man were already in the boat.

"Sorell, will you stroke the other boat?" said Pryce, "and Miss Nora, will you have a cushion in the bows? Now I think we're made up. No—we want another lady. And running his eyes over those still standing on the bank, he called a plump little woman, the wife of a Llandaff tutor, who had been walking with Mrs. Hooper.

"Mrs. Maddison, will you come with us? I think that will about trim us."

Mrs. Maddison obeyed him with alacrity, and the first boat pushed off. Mrs. Hooper, Alice, Sorell, two St. Cyprian undergraduates and Nora's girl friend, Miss Watson, followed in the second.

Then, while the June evening broadened and declined, the party wound in and out of the curves of the Cherwell. The silver river, brimming from a recent flood, lay sleepily like a gorged serpent between the hay meadows on either side. Flowers of the edge, meadow-sweet, ragged-robin and yellow flags, dipped into the water; willows spread their thin green over the embattled white and blue of the sky; here and there a rat plunged or a bird fled shrieking; bushes of wild roses flung out their branches, and everywhere the heat and the odours of a rich open land proclaimed the fulness of the midland summer.

Connie made the life of the leading boat. Something had roused her, and she began to reveal some of the "parlour-tricks," with which she had amused the Palazzo Barberini in her Roman days. A question from Pryce stirred her into quoting some of the folksongs of the Campagna, some comic, some tragic, fitting an action to them so lively and true that even those of her hearers who could not follow the dialect sat entranced. Then some one said—"But they ought to be sung!" And suddenly, though rather shyly, she broke into a popular *canzone* of the Garibaldian time, describing the day of Villa Gloria; the march of the morning, the wild hopes, the fanfaronade; and in the evening, a girl hiding a wounded lover and weeping both for him and "Italia" undone.

The sweet low sounds floated along the river.

"Delicious!" said Sorell, holding his oar suspended to listen. He remembered the song perfectly. He had heard her sing it in many places—Rome, Naples, Syracuse. It was a great favourite with her mother, for whom the national upheaval of Italy—the heroic struggle of the Risorgimento—had been a life-long passion.

"Why did Connie never tell us she could sing!" said Mrs. Hooper in her thin peevish voice. "Girls really shouldn't hide their accomplishments."

Sorell's oar dropped into the water with a splash.

At Marston Ferry, there was a general disembarking, a ramble along the river bank and tea under a group of elms beside a broad reach of the stream. Sorell noticed, that in spite of the regrouping of the two boat loads, as they mingled in the walk, Herbert Pryce never left Connie's side. And it seemed to him, and to others, that she was determined to keep him there. He must gather yellow flag and pink willow-herb for her, must hook a water-lily within reach of the bank with her parasol, must explain to her about English farms, and landlords, and why the labourers were discontented—why there were no peasant owners, as in Italy—and so on, and so on. Round-faced Mrs. Maddison, who had never seen the Hoopers' niece before, watched her with amusement, deciding that, distinguished and refined as the girl was, she was bent on admiration, and not too critical as to whence it came. The good-natured, curly-haired Meyrick, who was discontentedly reduced to helping Alice and Nora with the tea, and had never been so bored with a river picnic before, consoled himself by storing up rich materials for a "chaff" of Douglas when they next met—perhaps that evening, after hall? Alice meanwhile laughed and talked with the freshman whom Meyrick had brought with him from Marmion. Her silence and pallor had gone; she showed a kind of determined vivacity. Sorell, with his strange gift of sympathy, found himself admiring her "pluck."

When the party returned to the boat-house in the evening, Sorell, whose boat had arrived first at the landing-stage, helped Constance to land. Pryce, much against his will, was annexed by Nora to help her return the boats to the Isis; the undergraduates who had brought them being due at various engagements in Oxford. Sorell carried Constance off. He thought that he had never seen her look more radiant. She was flushed with success and praise, and the gold of the river sunset glorified her as she walked. Behind them, dim figures in the twilight, followed Mrs. Hooper and Alice, with the two other ladies, their cavaliers having deserted them.

"I am so glad you like Mr. Pryce," said Sorell suddenly.

Constance looked at him in astonishment.

"But why? I don't like him very much!"

"Really? I was glad because I suppose—doesn't everybody suppose?"—he looked at her smiling—"that there'll be some news in that quarter presently?"

Constance was silent a moment. At last, she said—

"You mean—he'll propose to Alice?"

"Isn't that what's expected?" He too had reddened. He was a shy man, and he was suddenly conscious that he had done a marked thing.

Another silence. Then Constance faced him, her face now more than flushed—aflame.

"I see. You think I have been behaving badly?"

He stammered.

"I didn't know perhaps—whether—you have been such a little while here—whether you had come across the Oxford gossip. I wish sometimes—you know I'm an old friend of your uncle—that it could be settled. Little Miss Alice has begun to look very worn."

Constance walked on, her eyes on the ground. He could see the soft lace on her breast fluttering. What foolish quixotry—what jealousy for an ideal—had made him run this hideous risk of offending her? He held his breath till she should look at him again. When she did, the beauty of the look abashed him.

"Thank you!" she said quietly. "Thank you very much. Alice annoyed me—she doesn't like me, you see—and I took a mean revenge. Well, now you understand—how I miss mamma!"

She held out her hand to him impulsively, and he enclosed it warmly in his; asking her, rather incoherently, to forgive his impertinence. Was it to be Ella Risborough's legacy to him—this futile yearning to help—to watch over—her orphaned child?

Much good the legacy would do him, when Connie's own will was really engaged! He happened to know that Douglas Falloden was already in Oxford again, and in a few more days Greats would be over, and the young man's energies released. What possible justification had he, Sorell, for any sort of interference in this quarter? It seemed to him, indeed, as to many others, that the young man showed every sign of a selfish and violent character. What then? Are rich and handsome husbands so plentiful? Have the moralists ever had their way with youth and sex in their first turbulent hour?

VIII

THIS LITTLE scene with Sorell, described in the last chapter, was of great importance to Connie's after history. It had placed her suddenly on a footing of intimacy with a man of poetic and lofty character, and had transformed her old childish relation to him—which had alone made the scene possible—into something entirely different. It produced a singular effect upon her that such a man should care enough what befell her to dare to say what he had said to her. It had been—she admitted it—a lesson in scrupulousness, in high delicacy of feeling, in magnanimity. "You are trifling with what may be the life of another—just to amuse yourself—or to pay off a moment's offence. Only the stupid or cruel souls do such things—or think lightly of them. But not you—your mother's daughter!"

That had been the meaning of his sudden incursion. The more Connie thought of it, the more it thrilled her. It was both her charm and her weakness, at this moment, that she was so plastic, so responsive both for good and evil. She said to herself that she was fortunate to have such a friend; and she was conscious of a new and eager wish to win his praise, or to avoid his blame.

At the same time it did not occur to her to tell him anything of her escapade with Douglas Falloden. But the more closely she kept this to herself, the more eager she was to appease her conscience and satisfy Sorell, in the matter of Alice and Herbert Pryce. Her instinct showed her what to do, and Sorell watched her struggling with the results of her evening's flirtation with much secret amusement and applause. Herbert Pryce having been whistled on, had to be whistled off, and Alice had to be gently and gradually reassured; yet without any obvious penitence on Connie's part, which would only have inflicted additional wounds on Alice's sore spirit.

And Connie did it, broadly speaking, during the week of Falloden's schools. Sorell himself was busy every day and all day as one of the Greats examiners. He scarcely saw her for more than two half-hours during a hideously strenuous week, through which he sat immersed in the logic and philosophy papers of the disappearing generation of Honour men. Among the papers of the twenty or thirty men who were the certain Firsts of the year, he could not help paying a special attention to Douglas Falloden's. What a hard and glittering mind the fellow had!—extraordinarily competent and well-trained; extraordinarily lacking, as it seemed to Sorell, in width or pliancy, or humanity. One of the ablest essays sent in, however, was a paper by Falloden on the "Sentimentalisms of Democracy"—in which a reasoned and fierce contempt for the popular voice, and a brilliant glorification of war and of a military aristocracy, made very lively reading.

On the later occasion, when Sorell and Constance met during the week, he found Radowitz in the Hoopers' drawing-room. Sorell had gone in after dinner to consult with Ewen Hooper, one of his fellow examiners, over some doubtful papers, and their business done, the two men allowed themselves an interval of talk and music with the ladies before beginning work again till the small hours.

Constance, in diaphanous black, was at the piano, trying to recall, for Radowitz's benefit, some of the Italian folk-songs that had delighted the river-party. The room was full of a soft mingled light from the still uncurtained windows and the lamp which had been just brought in. It seemed to be specially concentrated on the hair, "golden like ripe corn," of the young musician, and on Connie's white neck and arms. Radowitz lay back in a low chair gazing at her with all his eyes.

On the further side of the room Nora was reading, Mrs. Hooper was busy with the newspaper, and Alice and Herbert Pryce were talking with the air of people who are, rather uncomfortably, making up a quarrel.

Sorell spent his half-hour mostly in conversation with Mrs. Hooper and Nora, while his inner mind wondered about the others. He stood with his back to the mantelpiece, his handsome pensive face, with its intensely human eyes, bent towards Nora, who was pouring out to him some grievances of the "home-students," to which he was courteously giving a jaded man's attention.

When he left the room Radowitz broke out—

"Isn't he like a god?"

Connie opened astonished eyes.

"Who?"

"My tutor—Mr. Sorell. Ah, you didn't notice—but you should. He is like the Hermes—only grown older, and with a soul. But there is no Greek sculptor who could have done him justice. It would have wanted a Praxiteles; but with the mind of Euripides!"

The boy's passionate enthusiasm pleased her. But she could think of nothing less conventional in reply than to ask if Sorell were popular in college.

"Oh, they like him well enough. They know what trouble he takes for them, and there's nobody dares cheek him. But they don't understand him. He's too shy. Wasn't it good fortune for me that he happens to be my friend?"

And he began to talk at headlong speed, and with considerable eloquence, of Sorell's virtues and accomplishments. Constance, who had been brought up in a southern country, liked the eloquence. Something in her was already tired of the slangy brevities that do duty in England for conversation. At the same time she thought she understood why Falloden, and Meyrick, and others called the youth a *poseur*, and angrily wished to snub him. He possessed besides, inbred, all the foreign aids to the mere voice—gesticulation of hands and head, movements that to the Englishman are unexpected and therefore disagreeable. Also there, undeniably, was the frilled dress-shirt, and the two diamond studs, much larger and more conspicuous than Oxford taste allowed, which added to its criminality. And it was easy to see too that the youth was inordinately proud of his Polish ancestry, and inclined to rate all Englishmen as *parvenus* and shopkeepers.

"Was it in Paris you first made friends with Mr. Sorell?" Connie asked him.

Radowitz nodded.

"I was nineteen. My uncle had just died. I had nobody. You understand, my father was exiled twenty years ago. We belong to German Poland; though there has always been a branch of the family in Cracow. For more than a hundred years these vile Germans have been crushing and tormenting us. They have taken our land, they have tried to kill our language and our religion. But they can not. Our soul lives. Poland lives. And some day there will be a great war—and then Poland will rise again. From the East and the West and the South they will come—and the body that was hewn asunder will be young and glorious again." His blue eyes shone. "Some day, I will play you that in music. Chopin is full of it—the death of Poland—and then her soul, her songs, her hopes, her rising again. Ah, but Sorell!—I will explain. I saw him one night at a house of kind people—the master of it was the Directeur of the Ecole des Sciences Politiques—and his wife. She was so beautiful, though she was not young; and gentle, like a child; and so good. I was nothing to them—but I went to some lectures at the school, while I was still at the Conservatoire, and I used to go and play to them sometimes. So when my uncle died, they said, 'Come and stay with us.' I had really nobody. My father and mother died years ago. My mother, you understand, was half English; I always spoke English with her. She knew I must be a musician. That was settled when I was a child. Music is my life. But if I took it for a profession, she made me promise to see some other kinds of life first. She often said she would like me to go to Oxford. She had some old engravings of the colleges she used to show me. I am not a pauper, you see,—not at all. My family was once a very great family; and I have some money—not very much, but enough. So then Mr. Sorell and I began to talk. And I had suddenly the feeling—'If this man will tell me what to do, I will do it.' And then he found I was thinking of Oxford, and he said, if I came, he would be my friend, and look after me. And so he advised me to go to Mannion, because some of the tutors there were great friends of his. And that is why I went. And I have been there nearly a year."

"And you like it?" Connie, sitting hunched on the music-stool, her chin on her hand, was thinking of Falloden's outburst, and her own rebuff in Lathom Woods.

The boy shrugged his shoulders. He looked at Connie with his brilliant eyes, and she seemed to see that he was on the point of confiding in her, of complaining of his treatment, and then proudly checked himself.

"Oh, I like it well enough," he said carelessly. "I am reading classics. I love Greek. There is a soul in Greek. Latin—and Rome—that is too like the Germans! Now let me play to you—something from Poland."

He took her seat at the piano, and began to play—first in a dreamy and quiet way, passing from one plaintive folk-song to another; then gradually rising into passion, defiance, tragedy. Constance stood listening to him in amazement—entranced. Music was a natural language to her as it was to Radowitz, though her gift was so small and slight compared to his. But she understood and followed him; and there sprang up in her, as she sat turning her delicate face to the musician, that sudden, impassioned delight, that sense of fellowship with things vast and incommunicable—"exultations, agonies, and love, and man's unconquerable mind"—which it is the glorious function of music to kindle in the human spirit.

The twilight darkened. Every sound in the room but Radowitz's playing had ceased; even Mrs. Hooper had put down her newspaper. Nora, on the further side of the room, was absorbed in watching the two beautiful figures under the lamplight, the golden-haired musician and the listening girl.

Suddenly there was a noise of voices in the hall outside. The drawing-room door was thrown open, and the parlourmaid announced:

"Mr. Falloden."

Mrs. Hooper rose hastily. Radowitz wavered in a march finale he was improvising, and looked round.

"Oh, go on!" cried Constance.

But Radowitz ceased playing. He got up, with an angry shake of his wave of hair, muttered something about "another couple of hours' work" and closed the piano.

Constance remained sitting, as though unaware of the new arrival in the room.

"That was wonderful!" she said, with a long breath, her eyes raised to Radowitz. "Now I shall go and read Polish history!"

A resonant voice said:

"Hullo—Radowitz! Good-evening, Lady Connie. Isn't this a scandalous time to call? But I came about the ball-tickets for next Wednesday—to ask how many your aunt wants. There seems to be an unholy rush on them."

Connie put out a careless hand.

"How do you do? We've been having the most divine music! Next Wednesday? Oh, yes, I remember!" And as she recovered her hand from Falloden, she drew it across her eyes, as though trying to dispel the dream in which Radowitz's playing had wrapped her. Then the hand dropped, and she saw the drawing-room door closing on the player.

Falloden looked down upon her with a sarcastic mouth, which, however, worked nervously.

"I'm extremely sorry to bring you down to earth. I suppose he's awfully good."

"It's genius," said Connie, breathlessly—"just that—genius! I had no idea he had such a gift." Falloden shrugged his shoulders without reply. He threw himself into a chair beside her, his knees crossed, his hands on the topmost knee, with the finger-tips lightly touching, an attitude characteristic of him. The lamp which had been brought in to light the piano shone full upon him, and Constance perceived that, in spite of his self-confident ease of bearing, he looked haggard and pale with the long strain of the schools. Her own manner relaxed.

"Have you really done?" she asked, more graciously.

"I was in for my last paper this afternoon. I am now a free man."

"And you've got your First?"

He laughed.

"That only the gods know. I may just squeak into it."

"And now you've finished with Oxford?"

"Oh, dear, no! There's a fortnight more. One keeps the best—for the last."

"Then your people are coming up again for Commem.?" The innocence of the tone was perfect.

His sparkling eyes met hers.

"I have no domestic prospects of that sort," he said drily. "What I shall do with this fortnight depends entirely—on one person."

The rest of the room seemed full of a buzz of conversation which left them unobserved. Connie had taken up her large lace fan and was slowly opening and closing it. The warm pallor of her face and throat, the golden brown of her hair, the grace of her neck and shoulders, enchanted the man beside her. For three weeks he had been holding desire in check with a strong hand. The tide of it rushed back upon him, with the joy of a released force. But he knew that he must walk warily.

"Will you please give me some orders?" he went on, smiling, seeing that she did not reply. "How has the mare been behaving?"

"She is rather tame—a little too much of the sheep in her composition."

"She wants a companion. So do I—badly. There is a little village beyond the Lathom Woods—which has a cottage—for tea—and a strawberry garden. Shall we sample it?"

Constance shook her head laughing.

"We haven't an hour. Everybody asks us to parties, all day and all night long. London is a joke to Oxford."

"Don't go!" said Falloden impatiently. "I have been asked to meet you—three times—at very dull houses. But I shall go, of course, unless I can persuade you to do something more amusing."

"Oh, dear, no! We're in for it. But I thought people came here to read books?"

"They do read a few; but when one has done with them one feels towards them like enemies whom one has defeated—and insults.

I chucked my Greek lexicon under the sofa, first thing, when I got back from the schools this afternoon."

"Wasn't that childish—rather? I am appalled to think how much you know."

He laughed impatiently.

"Now one may begin to learn something. Oxford is precious little use. But it's not worth while being beaten—in anything. Shall we say Thursday, then?—for our ride?"

Constance opened her eyes in pretended astonishment.

"After the ball? Shall I be awake? Let's settle it on Wednesday!"

He could get no more definite promise from her, and must needs take his leave. Before he went, he asked her to keep the first four dances for him at the Marmion ball, and two supper-dances. But Constance evaded a direct assent. She would do her best. But she had promised some to Mr. Pryce, and some to Mr. Radowitz.

Falloden's look darkened.

"You should not allow him to dance with you," he said imperiously. "He is too eccentric. He doesn't know how to behave; and he makes his partners conspicuous."

Constance too had risen, and they confronted each other—she all wilfulness.

"I shall certainly dance with him!" she said, with a little determined air. "You see, I like foreign ways!"

He said good night abruptly. As he stood a few minutes on the further side of the room, making a few last arrangements as to the ball with Mrs. Hooper and Alice, Constance, still standing by the piano, and apparently chatting with Herbert Pryce, was really aware of Falloden's every movement. His manner to her aunt was brusque and careless; and he forgot, apparently, to say good night either to Alice or Nora. Nobody in the room, as she well knew, except herself, found any pleasure in his society. Nora's hostile face in the background was a comic study. And yet, so long as he was there, nobody could forget or overlook him; so splendid was the physical presence of the man, and so strong the impression of his personality—even in trivial things.

*

Meanwhile, everybody in the house had gone to bed, except Nora and her father. She had lit a little fire in his study, as the night had grown chilly; she had put a little tray with tea on it by his side, and helped him to arrange the Greats papers, in which he was still immersed, under his hand. And finally she brought his pipe and filled it for him.

"Must you sit up long, father?"

"An hour or two," said Ewen Hooper wearily. "I wish I didn't get so limp. But these Honour exams take it out of one. And I have to go to Winchester to-morrow."

"For the scholarship?"

He nodded.

"Father! you work a great deal too hard—you look dog-tired!" cried Nora in distress. "Why do you do so much?"

He shook his head sadly.

"You know, darling."

Nora did know. She knew that every pound was of importance to the household, that the temporary respite caused by the legacy from Lord Risborough and by Connie's prepayment would very soon come to an end, and that her father seemed to be more acutely aware of the position than he had yet been. Her own cleverness, and the higher education she was steadily getting for herself enabled her to appreciate, as no one else in the family could or did, her father's delicate scholarly gifts, which had won him his reputation in Oxford and outside. But the reputation might have been higher, if so much time had not been claimed year after year by the sheer pressure of the family creditors. With every year, Nora had grown up into a fuller understanding of her father's tragedy; a more bitter, a more indignant understanding. They might worry through; one way or another she supposed they would worry through. But her father's strength and genius were being sacrificed. And this child of seventeen did not see how to stop it.

After she had brought him his pipe, and he was drawing at it contentedly over the fire, she stood silent beside him, bursting with something she could not make up her mind to say. He put out an arm, as she stood beside his chair, and drew her to him.

"Dear little Trotty Veck!" It had been his pet name for her as a child. Nora, for answer, bent her head, and kissed him.

"Father"—she broke out—"I've got my first job!"

He looked up enquiringly.

"Mr. Hurst"—she named her English Literature tutor, a fellow of Marmion—"has got it for me. I've been doing some Norman-French with him; and there's a German professor has asked him to get part of a romance copied that's in the Bodleian—the only manuscript. And Mr. Hurst says he'll coach me—I can easily do it—and I shall get ten pounds!"

"Well done, Trotty Veck!" Ewen Hooper smiled at her affectionately. "But won't it interfere with your work?"

"Not a bit. It will help it. Father!—I'm going to earn a lot before long. If it only didn't take such a long time to grow up! " said Nora impatiently. "One ought to be as old as one feels—and I feel quite twenty-one!"

Ewen Hooper shook his head.

"That's all wrong. One should be young—and taste being young, every moment, every day that one can. I wish I'd done it—now that I'm getting old."

"You're not old!" cried Nora. "You're not, father! You're not to say it!"

And kneeling down by him, she laid her cheek against his shoulder, and put one of his long gaunt hands to her lips.

Her affection was very sweet to him, but it could not comfort him. There are few things, indeed, in which the old can be comforted by the young—the old, who know too much, both of life and themselves.

But he pulled himself together.

"Dear Trotty Veck, you must go to bed, and let me do my work. But—one moment! " He laid a hand on her shoulder, and abruptly asked her whether she thought her Cousin Constance was in love with Douglas Falloden. "Your mother's always talking to me about it," he said, with a wearied perplexity.

"I don't know," said Nora, frowning. "But I shouldn't wonder."

"Then I shall have to make some enquiries," said Connie's guardian, with resignation. "She's a masterful young woman. But she can be very sweet when she likes. Do you see what she gave me to-day?"

He pointed to a beautiful Viennese edition of Aeschylus, in three sumptuous volumes, which had just appeared and was now lying on the Reader's table.

Nora took it up with a cry of pleasure. She had her father's passion for books.

"She heard me say to Sorell, apparently, that I would give my eyes for it, and couldn't afford it. That was a week ago. And to-day, after luncheon, she stole in here like a mouse—you none of you saw or heard her—holding the books behind her—and looking as meek as milk. You would have thought she was a child, coming to say she was sorry! And she gave me the books in the prettiest way—just like her mother!—as though all the favour came from me. I'm beginning to be very fond of her. She's so nice to your old father. I say, Nora!"—he held her again—"you and I have got to prevent her from marrying the wrong man!"

Nora shook her head, with an air of middle-aged wisdom.

"Connie will marry whomever she has a mind to!" she said firmly. "And it's no good, father, you imagining anything else."

Ewen Hooper laughed, released her, and sent her to bed.

The days that followed represented the latter part of the interval between the Eights and Commemoration, before Oxford plunged once more into high festival.

It was to be a brilliant Commem.; for an ex-Viceroy of India, a retired Ambassador, England's best General, and five or six foreign men of science and letters, of rather exceptional eminence, were coming to get their honorary degrees. When Mrs. Hooper, *Times* in hand, read out at the breakfast-table the names of Oxford's expected guests, Constance Bledlow looked up in surprised amusement. It seemed the Ambassador and she were old friends; that she had sat on his knee as a baby through various Carnival processions in the Corso, showing him how to throw *confetti*; and that he and Lady F.

had given a dance at the Embassy for her coming-out, when Connie, at seventeen, and His Excellency—still the handsomest man in the room, despite years and gout—had danced the first waltz together, and a subsequent minuet; which—though Connie did not say so—had been the talk of Rome.

As to the ex-Viceroy, he was her father's first cousin, and had passed through Rome on his way east, staying three or four days at the Palazzo Barberini. Constance, however, could not be induced to trouble her head about him. "He bored Mamma and me dreadfully," she said—"he had seven pokers up his back, and was never human for a minute. I don't want to see him at all." Oxford, however, seemed to be of the opinion that ex-viceroys do want to see their cousins; for the Hooper party found themselves asked as a matter of course to the All Souls' luncheon, the Vice-Chancellor's garden-party, and to a private dinner-party in Christ Church on the day of the Encænia, at which all the new-made doctors were to be present. As for the ball-tickets for Commem. week, they poured in; and meanwhile there were endless dinner-parties, and every afternoon had its river picnic, now on the upper, now on the lower river.

It was clear, indeed, both to her relations and to Oxford in general, that Constance Bledlow was to be the heroine of the moment. She would be the "star" of Commem., as so many other pretty or charming girls had been before her. But in her case, it was no mere undergraduate success. Old and young alike agreed to praise her. Her rank inevitably gave her precedence at almost every dinner-party, Oxford society not being rich in the peerage. The host, who was often the head of a college and grey-haired, took her in; and some other University big-wig, equally mature, flanked her on the right. When she was undressing in her little room after these entertainments, she would give Annette a yawning or plaintive account of them. "You know, Annette, I never talk to anybody under fifty now!" But at the time she never failed to play her part. She was born with the wish to please, which, as every one knows, makes three parts of the art of pleasing.

Meanwhile Sorell, who was at all times a very popular man, in great request, accepted many more invitations than usual in order to see as much as he could of this triumphal progress of Lady Risborough's daughter. Oxford society was then much more limited than now, and he and she met often. It seemed to him whenever he came across Douglas Falloden in Connie's company during these days, that the young man's pursuit of Constance, if it was a pursuit, was making no progress at all, and that his temper suffered accordingly. Connie's endless engagements were constantly in the way. Sorell thought he detected once or twice that Falloden had taken steps to procure invitations to houses where Constance was expected; but when they did meet it was evident that he got but a small share of her attention.

Once Sorell saw them in what appeared intimate conversation at a Christ Church party. Falloden—who was flushed and frowning—was talking rapidly in a low voice; and Constance was listening to him with a look half soft, half mocking. Her replies seemed to irritate her companion, for they parted abruptly, Constance looking back to smile a sarcastic good-bye.

Again, on the Sunday before the Encænia, a famous high churchman preached in the University church. The church was densely crowded, and Sorell, sitting in the masters' seats under the pulpit, saw Constance dimly, in the pews reserved for wives and families of the University doctors and masters, beneath the gallery. Immediately to her right, in the very front of the undergraduates' gallery, he perceived the tall form and striking head of Douglas Falloden; and when the sermon was over he saw that the young man was one of the first to push his way out.

"He hopes to waylay her," thought Sorell.

If so, he was unsuccessful. Sorell emerging with the stream into the High Street saw Connie's black and white parasol a little ahead. Falloden was on the point of overtaking her, when Radowitz, the golden-haired, the conspicuous, crossed his path. Constance looked round, smiled, shook hands with Radowitz, and apparently not seeing Falloden in her rear, walked on, in merry talk with the beaming musician. Sorell, perhaps, was the only person who noticed the look of pale fury with which Falloden dropped out of the crowded pathway, crossed the street, and entered a smart club opposite, exclusively frequented by "bloods."

Commem. week itself, however, would give a man in love plenty of chances. Sorell was well aware of it. Monday dawned with misty sunshine after much rain. In the Turl after luncheon, Sorell met Nora Hooper hurrying along with note-books under her arm. They turned down Brasenose Lane together, and she explained that she was on her way to the Bodleian where she was already at work on her first paid job. Her pleasure in it, and the childish airs she gave herself in regard to it, touched and amused Sorell, with whom—through the Greek lessons—she had become a great favourite.

As they parted at the doorway leading to the Bodleian, she said with a mischievous look—

"Did you know Mr. Falloden's party is off?"

And she explained that for the following day, Falloden had arranged the most elaborate and exclusive of river-parties, with tea in the private gardens of a famous house, ten miles from Oxford. His mother and sister had been coming down for it, and he had asked other people from London.

"It was all for Connie—and Connie's had to scratch! And Mr. Falloden has put it all off. He says his mother, Lady Laura, has a chill and can't come, but every one knows—it's Connie!"

She and Sorell smiled at each other. They had never had many words on the subject, but they understood each other perfectly.

"What made her scratch?" asked Sorell, wondering.

"Royalties," said Nora shortly, with a democratic nose in air.

It appeared that a certain travelled and artistic Princess had been spending the week-end in a ducal house in the neighbourhood. So, too, had the ex-Viceroy. And hearing from him that the only daughter "of those dear Risboroughs" was at Oxford, twelve miles off, her Royal Highness, through him, had "commanded" Constance for tea under the ducal roof on Tuesday. A carriage was to be sent for her, and the ex-Viceroy undertook to convey her back to Oxford afterwards, he being due himself to dine and sleep at the Vice-Chancellor's the night before the Encænia.

"Constance didn't want to go a bit. She was dreadfully annoyed. But father and mother made her. So she sent a note to Mr. Falloden, and he came round. She was out, but Alice saw him. Alice says he scarcely said a word, but you could feel he was in a towering rage."

"Poor Falloden!" said Sorell.

Nora's eyes twinkled.

"Yes, but so good for him! I'm sure he's always throwing over other people. Now he knows

'Golden lads and lasses must
Like chimney-sweepers come to dust.'"

"Vandal!" cried Sorell—"to twist such a verse!"

Nora laughed, threw him a friendly nod, and vanished up the steps of the Bodleian.

But Falloden's hour came.

The Encænia went off magnificently. Connie, sitting beside Mrs. Hooper in the semicircle of the Sheldonian Theatre, drew the eyes of the crowd of graduates as they surged into the arena, and tantalised the undergraduates in the gallery, above the semicircle, who were well aware that the "star" was there, but could not see her. As the new doctors' procession entered through the lane made for it by the bedells, as the whole assembly rose, and as the organ struck up, amid the clapping and shouting of the gods in the gallery, Connie and the grey-haired Ambassador, who was walking second in the red and yellow line, grinned openly at each other, while the ex-Viceroy in front, who had been agreeably flattered by the effect produced by his girl-cousin in the august circles of the day before, nodded and smiled at the young lady in the white plumes and pale mauve dress.

"Do you know my cousin, Lady Constance Bledlow?—the girl in mauve there?" he said, complacently in the ear of the Public Orator, as they stood waiting till the mingled din from the organ and the undergraduates' gallery overhead should subside sufficiently to allow that official to begin his arduous task of introducing the doctors-elect.

The Public Orator, in a panic lest one of the Latin puns in his forthcoming address should escape him, said hurriedly—"Yes!"—and then "No"—being quite uncertain to which girl in mauve the great man referred, and far too nervous to find out. The great man smiled, and looked up blandly at the shrieking gallery overhead, wondering—as all persons in his position do wonder in each succeeding generation—whether the undergraduates were allowed to make quite such an infernal noise when he was "up."

Meanwhile, Constance herself was only conscious of one face and figure in the crowded theatre. Falloden had borrowed a master's gown, and as the general throng closed up behind the doctors' procession, he took up a position in the rear, just in front of the great doors under the organ loft, which, as the day was very hot, remained unclosed. His dark head and athlete's figure, scarcely disguised by the ampler folds of the borrowed gown, showed in picturesque relief against the grey and sunlit background of the beautiful Divinity School, which could be seen through the doorway. Constance knew that his eyes were on her; and she guessed that he was only conscious of her, as she at that moment was only conscious of him. And again that tremor, that premonition of some coming attack upon her will which she half dreaded, and half desired, swept over her. What was there in the grave and slightly frowning face that drew her through all repulsion? She studied it. Surely the brow and eyes were beautiful—shaped for high thought, and generous feeling? It was the disdainful sulky mouth, the haughty carriage of the head, that spoilt a noble aspect. Yet she had seen the mouth quiver into softness; and those broad shoulders had once stood between her and danger—possibly death. Her heart trembled. "What do you want of me?" it was asking—helplessly—of the distant man; "and can I—dare I—give it?"

Then her thoughts flew onward to the ball of the evening, for it was the night of the Marmion ball. No more escape! If she went—and nothing should prevent her from going—it would be Falloden's evening, Falloden's chance. She had been perfectly conscious of evading and thwarting him during the previous week. There had been some girlish mischief, but more excitement in it. Now, would he take his revenge?

Her heart beat fast. She had never yet danced with him. To-night she would feel his arm round her in the convention of the waltz. And she knew that for her it would be no convention; but something either to be passionately accepted—or impatiently endured.

Oxford went early to the Marmion ball. It was a very popular gathering. So that before ten o'clock the green quadrangle was crowded with guests waiting to see other guests come in; while the lights from the Gothic hall, and the notes of the "Blue Danube," then in its first prime, flung out their call to youth and sex.

In they thronged—young men and maidens—a gay procession through the lawns and quadrangles, feeling the world born anew for them, and for them only, as their fathers and mothers had felt before them.

Falloden and Meyrick, with half a dozen other chosen spirits, met Constance at the entrance and while Mrs. Hooper and Alice followed, pleased against their will by the reflected fame which had fallen upon them also, the young men formed a body-guard round Constance, and escorted her like a queen to the hall.

Sorell, eagerly waiting, watched her entrance into the beautiful and spacious room, with its throng of dancers. She came in, radiant, with that aureole of popular favour floating round her, which has so much to do with the loveliness of the young. All the world smiled on her; she smiled in return; and that sarcastic self behind the smile, which Nora's quick sense was so often conscious of, seemed to have vanished. She carried, Sorell saw, a glorious bunch of pale roses. Were they Falloden's gift?

That Douglas Falloden danced with her repeatedly, that they sat out together through most of the supper-dances, that there was a sheltered corner in the illuminated quad, beside the Græco-Roman fountain which an archæological warden had given to the college, where, involuntarily, his troubled eyes discovered them more than once:—this at least Sorell knew, and could not help knowing. He saw that she danced twice with Radowitz, and that Falloden stood meanwhile in the doorway of the hall, twisting his black moustache, and chaffing Meyrick, yet all the time with an eye on the ballroom. And during one long disappearance, he found himself guessing that Falloden had taken her to the library for greater seclusion. Only a very few people seemed to know that the fine old room was open.

"Where is Connie?" said poor Mrs. Hooper fretfully—when three o'clock had long struck. "I can't keep awake!"

And now a midsummer sun was rising over Oxford. The last carriage had rumbled through the streets; the last merry group of black-coated men, and girls in thin shoes and opera-cloaks had vanished. The summer dawn held the whole beautiful and silenced city in its peace.

Constance, in her dressing-gown, sat at the open window, looking out over the dewy garden, and vaguely conscious of its scents as one final touch of sweetness in a whole of pleasure which was still sending its thrill through all her pulses.

At last, she found pen and paper on her writing-table, and wrote an instruction for Annette upon it.

"Please send early for the horses. They should be here at a quarter to nine. Call me at eight. Tell Aunt Ellen that I have gone for a ride, and shall be back by eleven. It was quite a nice ball."

Then, with a silent laugh at the last words, she took the sheet of paper, stole noiselessly out of her room, and up the stairs to Annette's room, where she pushed the message under the door. Annette had not been well the day before, and Connie had peremptorily forbidden her to sit up.

IX

THE DAY was still young in Lathom Woods. A woodcutter engaged in cutting coppice on the wood's eastern skirts, hearing deep muffled sounds from "Tom" clock-tower, borne to him from Oxford on the light easterly breeze, stopped to count the strokes.

Ten o'clock.

He straightened himself, wiped the sweat from his brow, and was immediately aware of certain other sounds approaching from the wood itself. Horses—at a walk. No doubt the same gentleman and lady who had passed him an hour earlier, going in a contrary direction.

He watched them as they passed him again, repeating his reflection that they were a "fine-lookin' couple"—no doubt sweethearts. What else should bring a young man and a young woman riding in Lathom Woods at that time in the morning? "Never seed 'em doin' it before, anyways."

Connie threw the old man a gracious "Good morning!"—to which he guardedly responded, looking full at her, as he stood leaning on his axe.

"I wonder what the old fellow is thinking about us!" she said lightly, when they had moved forward. Then she flushed, conscious that the remark had been ill-advised.

Falloden, who was sitting erect and rather sombre, his reins lying loosely on his horse's neck, said slowly—

"He is probably thinking all sorts of foolish things, which aren't true. I wish they were."

Connie's eyes were shining with a suppressed excitement.

"He supposes at any rate we have had a good time, and in fact—we haven't. Is that what you mean?"

"If you like to put it so."

"And we haven't had a good time, because—unfortunately—we've quarrelled!"

"I should describe it differently. There are certain proofs and tests of friendship that any friend may ask for. But when they are all refused——"

"Friendship itself is strained!" laughed Constance, looking round at her companion. She was breathing quickly. "In other words, we have been quarrelling—about Radowitz—and there seems no way of making it up."

"You have only to promise me the very little thing I asked," said Falloden stiffly.

"That I shouldn't dance with him to-night, or again this week? You call that a little thing?"

"I should have thought it a small thing, compared——"

He turned and faced her. His dark eyes were full of proud agitation—of things unspoken. But she met them undaunted.

"Compared to—friendship?"

He was silent, but his eyes held her.

"Well then"—said Constance—"let me repeat that—in my opinion, friendship which asks unreasonable things—is not friendship—but tyranny!"

She drew herself up passionately, and gave a smart touch with her whip to the mare's flank, who bounded forward, and had to be checked by Falloden's hand on her bridle.

"Don't get run away with, while you are denouncing me!" he said, smiling, as they pulled up.

"I really didn't want any help!" said Constance, panting. "I could have stopped her quite easily."

"I doubt it. She is really not the lamb you think her!"

"Nor is her mistress: I return the remark."

"Which has no point. Because only a madman——"

"Could have dreamed of comparing me—to anything soft and docile?" laughed Constance.

There was another silence. Before them at the end of a long green vista the gate opening on the main road could be seen.

Constance broke it. Wounded pride, and stubborn will were hot within her.

"Well, it is a great pity we should have been sparring like this. I can't remember who began it. But now I suppose I may do what I like with the dances I promised you?"

"I keep no one to their word who means to break it," said Falloden coldly.

Constance grew suddenly white.

"That"—she said quietly—"was unpardonable!"

"It was. I retract it."

"No. You have said it—which means that you could think it. That decides it."

They rode on in silence. As they neared the gate, Constance, whose face showed agitation and distress, said abruptly—

"Of course I know I must seem very ungrateful——"

A sound, half bitter, half scornful from Falloden stopped her. She threw her head back defiantly.

"All the same I could be grateful enough, in my own way, if you would let me. But what you don't understand is that men can't lord it over women now as they used to do. You say—you"—she stammered a little—"you love me. I don't know yet—what I feel. I feel many different things. But I know this: A man who forbids me to do this and that—to talk to this person—or dance with some one else—a man who does not trust and believe in me—if I were ever so much in love with him, I would not marry him! I should feel myself a coward and a slave!"

"One is always told"—said Falloden hoarsely—"that love makes it easy to grant even the most difficult things. And I have begged the merest trifle."

"'Begged'?" said Constance, raising her eyebrows. "You issued a decree. I am not to dance with Radowitz—and I am not to see so much of Mr. Sorell—if I am to keep your—friendship. I demurred.

You repeated it—as though you were responsible for what I do, and had a right to command me. Well, that does not suit me. I am perfectly free, and I have given you no right to arrange my life for me. So now let us understand each other."

Falloden shrugged his shoulders.

"You have indeed made it perfectly plain!"

"I meant to," said Constance vehemently.

But they could not keep their eyes from each other. Both were pale. In both the impulse to throw away pride and hold out a hand of yielding was all but strong enough to end their quarrel. Both suffered, and if the truth were told, both were standing much deeper than before in the midstream of passion. But neither spoke another word—till the gate was reached.

Falloden opened it, and backed his horse out of Connie's way. In the road outside, at a little distance, the groom was waiting.

"Good-bye," said Falloden, with ceremonious politeness. "I wish I had not spoilt your ride. Please do not give up riding in the woods, because you might be burdened with my company. I shall never intrude upon you. All the woodmen and keepers have been informed that you have full permission. The family will be all away till the autumn. But the woodmen will look after you, and give you no trouble."

"Thank you!" said Constance, lightly, staying the mare for a moment. "But surely some of the rides will be wanted directly for the pheasants? Anyway I think I shall try the other side of Oxford. They say Bagley is delightful. Good-bye!"

She passed through, made a signal to Joseph, and was soon trotting fast towards Oxford.

On that return ride, Constance could not conceal from herself that she was unhappy. Her lips quivered, her eyes had much ado to keep back the onset of tears—now that there was no Falloden to see her, or provoke her. How brightly their ride had begun!—how miserably it had ended! She thought of that first exhilaration; the early sun upon the wood; the dewy scents of moss and tree; Falloden's face of greeting—"How can you look so fresh! You can't have slept more than four hours—and here you are! Wonderful! 'Did ever Dian so become a grove'——"

An ominous quotation, if she had only remembered at the time where it came from! For really his ways were those of a modern Petruchio—ways that no girl of any decent spirit could endure.

Yet how frank and charming had been his talk as they rode into the wood!—talk of his immediate plans, which he seemed to lay at her feet, asking for her sympathy and counsel; of his father and his two sisters; of the Hoopers even. About them, his new tone was no doubt a trifle patronising, but still, quite tolerable. Ewen Hooper, he vowed, was "a magnificent scholar," and it was too bad that Oxford had found nothing better for him than "a scrubby readership." But "some day, of course, he'll have the regius professorship." Nora was "a plucky little thing—though she hates me!" And he, Falloden, was not so sure after all that Miss Alice would not land her Pryce. "Can't we bring it about?"

And Falloden ran, laughing, through a catalogue of his own smart or powerful relations, speculating what could be done. It was true, wasn't it, that Pryce was anxious to turn his back on Oxford and the higher mathematics, and to try his luck in journalism, or politics? Well, Falloden happened to know that an attractive post in the Conservative Central Office would soon be vacant; an uncle of his was a very important person on the Council; that and other wires might be pulled. Constance, eagerly, began to count up her own opportunities of the same kind; and between them, they had soon—in imagination—captured the post. Then, said Falloden, it would be for Constance to clinch the matter. No man could do such a thing decently. Pryce would have to be told—" 'The world's your oyster—but before you open it, you will kindly go and propose to my cousin!—which of course you ought to have done months ago!' "

And so laughing and plotting like a couple of children they had gone rambling through the green rides and glades of the wood, occasionally putting their horses to the gallop, that the pulse of life might run still faster.

But a later topic of conversation had brought them into even closer contact. Connie spoke of her proposed visit to her aunts. Falloden, radiant, could not conceal his delight.

"You will be only five miles from us. Of course you must come and stay at Flood! My mother writes they have collected a jolly party for the 12th. I will tell her to write to you at once. You must come! You must! Will you promise?"

And Constance, wondering at her own docility, had practically promised. "I want you to know my people—I want you to know my father!" And as he plunged again into talk about his father, the egotistical man of fashion disappeared; she seemed at last to have reached something sincere and soft, and true.

And then—what had begun the jarring? Was it—first—her account of her Greek lessons with Sorell? Before she knew what had happened, the brow beside her had clouded, the voice had changed. Why did she see so much of Sorell? He, like Radowitz, was a *poseur*—a wind-bag. That was what made the attraction between them. If she wished to learn Greek——

"Let me teach you!" And he had bent forward, with his most brilliant and imperious look, his hand upon her reins.

But Constance, surprised and ruffled, had protested that Sorell had been her mother's dear friend, and was now her own. She could not and would not give up her lessons. Why indeed should she?

"Because friends"—Falloden had laid a passionate emphasis on the word—"must have some regard—surely—to each other's likes and dislikes. If you have an enemy, tell me—he or she shall be mine—instantly! Sorell dislikes me. You will never hear any good of me from him. And, of course, Radowitz hates me. I have given him good cause. Promise—at least—that you will not dance with Radowitz again. You don't know what I suffered last night. He has the antics of a monkey!"

Whereupon the quarrel between them had broken like thunder, Constance denouncing the arrogance and unkindness that could ask such promises of her; Falloden steadily, and with increasing bitterness, pressing his demand.

And so to the last scene between them, at the gate.

Was it a breach?—or would it all be made up that very night at the Magdalen ball?

No!—it was and should be a breach! Constance fought back her tears, and rode proudly home.

"What are you going to wear to-night?" said Nora, putting her head in at Constance's door. Constance was lying down by Annette's strict command, in preparation for her second ball, which was being given by Magdalen, where the college was reported to have surpassed itself in the lavishness of all the preparations made for lighting up its beautiful walks and quadrangles.

Constance pointed languidly to the sofa, where a creation in white silk and tulle, just arrived from London, had been laid out by the reverential hands of Annette.

"Why on earth does one go to balls?" said Constance, gloomily pressing both hands upon a pair of aching temples.

Nora shut the door behind her, and came to the side of the bed.

"It's time to dress," she said firmly. "Alice says you had a *succès fou* last night."

"Go away, and don't talk nonsense!" Constance turned on her side, and shut her eyes.

"Oh, Alice hadn't a bad time either!" said Nora, complacently, sitting on the bed. "Herbert Pryce seems to have behaved quite decently. Shall I tell you something?" The laughing girl stooped over Connie, and said in her ear—"Now that Herbert knows it would be no good proposing to you, he thinks it might be a useful thing to have you for a relation."

"Don't be horrid?" said Constance. "If I were Alice——"

"You'd punch my head?" Nora laughed. "All very well. But Alice doesn't much care why Herbert Pryce marries her, so long as he does marry her."

Constance did not reply. She continued to feign a headache. But all the time she was thinking of the scene in the wood that morning, when she and Falloden had—to amuse themselves—plotted the rise in life, and the matrimonial happiness, of Herbert and Alice. How little they had cared for what they talked about! They talked only that they might laugh together—hear each other's voices, look into each other's eyes——

"Where did you ride this morning?" said Nora suddenly.

"Somewhere out towards Godstowe," said Constance vaguely.

"I saw Mr. Falloden riding down the High this morning, when I was on the way to the Bodleian. He just looks splendid on horseback—I must give him that. Why doesn't he ride with you sometimes, as he chose your horse?"

"I understand the whole of Oxford would have a fit if a girl went out riding with an undergraduate," said Constance, her voice muffled in the pillow. Then, after a moment she sprang up, and began to brush her hair.

"Mr. Falloden's not an undergraduate now. He can do what he likes," said Nora.

Constance made no reply. Nora observed her with a pair of shrewd brown eyes.

"There are two bouquets for you downstairs," she said abruptly.

Constance turned round startled, almost hidden by the thick veil of her brown hair.

"Who's sent them?"

"One comes from Mr. Radowitz—a beauty. The other's from Lord Meyrick. Isn't he a jolly boy?"

Constance turned back to the dressing-table, disappointed. She had half expected another name. And yet she would have felt insulted if Falloden had dared to send her flowers that evening, without a word of apology—of regret for their happy hour, spoilt by his absurd demands.

"Well, I can't carry them both; and one will be offended."

"Oh, you must take Radowitz's!" cried Nora. "Just to show that you stand by him. Mr. Sorell says everybody likes him in college—except Mr. Falloden's horrid set, who think themselves the lords of creation. They say that Otto Radowitz made such an amusing speech last week in the college debating society attacking 'the bloods.' Of course they didn't hear it, because they have their own club, and turn up their nose at the college society. But it's going to be printed somewhere, and then it'll make them still more furious with him. They'll certainly pay him out some time."

"All right," said Constance, who had suddenly recovered colour and vivacity. "I'll take Mr. Radowitz's bouquet."

"Then, of course, Lord Meyrick will feel snubbed. Serve him right! He shouldn't be so absurdly fond of Mr. Falloden!"

Nora was quite aware that she might be provoking Constance. She did it with her eyes open. Her curiosity and concern after what Alice had told her of the preceding night's ball were becoming hard to conceal. Would Connie really engage herself to that horrid man?

But no rise could be got out of Constance. She said nothing. Annette appeared, and the important business of hair-dressing went forward. Nora, however, had yet another fly to throw.

"Alice passed Mr. Falloden on the river this afternoon—he was with the Mansons, and another lady, an awfully pretty person. Mr. Falloden was teaching her to row. Nobody knew who she was. But she and he seemed great friends. Alice saw them also walking about together at Iffley, while the others were having tea."

"Indeed?" said Constance. "Annette, I think I'll wear my black after all—the black tulle, and my pearls."

Annette unwillingly hung up the "creation." "You'd have looked a dream in it, my lady. Why ever won't you wear it?"

But Constance was obstinate. And very soon she stood robed in clouds of black tulle and jet, from which her delicate neck and arms, and her golden-brown head stood out with brilliant effect. Nora, still sitting on the bed, admired her hugely. "She'll look like that when she's married," she thought, by which she meant that the black had added a certain proud—even a sombre—stateliness to Connie's good looks.

"Now my pearls, Annette."

"Won't you have some flowers, my lady?"

"No. Not one. Only my pearls."

Annette brought them, from the locked dressing-case under her own bed where she jealously kept them. They were famous pearls and many of them. One string was presently wound in and out through the coils of hair that crowned the girl's delicate head; the other string coiled twice round her neck and hung loose over the black dress. They were her only ornament of any kind, but they were superb.

Connie looked at herself uneasily in the glass.

"I suppose I oughtn't to wear them," she said doubtfully.

"Why?" said Nora, staring with all her eyes. "They're lovely!"

"I suppose girls oughtn't to wear such things. I—I never have worn them, since—mamma's death."

"They belonged to her?"

"Of course. And to papa's mother. She bought them in Rome. It was said they belonged to Marie Antoinette. Papa always believed they were looted at the sack of the Tuileries in the Revolution."

Nora sat stupefied. How strange that a girl like Connie should possess such things!—and others, nothing!

"Are they worth a great deal of money?"

"Oh, yes, thousands," said Connie, still looking at herself, in mingled vanity and discomfort. "That's why I oughtn't to wear them. But I shall wear them!" She straightened her tall figure imperiously. "After all they were mamma's. I didn't give them myself."

Popular as the Marmion ball had been, the Magdalen ball on the following night was really the event of the week. The beauty of its cloistered quadrangle, its river walks, its President's garden, could not be rivalled elsewhere; and Magdalen men were both rich and lavish, so that the illuminations easily surpassed the more frugal efforts of other colleges. The midsummer weather still held out, and for all the young creatures, plain and pretty, in their best dancing frocks, whom their brothers and cousins and friends were entertaining, this particular ball struck the top note of the week's romance.

"Who is that girl in black?" said his partner to Douglas Falloden, as they paused to take breath after the first round of waltzing.

"And—good heavens, what pearls! Oh, they must be sham. Who is she?"

Falloden looked round, while fanning his partner. But there was no need to look. From the moment she entered the room, he had been aware of every movement of the girl in black.

"I suppose you mean Lady Constance Bledlow."

The lady beside him raised her eyebrows in excited surprise.

"Then they're not sham! But how ridiculous that an unmarried girl should wear them! Yes they are—the Risborough pearls! I saw them once, before I married, on Lady Risborough, at a gorgeous party at the Palazzo Farnese. Well, I hope that girl's got a trustworthy maid!"

"I dare say Lady Constance values them most because they belonged to her mother!" said Falloden drily.

The lady sitting beside him laughed, and tapped him on the arm.

"Sentimentalist! Don't you know that girls nowadays—babes in the schoolroom—know the value of everything? Who is she staying with?"

Falloden briefly explained and tried to change the subject. But Mrs. Glendower could not be persuaded to leave it. She was one of the reigning beauties of the moment, well acquainted with the Falloden family, and accustomed since his Eton days to lay violent hands on Douglas whenever they met. She and her husband had lately agreed to live apart, and she was now pursuing amusement wherever it was to be had. A certain Magdalen athlete was at the moment her particular friend, and she had brought down a sister to keep her in countenance. She had no intention, indeed, of making scandal, and Douglas Falloden was a convenient string to her bow.

Falloden was quite aware of the situation. But it suited him to dance with Mrs. Glendower, and to dance with her a great deal. He and Constance exchanged greetings; he went through the form of asking her to dance, knowing very well that she would refuse him; and then, for the rest of the evening, when he was not dancing with Mrs. Glendower, he was standing about, "giving himself airs," as Alice repeated to her mother, and keeping a sombre watch on Constance.

"My dear—what has happened to Connie!" said Mrs. Hooper to Alice in bewilderment. Lord Meyrick had just good-naturedly taken Aunt Ellen into supper, brought her back to the ballroom, and bowed himself off, bursting with conscious virtue, and saying to himself that Constance Bledlow must now give him at least two more dances.

Mrs. Hooper had found Alice sitting solitary, and rather drooping. Nobody had offered her supper; Herbert Pryce was not at the ball; her other friends had not showed her any particular attention, and her prettiness had dribbled away, like a bright colour washed out by rain. Her mother could not bear to see her—and then to look at Connie across the room, surrounded by all those silly young men, and wearing the astonishing jewels that were the talk of the ball, and had only been revealed to Mrs. Hooper's bewildered gaze, when the girl threw off her wraps in the cloak-room.

Alice answered her mother's question with an irritable shake of the head, meant to indicate that Connie was nothing to her.

Whereupon Mrs. Hooper settled herself carefully in the chair which she meant to keep for the rest of the evening, smoothing the bright folds of the new dress over her knee. She was much pleased with the new dress; and, of course, it would be paid for some time. But she was almost forgetting it in the excitement of Connie's behaviour.

"She has never danced once with Mr. Falloden!" she whispered in Alice's ear. "It has been all Mr. Radowitz. And the talk!" She threw up her hands maliciously.

"It's the way they dance—that makes people talk!" said Alice. "As for Mr. Falloden—perhaps she's found out what a horrid creature he is."

The band struck up. It was a mazurka with a swinging tune. Radowitz opposite sprang to his feet, with a boyish gesture of delight.

"Come!" he said to Constance; and they took the floor. Supper had thinned the hall, and the dancers who stood in the doorways and along the walls involuntarily paused to watch the pair. Falloden and Mrs. Glendower had just returned from supper. They too stood among the spectators.

The dance they watched was the very embodiment of youth, and youth's delight in itself. Constance knew, besides, that Falloden was looking on, and the knowledge gave a deeper colour to her cheek, a touch of wildness to her perfect grace of limb and movement. Radowitz danced the Polish dance with a number of steps and gestures unknown to an English ballroom, as he had learnt them in his childhood from a Polish dancing-mistress; Constance, with the instinct of her foreign training, adapted herself to him, and the result was enchanting. The slim girl in black, and the handsome youth, his golden hair standing up straight, *en brosse*, round his open brow and laughing eyes, seemed, as dancers, made for each other. They were absorbed in the poetry of concerted movement, the rhythm of lilting sound.

"Mountebank!" said Falloden to Meyrick, contemptuously, as the couple passed.

Radowitz saw his enemy, and though he could not hear what was said, was sure that it was something insulting. He drew himself up, and as he passed on with Constance he flung a look of mingled triumph and defiance at the group of "bloods" standing together, at Falloden in particular. Falloden had not danced once with her, had not been allowed once to touch her white hand. It was he, Radowitz, who had carried her off—whom she had chosen—whom she had honoured. The boy's heart swelled with joy and pride; the artist in him, of another race than ours, realising and sharpening the situation, beyond the English measure.

And, afterwards, he danced with her again—many times. Moreover with him and an escort of his friends—for in general the young Pole with his musical gift and his romantic temperament was popular in Oxford—Constance made the round of the illuminated river-walks and the gleaming cloisters, moving like a goddess among the bevy of youths who hung upon her smiles. The intoxication of it banished thought and silenced regret.

But it was plain to all the world, no less than to Mrs. Hooper, that Falloden of Marmion, who had seemed to be in possession of her the night before, had been brusquely banished from her side; that Oxford's charming newcomer had put her supposed suitor to open contumely; and that young Radowitz reigned in his stead.

*

Radowitz walked home in a whirl of sensations and recollections that made of the Oxford streets an "insubstantial fairy place," where only Constance lived.

He entered Marmion about four o'clock in a pearly light of dawn. Impossible to go to bed or to sleep! He would change his clothes, go out for a bathe, and walk up into the Cumnor hills.

In the quadrangle he passed a group of men in evening dress returned like himself from the ball. They were talking loudly, and reading something which was being passed from hand to hand. As he approached, there was a sudden dead silence. But in his abstraction and excitement he noticed nothing.

When he had vanished within the doorway of his staircase, Meyrick, who had had a great deal too much champagne, said fiercely—

"I vote we give that young beggar a lesson! I still owe him one for that business of a month ago."

"When he very nearly settled you, Jim," laughed a Wykehamist, a powerfully built fellow, who had just got his Blue for the Eleven, had been supping freely and was in a mood for any riotous deed.

"That was nothing," said Meyrick—"but this can't be stood!"

And he pointed to the sheet that Falloden, who was standing in the centre of the group, was at the moment reading. It was the latest number of an Oxford magazine, one of those *éphémérides* which are born, and flutter, and vanish with each Oxford generation. It contained a verbatim report of the attack on the Mannion "bloods" made by Radowitz at the dinner of the college debating society about a fortnight earlier. It was witty and damaging in the highest degree, and each man as he read it had vowed vengeance. Falloden had been especially mocked in it. Some pompous tricks of manner peculiar to Falloden in his insolent moods, had been worked into a pseudoscientific examination of the qualities proper to a "blood," with the happiest effect. Falloden grew white as he read it. Perhaps on the morrow it would be in Constance Bledlow's hands. The galling memories of the evening just over were burning too in his veins. That open humiliation in the sight of Oxford had been her answer to his prayer—his appeal. Had she not given him a right to make the appeal? What girl could give two such rendezvous to a man, and not admit some right on his part to advise, to influence her? It was monstrous she should have turned upon him so!

And as for this puppy!—

A sudden gust of passion, of hot and murderous wrath, different from anything he had ever felt before, blew fiercely through the man's soul. He wanted to crush—to punish—to humiliate. For a moment he saw red. Then he heard Meyrick say excitedly: "This is our last chance! Let's cool his head for him—in Neptune."

Neptune was the Græco-Roman fountain in the inner quad, which a former warden had presented to the college. The sea god with his trident, surrounded by a group of rather dilapidated nymphs, presided over a broad basin, filled with running water and a multitude of goldfish.

There was a shout of laughing assent, and a rush across the grass to Radowitz's staircase. College was nearly empty; the Senior Tutor had gone to Switzerland that morning; and those few inmates who still remained, tired out with the ball of the night before, were fast asleep. The night porter, having let everybody in and closed the gate, was dozing in his lodge.

There was a short silence in the quadrangle. Then the rioters who had been for a few minutes swallowed up in a distant staircase on the western side of the quadrangle reëmerged, with muffled shouts and laughter, bringing their prey with them—a pale, excited figure.

"Let me alone, you cowardly bullies!—ten of you against one!"

But they hurried him along, Radowitz fighting all the way, and too proud to call for help. The intention of his captors—of all save one—was mere rowdy mischief. To duck the offender and his immaculate white flannels in Neptune, and then scatter to their beds before any one could recognise or report them, was all they meant to do.

But when they reached the fountain, Radowitz, whose passion gave him considerable physical strength, disengaged himself, by a sudden effort, from his two keepers, and leaping into the basin of the fountain, he wrenched a rickety leaden shell from the hand of one of Neptune's attendant nymphs and began to fling the water in the faces of his tormentors. Falloden was quickly drenched, and Meyrick and others momentarily blinded by the sudden deluge in their eyes. Robertson, the Winchester Blue, was heavily struck. In a wild rage he jumped into the fountain and closed with Radowitz. The Pole had no chance against him, and after a short struggle, Radowitz fell heavily, catching in his fall at a piece of rusty piping, part of some disused machinery of the fountain.

There was a cry. In a moment it sobered the excited group of men. Falloden, who had acted as leader throughout, called peremptorily to Robertson.

"Is he hurt? Let him up at once."

Robertson in dismay stooped over the prostrate form of Radowitz, and carried him to the edge of the fountain. There it was seen that the lad had fainted, and that blood was streaming from his right hand.

"He's cut it on that beastly piping—it's all jagged," gasped Robertson. "I say, can anybody stop the bleeding?"

One Desmond, an Etonian who had seen one or two football accidents, knelt down, deadly pale, by Radowitz and rendered a rough first-aid. By a tourniquet of handkerchiefs he succeeded in checking the bleeding. But it was evident that an artery was injured.

"Go for a doctor," said Falloden to Meyrick, pointing to the lodge. "Tell the porter that somebody's been hurt in a lark. You'll probably find a cab outside. We'll carry him up."

In a few minutes they had laid the blood-stained and unconscious Radowitz on his bed, and were trying in hideous anxiety to bring him round. The moment when he first opened his eyes was one of unspeakable relief to the men who in every phase of terror and remorse were gathered round him. But the eyelids soon fell again.

"You'd better go, you fellows," said Falloden, looking round him. "Robertson and I and Desmond will see the doctor."

The others stole away. And the three men kept their vigil. The broad-shouldered Wykehamist, utterly unnerved, sat by the bed trembling from head to foot. Desmond kept watch over the tourniquet.

Falloden stood a little apart, in a dead silence, his eyes wandering occasionally from the figure on the bed to the open window, through which could be seen the summer sky, and a mounting sun, just touching the college roofs. The college clock struck half past four. Not two hours since Radowitz and Constance Bledlow had held the eyes of Oxford in the Magdalen ballroom.

X

Radowitz woke up the following morning, after the effects of the dose of morphia administered by the surgeon who had dressed his hand had worn off, in a state of complete bewilderment. What had happened to him? Why was he lying in this strange, stiff position, propped up with pillows?

He moved a little. A sharp pain wrung a groan from him. Then he perceived his bandaged hand and arm; and the occurrences of the preceding night began to rush back upon him. He had soon reconstructed them all; up to the moment of his jumping into the fountain. After that he remembered nothing.

He had hurt himself somehow in the row, that was clear. A sudden terror ran through him. "It's my right hand!—Good God! if I lost my hand!—if I couldn't play again!" He opened his eyes, trembling, and saw his little college room; his clothes hanging on the door, the photographs of his father and mother, of Chopin and Wagner on the chest of drawers. The familiar sight reassured him at once, and his natural buoyancy of spirit began to assert itself.

"I suppose they got a doctor. I seem to remember somebody coming. Bah, it'll be all right directly. I heal like a baby. I wonder who else was hurt. Who's that? Come in!"

The door opened, and his scout looked in cautiously. "Thought I heard you moving, sir. May the doctor come in?"

The young surgeon appeared who had been violently rung up by Meyrick some five hours earlier. He had a trim, confident air, and pleasant eyes. His name was Fanning.

"Well, how are you? Had some sleep? You gave yourself an uncommonly nasty wound. I had to set a small bone, and put in two or three stitches. But I don't think you knew much about it."

"I don't now," said Radowitz vaguely. "How did I do it?"

"There seems to have been a 'rag' and you struck your hand against some broken tubing. But nobody was able to give a clear account." The doctor eyed him discreetly, having no mind to be more mixed up in the affair than was necessary.

"Who sent for you?"

"Lord Meyrick rang me up, and when I got here I found Mr. Falloden and Mr. Robertson. They had done what they could."

The colour rushed back into the boy's pale cheeks.

"I remember now," he said fiercely. "Damn them!"

The surgeon made no reply. He looked carefully at the bandage, asked if he could ease it at all—took pulse and temperature, and sat some time in silence, apparently thinking, by the bed. Then rising, he said:

"I shan't disturb the dressing unless it pains you. If it does, your scout can send a message to the surgery. You must stay in bed—you've got a little fever. Take light food—I'll tell your scout all about that—and I'll come in again to-night."

He departed. The scout brought warm water and a clean sheet. Radowitz was soon washed and straightened as well as masculine fingers could achieve it.

"You seem to have lost a lot of blood, sir, last night!" said the man involuntarily, as he became aware in some dismay of the white flannels and other clothes that Radowitz had been wearing when the invaders broke into his room, which were now lying in a corner, where the doctor had thrown them.

"That's why I feel so limp!" said Radowitz, shutting his eyes again. "Please get me some tea, and send a message round to St. Cyprian's—to Mr. Sorell—that I want to see him as soon as he can come."

The door closed on the scout.

Left alone Radowitz plunged into a tumult of feverish thought. He seemed to be standing again, just freshly dressed, beside his bed—to hear the noise on the stairs, the rush into his sitting-room. Falloden, of course, was the leader—insolent brute! The lad, quivering once more with rage and humiliation, seemed to feel again Falloden's iron grip upon his shoulders—to remember the indignity of his forced descent into the quad—the laughter of his captors. Then he recollected throwing the water—and Robertson's spring upon him—

If *she* had seen it! Whereupon, a new set of images displaced the first. He was in the ballroom again, he had her hand in his; her charming face with its small features and its beautiful eyes was turned to him. How they danced, and how deliciously the music ran! And there was Falloden in the doorway, with his dark face,—looking on. The rag on his part, had been mere revenge; not for the speech, but for the ball.

Was she in love with him? Impossible! How could such a hard, proud being attract her? If she did marry him he would crush and wither her. Yet of course girls did do—every day—such idiotic things. And he thought uncomfortably of a look he had surprised in her face, as he and she were sitting in the New Quad under the trees and Falloden passed with a handsome dark lady—one of the London visitors. It had been something involuntary—a flash from the girl's inmost self. It had chilled and checked him as he sat by her. Yet the next dance had driven all recollection of it away.

"She can't ever care for me," he thought despairingly. "I know that. I'm not her equal. I should be a fool to dream of it. But if she's going to throw herself away—to break her heart for that fellow—it's—it's devilish! Why aren't we in Paris—or Warsaw—where I could call him out?"

He tossed about in pain and fever, irritably deciding that his bandage hurt him, and he must recall the doctor, when he heard Sorell's voice at the door. It quieted him at once.

"Come in!"

Sorell came in with a scared face.

"My dear boy—what's the matter?"

"Oh, there was a bit of a row last night. We were larking round the fountain, trying to push each other in, and I cut my hand on one of those rotten old pipes. Beastly luck! But Fanning's done everything. I shall be all right directly. There's a little bone broken."

"A bone broken!—your hand!" ejaculated Sorell, who sat down and looked at him in dismay.

"Yes—I wish it had been my foot! But it doesn't matter. That kind of thing gets well quickly, doesn't it?" He eyed his visitor anxiously. "You see I never was really ill in my life."

"Well, we can't run any risks about it," said Sorell decidedly. "I shall go and see Fanning. If there's any doubt about it, I shall carry you up to London, and get one of the crack surgeons to come and look at it. What was the row about?"

Radowitz's eyes contracted so that Sorell could make nothing out of them.

"I really can't remember," said the lad's weary voice. "There's been a lot of rowing lately."

"Who made the row?"

"What's the good of asking questions?" The speaker turned irritably away. "I've had such a lot of beastly dreams all night, I can't tell what happened, and what didn't happen. It was just a jolly row, that's all I know."

Sorell perceived that for some reason Radowitz was not going to tell him the story. But he was confident that Douglas Falloden had been at the bottom of it, and he felt a fierce indignation. He had however to keep it to himself, as it was clear that questions excited and annoyed the patient.

He sat by the boy a little, observing him. Then he suggested that Bateson the scout and he should push the bed into the sitting-room, for greater air and space. Radowitz hesitated, and then consented. Sorell went out to speak to Bateson.

"All right, sir," said the scout. "I've just about got the room straight; but I had to get another man to help me. They must have gone on something fearful. There wasn't an article in the room that wasn't knocked about."

"Who did it?" said Sorell shortly.

The scout looked embarrassed.

"Well, of course, sir, I don't know for certain. I wasn't there to see. But I do hear Mr. Falloden, and Lord Meyrick, and Mr. Robertson were in it—and there were some other gentlemen besides. There's been a deal of ragging in this college lately, sir. I do think, sir, as the fellows should stop it."

Sorell agreed, and went off to the surgery, thinking furiously. Suppose the boy's hand—and his fine talent—had been permanently injured by that arrogant bully, Falloden, and his set! And Constance Bledlow had been entangling herself with him—in spite of what anybody could say! He thought with disgust of the scenes of the Marmion ball, of the reckless way in which Constance had encouraged Falloden's pursuit of her, of the talk of Oxford. His work with the Greats' papers had kept him away from the Magdalen ball, and he had heard nothing of it. No doubt that foolish child had behaved in the same way there. He was thankful he had not been there to see. But he vowed to himself that he would find out the facts of the attack on Radowitz, and that she should know them.

Yet the whole thing was very surprising. He had seen on various occasions that Falloden was jealous of Connie's liking for Radowitz, of the boy's homage, and of Connie's admiration for his musical gift. But after the Marmion night, and the triumph she had so unwisely given the fellow—to behave in this abominable way! There couldn't be a spark of decent feeling in his composition.

Radowitz lay still—thinking always of Falloden, and Lady Constance.

Another knock at his door—very timid and hesitating. Radowitz said "Come in."

The door opened partially, and a curly head, was thrust in. Another head appeared behind it.

"May we come in?" said a muffled voice. "It's Meyrick—and Robertson."

"I don't care if you do," said Radowitz coldly. "What do you want?"

The two men came in, stepping softly. One was fair and broad-shouldered. The other exceedingly dark and broad-shouldered. Each was a splendid specimen of the university athlete. And two more sheepish and hang-dog individuals it would have been difficult to find.

"We've come to apologise," said Meyrick, standing by the bed, his hands in his pockets, looking down on Radowitz. "We didn't mean to hurt you of course, and we're awfully sorry—aren't we, Robertson?"

Robertson, sheltering behind Meyrick, murmured a deep-voiced assent.

"If we hadn't been beastly drunk we should never have done it," said Meyrick; "but that's no excuse. How are you? What does Fanning say?"

They both looked so exceedingly miserable that Radowitz, surveying them with mollified astonishment, suddenly went into a fit of hysterical laughter. The others watched him in alarm.

"Do sit down, you fellows!—and don't bother!" said Radowitz, as soon as he could speak. "I gave it to you both as hard as I could in my speech. And you hit back. We're quits. Shake hands."

And he held out his left hand, which each of them gingerly shook. Then they both sat down, extremely embarrassed, and not knowing what to say or do next, except that Meyrick again enquired as to Fanning's opinion.

"Let's have some swell down," said Meyrick urgently. "We could get him in a jiffy."

But Radowitz impatiently dismissed the subject. Sorell, he said, had gone to see Fanning, and it would be all right. At the same time it was evident through the disjointed conversation which followed that he was suffering great pain. He was alternately flushed and deadly pale, and could not occasionally restrain a groan which scared his two companions. At last they got up to go, to the relief of all three.

Meyrick said awkwardly:

"Falloden's awfully sorry too. He would have come with us—but he thought perhaps you wouldn't want him."

"No, I don't want him!" said Radowitz vehemently. "That's another business altogether."

Meyrick hummed and hawed, fidgeting from one foot to the other.

"It was I started the beastly thing," he said at last. "It wasn't Falloden at all."

"He could have stopped it," said Radowitz shortly. "And you can't deny he led it. There's a long score between him and me. Well, never mind, I shan't say anything. And nobody else need. Good-bye."

A slight ghostly smile appeared in the lad's charming eyes as he raised them to the pair, again holding out his free hand. They went away feeling, as Meyrick put it, "pretty beastly."

By the afternoon various things had happened. Falloden, who had not got to bed till six, woke towards noon from a heavy sleep in his Beaumont Street "diggings," and recollecting in a flash all that had happened, sprang up and opened his sitting-room door. Meyrick was sitting on the sofa, fidgeting with a newspaper.

"Well, how is he?"

Meyrick reported that the latest news from Marmion was that Sorell and Fanning between them had decided to take Radowitz up to town that afternoon—for the opinion of Sir Horley Wood, the great surgeon.

"Have you seen Sorell?"

"Yes. But he would hardly speak to me. He said we'd perhaps spoilt his life."

"Whose?"

"Radowitz's."

Falloden's expression stiffened.

"That's nonsense. If he's properly treated, he'll get all right. Besides it was a pure accident. How could any of us know those broken pipes were there? "

"Well, I shall be glad when we get Wood's opinion," said Meyrick gloomily. "It does seem hard lines on a fellow who plays that it should have been his hand. But of course—as you say, Duggy—it'll probably be all right. By the way, Sorell told me Radowitz had absolutely refused to let anybody in college know—any of the dons—and had forbidden Sorell himself to say a word."

"Well of course that's more damaging to us than any other line of action," said Falloden drily. "I don't know that I shall accept it—for myself. The facts had better be known."

"Well, you'd better think of the rest of us," said Meyrick. "It would hit Robertson uncommonly hard if he were sent down. If Radowitz is badly hurt, and the story gets out, they won't play him for the Eleven——"

"If he's badly hurt, it will get out," said Falloden coolly.

"Well, let it alone, anyway, till we see."

Falloden nodded—"Barring a private friend or two. Well, I must dress."

When he opened the door again, Meyrick was gone.

In an unbearable fit of restlessness, Falloden went out, passed Marmion, looked into the quad which was absolutely silent and deserted, and found his way aimlessly to the Parks.

He must see Constance Bledlow, somehow, before the story reached her from other sources, and before everybody separated for the vac. A large Nuneham party had been arranged by the Mansons for the following day in honour of the ex-Ambassador and his wife, who were prolonging their stay in Christ Church so as to enjoy the river and an Oxford without crowds or functions. Falloden was invited, and he knew that Constance had been asked. In his bitterness of the day before, after their quarrel in the wood, he had said to himself that he would certainly go down before the party. Now he thought he would stay.

Suddenly, as he was walking back along the Cherwell edge of the park, under a grey sky with threatening clouds, he became aware of a lady in front of him. Annoying or remorseful thought became in a moment excitement. It was impossible to mistake the springing step and tall slenderness of Constance Bledlow.

He rapidly weighed the pros and cons of overtaking her. It was most unlikely that she had yet heard of the accident. And yet she might have seen Sorell.

He made up his mind and quickened his pace. She heard the steps behind her and involuntarily looked round. He saw, with a passionate delight, that she could not immediately hide the agitation with which she recognised him.

"Whither away?" he said as he took off his hat. "Were you up as late as I? And are balls worth their headaches?"

She was clearly surprised by the ease and gaiety of his manner, and at the same time—he thought—inclined to resent his interruption of her walk, before she had made up her mind in what mood, or with what aspect to meet him next. But he gave her no time for further pondering. He walked beside her, while she coldly explained that she had taken Nora to meet some girl friends at the Cherwell boat-house, and was now hurrying back herself to pay some calls with her aunt in the afternoon.

"What a week you have had!" he said when she paused. "Is there anything left of you? I saw that you stayed very late last night."

She admitted it.

"As for me, of course, I thought the ball—intolerable. But that of course you know—you must know!" he added with a sudden vehement emphasis. "May I not even say that you intended it? You meant to scourge me, and you succeeded."

Constance laughed, though he perceived that her lip trembled a little.

"The scourging had, I think—compensations."

"You mean I took refuge with Mrs. Glendower? Yes, she was kind—and useful. She is an old friend—more of the family than mine. She is coming to stay at Flood in August."

"Indeed?" The tone was as cool as his own. There was a moment's pause. Then Falloden turned another face upon her.

"Lady Constance!—I have something rather serious and painful to tell you—and I am glad of this opportunity to tell you before you hear it from any one else. There was a row in college last night, or rather this morning, after the ball, and Otto Radowitz was hurt."

The colour rushed into Connie's face. She stopped. All around them the park stretched, grey and empty. There was no one in sight on the path where they had met.

"But not seriously," she breathed.

"His hand was hurt in the scuffle!"

Constance gave a cry.

"His hand!"

"Yes. I knew you'd feel that. It was a horrible shame—and a pure accident. But you'd better know the whole truth. It was a rag, and I was in it. But, of course, nobody had the smallest intention of hurting Radowitz."

"No—only of persecuting and humiliating him!" cried Constance, her eyes filling with tears. "His hand!—oh, how horrible! If it were really injured, if it hindered his music—if it stopped it—it would just kill him!"

"Very likely it is only a simple injury which will quickly heal," said Falloden coldly. "Sorell has taken him up to town this afternoon to see the best man he can get. We shall know to-morrow, but there is really no reason to expect anything—dreadful."

"How did it happen?"

"We tried to duck him in Neptune—the college fountain. There was a tussle, and his hand was cut by a bit of broken piping. You perhaps don't know that he made a speech last week, attacking several of us in a very offensive way. The men in college got hold of it last night. A man who does that kind of thing runs risks."

"He was only defending himself!" cried Constance. "He has been ragged, and bullied, and ill-treated—again and again—just because he is a foreigner and unlike the rest of you. And you have been the worst of any—you know you have! And I have begged you to let him alone! And if—if you had really been my friend—you would have done it—only to please me!"

"I happened to be more than your friend!"—said Falloden passionately. "Now let me speak out! You danced with Radowitz last night, dance after dance—so that it was the excitement, the event of the ball—and you did it deliberately to show me that I was nothing to you—nothing!—and he, at any rate, was something. Well!—I began to see red. You forget—that"—he spoke with difficulty—"my temperament is not exactly saintly. You have had warning, I think, of that often. When I got back to college, I found a group of men in the quad reading the skit in *The New Oxonian*. Suddenly Radowitz came in upon us. I confess I lost my head. Oh, yes, I could have stopped it easily. On the contrary, I led it. But I must ask you—because I have so much at stake!—was I alone to blame?—Was there not some excuse?—had you no part in it?"

He stood over her, a splendid accusing figure, and the excited girl beside him was bewildered by the adroitness with which he had carried the war into her own country.

"How mean!—how ungenerous!" Her agitation would hardly let her speak coherently. "When we were riding, you ordered me—yes, it was practically that!—you warned me, in a manner that nobody—*nobody*—has any right to use with me—unless he were my fiancé or my husband—that I was not to dance with Otto Radowitz—I was not to see so much of Mr. Sorell. So just to show you that I was really not at your beck and call—that you could not do exactly what you liked with me—I danced with Mr. Radowitz last night, and I refused to dance with you. Oh, yes, I know I was foolish—I daresay I was in a temper too—but how you can make that any excuse for your attack on that poor boy—how you can make me responsible, if——"

Her voice failed her. But Falloden saw that he had won some advantage, and he pushed on.

"I only want to point out that a man is not exactly a stock or a stone to be played with as you played with me last night. Those things are dangerous! Can you deny—that you have given me some reason to hope—since we met again—to hope confidently, that you might change your mind? Would you have let me arrange those rides for you—unknown to your friends—would you have met me in the woods, those heavenly times—would you have danced with me as you did—would you have let me pay you in public every sort of attention that a man can pay to a girl, when he wants to marry her, the night of the Marmion ball—if you had not felt something for me—if you had not meant to give me a little hope—to keep the thing at least uncertain? No!—if this business does turn out badly, I shall have remorse enough, God knows—but you can't escape! If you punish me for it, if I alone am to pay the penalty, it will be not only Radowitz that has a grievance—not only Radowitz whose life will have been spoilt!"

She turned to him—hypnotised, subdued, by the note of fierce accusation—by that self-pity of the egotist—which looked out upon her from the young man's pale face and tense bearing.

"No"—she said trembling—"no—it is quite true—I have treated you badly. I have behaved wilfully and foolishly. But that was no reason—no excuse——"

"What's the good of talking of 'reason'—or 'excuse'?" Falloden interrupted violently. "Do you understand that I am in love with you—and what that means to a man? I tore myself away from Oxford, because I knew that if I stayed another day within reach of you—after that first ride—I should lose my class—disappoint my father—and injure my career. I could think of nothing but you—dream of nothing but you. And I said to myself that my success—my career—might after all be your affair as well as mine. And so I went. And I'm not going to boast of what it cost me to go, knowing that other people would be seeing you—influencing you—perhaps setting you against me—all the time I was away. But then when I came back, I couldn't understand you. You avoided me. It was nothing but check after check—which you seemed to enjoy inflicting. At last, on the night of our ball I seemed to see clear. On that night, I did think—yes, I did think, that I was something to you!—that you could not have been so sweet—so adorable—in the sight of the whole world—unless you had meant that—in time it would all come right. And so next day, on our ride, I took the tone I did. I was a fool, of course. All men are, when they strike too soon. But if you had had any real feeling in your heart for me—if you had cared one ten-thousandth part for me, as I care for you, you couldn't have treated me as you did last night—so outrageously—so cruelly!"

The strong man beside her was now trembling from head to foot. Constance, hard-pressed, conscience-struck, utterly miserable, did not know what to reply. Falloden went on impetuously:

"And now at least don't decide against me without thinking—without considering what I have been saying. Of course the whole thing may blow over. Radowitz may be all right in a fortnight. But if he is not—if between us, we've done something sad and terrible, let's stand together, for God's sake!—let's help each other. Neither of us meant it. Don't let's make everything worse by separating and stabbing each other. I shall hear what has happened by to-night. Let me come and bring you the news. If there's no great harm done—why—you shall tell me what kind of letter to write to Radowitz. I'm in your hands. But if it's bad—if there's blood-poisoning and Radowitz loses his hand—that they say is the worst that can happen—I of course shall feel like hanging myself—everybody will, who was in the row. But next to him, to Radowitz himself, whom should you pity more than—the man—who—was three parts to blame—for injuring him?"

His hoarse voice dropped. They came simultaneously, involuntarily to a standstill. Constance was shaken by alternate waves of feeling. Half of what he said seemed to her insolent sophistry; but there was something else which touched—which paralysed her. For the first time she knew that this had been no mere game she had been playing with Douglas Falloden. Just as Falloden in his careless selfishness might prove to have broken Otto Radowitz's life, as a passionate child breaks a toy, so she had it in her power to break Falloden.

They had wandered down again, without knowing it, to the banks of the river, and were standing in the shelter of a group of young chestnuts, looking towards the hills, over which hung great thunder-clouds.

At last Constance held out her hand.

"Please go now," she said pleadingly. "Send me word to-night. But don't come. Let's hope. I—I can't say any more."

And indeed he saw that she could bear no more. He hesitated—yielded—took her unresisting hand, which he pressed violently to his lips—and was gone.

*

Hour after hour passed. Falloden had employed Meyrick as an intermediary with a great friend of Sorell's, one Benham, another fellow of St. Cyprian's, who had—so Meyrick reported—helped Sorell to get Radowitz to the station in time for the two o'clock train to London. The plan, according to Benham, was to go straight to Sir Horley Wood, who had been telegraphed to in the morning, and had made an appointment for 4:30. Benham was to hear the result of the great surgeon's examination as soon as possible, and hoped to let Meyrick have it somewhere between seven and eight.

Four or five other men, who had been concerned in the row, including Desmond and Robertson, hung about college, miserably waiting. Falloden and Meyrick ordered horses and went off into the country, hardly speaking to each other during the whole of the ride. They returned to their Beaumont Street lodgings about seven, and after a sombre dinner Meyrick went out to go and enquire at St. Cyprian's.

He had scarcely gone when the last Oxford post arrived, and a letter was brought up for Falloden. It was addressed in his father's hand-writing. He opened it mechanically; and in his preoccupation, he read it several times before he grasped his meaning.

"My dear Son,"—wrote Sir Arthur Falloden—"We expected you home early this week, for you do not seem to have told us that you were staying up for Commem. In any case, please come home at once. There are some very grave matters about which I must consult with you, and which will I fear greatly affect your future. You will find me in great trouble, and far from well. Your poor mother means very kindly, but she can't advise me. I have long dreaded the explanations which can not now be avoided. The family situation has been going from bad to worse,—and I have said nothing—hoping always to find some way out. But now it is precisely my fear that—if we can't discover it—you will find yourself, without preparation, ruined on the threshold of life, which drives me to tell you everything. Your head is a cleverer one than mine. You may think of something. It is of course the coal-mining that has come to grief, and dragged in all the rest. I have been breaking down with anxiety. And you, my poor boy!—I remember you said when we met last, that you hoped to marry soon—perhaps this year—and go into Parliament. I am afraid all that is at an end, unless you can find a girl with money, which of course you ought to have no difficulty in doing, with your advantages.

"But it is no good writing. Come to-morrow, and wire your train.

"Your loving father,
"ARTHUR FALLODEN."

"'Ruined on the threshold of life'—what does he mean?"—thought Falloden impatiently. "Father always likes booky phrases like that. I suppose he's been dropping a thousand or two as he did last year—hullo!"

As he stood by the window, he perceived the Hoopers' parlour-maid coming up Beaumont Street and looking at the numbers on the houses. He ran out to meet her, and took a note from her hand.

"I will send or bring an answer. You needn't wait." He carried it into his own room, and locked the door before opening it.

"Dear Mr. Falloden,—Mr. Sorell has just been here. He left Mr. Radowitz at a nursing home after seeing the surgeons. It is all terrible. The hand is badly poisoned. They hope they may save it, but the injuries will make it impossible for him ever to play again as he has done. He may use it again a little, he may compose of course, but as a performer it's all over. Mr. Sorell says he is in despair—and half mad. They will watch him very carefully at the home, lest he should do himself any mischief. Mr. Sorell goes back to him to-morrow. He is himself broken-hearted.

"I am very, very sorry for you—and for Lord Meyrick,—and everybody. But I can't get over it—I can't ever forget it. There is a great deal in what you said this afternoon. I don't deny it. But, when it's all said, I feel I could never be happy with you; I should be always afraid of you—of your pride and your violence. And love mustn't be afraid.

"This horrible thing seems to have opened my eyes. I am of course very unhappy. But I am going up to-morrow to see Mr. Radowitz, who has asked for me. I shall stay with my aunt, Lady Langmoor, and nurse him as much as they will let me. Oh, and I must try and comfort him! His poor music!—it haunts me like something murdered. I could cry—and cry.

"Good night—and good-bye!

"CONSTANCE BLEDLOW."

The two notes fell at Falloden's feet. He stood looking out into Beaumont Street. The long narrow street, which only two days before had been alive with the stream of Commemoration, was quiet and deserted. A heavy thunder rain was just beginning to plash upon the pavements; and in the interval since he had taken the note from the maid's hand, it seemed to Falloden that the night had fallen.

PART II

XI

"SO, CONNIE, you don't want to go out with me this afternoon?" said Lady Langmoor, bustling into the Eaton Square drawing-room, where Connie sat writing a letter at a writing-table near the window, and occasionally raising her eyes to scan the street outside.

"I'm afraid I can't, Aunt Sophia. You remember, I told you, Mr. Sorell was coming to fetch me."

Lady Langmoor looked rather vague. She was busy putting on her white gloves, and inspecting the fit of her grey satin dress, as she saw it in the mirror over Connie's head.

"You mean—to see the young man who was hurt? Dreadfully sad of course, and you know him well enough to go and see him in bed? Oh, well, of course, girls do anything nowadays. It is very kind of you."

Connie laughed, but without irritation. During the week she had been staying in the Langmoors' house, she had resigned herself to the fact that her Aunt Langmoor—as it seemed to her—was a very odd and hardly responsible creature, the motives of whose existence she did not even begin to understand. But both her aunt and Lord Langmoor had been very kind to their new-found niece. They had given a dinner-party and a tea-party in her honour; they had taken her to several crushes a night, and introduced her to a number of their own friends. And they would have moved Heaven and earth to procure her an invitation to the Court ball they themselves attended, on the day after Connie's arrival, if only, as Lady Langmoor plaintively said—"Your poor mother had done the right thing at the right time." By which she meant to express—without harshness towards the memory of Lady Risborough—how lamentable it was that, in addition to being christened, vaccinated and confirmed, Constance had not also been "presented" at the proper moment. However Constance probably enjoyed the evening of the Court ball more than any other in the week, since she went to the Italian Embassy after dinner to help her girl friend, the daughter of Italy's new Prime Minister, Elisa Bardinelli, to dress for the function; and the two girls were so enchanted to see each other, and had so much Roman gossip to get through, that Donna Elisa was scandalously late, and the Ambassador almost missed the Royal Procession.

But that had been the only spot of pleasure in Connie's fortnight. Lady Langmoor was puzzled by her pale looks and her evident lack of zest for the amusements offered her. She could only suppose that her niece was tired out with the balls of Commem., and Connie accepted the excuse gratefully. In reality she cared for nothing day after day but the little notes she got from Sorell night and morning giving her news of Radowitz. Till now he had been too ill to see her. But at last the doctor had given leave for a visit, and as soon as Lady Langmoor had gone off on her usual afternoon round of concerts and teas, Connie moved to the window, and waited for Sorell.

How long was it since she had first set foot in England and Oxford? Barely two months! And to Constance it seemed as if these months had been merely an unconscious preparation for this state of oppression and distress in which she found herself. Radowitz in his misery and pain—Falloden on the Cherwell path, defending himself by those passionate retorts upon her of which she could not but admit the partial justice—by these images she was perpetually haunted. Certainly she had no reason to look back with pleasure or self-approval on her Oxford experiences. In all her dealings with Falloden she had behaved with a reckless folly of which she was now quite conscious; courting risks; in love with excitement rather than with the man; and careless whither the affair might lead, so long as it gratified her own romantic curiosities as to the power of woman over the masculine mind.

Then, suddenly, all this had become serious. She was like the playing child on whose hand the wasp sat down. But in this case the moral sting of what had happened was abidingly sharp and painful. The tragedy of Radowitz, together with the charm interwoven with all her few recollections of him, had developed in Connie feelings of unbearable pity and tenderness, altogether new to her. Yet she was constantly thinking of Falloden; building up her own harrowed vision of his remorse, or dreaming of the Marmion ball, and the ride in the bluebell wood,—those two meetings in which alone she had felt happiness with him, something distinct from vanity, and a challenging love of power. Now it was all over. They would probably not meet again, till he had forgotten her, and had married some one else. She was quite aware of his fixed and businesslike views for himself and his career—as to marriage, travel, Parliament and the rest; and it had often pleased her wilfulness to think of modifying or upsetting them. She had now far more abundant proof of his haughty self-centredness than their first short acquaintance on the Riviera had given her; and yet—though she tried to hide it from herself—she was far more deeply absorbed in the thought of him. When all was said, she knew that she had treated him badly. The effect of his violence and cruelty towards Radowitz had been indeed to make her shudder away from him. It seemed to her still that it would be impossible to forgive herself should she ever make friends with Douglas Falloden again. She would be an accomplice in his hardness of heart and deed. Yet she recognised guiltily her own share in that hardness. She had played with and goaded him; she had used Radowitz to punish him; her championship of the boy had become in the end mere pique with Falloden; and she was partly responsible for what had happened. She could not recall Falloden's face and voice on their last walk without realising that she had hit him recklessly hard, and that her conduct to him had been one of the causes of the Marmion tragedy.

She was haunted by these thoughts, and miserable for lack of some comforting, guiding, and—if possible—absolving voice. She missed her mother childishly day and night, and all that premature self-possession and knowledge of the world, born of her cosmopolitan training, which at Oxford had made her appear so much older than other English girls of twenty, seemed to have broken away, and left her face to face with feelings she could not check, and puzzles she wanted somebody else to judge.

For instance—here was this coming visit to her aunts in Yorkshire. Their house in Scarfedale was most uncomfortably near to Flood Castle. The boundaries of the Falloden estate ran close to her aunts' village. She would run many chances of coming across Douglas himself, however much she might try to avoid him. At the same time Lady Marcia wrote continually, describing the plans that were being made to entertain her—eager, affectionate letters, very welcome in spite of their oddity to the girl's sore and orphaned mood. No she really couldn't frame some clumsy excuse, and throw her aunts over. She must go, and trust to luck.

And there would be Sorrell and Otto to fall back upon—to take refuge with. Sorell had told her that the little rectory on the moors, whither he and Otto were bound as soon as the boy could be moved, stood somewhere about midway between her aunts' house and Flood, on the Scarfedale side of the range of moors girdling the Flood Castle valley.

It was strange perhaps that she should be counting on Sorell's neighbourhood. If she had often petulantly felt at Oxford that he was too good, too high above her to be of much use to her, she might perhaps have felt it doubly now. For although in some undefined way, ever since the night of the Vice-Chancellor's party, she had realised in him a deep interest in her, even a sense of responsibility for her happiness, which made him more truly her guardian than poor harassed Uncle Ewen, she knew very well that she had disappointed him, and she smarted under it. She wanted to have it out with him, and didn't dare! As she listened indeed to his agitated report on Radowitz's injuries, after the first verdict of the London surgeons, Connie had been conscious of a kind of moral terror. In the ordinary man of the world, such an incident as the Marmion ragging of a foreign lad, who had offended the prejudices of a few insolent and lordly Englishmen, would have merely stirred a jest. In Sorell it roused the same feelings that made him a lover of Swinburne and Shelley and the nobler Byron; a devoted reader of everything relating to the Italian Risorgimento; and sent him down every long vacation to a London riverside parish to give some hidden service to those who were in his eyes the victims of an unjust social system. For him the quality of behaviour like Falloden's towards Otto Radowitz was beyond argument. The tyrannical temper in things great or small, and quite independent of results, represented, for him, the worst treason that man can offer to man. In this case it had ended in hideous catastrophe to an innocent and delightful being, whom he loved. But it was not thereby any the worse; the vileness of it was only made manifest for all to see.

This hidden passion in him, as he talked, seemed to lay a fiery hand on Constance, she trembled under it, conscience-stricken. "Does he see the same hateful thing in me?—though he never says a word to hurt me?—though he is so gentle and so courteous?"

A tall figure became visible at the end of the street. Connie shut up her writing and ran upstairs to put on her things. When she came down, she found Sorell waiting for her with a furrowed brow.

"How is he?" She approached him anxiously. Sorell's look changed and cleared. Had she put on her white dress, had she made herself a vision of freshness and charm, for the poor boy's sake? He thought so; and his black eyes kindled.

"Better in some ways. He is hanging on your coming. But these are awfully bad times for the nurses—for all of us."

"I may take him some roses?" she said humbly, pointing to a basket she had brought in with her.

Sorell smiled assent and took it from her. As they were speeding in a hansom towards the Portland Place region, he gave her an account of the doctors' latest opinion. It seemed that quite apart from the blood-poisoning, which would heal, the muscles and nerves of the hand were fatally injured. All hope of even a partial use of it was gone.

"Luckily he is not a poor man. He has some hundreds a year. But he had a great scheme, after he had got his Oxford degree, of going to the new Leschetizsky school in Vienna for two years, and then of giving concerts in Warsaw and Cracow, in aid of the great Polish museum now being formed at Cracow. You know what a wild enthusiasm he has for Polish history and antiquities. He believes his country will rise again, and it was his passion—his most cherished hope—to give his life and his gift to her. Poor lad!"

The tears stood in Connie's eyes.

"But he can still compose?" she urged piteously.

Sorell shrugged his shoulders.

"Yes, if he has the heart—and the health. I never took much account before of his delicacy. One can see, to look at him, that he's not robust. But somehow he was always so full of life that one never thought of illness in connection with him. But I had a long talk with one of the doctors last week, who takes rather a gloomy view. A shock like this sometimes lets loose all the germs of mischief in a man's constitution. And his mother was undoubtedly consumptive. Well, we must do our best."

He sighed. There was silence till they turned into Wimpole Street and were in sight of the nursing home. Then Connie said in a queer, strained voice: "You don't know that it was partly I who did it."

Sorell turned upon her with a sudden change of expression. It was as though she had said something he had long expected, and now that it was said a great barrier between them had broken down. He looked at her with shining eyes from which the veil of reserve had momentarily lifted. She saw in them both tenderness and sorrow.

"I don't think you need feel that," he said gently. Her lips trembled. She looked straight before her into the hot vista of the street.

"I just played with him—with his whole future, as it's turned out—without a thought."

Sorell knew that she was thinking of the Magdalen ball, of which he had by now heard several accounts. He guessed she meant that her provocation of Falloden had contributed to the tragedy, and that the thought tormented her. But neither of them mentioned Falloden's name. Sorrell put out his hand and grasped hers. "Otto's only thought about you is that you gave him the happiest evening he ever spent in England," he said with energy. "You won't misunderstand."

Her eyes filled with tears. But there was no time to say more. The hansom drew up.

They found Radowitz lying partly dressed on the balcony of his back room, which overlooked a tiny walled patch of grass and two plane-trees. The plane-tree seems to have been left in pity to London by some departing rural deity. It alone flourishes amid the wilderness of brick; and one can imagine it as feeling a positive satisfaction, a quiet triumph, in the absence of its stronger rivals, oak and beech and ash, like some gentle human life escaped from the tyrannies of competition. These two great trees were the guardian genii of poor Otto's afternoons. They brought him shade and coolness, even in the hottest hours of a burning June.

Connie sat down beside him, and they looked at each other in silence. Sorell, after a few gay words, had left them together. Radowitz held her hand in his own left. The other was bandaged and supported on a pillow. When she got used to the golden light filtering through the plane leaves, she saw that he was pale and shrunken, that his eyes were more living and blue than ever, and his hair more like the burnished halo of some Florentine or Siennese saint. Yet the whole aspect was of something stricken. She felt a foreboding, a terror, of which she knew she must let nothing appear.

"Do you mind my staring?" he said presently, with his half-sad, half-mischievous smile. "You are so nice to look at."

She tried to laugh.

"I put on my best frock. Do you like it?"

"For me?" he said, wondering. "And you brought me these roses?"

He lifted some out of the basket, looked at them, then let them drop listlessly on his knee. "I am afraid I don't care for such things, as I used to do. Before—this happened, I had a language of my own, in which I could express everything—as artists or poets can. Now—I am struck dumb. There is something crying in me—that can find no voice. And when one can't express, one begins not to feel!"

She had to check the recurring tears before she could reply.

"But you can still compose?"

Her tone, in repeating the same words she had used to Sorell, fell into the same pleading note.

He shook his head, almost with irritation.

"It was out of the instrument—out of improvisation—that all my composing grew. Do you remember the tale they tell of George Sand, how when she began a novel, she made a few dots and scratches on a sheet of paper, and as she played with them they ran into words, and then into sentences—that suggested ideas—and so, in half an hour, she had sketched a plot, and was ready to go to work? So it was with me. As I played, the ideas came. I am not one of your scientific musicians who can build up everything *in vacuo*. I must translate everything into sound—through my fingers. It was the same with Chopin." He pointed to a life of Chopin that was lying open on the couch beside him.

"But you will do wonders with your left hand. And your right will perhaps improve. The doctors mayn't know," she pleaded, catching at straws. "Dear Otto—don't despair!"

He flushed and smiled. His uninjured hand slipped back into hers again.

"I like you to call me Otto. How dear that was of you! May I call you Constance?"

She nodded. There was a sob in her throat that would not let her speak.

"I don't despair—now," he said, after a moment. "I did at first. I wanted to put an end to myself. But, of course, it was Sorell who saved me. If my mother had lived, she could not have done more."

He turned away his face so that Constance should not see it. When he looked at her again, he was quite calm and smiling.

"Do you know who come to see me almost every day?"

"Tell me."

"Meyrick—Lord Meyrick, and Robertson. Perhaps you don't know him. He's a Winchester man, a splendid cricketer. It was Robertson I was struggling with when I fell. How could he know I should hurt myself? It wasn't his fault and he gave up his 'choice' for the Oxford Eleven. They put him in at the last moment. But he wouldn't play. I didn't know till afterwards. I told him he was a great fool."

There was a pause. Then Connie said—with difficulty—"Did—did Mr. Falloden write? Has he said anything?"

"Oh yes, he sent a message. After all, when you run over a dog, you send a message, don't you?" said the lad with sudden bitterness. "And I believe he wrote a letter—after I came here. But I didn't open it. I gave it to Sorell."

Then he raised himself on his pillows and looked keenly at Connie.

"You see the others didn't mean any harm. They were drunk, and it was a row. But Falloden wasn't drunk—and he did mean——"

"Oh, not to hurt you so?" cried Connie involuntarily.

"No—but to humble and trample on me," said the youth with vehemence, his pale cheeks flaming. "He knew quite well what he was about. I felt that when they came into my room. He is cruel—he has the temper of the torturer—in cold blood——"

A shudder of rage went through him. His excitable Slav nature brought everything back to him—as ugly and as real as when it happened.

"Oh, no—no!" said Constance, putting her hand over her eyes.

Radowitz controlled himself at once.

"I won't say any more," he said in a low voice, breathing deep—"I won't say any more." But a minute afterwards he looked up again, his brow contracting—"Only, for God's sake, don't marry him!"

"Don't be afraid," said Constance. "I shall never marry him!"

He looked at her piteously. "Only—if you care for him—what then? You are not to be unhappy!—you are to be the happiest person in the world. If you did care for him—I should have to see some good in him—and that would be awful. It is not because he did me an injury, you understand. The other two are my friends—they will be always my friends. But there is something in Falloden's soul that I hate—that I would like to fight—till either he drops or I. It is the same sort of feeling I have towards those who have killed my country."

He lay frowning, his blue eyes sombrely fixed and strained.

"But now"—he drew himself sharply together—"you must talk of something else, and I will be quite quiet. Tell me where you have been—what you have seen—the theatre—the opera—everything!"

She did her best, seeing already the anxious face of the nurse in the window behind. And as she got up to go, she said, "I shall come again very soon. And when you go to Yorkshire, I shall see you perhaps every day."

He looked up in astonishment and delight, and she explained that at Scarfedale Manor, her aunts' old house, she would be only two or three miles from the high moorland vicarage whither he was soon to be moved.

"That will do more for me than doctors!" said Radowitz with decision. Yet almost before she had reached the window opening on the balcony, his pain, mental and physical, had clutched him again. He did not look up as she waved farewell; and Sorell hurried her away.

Thenceforward she saw him almost every day, to Lady Langmoor's astonishment. Sorell too, and his relation to Connie, puzzled her greatly. Connie assured her with smiles that she was not in love with the handsome young don, and never thought of flirting with him. "He was mother's friend, Aunt Sophia," she would say, as though that settled the matter entirely. But Lady Langmoor could not see that it settled it at all. Mr. Sorell could not be much over thirty—the best time of all for falling in love. And here was Connie going to pictures with him, and the British Museum, and to visit the poor fellow in the nursing home. It was true that the aunt could never detect the smallest sign of love-making between them. And Connie was always putting forward that Mr. Sorell taught her Greek. As if that kind of thing wasn't one of the best and oldest gambits in the great game of matrimony! Lady Langmoor would have felt it her solemn duty to snub the young man had it been at all possible. But it was really not possible to snub any one possessed of such a courteous self-forgetting dignity. And he came of a good Anglo-Irish family too. Lady Langmoor had soon discovered that she knew some of his relations, and placed him socially to a T. But, of course, any notion of his marrying Connie, with her money, her rank, and her good looks, would be simply ridiculous, so ridiculous that Lady Langmoor soon ceased to think about it, accepted his visits, and began to like him on her own account.

One evening towards the end of the first week in July, a hansom drew up before a house in Portman Square. Douglas Falloden emerged from it, as the door was opened by a maidservant.

The house, which had been occupied at the beginning of the season by the family, was given over now to a charwoman and a couple of housemaids, the senior of whom looked a little scared at the prospect of having to wait on the magnificent gentleman who had just entered the house. In general, when Mr. Douglas came up to town in the absence of his family, he put up at his own very expensive club, and the servants in Portman Square were not troubled with him. But they, like every one else, knew that something was going wrong with the Fallodens.

Falloden walked into the deserted and dust-sheeted house, while the cabman brought in his portmanteau. "Is Mr. Gregory here?" he enquired of the maid.

"Yes, sir, he is in the library. Please, sir, Mrs. O'Connor wants to know if you'll want dinner."

Falloden impatiently said "No," and walked on down a long passage to the library, which had been built out at the back of the house. Here the blinds had been drawn up, only to reveal the dusty desolation of an unused room, in which a few chairs had been uncovered, and a table cleared. A man rose from a chair beside the table, and he and Falloden shook hands. He was a round-faced and broad-shouldered person, with one of the unreadable faces developed by the life of a prominent solicitor, in contact with all sorts of clients and many varieties of business; and Falloden's sensitive pride had soon detected in his manner certain shades of expression to which the heir of Flood Castle was not accustomed.

"I am sorry to hear Sir Arthur is not well." Mr. Gregory spoke politely, but perhaps without that accent of grave and even tragic concern which six months earlier he would have given to the same words. "There is a great deal of heavy, and, I am afraid, disagreeable business to be done."

"My father is not fit for it," said Falloden abruptly. "I must do the best I can."

Mr. Gregory gave a sign of assent. He drew a packet of documents from his pocket, and spreading out a letter from Sir Arthur Falloden on the table, proceeded to deal with the points in it seriatim. Falloden sat beside him, looking carefully through the various documents handed to him, asking questions occasionally, and making notes of his own. In the dusty northern light of the room, his face had a curiously purple and congested look; and his eyes were dead tired. But he showed so much shrewdness in his various remarks that the solicitor secretly admitted his capacity, reflecting indeed once or twice that, young as he was, it would have been a good thing if his father had taken him into counsel earlier. After the discussion had lasted half an hour, Falloden pushed the papers away.

"I think I see. The broad facts are that my father can raise no more money, either on his securities, or on the land; his two banks are pressing him; and the Scotch mortgages must be paid. The estates, of course, will have to be sold. I am quite willing."

"So I understand. But it will take time and the bank overdrafts are urgent. Mason's Bank declare that if their debt is not paid—or freshly secured—within a month from now, they will certainly take proceedings. I must remind you they have been exceedingly forbearing."

"And the amount?" Falloden consulted his papers.

"Forty thousand. The securities on which Sir Arthur obtained it are now not worth more than eight."

The lawyer paused a moment, looked at his companion, and at last said—

"There are, of course, your own expectations from Lord Dagnall. I do not know whether you and your father have considered them. But I imagine it would be possible to raise money on them."

Falloden laughed. The sound was a mixture of irritation and contempt.

"Uncommonly little! The fact is my uncle—at seventy-two—is philandering with a lady-housekeeper he set up a year ago. She seems to be bent on netting him, and my father thinks she'll do it. If she does, my uncle will probably find himself with an heir of his own. Anyway the value of my prospects is enormously less than it was. All the neighbours are perfectly aware of what is going on. Oh, I suppose he'll leave me something—enough to keep me out of the workhouse. But there's nothing to be got out of it now."

There was another silence. Falloden pondered the figures before him.

"There are always the pictures," he said at last, looking up.

The lawyer's face lightened.

"If you and Sir Arthur will sell! But as you know they are heirlooms, and you could stop it."

"On the contrary, I am ready to agree to it," said Falloden briefly. "But there will be a lot of legal business, won't there?"

"Certainly. But it can all be put through in time. And directly it was known that you would sell, the whole situation would be changed."

"We might save something out of the wreck?" said Falloden, looking up.

The lawyer nodded gravely.

"Something—certainly."

"What are they worth?" said Falloden, taking a note-book from his pocket, and looking at a list scribbled on its first page.

Mr. Gregory laughed.

"There is no market in the ordinary sense for such pictures as yours. There are only half a dozen millionaires in the world who could buy them—and one or two museums." He paused a moment, looking thoughtfully at the young man before him. "There happens, however,"—he spoke slowly—"to be a buyer at this moment in London, whom it would be difficult to beat—in the matter of millions."

He mentioned the name.

"Not an American? Well, send him along." Falloden raised his eyebrows. "If my father doesn't feel able to see him, I can tackle him. He can choose his own day and hour. All our best pictures are at Flood."

"And they include——"

"Four Rembrandts," said Falloden, looking at his list, "two Titians, two Terburgs, a Vermeer of Delft, heaps of other Dutchmen—four full-length Gainsboroughs, and three half-lengths—two full-length Reynoldses, three smaller—three Lawrences, a splendid Romney, three Hoppners, two Constables, etc. The foreign pictures were bought by my grandfather from one of the Orléans collections about 1830. The English pictures—the portraits—have all been at Flood since they were painted, and very few of them have ever been exhibited. I scribbled these few facts down before I left home. There is, of course, an elaborate catalogue."

For the first time the lawyer's countenance as he listened showed a flash of active sympathy. He was himself a modest collector, and his house at Richmond contained a number of pretty things.

"Sir Arthur will mind parting with them very much, I fear," he said with real concern. "I wish with all my heart it had been possible to find some other way out. But we have really done our best."

Falloden nodded. He sat looking straight before him, one hand drumming on the table. The whole attitude was haughtily irresponsive. The slight note of compassion in Mr. Gregory's tone was almost intolerable to him, and the lawyer guessed it.

"Insolent cub!" he thought to himself; and thenceforward allowed himself no departure from a purely business tone. It was settled that the buyer—with legal caution, Mr. Gregory for the moment threw no further light upon him—was, if possible, to be got hold of at once, and an appointment was to be made for Flood Castle, where Falloden, or his father, would receive him.

Then the solicitor departed, and Falloden was left to pace up and down the dismal room, his hands in his pockets—deep in thought.

He looked back upon a fortnight of unbroken worry and distress. The news with which his father had received him on his return from Oxford had seemed to him at first incredible. But the facts on which it was based were only too substantial, and his father, broken in health and nerve, now that silence was once thrown aside, poured out upon his son a flood of revelation and confession that soon made what had happened tragically clear. It was the familiar story of wealth grasping at yet more wealth, of the man whose judgment and common sense begin to play him false, when once the intoxication of money has gone beyond a certain point. Dazzled by some first speculative successes, Sir Arthur had become before long a gambler over half the world, in Canada, the States, Egypt, Argentina. One doubtful venture supported another, and the City, no less than the gambler himself, was for a time taken in. But the downfall of a great Egyptian company, which was to have extracted untold wealth from a strip of Libyan desert, had gradually but surely brought down everything else in its train. Blow after blow fell, sometimes rapidly, sometimes tardily. Sir Arthur tried every expedient known to the financier *in extremis*, descending ever lower in the scale of credit and reputation; and in vain. One tragic day in June, after a long morning with the Gregory partners, Sir Arthur came home to the splendid house in Yorkshire, knowing that nothing now remained but to sell the estates, and tell Douglas that his father had ruined him. Lady Laura's settlement was safe; and on that they must live.

The days of slow realisation, after Douglas's return, had tried both father and son severely. Sir Arthur was worn out and demoralised by long months of colossal but useless effort to retrieve what he had done. Falloden, with his own remorse, and his own catastrophe to think over, was called on to put it aside, to think for and help his father. He had no moral equipment—no trained character—equal to the task. But mercifully for them both, his pride came into play; his shrewd intelligence also, and his affection for his father—the most penetrable spot so far in his hard and splendid youth. He had done his best—a haughty, ungracious best—but still he had done it, and in the course of a few days, now that the tension of concealment was over, Sir Arthur had become almost childishly dependent upon him.

A church clock struck somewhere in the distance. Falloden looked at his watch. Time to go to some restaurant and dine. With Gregory's figures running in his head, he shrank from his Club where he would be sure to meet a host of Harrow and Oxford acquaintance, up for the Varsity match, and the latter end of the season. After dinner he would look into a music-hall, and about eleven make his way to the Tamworth House ball.

He must come back, however, to Portman Square sometime to dress. Lady Tamworth had let it be known privately that the Prince and Princess were coming to her ball, and that the men were expected to appear in knee-breeches and silk stockings. He had told his valet at Flood to pack them; and he supposed that fool of a housemaid would be equal to unpacking for him, and putting out his things.

"How do you do, Douglas?" said Lady Tamworth, an imposing, bejewelled figure standing at the head of the galleried staircase of Tamworth House. "Saw your father yesterday and thought him looking very seedy."

"Yes, he's not the thing," said Douglas. "We shall have to get him away to Marienbad, or somewhere of that kind."

Lady Tamworth looked at him closely, her eyelids fluttering just a little. Douglas noticed the flutter, and knew very well what it meant. Lady Tamworth and his father were first cousins. No doubt all their relations were busy discussing their affairs day and night; the City, he knew, was full of rumours, and certain newspapers had already scented the quarry ahead, and were beginning to make ghoulish hints and gibberings. As he passed on into the ballroom, every nerve in him was sensitive and alive. He seemed to have eyes at the back of his head, to catch everywhere the sudden attention, the looks of curiosity, sometimes of malice, that followed him through the crowd. He spoke to a great many acquaintance, to girls he had been accustomed to dance with and their mothers. The girls welcomed him just as usual; but the casual or interrupted conversation, which was all the mothers could spare him, showed him very soon how much was known or guessed of the family disasters. He understood that he was no longer in the running for these exquisite creatures in their silks and satins. The campaigning mothers had already dropped him out of their lists. His pride recoiled in self-contempt from its own smart. But he had been accustomed to walk this world as one of its princelings, and indifference to what it might think of him was not immediately attainable.

All the same, he was still handsome, distinguished, and well born. No one could overlook him in a ballroom, and few women could be quite indifferent to his approach. He danced as much as he wished, and with the prettiest girls. His eyes meanwhile were always wandering over the crowd, searching in vain for a delicate face, and a wealth of brown hair. Yet she had told him herself that Lady Langmoor was to bring her to this ball. He only wanted to see her—from a distance—not to speak to her—or be spoken to.

"Douglas," said a laughing voice in his ear—"will you dance the royal quadrille with me? Something's happened to my partner. Mother sent me to ask you."

He turned and saw the youngest daughter of the house, Lady Alice, with whom he had always been on chaffing, cousinly terms; and as she spoke a sudden stir and hush in the room showed that the royal party had arrived, and were being received in the hall below.

Falloden's first irritable instinct was to refuse. Why should he go out of his way to make himself a show for all these eyes? Then a secret excitement—an expectation—awoke in him, and he nodded a laughing comment to Lady Alice, who just stayed to throw him a mocking compliment on his knee-breeches, and ran away. Immediately afterwards, the royal party came through the lane made for them, shaking hands with their acquaintance, and bowing right and left. As they disappeared into the room beyond, which had been reserved for them, the crowd closed up behind them. Falloden heard a voice at his elbow.

"How are you? I hear you're to be in the quadrille. You'll have the pretty lady we saw at Oxford for a colleague."

He turned to see Mrs. Glendower, very much made-up and glittering with diamonds. Her face seemed to him to have grown harder and plainer, her smile more brazen since their Oxford meeting. But she filled up time agreeably till the quadrille was ready. She helped him to pin on the small rosette made of the Tamworth colours which marked all the dancers in the royal quadrille, and she told him that Constance Bledlow was to dance it with the Tamworths' eldest son, Lord Bletchley.

"There's a great deal of talk about her, as perhaps you know. She's very much admired. The Langmoors are making a great fuss about her, and people say she'll have all their money as well as her own some day—not to speak of the old aunts in Yorkshire. I shouldn't wonder if the Tamworths had their eye upon her. They're not really well off."

Falloden gaily declared that he would back his cousin Mary Tamworth to get anything she wanted. Mrs. Glendower threw him a sudden, sharp look. Then she was swept into the crowd. A couple of men in brilliant uniform came by, clearing a space in the centre of the room, and Falloden saw Lady Alice beckoning.

In another minute or two he and she were in their places, and what the newspapers who record these things call "a brilliant scene" was in full tide:—the Prince and Princess dancing with the master and mistress of the house, and the rest of the quadrille made up of the tallest men and handsomest women that Lady Tamworth, with a proper respect both to rank and to looks, had been able to collect.

The six-foot-three Falloden and his fairylike partner were much observed, and Lady Alice bubbling over with fun and spirits, found her cousin Douglas, whom in general she disliked, far better company than usual. As for him, he was only really conscious of one face and form in the stately dance itself, or in the glittering crowd which was eagerly looking on. Constance Bledlow, in filmy white, was his *vis-à-vis*. He saw her quick movement as she perceived him. Then she bowed slightly, he ceremoniously. Their hands touched at intervals, and not a few of the spectators noticed these momentary contacts with a thrill of pleasure—the splendid physique of the young man, the flowerlike grace of the girl. Once or twice, as they stood together in the centre of the "chain," a few words would have been possible. But Constance never spoke, nor did Falloden. He had thought her very pale at first sight. But her cheek flushed with dancing; and with every minute that passed she seemed to him more lovely and more remote, like a spirit from another world, into which he could not pass.

"Isn't she pretty!—Connie Bledlow?" said Lady Alice enthusiastically. "She's having a great success. Of course other people are much handsomer, but there's something——"

Yes, there was something!—and something which, like an exquisite fluttering bird, had just escaped from Douglas Falloden, and would now, he supposed, forever escape him.

When the quadrille was over he watched her delicate whiteness disappear amid the uniforms, the jewels, and the festoons or roses hanging across the ballroom. The barbaric, overdecorated scene, with all its suggestions of a luxurious and self-confident world, where every one was rich and privileged, or hunting riches and privilege—a world without the smallest foreboding of change, the smallest doubt of its own right to exist—forced upon him by contrast the recollection of the hour he had just spent with Mr. Gregory in his father's dusty dismantled library. He and his were, it seemed, "ruined"—as many people here already guessed. He looked at the full-length Van Dycks on the wall of the Tam worths' ballroom, and thought, not without a grim leap of humour, that he would be acting showman and auctioneer, within a few days perhaps, to his father's possessions of the same kind.

But it was not the loss of money or power that was separating him from Constance Bledlow. He knew her well enough by now to guess that in spite of her youth and her luxurious bringing up, there was that in her which was rapidly shaping a character capable of fighting circumstance, as her heart might bid. If she loved a man she would stand by him. No, it was something known only to her and himself in all those crowded rooms. As soon as he set eyes on her, the vision of Radowitz's bleeding hand and prostrate form had emerged in consciousness—a haunting presence, blurring the many-coloured movements of the ballroom.

And yet it was not that maimed hand, either, which stood between himself and Constance. It was rather the spiritual fact behind the visible—that instinct of fierce, tyrannical cruelty which he had felt as he laid his hands on Radowitz in the Oxford dawn a month ago. He shrank from it now as he thought of it. It blackened and degraded his own image of himself. He remembered something like it years before, when he had joined in the bullying of a small boy at school—a boy who yet afterwards had become his good friend. If there is such a thing as "possession," devilish possession, he had pleaded it on both occasions. Would it, however, have seemed of any great importance to him now, but for Constance Bledlow's horror-struck recoil? All men of strong and vehement temperament—so his own defence might have run—are liable to such gusts of violent, even murderous feeling; and women accept it. But Constance Bledlow, influenced, no doubt, by a pale-blooded sentimentalist like Sorell, had refused to accept it.

"I should be always afraid of you—of your pride and your violence—and love mustn't be afraid. Good-bye!"

He tried to scoff, but the words had burnt into his heart.

XII

IT WAS in the early morning, a few days after her arrival at Scarfedale Manor, the house of her two maiden aunts, that Connie, while all the Scarfedale household was still asleep, took pen and paper and began a letter to Nora Hooper.

On the evening before Connie left Oxford there had been a long and intimate scene between these two. Constance, motherless and sisterless, and with no woman friend to turn to more understanding than Annette, had been surprised in passionate weeping by Nora, the night after the Marmion catastrophe. The tact and devotion of the younger girl had been equal to the situation. She humbly admired Connie, and yet was directly conscious of a strength in herself, in which Connie was perhaps lacking, and which might be useful to her brilliant cousin. At any rate on this occasion she showed so much sweetness, such power, beyond her years, of comforting and understanding, that Connie told her everything, and thenceforward possessed a sister and a confidante. The letter ran as follows:—

"DEAREST NORA,—I have only been at Scarfedale Manor a week, and already I seem to have been living here for months. It is a dear old house, very like the houses one used to draw when one was four years old—a doorway in the middle, with a nice semicircular top, and three windows on either side; two stories above with seven windows each, and a pretty dormered roof, with twisted brick chimneys, and a rookery behind it; also a walled garden, and a green oval grass-plot between it and the road. It seems to me that everywhere you go in England you find these houses, and, I dare say, people like my aunts living in them.

"They are very nice to me, and as different as possible from each other. Aunt Marcia must have been quite good-looking, and since she gave up wearing a rational dress which she patented twenty-five years ago, she has always worn either black silk or black satin, a large black satin hat, rather like the old 'pokes,' with black feathers in winter and white feathers in summer, and a variety of lace scarves—real lace—which she seems to have collected all over the world. Aunt Winifred says that the 'Unipanta loonicoat'—the name of the patented thing—lost Aunt Marcia all her lovers. They were scared by so much strength of character, and could not make up their minds to tackle her. She gave it up in order to capture the last of them—a dear old general who had adored her—but he shook his head, went off to Malta to think it out, and there died of Malta fever. She considers herself his widow and his portrait adorns her sitting-room. She has a poor opinion of the lower orders, especially of domestic servants. But her own servants don't seem to mind her much. The butler has been here twenty years, and does just what he pleases. The amusing thing is that she considers herself extremely intellectual, because she learnt Latin in her youth—she doesn't remember a word of it now!—because she always read the reviews of papa's books—and because she reads poetry every morning before breakfast. Just now she is wrestling with George Meredith; and she asks me to explain 'Modern Love' to her. I can't make head or tail of it. Nor can she. But when people come to tea she begins to talk about Meredith, and asks them if they don't think him very obscure. And as most people here who come to tea have never heard of him, it keeps up her dignity. All the same, she is a dear old thing—and she put a large case of chocolate in my room before I arrived!

"Aunt Winifred is quite different Aunt Marcia calls her a 'reactionary,' because she is very high church and great friends with all the clergy. She is a very quiet little thing, short and fair, with a long thin nose and eyes that look you through. Her two great passions are—curates, especially consumptive curates—and animals. There is generally a consumptive curate living the open-air life in the garden. Mercifully the last patient has just left. As for animals, the house is full of stray dogs and tame rabbits and squirrels that run up you and look for nuts in your pocket. There is also a mongoose, who pulled the cloth off the tea-table yesterday and ran away with all the cakes. Aunt Marcia bears it philosophically, but the week before I came there was a crisis. Aunt Winifred met some sheep on the road between here and our little town. She asked where they were going to. And the man with them said he was taking them to the slaughter-house. She was horrified, and she bought them all—there and then! And half an hour later, she appeared here with the sheep, and Aunt Marcia was supposed to put them up in the garden. Well, that was too much, and the aunts had words. What happened to the sheep I don't know. Probably Aunt Winifred has eaten them since without knowing it.

"Dear Nora—I wonder why I write you all these silly things when there is so much else to say—and I know you want to hear it. But it's horribly difficult to begin.—Well, first of all, Mr. Sorell and Otto Radowitz are about three miles from here, in a little vicarage that has a wide lookout upon the moors and a heavenly air. The aunts have found me a horse, and I go there often. Otto is in some ways very much better. He lives an ordinary life, walks a fair amount, and is reading some classics and history with Mr. Sorell, besides endless books of musical theory and biography. You know he passed his first musical exam last May. For the second, which will come off next year, he has to write a composition in five-part harmony for at least five stringed instruments, and he is beginning work for it now. He writes and writes, and his little study at the vicarage is strewn deep in scribbled music-paper. With his left hand and his piano he does wonders, but the poor right hand is in a sling and quite useless, up to now. He reads scores endlessly, and he said to me yesterday that he thought his intellectual understanding of music—his power of grasping it through the eye—of hearing it with the mind—'ditties of no tone!'—had grown since his hand was injured. But the pathetic thing is that the sheer pleasure—the joy and excitement—of his life is gone; those long hours of dreaming and composing with the piano, when he could not only make himself blissfully happy, but give such exquisite pleasure to others.

"He is very quiet and patient now—generally—and quite determined to make a name for himself as a composer. But he seems to me extraordinarily frail. Do you remember that lovely French poem of Sully Prudhomme's I read you one night—'*Le Vase Brisé*'? The vase has had a blow. No one knew of it. But the little crack widens and grows. The water ebbs away—the flowers die. '*Il est brisé—n'y touchez pas!*' I can see it is just that Mr. Sorell feels about Otto.

"What makes one anxious sometimes, is that he has hours of a kind of fierce absent-mindedness, when his real self seems to be far away—as though in some feverish or ugly dream. He goes away and wanders about by himself. Mr. Sorell does not attempt to follow him, though he is always horribly anxious. And after some hours he comes back, limp and worn out, but quite himself again—as though he had gone through some terrible wrestle and escaped.

"Mr. Sorell gave him, a little while ago, a wonderful new automatic thing—a piano-player, I think they call it. It works with a roll like a musical box and has pedals. But Otto can't do much with it. To get any expression out of it you must use your hands—both hands; and I am afraid it has been more disappointment than joy. But there are rumours of some development—something electric—that plays itself. They say there is an inventor at work in Paris, who is doing something wonderful. I have written to a girl I know at the Embassy to ask her to find out. It might just help him through some weary hours—that's all one can say.

"The relation between him and Mr. Sorell is wonderful. Oh, what an angel Mr. Sorell is! How can any human being, and with no trouble at all apparently, be so unselfish, so self-controlled? What will any woman do who falls in love with him? It won't make any difference that he'll think her so much better than himself—because she'll know the truth. I see no chance for her. My dear Nora, the best men are better than the best women—there! But—take note!—I am not in love with him, though I adore him, and when he disapproves of me, I feel a worm.

"I hear a good deal of the Fallodens, but nobody sees them. Every one shrinks from pestering them with society—not from any bad feeling—but because every one knows by now that they are in hideous difficulties, and doesn't want to intrude. Lady Laura, they say, is very much changed, and Sir Arthur looks terribly ill and broken. Aunt Marcia hears that Douglas Falloden is doing all the business, and impressing the lawyers very much. Oh, I do hope he is helping his father!

"I can't write about him, Nora darling. You would wonder how I can feel the interest in him I do. I know that. But I can't believe, as Otto does, that he is deliberately cruel—a selfish, hard-hearted monster. He has been a spoilt child all his life. But if some great call were made upon him, mightn't it stir up something splendid in him, finer things than those are capable of 'who need no repentance'?

"There—something has splashed on my paper. I have written enough. Now you must tell me of yourselves. How is your father? Does Aunt Ellen like Ryde? I am so delighted to hear that Mr. Pryce is actually coming. Tell him that, of course, I will write to Uncle Langmoor, and Lord Glaramara, whenever he wishes, about that appointment. I am sure something can be done. Give Alice my love. I thought her new photographs charming. And you, darling, are you looking after everybody as usual? I wish I could give you a good hug. Good-bye."

To which Nora replied, a couple of days later—

"Your account of Aunt Marcia and Aunt Winifred amused father tremendously. He thinks, however, that he would like Aunt Marcia better than Aunt Winifred, as he—and I—get more anticlerical every year. But we keep it to ourselves. Mamma and Alice wouldn't understand. Ryde is very full, and mamma and Alice want nothing more than the pier and the sands and the people. Papa and I take long walks along the coast, or across the island. We find a cliff to bask on, or a wood that comes down to the water, and then papa gets out a Greek book and translates to me. Sometimes I listen to the sea, instead of to him, and go to sleep. But he doesn't mind. He is looking better, but work is loading up for him again as soon as we get back to Oxford about a week from now. If only he could get rid of drudgery, and write his best about the things he loves. Nobody knows what a mind he has. He is not only a scholar—he is a poet. He could write things as beautiful as Mr. Pater's, but his life is ground out of him.

"I won't go on writing this—it's no good.

"Herbert Pryce came down yesterday, and has taken mother and Alice out boating to-day. If he doesn't mean to propose to Alice, it is very odd he should take the trouble to come here. But he doesn't say anything definite; he doesn't propose; and her face often makes me furious. His manner to mamma—and to me—is often brusque and disagreeable. It is as though he felt that in marrying Alice—if he is going to marry her—he is rather unfairly burdened with the rest of us. And it is no good shirking the fact that you count for a good deal in the matter. He was delighted with your message, and if you can help him he will propose to Alice. Goodness, fancy marrying such a man!

"As to Mr. Falloden, I don't believe he will ever be anything but hard and tyrannical. I don't believe in conversion and change of heart, and that kind of thing. I don't—I don't! You are not to be taken in, Connie! You are not to fall in love with him again out of pity. If he does lose all his money, and have to work like anybody else, what does it matter? He was as proud as Lucifer—let him fall like Lucifer. You may be sure he won't fall so very far. That kind never does. No, I want him put down. I want him punished. He won't repent—he can't repent—and there was never any one less like a lost sheep in the world.

"After which I think I will say good-night!"

A few days later, Connie, returning from a ramble with one of Lady Winifred's stray dogs along the banks of the Scarfe, found her two aunts at tea in the garden.

"Sit down, my dear Connie," said Lady Marcia, with a preoccupied look." We have just heard distressing news. The clergy are such gossips!"

The elevation of Aunt Winifred's sharp nose showed her annoyance.

"And you, Marcia, are always so dreadfully unfair to them. You were simply dying for Mr. Latimer to tell you all he knew, and then you abuse him."

"Perfectly true," said Lady Marcia provokingly, "but if he had snubbed me, I should have respected him more."

Whereupon it was explained to Connie that a Mr. Latimer, rector of the Fallodens' family living of Flood Magna, had just been paying a long visit to the two ladies. He was a distant cousin and old crony of theirs, and it was not long before they had persuaded him to pour out all he knew about the Falloden affairs. "They must sell everything!" said Lady Marcia, raising her hands and eyes in protest—"the estates, the house, the pictures—my dear, think of the pictures! The nation of course ought to buy them, but the nation never has a penny. And however much they sell, it will only just clear them. There'll be nothing left but Lady Laura's settlement—and that's only two thousand a year."

"Well, they won't starve," said Aunt Winifred, with a sniff, applying for another piece of tea-cake. "It's no good, Marcia, your trying to stir us up. The Fallodens are not beloved. Nobody will break their hearts—except of course we shall all be sorry for Lady Laura and the children. And it will be horrid to have new people at Flood."

"My dear Connie, it is a pity we haven't been able to take you to Flood," said Lady Marcia to her niece, handing a cup of tea. "You know Douglas, so of course you would have been shown everything. Such pictures! Such lovely old rooms! And then the grounds—the cedars—the old gardens! It really is a glorious place. I can't think why Winifred is so hard-hearted about it!"

Lady Winifred pressed her thin lips together.

"Marcia, excuse me—but you really do talk like a snob. Before I cry over people who have lost their property, I ask myself how they have lost it, and also how they have used it." The little lady drew herself up fiercely.

"We have all got beams in our own eyes," cried Aunt Marcia. "And of course we all know, Winifred, that Sir Arthur never would give you anything for your curates."

"That has nothing to do with it," said Lady Winifred angrily. "I gave Sir Arthur a sacred opportunity—which he refused. That's his affair. But when a man gambles away his estates, neglects his duties and his poor people, wastes his money in riotous living, and teaches his children to think themselves too good for this common world, and then comes to grief—I am not going to whine and whimper about it. Let him take it like a man!"

"So he does," said her sister warmly. "You know Mr. Latimer said so, and also that Douglas was behaving very well."

"What else can he do? I never said he wasn't fond of his father. Well, now let him look after his father."

The two maiden ladies, rather flushed and agitated, faced each other nervously. They had forgotten the presence of their niece. Constance sat in the shade, her beautiful eyes passing intently from one sister to the other, her lips parted. Aunt Marcia, by way of proving to her sister Winifred that she was a callous and unkind creature, began to rake up inconsequently a number of incidents throwing light on the relations of father and son; which Lady Winifred scornfully capped by another series of recollections intended to illustrate the family arrogance, and Douglas Falloden's full share in it. For instance:

Marcia—"I shall never forget that charming scene when Douglas made a hundred, not out, the first day of the Flood cricket week, when he was sixteen. Sir Arthur's face! And don't you remember how he went about half the evening with his arm round the boy's shoulders?"

Winifred—"Yes, and how Douglas hated it! I can see him wriggling now. Do you remember that just a week after that, Douglas broke his hunting-whip beating a labourer's boy, whom he found trespassing in one of the coverts, and how Sir Arthur paid fifty pounds to get him out of the scrape?"

Marcia, indignantly—"Of course that was just a lad's high spirits! I have no doubt the labourer's boy richly deserved it."

Winifred—"Really, Marcia, your tone towards the lower orders! You don't allow a labourer's boy any high spirits!—not you! And I suppose you've quite forgotten that horrid quarrel between the hunt and the farmers which was entirely brought about by Douglas's airs. 'Pay them!—pay them!' he used to say—'what else do the beggars want?' As if money could settle everything! And I remember a farmer's wife telling me how she had complained to Douglas about the damage done by the Flood pheasants in their fields. And he just mocked at her. 'Why don't you send in a bigger bill?' 'But it's not only money, my lady,' she said to me. 'The fields are like your children, and you hate to see them wasted by them great birds—money or no money. But what's the good of talking? Fallodens always best it!' "

Marcia—with the air of one defending the institutions of her country—"Shooting and hunting have to be kept up, Winifred, for the sake of the physique of our class; and it's the physique of our class that maintains the Empire. What do a few fields of corn matter compared with that! And what young man could have done a more touching—a more heroic thing—than——"

Winifred, contemptuously—"What?—Sir Arthur's accident? You always did lose your head about that, Marcia. Nothing much, I consider, in the story. However, we shan't agree, so I'd better go to my choir practice."

When she was out of sight, and Marcia, who was always much agitated by an encounter with her sister, was still angrily fanning herself, Connie laid a hand on her aunt's knee. "What was the story, Aunt Marcia?"

Lady Marcia composed herself. Connie, in a thin black frock, with a shady hat and a tea-rose at her waist, was looking up at the elder lady with a quiet eagerness. Marcia patted the girl's hand.

"Winifred never asked your opinion, my dear!—and I expect you know him a great deal better than either of us."

"I never knew him before this year. That's a very little while. I—I'm sure he's difficult to know. Perhaps he's one of the people—who"—she laughed—"who want keeping."

"That's it!" cried Lady Marcia, delighted. "Of course that's it. It's like a rough fruit that mellows. Anyway I'm not going to damn him for good at twenty-three, like Winifred. Well, Sir Arthur was very badly thrown, coming home from hunting, six years ago now and more, when Douglas was seventeen. It was in the Christmas holidays. They had had a run over Leman Moor and Sir Arthur and Douglas got separated from the rest, and were coming home in the dark through some very lonely roads—or tracks—on the edge of the moor. They came to a place where the track went suddenly into a wood, and a pheasant was startled by the horses, and flew right across Sir Arthur, almost in his face. The horse—it was always said no one but Sir Arthur Falloden could ride it—took fright, bolted, dashed in among the trees, threw Sir Arthur, and made off. When Douglas came up he found his father on the ground, covered with blood, and insensible. There was no one anywhere near. The boy shouted—no one came. It was getting dark and pouring with rain—an awful January night—I remember it well! Douglas tried to lift his father on his own horse, but the horse got restive, and it couldn't be done. If he had ridden back to a farm about a mile away he could have got help. But he thought his father was dying, and he couldn't make up his mind, you see, to leave him. Then—imagine!—he somehow was able—of course he was even then a splendid young fellow, immensely tall and strong for his age—to get Sir Arthur on his back, and to carry him through two fields to a place where he thought there was a cottage. But when he got there, the cottage was empty—no lights—and the door padlocked. He laid his father down under the shelter of the cottage, and called and shouted. Not a sign of help! It was awfully cold—a bitter north wind—blowing great gusts of rain. Nobody knows quite how long they were there, but at last they were found by the vicar of the village near, who was coming home on his bicycle from visiting a sick woman at the farm. He told me that Douglas had taken off his own coat and a knitted waistcoat he wore, and had wrapped his father in them. He was sitting on the ground with his back to the cottage wall, holding Sir Arthur in his arms. The boy himself was weak with cold and misery. The vicar said he should never forget his white face, when he found them with his lamp, and the light shone on them. Douglas was bending over his father, imploring him to speak to him—in the tenderest, sweetest way. Then, of course, when the vicar, Mr. Burton, had got a cart and taken them to the farm, and a carriage had come from Flood with two doctors, and Sir Arthur had begun to recover his senses, Douglas—looking like a ghost—was very soon ordering everybody about in his usual lordly manner. 'He slanged the farmer,' said Mr. Burton, 'for being slow with the cart; he sent me off on errands as though I'd been his groom; and when the doctors came, you'd have thought he was more in charge of the case than they were. They thought him intolerable; so he was. But I made allowances, because I couldn't forget how I had seen them first—the boy's face, and his chattering teeth, and how he spoke to his father. He's spoilt, that lad! He's as proud as Satan. If his father and mother don't look out, he'll give them sore hearts some day. But he can feel!—and—if he could have given his life for his father's that night, he would have done it with joy.'—Well, there it is, Connie!—it's a true story anyway, and why shouldn't we remember the nice things about a young man, as well as the horrid ones?"

"Why not, indeed?" said Connie, her chin on her hands, her eyes bent on the ground.

Lady Marcia was silent a moment, then she said with a tremulous accent that belied her height, her stateliness and her black satin gown:

"You see, Connie, I know more about men than Winifred does. We have had different experiences."

"She's thinking about the General," thought Connie. "Poor old dear!" And she gently touched her aunt's long thin hand.

Lady Marcia sighed.

"One must make allowances for men," she said slowly.

Connie offered no reply, and they sat together a few more minutes in silence. Then Connie rose.

"I told the coachman, Aunt Marcia, I should ride for an hour or so after tea. If I take the Lawley road, does that go anywhere near Flood?"

"It takes you to the top of the moor, and you have a glorious view of the castle and all its woods. Yes, do go that way. You'll see what the poor things have lost. You did like Douglas, didn't you?"

"'Like' is not exactly the word, is it?" said Constance with a little laugh, vexed to feel that she could not keep the colour out of her cheeks. "And he doesn't care whether you like him or not!"

She went away, and her elderly aunt watched her cross the lawn. Lady Marcia looked puzzled. After a few moments' meditation a half light broke on her wrinkled face. "Is it possible? Oh, no!"

It was a rich August evening. In the fields near the broad river the harvest had begun, and the stubbles with their ranged stocks alternated with golden stretches still untouched. The air was full of voices—the primal sounds of earth, and man's food-gathering; calling reapers, clattering carts, playing children. And on the moors that closed the valley there were splashes and streaks of rose colour, where the heather spread under the flecked evening sky.

Constance rode in a passion of thought. "On the other side of that moor—five miles away—there he is! What is he doing now—at this moment? What is he thinking of?"

Presently the road bent upward, and she followed it, soothed by the quiet movement of her horse and by the evening air. She climbed and climbed, till the upland farms fell behind, and the road came out upon the open moor. The distance beyond began to show—purple woods in the evening shadow, dim valleys among them, and wide grassy stretches. A little more, and she was on the crest. The road ran before her—westward—a broad bare whiteness through the sun-steeped heather. And, to the north, a wide valley, where wood and farm and pasture had been all fashioned by the labour of generations into one proud setting for the building in its midst. Flood Castle rose on the green bottom of the valley, a mass of mellowed wall and roof and tower, surrounded by its stately lawns and terraces, and girdled by its wide "chase," of alternating wood and glade—as though wrought into the landscape by the care of generations, and breathing history. A stream, fired with the sunset, ran in loops and windings through the park, and all around the hills rose and fell, clothed with dark hanging woods.

Constance held in her horse, feeding her eyes upon the castle and its woods. Her mind, as she looked, was one riot of excuse for Douglas Falloden. She knew very well—her own father had been an instance of it—that a man can be rich and well-born, and still remain modest and kind. But—but—"How hardly shall they that have riches——!"

She moved slowly on, thinking and gazing, till she had gone much further than she intended, and the light had begun to fail. She would certainly be late for dinner. Looking round her for her bearings, she saw on the Scarfedale side of the hill, about three miles away, what she took to be her aunts' house. Surely there must be a short cut to it. Yes! there was a narrow road to be seen, winding down the hill, and across the valley, which must certainly shorten the distance. And almost immediately she found herself at the entrance to it, where it abutted on the moor; and a signpost showed the name of Hilkley, her aunts' village. She took the road at once, and trotted briskly along, as the twilight deepened.

A gate ahead! Well, never mind. The horse was quiet; she could easily manage any ordinary latch.

But the gate was difficult, and she fumbled at it. Again and again, she brought up her horse, only to fail. And the cob began to get nervous and jump about—to rear a little. Whenever she stooped towards the gate, it would swerve violently, and each unsuccessful attempt made it more restive. She began to get nervous herself.

"How abominable! Must I go back? Suppose I get off? But if I do, can I get on again?" She looked round her for a log or a stone.

Who was that approaching? For suddenly she saw a horse and rider coming from the Hilkley direction towards the gate. A moment—then through the dusk she recognised the rider; and agitation—suffocating, overwhelming—laid hold upon her.

A sharp movement on the part of the horseman checked his horse. Falloden pulled up in amazement on the further side of the gate.

"You?—Lady Constance!"

She controlled herself, with a great effort.

"How do you do? My horse shies at the gate. He's so tiresome—I was just thinking of getting off. It will be most kind if you will let me through."

She drew aside, quieting and patting the cob, while he opened the gate. Then she passed through and paused, looking back.

"Thank you very much. Are there any more gates?"

"Two more I am afraid," he said formally, as he turned and joined her. "Will you allow me to open them for you?"

"It would be very good of you," she faltered, not knowing how to refuse, or what to say.

They walked their horses side by side, through the gathering darkness. An embarrassed and thrilling silence reigned between them, till at last he said: "You are staying at Scarfedale—with your aunts?"

"Yes."

"I heard you were there. They are only five miles from us."

She said nothing. But she seemed to realise, through every nerve, the suppressed excitement of the man beside her.

Another couple of minutes passed. Then he said abruptly:

"I should like to know that you read my last letter to you—only that! I of course don't ask for—for any comments upon it."

"Yes, I received it. I read it."

He waited a little, but she said no more. He sharply realised his disappointment, and its inconsequence. The horses slowly descended the long hill. Falloden opened another gate, with the hurried remark that there was yet one more. Meanwhile he saw Connie's slender body, her beautiful loosened hair and black riding-hat outlined against the still glowing sky behind. Her face, turned towards the advancing dusk, he could hardly see. But the small hand in its riding-glove, so close to him, haunted his senses. One movement, and he could have crushed it in his.

Far away the last gate came into sight. His bitterness and pain broke out.

"I can't imagine why you should feel any interest in my affairs," he said, in his stiffest manner, "but you kindly allowed me to talk to you sometimes about my people. You know, I presume, what everybody knows, that we shall soon be leaving Flood, and selling the estates."

"I know." The girl's voice was low and soft. "I am awfully, awfully sorry!"

"Thank you. It doesn't of course matter for me. I can make my own life. But for my father—it is hard. I should like you to know"—he spoke with growing agitation—"that when we met—at Cannes—and at Oxford—I had no knowledge—no idea—of what was happening."

She raised her head suddenly, impetuously.

"I don't know why you say that!"

He saw instantly that his wounded pride had betrayed him into a blunder—that without meaning it, he had seemed to suggest that she would have treated him differently, if she had known he was not a rich man.

"It was a stupid thing to say. Please consider it unsaid."

The silence deepened, till she broke it again—

"I see Mr. Radowitz sometimes. Won't you like to know that he is composing a symphony for his degree? He is always working at it. It makes him happy—at least—contented."

"Yes, I am glad. But nothing can ever make up to him. I know that."

"No—nothing," she admitted sadly.

"Or to me!"

Constance started. They had reached the last gate.

Falloden threw himself off his horse to open it and as she rode through, she looked down into his face. Its proud regularity of feature, its rich colour, its brilliance, seemed to her all blurred and clouded. A flashing insight showed her the valley of distress and humiliation through which this man had been passing. His bitter look, at once of challenge and renunciation, set her trembling; she felt herself all weakness; and suddenly the woman in her—dumbly, unguessed—held out its arms.

But he knew nothing of it. Rather her attitude seemed to him one of embarrassment—even of *hauteur.* It was suddenly intolerable to him to seem to be asking for her pity. He raised his hat, coldly gave her a few directions as to her road home, and closed the gate behind her. She bowed and in another minute he was cantering away from her, towards the sunset.

Connie went on blindly, the reins on her horse's neck, the passionate tears dropping on her hands.

XIII

DOUGLAS FALLODEN rode home rapidly after parting from Connie. Passion, impatience, bitter regret consumed him. He suffered, and could not endure to suffer. That life, which had grown up with him as a flattering and obsequious friend, obeying all his whims, yielding to all his desires, should now have turned upon him in this traitorous way, inflicting such monstrous reprisals and rebuffs, roused in him the astonishment and resentment natural to such a temperament.

He, too, drew rein for a moment at the spot where Connie had looked out over Flood Castle and its valley. The beautiful familiar sight produced in him now only a mingling of pain and irritation. The horrid thing was settled, decided. There was no avoiding ruin, or saving his inheritance. Then why these long delays, these endless discomforts and humiliations? The lawyers prolonged things because it paid them to do so; and his poor father wavered and hesitated from day to day, because physically and morally he was breaking up. If only his father and mother would have cleared out of Flood at once—they were spending money they could not possibly afford in keeping it up—and had left him, Douglas, to do the odious things, pay the creditors, sell the place, and sweep up the whole vast mess, with the help of the lawyers, it would have been infinitely best. His own will felt itself strong and determined enough for any such task. But Sir Arthur, in his strange, broken state, could not be brought to make decisions, and would often, after days of gloom and depression, pass into a fool's mood, when he seemed for the moment to forget and ignore the whole tragedy. Since he and Douglas had agreed with the trustees to sell the pictures, that sheer bankruptcy might just be escaped, Sir Arthur had been extravagantly cheerful. Why not have their usual shooting-party after all?—one last fling before the end! He supposed he should end his days in a suburban villa, but till they left Flood the flag should be kept flying.

During all this time of tension indeed, he was a great trial to his son. Douglas's quick and proud intelligence was amazed to find his father so weak and so incompetent under misfortune. All his boyish life he had looked up to the slender, handsome man, whom he himself so much resembled, on a solider, more substantial scale, as the most indulgent of fathers, the princeliest of hosts, the best of shots and riders, chief indeed of the Falloden clan and all its glories, who, like other monarchs, could do no wrong.

But now the glamour which must always attend the central figure of such a scene withered at the touch of poverty and misfortune. And, in its absence, Douglas found himself dealing with an enthusiastic, vain, self-confident being, who had ruined himself and his son by speculations, often so childishly foolish that Douglas could not think of them without rage. Intellectually, he could only despise and condemn his father.

Yet the old bond held. Till he met Constance Bledlow, he had cared only for his own people, and among them, preeminently, for his father. In this feeling, family pride and natural affection met together. The family pride had been sorely shaken, the affection, steeped in a painful, astonished pity, remained. For the first time in his life Douglas had been sleeping badly. Interminable dreams pursued him, in which the scene in Mannion quad, his last walk with Constance along the Cherwell, and the family crash, were all intermingled, with the fatuity natural to dreams. And his wakings from them were almost equally haunted by the figures of Constance and Radowitz, and by a miserable yearning over his father, which no one who saw his hard, indifferent bearing during the day could possible have guessed. "Poor—poor old fellow!"—he had once or twice raised himself from his bed in the early morning, as though answering this cry in his ears, only to find that he himself had uttered it.

He had told his people nothing of Constance Bledlow beyond the bare fact of his acquaintance with her, first at Cannes, and then at Oxford. And they knew nothing of the Radowitz incident. Very few people indeed were aware of the true history of that night which had marred an artist's life. The college authorities had been painfully stirred by the reports which had reached them; but Radowitz himself had written to the Head maintaining that the whole thing was an accident and a frolic, and insisting that no public or official notice should be taken of it, a fact which had not prevented the Head from writing severely to Falloden, Meyrick, and Robertson, or the fellows of the college from holding a college meeting, even in the long vacation, to discuss what measures should be taken in the October term to put down and stamp out ragging.

Falloden had replied to the Head's letter expressing his "profound regret" for the accident to Otto Radowitz, and declaring that nobody in the row had the smallest intention of doing him any bodily harm.

What indeed had anybody but himself to do with his own malignant and murderous impulse towards Radowitz? It had had no casual connection whatever with the accident itself. And who but he—and Constance Bledlow—was entitled to know that, while the others were actuated by nothing but the usual motives of a college rag, quickened by too much supping, he himself had been impelled by a mad jealousy of Radowitz, and a longing to humiliate one who had humiliated him? All the same he hated himself now for what he had said to Constancc on their last walk. It had been a mean and monstrous attempt to shift the blame from his own shoulders to hers; and his sense of honour turned from the recollection of it in disgust.

How pale she had looked, beside that gate, in the evening light—how heavy-eyed! No doubt she was seeing Radowitz constantly, and grieving over him; blaming herself, indeed, as he, Falloden, had actually invited her to do. With fresh poignancy, he felt himself an outcast from her company. No doubt they sometimes talked of him—his bitter pride guessed how!—she, and Sorell, and Radowitz together. Was Sorell winning her? He had every chance. Falloden, in his sober senses, knew perfectly well that she was not in love with Radowitz; though no one could say what pity might do with a girl so sensitive and sympathetic.

Well, it was all over!—no good thinking about it. He confessed to himself that his whole relation to Constance Bledlow had been one blunder from beginning to end. His own arrogance and self-confidence with regard to her, appeared to him, as he looked back upon them, not so much a fault as an absurdity. In all his dealings with her he had been a conceited fool, and he had lost her. "But I had to be ruined to find it out!" he thought, capable at last of some ironic reflection on himself.

He set his horse to a gallop along the moorland turf. Let him get home, and do his dreary tasks in that great house which was already becoming strange to him; which, in a sense, he was now eager to see the last of. On the morrow, the possible buyer of the pictures—who, by the way, was not an American at all, but a German shipping millionaire from Bremen—was coming down, with an "expert." Hang the expert! Falloden, who was to deal with the business, promised himself not to be intimidated by him, or his like; and amid his general distress and depression, his natural pugnacity took pleasure in the thought of wrestling with the pair.

When he rode up to the Flood gateway everything appeared as usual. The great lawns in front of the house were as immaculately kept as ever, and along the shrubberies which bordered the park there were gardeners still at work pegging down a broad edge of crimson rambler roses, which seemed to hold the sunset. Falloden observed them. "Who's paying for them?" he thought. At the front door two footmen received him; the stately head butler stood with a detached air in the background.

"Sir Arthur's put off dinner half an hour, sir. He's in the library."

Douglas went in search of his father. He found him smoking and reading a novel, apparently half asleep.

"You're very late, Duggy. Never mind. We've put off dinner."

"I found Sprague had a great deal to say."

Sprague was the subagent living on the further edge of the estate. Douglas had spent the day with him, going into the recent valuation of an important group of farms.

"I dare say," said Sir Arthur, lying back in his armchair. "I'm afraid I don't want to hear it."

Douglas sat down opposite his father. He was dusty and tired, and there were deep pits under his eyes.

"It will make a difference of a good many thousands to us, father, if that valuation is correct," he said shortly.

"Will it? I can't help it. I can't go into it. I can't keep the facts and figures in my head, Duggy. I've done too much of them this last ten years. My brain gives up. But you've got a splendid head, Duggy—wonderful for your age. I leave it to you, my son. Do the best you can."

Douglas looked at his father a moment in silence. Sir Arthur was sitting near the window, and had just turned on an electric light beside him. Douglas was struck by something strange in his father's attitude and look—a curious irresponsibility and remoteness. The deep depression of their earlier weeks together had apparently disappeared. This mood of easy acquiescence—almost levity—was becoming permanent. Yet Douglas could not help noticing afresh the physical change in a once splendid man—how shrunken his father was, and how grey. And he was only fifty-two. But the pace at which he had lived for years, first in the attempt to double his already great wealth by adventures all over the world, and latterly in his frantic efforts to escape the consequences of these adventures, had rapidly made an old man of him. The waste and pity—and at the same time the irreparableness of it all—sent a shock, intolerably chill and dreary, through the son's consciousness. He was too young to bear it patiently. He hastily shook it off.

"Those picture chaps are coming to-morrow," he said, as he got up, meaning to go and dress.

Sir Arthur put his hands behind his head, and didn't reply immediately. He was looking at a picture on the panelled wall opposite, on which the lingering western glow still shone through the mullioned window on his right. It was an enchanting Romney—a young woman in a black dress holding a spaniel in her arms. The picture breathed a distinction, a dignity beyond the reach of Romney's ordinary mood. It represented Sir Arthur's great-grandmother, on his father's side, a famous Irish beauty of the day.

"Wonder what they'll give me for that," he said quietly, pointing to it. "My father always said it was the pick. You remember the story that she—my great-grandmother—once came across Lady Hamilton in Romney's studio, and Emma Hamilton told Romney afterwards that at last he'd found a sitter handsomer than herself. It's a winner. You inherit her eyes, Douglas, and her colour. What's it worth?"

"Twenty thousand perhaps." Douglas's voice had the cock-sureness that goes with new knowledge. "I've been looking into some of the recent prices."

"Twenty thousand!" said Sir Arthur, musing. "And Romney got seventy-five for it, I believe—I have the receipt somewhere. I shall miss that picture. What shall I get for it? A few shabby receipts—for nothing. My creditors will get something out of her—mercifully. But as for me—I might as well have cut her into strips. She looks annoyed—as though she knew I'd thrown her away. I believe she was a vixen."

"I must go and change, father," said Douglas.

"Yes, yes, dear boy, go and change. Douglas, you think there'll be a few thousands over, don't you, besides your mother's settlement, when it's all done?"

"Precious few," said Douglas, pausing on his way to the door. "Don't count upon anything, father. If we do well to-morrow, there may be something."

"Four or five thousand?—ten, even? You know, Duggy, many men have built up fortunes again on no more. A few weeks ago I had all sorts of ideas."

"That's no good," said Douglas, with emphasis. "For God's sake, father, don't begin again."

Sir Arthur nodded silently, and Douglas left the room.

His father remained sitting where his son had left him, his fingers drumming absently on the arms of his chair, his half-shut eyes wandering over the splendid garden outside, with its statues and fountains, and its masses of roses, all fused in the late evening glow.

The door opened softly. His wife came in.

Lady Laura had lost her old careless good humour. Her fair complexion had changed for the worse; there were lines in her white forehead, and all her movements had grown nervous and irritable. But her expression as she stood by her husband was one of anxious though rather childish affection.

"How are you, Arthur? Did you get a nap?"

"A beauty!" said her husband, smiling at her, and taking her hand. "I dreamt about Raby, and the first time I saw you there in the old Duke's day. What a pretty thing you were, Laura!—like a monthly rose, all pink."

He patted her hand; Lady Laura shrugged her shoulders rather pettishly.

"It's no good thinking about that now. . . . You're not really going to have a shooting-party, Arthur? I do wish you wouldn't!"

"But of course I am!" said her husband, raising himself with alacrity. "The grouse must be shot, and the estate is not sold yet! I've asked young Meyrick, and Lord Charles, and Robert Vere. You can ask the Charlevilles, dear, and if my lady doesn't come I shan't break my heart. Then there are five or six of the neighbours of course. And no whining and whimpering! The last shoot at Flood shall be a good one! The keeper tells me the birds are splendid!"

Lady Laura's lips trembled.

"You forget what Duggy and I shall be feeling all the time, Arthur. It's very hard on us."

"No—nonsense!" The voice was good-humouredly impatient. "Take it calmly, dear. What do places matter? Come to the Andes with me. Duggy must work for his fellowship; Nelly can stay with some of our relations; and we can send the children to school. Or what do you say to a winter in California? Let's have a second honeymoon—see something of the world before we die. This English country gentleman business ties one terribly. Life in one's own house is so jolly one doesn't want anything else. But now, if we're going to be uprooted, let's enjoy it!"

"Enjoy it!" repeated his wife bitterly. "How can you say such things, Arthur?"

She walked to the window, and stood looking out at the garden with its grandiose backing of hill and climbing wood, and the strong broken masses of the cedar trees—the oldest it was said in England—which flanked it on either side. Lady Laura was, in truth, only just beginning to realise their misfortunes. It had seemed to her impossible that such wealth as theirs should positively give out; that there should be nothing left but her miserable two thousand a year; that something should not turn up to save them from this preposterous necessity of leaving Flood. When Douglas came home, she had thrown herself on her clever son, confident that he would find a way out, and his sombre verdict on the hopelessness of the situation had filled her with terror. How could they live with nothing but the London house to call their own? How could they? Why couldn't they sell off the land, and keep the house and the park? Then they would still be the Fallodens of Flood. It was stupid—simply stupid—to be giving up everything like this.

So day by day she wearied her husband and son by her lamentations, which were like those of some petted animal in distress. And every now and then she had moments of shrinking terror—of foreboding—fearing she knew not what. Her husband seemed to her changed. Why wouldn't he take her advice? Why wouldn't Douglas listen to her? If only her father had been alive, or her only brother, they could have helped her. But she had nobody—nobody—and Arthur and Douglas would do this horrible thing.

Her husband watched her, half smiling—his shrunken face flushed, his eyes full of a curious excitement. She had grown stout in the last five years, poor Laura!—she had lost her youth before the crash came. But she was still very pleasant to look upon, with her plentiful fair hair, and her pretty mouth—her instinct for beautiful dress—and her soft appealing manner. He suddenly envisaged her in black—with a plain white collar and cuffs, and something white on her hair. Then vehemently shaking off his thought he rose and went to her.

"Dear—didn't Duggy want you to ask somebody for the shoot? I thought I heard him mention somebody."

"That was ages ago. He doesn't want anybody asked now," said Lady Laura resentfully. "He can't understand why you want a party."

"I thought he said something about Lady Constance Bledlow?"

"That was in June!" cried Lady Laura. "He certainly wouldn't let me ask her, as things are."

"Have you any idea whether he may have wanted to marry her?"

"He was very much taken with her. But how can he think about marrying, Arthur? You do say the strangest things. And after Dagnall's behaviour too."

"*Raison de plus!* That girl has money, my dear, and will have more, when the old aunts depart this life. If you want Duggy still to go into Parliament, and to be able to do anything for the younger ones, you'll keep an eye on her."

Lady Laura, however, was too depressed to welcome the subject. The gong rang for dinner, and as they were leaving the room, Sir Arthur said—

"There are two men coming down to-morrow to see the pictures, Laura. If I were you, I should keep out of the way."

She gave him a startled look. But they were already on the threshold of the dining-room, where a butler and two footmen waited. The husband and wife took their places opposite each other in the stately panelled room, which contained six famous pictures. Over the mantelpiece was a half-length Gainsborough, one of the loveliest portraits in the world, a miracle of shining colour and languid grace, the almond eyes with their intensely black pupils and black eyebrows looking down, as it seemed, contemptuously upon this after generation, so incurably lacking in its own supreme refinement. Opposite Lady Laura was a full-length Van Dyck of the Genoese period, a mother in stiff brocade and ruff, with an adorable child at her knee; and behind her chair was the great Titian of the house, a man in armour, subtle and ruthless as the age which bred him, his hawk's eye brooding on battles past, and battles to come, while behind him stretched the Venetian lagoon, covered dimly with the fleet of the great republic which had employed him. Facing the Gainsborough hung one of Cuyp's few masterpieces—a mass of shipping on the Scheldt, with Dordrecht in the background. For play and interplay of everything that delights the eye—light and distance, transparent water, and hovering clouds, the lustrous brown of fishing boats, the beauty of patched sails and fluttering flags—for both literary and historic suggestion, Dutch art had never done better. Impressionists and post-impressiopists came down occasionally to stay at Flood—for Sir Arthur liked to play Mæcenas—and were allowed to deal quite frankly with the pictures, as they wandered round the room at dessert, cigarette in hand, pointing out the absurdities of the Cuyp and the Titian. Their host, who knew that he possessed in that room what the collectors of two continents desired, who felt them buzzing outside like wasps against a closed window, took a special pleasure in the scoffs of the advanced crew. They supplied an agreeable acid amid a general adulation that bored him.

To-night the presence of the pictures merely increased the excitement which was the background of his mind. He talked about them a good deal at dinner, wondering secretly all the time, what it would be like to do without them—without Flood—without his old butler there—without everything.

Douglas came down late, and was very silent and irresponsive. He too was morbidly conscious of the pictures, though he wished his father wouldn't talk about them. He was conscious of everything that meant money—of his mother's pearls for instance, which she wore every evening without thinking about them. If he did well with the pictures on the morrow she might, perhaps, justly keep them, as a dowry for Nelly. But if not— He found himself secretly watching his mother, wondering how she would take it all when she really understood—what sort of person she would turn out to be in the new life to which they were all helplessly tending.

After dinner, he followed his father into the smoking room.

"Where is the catalogue of the pictures, father?"

"In the library, Duggy, to the right hand of the fire-place. I paid a fellow a very handsome sum for making it—a fellow who knew a lot—a real expert. But, of course, when we published it, all the other experts tore it to pieces."

"If I bring it, will you go through it with me?"

Sir Arthur shrugged his shoulders.

"I don't think I will, Duggy. The catalogue—there are a great many marginal notes on it which the published copies haven't got—will tell you all I know about them, and a great deal more. And you'll find a loose paper at the beginning, on which I've noted down the prices people have offered me for them from time to time. Like their impudence, I used to think! I leave it to you, old boy. I know it's a great responsibility for a young fellow like you. But the fact is—I'm pumped. Besides, when they make their offer, we can talk it over. I think I'll go and play a game of backgammon with your mother."

He threw away his cigar, and Douglas, angry at what seemed to him his father's shirking, stood stiffly aside to let him pass. Sir Arthur opened the door. He seemed to walk uncertainly, and he stooped a great deal. From the hall outside, he looked back at his son.

"I think I shall see M'Clintock next time I'm in town, Duggy. I've had some queer pains across my chest lately."

"Indigestion?" said Douglas. His tone was casual.

"Perhaps. Oh, they're nothing. But it's best to take things in time."

He walked away, leaving his son in a state of seething irritation. Extraordinary that a man could think of trumpery ailments at such a time! It was unlike his father too, whose personal fitness and soundness, whether on the moors, in the hunting field, or in any other sort of test, had always been triumphantly assumed by his family, as part of the general brilliance of Sir Arthur's rôle in life.

Douglas sombrely set himself to study the picture catalogue, and sat smoking and making notes till nearly midnight. Having by that time accumulated a number of queries to which answers were required, he went in search of his father. He found him in the drawing-room, still playing backgammon with Lady Laura.

"Oh Duggy, I'm so tired!" cried his mother plaintively, as soon as he appeared. "And your father will go on. Do come and take my place."

Sir Arthur rose.

"No, no, dear—we've had enough. Many thanks. If you only understood its points, backgammon is really an excellent game. Well, Duggy, ready to go to bed?"

"When I've asked you a few questions, father."

Lady Laura escaped, having first kissed her son with tearful eyes. Sir Arthur checked a yawn, and tried to answer Douglas's enquiries. But very soon he declared that he had no more to say, and couldn't keep awake.

Douglas watched him mounting the famous staircase of the house, with its marvellous *rampe*, bought under the Bourbon Restoration from one of the historic chateaux of France; and, suddenly, the young man felt his heart gripped. Was that shrunken, stooping figure really his father? Of course they must have M'Clintock at once—and get him away—to Scotland or abroad.

"The two gentlemen are in the red drawing-room, sir!" Douglas and his father were sitting together in the library, after lunch, on the following afternoon, when the butler entered.

"Damn them!" said Sir Arthur under his breath. Then he got up, smiling, as the servant disappeared. "Well, Duggy, now's your chance. I'm a brute not to come and help you, my boy. But I've made such a mess of driving the family coach, you'd really better take a turn. I shall go out for an hour. Then you can come and report to me."

Douglas went into the red drawing-room, one of the suite of rooms dating from the early seventeenth century which occupied the western front of the house. As he entered, he saw two men at the farther end closely examining a large Constable, of the latest "palette-knife" period, which hung to the left of the fire-place. One of the men was short, very stout, with a fringe of grey hair round his bald head, a pair of very shrewd and sparkling black eyes, a thick nose, full lips, and a double chin. He wore spectacles, and was using in addition, a magnifying glass with which he was examining the picture. Beside him stood a thin, slightly-bearded man, cadaverous in colour, who, with his hands in his pockets, was holding forth in a nonchalant, rather patronising voice.

Both of them turned at Douglas's entrance, surveying the son of the house with an evident and eager curiosity.

"You are, I suppose, Mr. Douglas Falloden?" said the short man, speaking perfect English, though with a slight German accent. "Your father is not able to see us?"

"My father will be pleased to see you, when you have been the round of the pictures," said Douglas stiffly. "He deputes me to show you what we have."

The short man laughed.

"I expect we know what you have almost as well as you. Let me introduce Mr. Miklos."

Douglas bowed, so did the younger man. He was, as Douglas already knew, a Hungarian by birth, formerly an official in one of the museums of Budapest, then at Munich, and now an "expert" at large, greatly in demand as the adviser of wealthy men entering the field of art collecting, and prepared to pay almost anything for success in one of the most difficult and fascinating *chasses* that exist.

"I see you have given this room almost entirely to English pictures," said Mr. Miklos politely. "A fine Constable!"—he pointed to the picture they had just been considering—"but not, I think, entirely by the master?"

"My great-grandfather bought it from Constable himself," said Douglas. "It has never been disputed by any one."

Mr. Miklos did not reply, but he shook his head with a slight smile, and walked away towards a Turner, a fine landscape of the middle period, hanging close to the Constable. He peered into it shortsightedly, with his strong glasses.

"A pity that it has been so badly relined," he said presently, to Douglas, pointing to it.

"You think so? Its condition is generally thought to be excellent. My father was offered eight thousand for it last year by the Berlin Museum."

Douglas was now apparently quite at his ease. With his thumbs in the armholes of his white waistcoat, he strolled along beside the two buyers, holding his own with both of them, thanks to his careful study of the materials for the history of the collection possessed by his father. The elder man, a Bremen shipowner,—one Wilhelm Schwarz—who had lately made a rapid and enormous fortune out of the Argentine trade, and whose chief personal ambition it now was to beat the New York and Paris collectors, in the great picture game, whatever it might cost, was presently forced to take some notice of the handsome curly-headed youth in the perfectly fitting blue serge suit, whose appearance as the vendor, or the vendor's agent, had seemed to him, at first, merely one more instance of English aristocratic stupidity.

As a matter of fact, Herr Schwarz was simply dazzled by the contents of Flood Castle. He had never dreamt that such virgin treasures still existed in this old England, till Miklos, instructed by the Falloden lawyer, had brought the list of the pictures to his hotel, a few days before this visit. And now he found it extremely difficult to conceal his excitement and delight, or to preserve, in the presence of this very sharp-eyed young heir, the proper "don't care" attitude of the buyer. He presently left the "running down" business almost entirely to Miklos, being occupied in silent and feverish speculations as to how much he could afford to spend, and a passion of covetous fear lest somehow A——, or Z——, or K——, the leading collectors of the moment, should even yet forestall him, early and "exclusive" as Miklos assured him their information had been.

They passed along through the drawing-rooms, and the whole wonderful series of family portraits, Reynolds,' Lawrences, Gainsboroughs, Romneys, Hoppners, looked down, unconscious of their doom, upon the invaders, and on the son of the house, so apparently unconcerned. But Douglas was very far from unconcerned. He had no artistic gift, and he had never felt or pretended any special interest in the pictures. They were part of Flood, and Flood was the inseparable adjunct of the Falloden race. When his father had first mooted the sale of them, Douglas had assented without much difficulty. If other things went, why not they?

But now that he was in the thick of the business, he found, all in a moment, that he had to set his teeth to see it through. A smarting sense of loss—loss hateful and irreparable, cutting away both the past and the future—burnt deep into his mind, as he followed in the track of the sallow and depreciatory Miklos or watched the podgy figure of Herr Schwarz, running from side to side as picture after picture caught his eye. The wincing salesman saw himself as another Charles Surface; but now that the predicament was his own it was no longer amusing. These fair faces, these mothers and babies of his own blood, these stalwart men, fighters by sea and land, these grave thinkers and churchmen, they thronged about him transformed, become suddenly alien and hostile, a crowd of threatening ghosts, the outraged witnesses of their own humiliation. "For what are you selling us?"—they seemed to say. "Because some one, who was already overfed, must needs grab at a larger mess of pottage—and we must pay! Unkind! degenerate!"

Presently, after the English drawing-rooms, and the library, with its one Romney, came the French room, with its precious Watteaus, its Latours, its two brilliant Nattiers. And here Herr Schwarz's coolness fairly deserted him. He gave little shrieks of pleasure, which brought a frown to the face of his companion, who was anxious to point out that a great deal of the Watteau was certainly pupil-work, that the Latours were not altogether "convincing" and the Nattiers though extremely pretty, "superficial." But Herr Schwarz brushed him aside.

"*Nein, nein, lieber freund!* Dat Nattier is as fine as anything at Potsdam. Dat I must have!" And he gazed in ecstasy at the opulent shoulders, the rounded forms, and gorgeous jewelled dress of an unrivalled Madame de Pompadour, which had belonged to her brother, the Marquis de Marigny.

"You will have all or nothing, my good sir!" thought Falloden, and bided his time.

Meanwhile Miklos, perceiving that his patron was irretrievably landed and considering that his own "expert" dignity had been sufficiently saved, relaxed into enthusiasm and small talk. Only in the later Italian rooms did his critical claws again allow themselves to scratch. A small Leonardo, the treasure of the house, which had been examined and written about by every European student of Milanese art for half a century, was suavely pronounced—

"A Da Predis, of course, but a very nice one!" A Bellini became a Rondinelli; and the names of a dozen obscure, and lately discovered painters, freely applied to the Tintorets, Mantegnas and Cimas on the walls, produced such an effect on Herr Schwarz that he sat down open-mouthed on the central ottoman, staring first at the pictures and then at the speaker; not knowing whether to believe or to doubt. Falloden stood a little apart, listening, a smile on his handsome mouth.

"We should know nothing about Rondinelli," said Miklos at last, sweetly—"but for the great Bode——"

"*Ach*, Bode!" said Herr Schwarz, nodding his head in complacent recognition at the name of the already famous assistant-director of the Berlin Museum.

Falloden laughed.

"Dr. Bode was here last year. He told my father he thought the Bellini was one of the finest in existence."

Miklos changed countenance slightly.

"Bode perhaps is a trifle credulous," he said in an offended tone.

But he went back again to the Bellini and examined it closely. Falloden, without waiting for his second thoughts, took Herr Schwarz into the dining-room.

At the sight of the six masterpieces hanging on its walls, the Bremen ship-owner again lost his head. What miraculous good-fortune had brought him, ahead of all his rivals, into this still unravaged hive? He ran from side to side,—he grew red, perspiring, inarticulate. At last he sank down on a chair in front of the Titian, and when Miklos approached, delicately suggesting that the picture, though certainly fine, showed traces of one of the later pupils, possibly Molari, in certain parts, Herr Schwarz waved him aside.

"*Nein, nein*!—Hold your tongue, my dear sir! Here must I judge for myself."

Then looking up to Falloden who stood beside him, smiling, almost reconciled to the vulgar, greedy little man by his collapse, he said abruptly—

"How much, Mr. Falloden, for your father's collection?"

"You desire to buy the whole of it?" said Falloden coolly.

"I desire to buy everything that I have seen," said Herr Schwarz, breathing quickly. "Your solicitors gave me a list of sixty-five pictures. No, no, Miklos, go away!"—he waved his expert aside impatiently.

"Those were the pictures on the ground floor," said Falloden. "You have seen them all. You had better make your offer in writing, and I will take it to my father."

He fetched pen and paper from a side-table and put them before the excited German. Herr Schwarz wrinkled his face in profound meditation. His eyes almost disappeared behind his spectacles, then emerged sparkling.

He wrote some figures on a piece of paper, and handed it to Douglas.

Douglas laughed drily, and returned it.

"You will hardly expect me to give my father the trouble of considering that."

Herr Schwarz puffed and blowed. He got up, and walked about excitedly. He lit a cigarette, Falloden politely helping him. Miklos advanced again.

"I have, myself, made a very careful estimate—" he began, insinuatingly.

"No, no, Miklos,—go away!—go away!" repeated Schwarz impatiently, almost walking over him. Miklos retreated sulkily.

Schwarz took up the paper of figures, made an alteration, and handed it to Falloden.

"It is madness," he said—"sheer madness. But I have in me something of the poet—the Crusader."

Falloden's look of slightly sarcastic amusement, as the little man breathlessly examined his countenance, threw the buyer into despair. Douglas put down the paper.

"We gave you the first chance, Herr Schwarz. As you know, nobody is yet aware of our intentions to sell. But I shall advise my father to-night to let one or two of the dealers know."

"*Ach, lieber Gott!*" said Herr Schwarz, and walking away to the window, he stood looking into the rose-garden outside, making a curious whistling sound with his prominent lips, expressive, evidently, of extreme agitation.

Falloden lit another cigarette, and offered one to Miklos.

At the end of two or three minutes, Schwarz again amended the figures on the scrap of paper, and handed it sombrely to Falloden.

"Dat is my last word."

Falloden glanced at it, and carelessly said—

"On that I will consult my father."

He left the room.

Schwarz and Miklos looked at each other.

"What airs these English aristocrats give themselves," said the Hungarian angrily—"even when they are beggars, like this young man!"

Schwarz stood frowning, his hands in his pockets, legs apart. His agitation was calming down, and his more prudent mind already half regretted his impetuosity.

"Some day—we shall teach them a lesson!" he said, under his breath, his eyes wandering over the rose-garden and the deer-park beyond. The rapidly growing docks of Bremen and Hamburg, their crowded shipping, the mounting tide of their business, came flashing into his mind—ran through it in a series of images. This England, with her stored wealth, and her command of the seas—must she always stand between Germany and her desires? He found himself at once admiring and detesting the English scene on which he looked. That so much good German money should have to go into English pockets for these ill-gotten English treasures! What a country to conquer—and to loot!

"And they are mere children compared to us—silly, thick-headed children! Yet they have all the plums—everywhere."

Falloden came back. The two men turned eagerly.

"My father thanks you for your offer, gentlemen. He is very sorry he is not able to see you as he hoped. He is not very well this afternoon. But I am to say that he will let you have an answer in twenty-four hours. Then if he agrees to your terms, the matter will have to go before the court. That, of course, our lawyers explained to you——"

"That will not suit me at all!" cried Herr Schwarz. "As far as your father is concerned, my offer must be accepted—or rejected—now."

He struck his open hand on the polished mahogany of the table beside him.

"Then I am very sorry you have had the trouble of coming down," said Falloden politely. "Shall I order your carriage?"

The great ship-owner stared at him. He was on the point of losing his temper, perhaps of withdrawing from his bargain, when over Falloden's head he caught sight of the Titian and the play of light on its shining armour; of the Van Dyck opposite. He gave way helplessly; gripped at the same moment by his parvenu's ambition, and by the genuine passion for beautiful things lodged oddly in some chink of his common and Philistine personality.

"I have the refusal then—for twenty-four hours?" he said curtly.

Falloden nodded, wrote him a statement to that effect, ordered whisky and soda, and saw them safely to their carriage.

Then pacing slowly through the rooms, he went back towards the library. His mind was divided between a kind of huckster's triumph and a sense of intolerable humiliation. All around him were the "tribal signs" of race, continuity, history—which he had taken for granted all his life. But now that a gulf had opened between him and them, his heart clung to them consciously for the first time. No good! He felt himself cast out—stripped—exposed. The easy shelter fashioned for him and his by the lives of generations of his kindred had fallen in fragments about him.

"Well—I never earned it!"—he said to himself bitterly, turning in disgust on his own self-pity.

When he reached the library he found his father walking up and down deep in thought. He looked up as his son entered.

"Well, that saves the bankruptcy, Duggy, and—as far as I can see—leaves a few thousands over—portions for the younger children, and what will enable you to turn round."

Douglas assented silently. After a long look at his son, Sir Arthur opened a side door which led from the library into the suite of drawing-rooms. Slowly he passed through them, examining the pictures steadily, one by one. At the end of the series, he turned and came back again to his own room, with a bent head and meditative step. Falloden followed him:

In the library, Sir Arthur suddenly straightened himself.

"Duggy, do you hate me—for the mess I've made—of your inheritance?"

The question stirred a quick irritation in Falloden. It seemed to him futile and histrionic; akin to all those weaknesses in his father which had brought them disaster.

"I don't think you need ask me that," he said, rather sharply, as he opened a drawer in his father's writing-table, and locked up the paper containing Herr Schwarz's offer.

Sir Arthur looked at him wistfully.

"You've been a brick, Duggy—since I told you. I don't know that I had any right to count upon it."

"What else could I do?" said Douglas, trying to laugh, but conscious—resenting it—of a swelling in the throat.

"You could have given a good many more twists to the screw—if you'd been a different sort," said his father slowly. "And you're a tough customer, Duggy, to some people. But to me"—He paused, beginning again in another tone—

"Duggy, don't be offended with me—but did you ever want to marry Lady Constance Bledlow? You wrote to me about her at Christmas."

Douglas gave a rather excited laugh.

"It's rather late in the day to ask me that question."

His father eyed him.

"You mean she refused you?"

His son nodded.

"Before this collapse?"

"Before she knew anything about it."

"Poor old Duggy!" said his father, in a low voice. "But perhaps—after all—she'll think better of it. By all accounts she has the charm of her mother, whom Risborough married to please himself and not his family."

Falloden said nothing. He wished to goodness his father would drop the subject. Sir Arthur understood he was touching things too sore to handle, and sighed.

"Well, shake hands, Duggy, old boy. You carried this thing through splendidly to-day. But it seems to have taken it out of me—which isn't fair. I shall go for a little walk. Tell your mother I shall be back in an hour or so."

The son took his father's hand. The strong young grasp brought a momentary sense of comfort to the older man. They eyed each other, both pale, both conscious of feelings to which it was easier to give no voice. Then their hands dropped. Sir Arthur looked for his hat and stick, which were lying near, and went out of the open glass door into the garden. He passed through the garden into the park beyond walking slowly and heavily, his son's eyes following him.

XIV

Out of sight of the house, at the entrance of the walk leading to the moor, Sir Arthur was conscious again of transitory, but rather sharp pains across the chest.

He sat down to rest, and they soon passed away. After a few minutes he pursued his walk, climbing towards the open stretches of heathery moor, which lay beyond the park, and a certain ghyll or hollow with a wild stream in it that cleft the moor high up—one of his favourite haunts.

He climbed through ferny paths, and amid stretches of heather just coming to its purple prime, up towards the higher regions of the moor where the millstone grit cropped out in sharp edges, showing gaunt and dark against the afternoon sky. Here the beautiful stream that made a waterfall within the park came sliding down shelf after shelf of yellowish rock, with pools of deep brown water at intervals, overhung with mountain ash and birch.

After the warm day, all the evening scents were abroad, carried by a gentle wind. Sir Arthur drank them in, with the sensuous pleasure which had been one of his gifts in life. The honey smell of the heather, the woody smell of the bracken, the faint fragrance of wood-smoke wafted from a bonfire in the valley below—they all carried with them an inexpressible magic for the man wandering on the moor. So did the movements of birds—the rise of a couple of startled grouse, the hovering of two kestrels, a flight of wild duck in the distance. Each and all reminded him of the halcyon times of life—adventures of his boyhood, the sporting pleasures of his manhood. By George!—how he had enjoyed them all!

Presently, to his left, on the edge of the heathery slope he caught sight of one of the butts used in the great grouse-shoots of the moor. What a jolly party they had had last year in that week of wonderful October weather! Two hundred brace on the home moor the first day, and almost as many on the Fairdale moor the following day. Some of the men had never shot better. One of the party was now Viceroy of India; another had been killed in one of the endless little frontier fights that are the price, month by month, which the British Empire pays for its existence. Douglas had come off particularly well. His shooting from that butt to the left had been magnificent. Sir Arthur remembered well how the old hands had praised it, warming the cockles of his own heart.

"I will have one more shoot," he said to himself with passion—"I will!"

Then, feeling suddenly tired, he sat down beside the slipping stream. It was fairly full, after some recent rain, and the music of it rang in his ears. Stretching out a hand he filled it full of silky grass and thyme, sniffing at it in delight. "How strange," he thought, "that I can still enjoy these things. But I shall—till I die."

Below him, as he sat, lay the greater part of his estate stretching east and west; bounded on the west by some of the high moors leading up to the Pennine range, lost on the east in a blue and wooded distance. He could see the towers of three village churches, and the blurred greys and browns of the houses clustering round them—some near, some far. Stone farm-buildings, their white-washed gables glowing under the level sun, caught his eye, one after the other—now hidden in wood, now standing out upon the fields or the moorland, with one sycamore or a group of yews to shelter them. And here and there were larger houses; houses of the middle gentry, with their gardens and enclosures. Farms, villages, woods and moors, they were all his—nominally his, for a few weeks or months longer. And there was scarcely one of them in the whole wide scene, with which he had not some sporting association; whether of the hunting field, or the big autumn shoots, or the jolly partridge drives over the stubbles.

But it suddenly and sharply struck him how very few other associations he possessed with these places spread below him in the declining August sunshine. He had not owned Flood more than fifteen years—enough however to lose it in! And he had succeeded a father who had been the beloved head of the county, a just and liberal landlord, a man of scrupulous kindness and honour, for whom everybody had a friendly word. His ruined son on the moorside thought with wonder and envy of his father's popular arts, which yet were no arts. For himself he confessed,—aware as he was, this afternoon, of the presence in his mind of a new and strange insight with regard to his own life and past, as though he were writing his own obituary—that the people living in these farms and villages had meant little more to him than the troublesome conditions on which he enjoyed the pleasures of the Flood estates, the great income he drew from them, and the sport for which they were famous. He had his friends among the farmers of course, though they were few. There were men who had cringed to him, and whom he had rewarded. And Laura had given away plentifully in the villages. But his chief agent he knew had been a hard man and a careless one; and he had always loathed the trouble of looking after him. Again and again he had been appealed to, as against his agent; and he had not even answered the letters. He had occasionally done some public duties; he had allowed himself to be placed on the County Council, but had hardly ever attended meetings; he had taken the chair and made a speech occasionally, when it would have cost him more effort to refuse than to accept; and those portions of the estate which adjoined the castle were in fairly good repair. But on the remoter farms, and especially since his financial resources had begun to fail, he knew very well that there were cottages and farmhouses in a scandalous state, on which not a farthing had been spent for years.

No, it could not be said he had played a successful part as a landowner. He had meant no harm to anybody. He had been simply idle and preoccupied; and that in a business where, under modern conditions, idleness is immoral. He was quite conscious that there were good men, frugal men, kind and God-fearing men, landlords like himself, though on a much smaller scale, in that tract of country under his feet, who felt bitterly towards him, who judged him severely, who would be thankful to see the last of him, and to know that the land had passed into other and better hands. Fifty-two years of life lived in that northern Vale of Eden; and what was there to show for them?—in honest work done, in peace of conscience, in friends? Now that the pictures were sold, there would be just enough to pay everybody, with a very little over. There was some comfort in that. He would have ruined nobody but himself and Duggy. Poor Laura would be quite comfortable on her own money, and would give him house-room no doubt—till the end.

The end? But he might live another twenty years. The thought was intolerable. The apathy in which he had been lately living gave way. He realised, with quickened breath, what this parting from his inheritance and all the associations of his life would mean. He saw himself as a tree, dragged violently out of its native earth—rootless and rotten.

Poor Duggy! Duggy was as proud and wilful as himself; with more personal ambition however, and less of that easy, sensuous recklessness, that gambler's spirit, which had led his father into such quagmires. Duggy had shown up well these last weeks. He was not a boy to talk, but in acts he had been good.

And through the man's remorseful soul there throbbed the one deep, disinterested affection of his life—his love for his son. He had been very fond of Laura, but when it came to moments like this she meant little to him.

He gave himself up to this feeling of love. How strange that it should both rend and soothe!—that it and it alone brought some comfort, some spermaceti for the inward bruise, amid all the bitterness connected with it. Duggy, in his arms, as a little toddling fellow, Duggy at school—playing for Harrow at Lord's—Duggy at college——

But of that part of his son's life, as he realised with shame, he knew very little. He had been too entirely absorbed, when it arrived, in the frantic struggle, first for money, and then for solvency. Duggy had become in some ways during the last two years a stranger to him—his own fault! What had he done to help him through his college life—to "influence him for good," as people said? Nothing. He had been enormously proud of his son's university distinctions; he had supplied him lavishly with money; he had concealed from him his own financial situation till it was hopeless; he had given him the jolliest possible vacation, and that was all that could be said.

The father groaned within himself. And yet again—how strangely!—did some fraction of healing virtue flow from his very distress?—from his remembrance, above all, of how Duggy had tried to help him?—during these few weeks since he knew?

Ah!—Tidswell Church coming out of the shadows! He remembered how one winter he had been coming home late on horseback through dark lanes, when he met the parson of that church, old and threadbare and narrow-chested, trudging on, head bent, against a spitting rain. The owner of Flood had been smitten with a sudden compunction, and dismounting he had walked his horse beside the old man. The living of Tidswell was in his own gift. It amounted, he remembered, to some £140 a year. The old man, whose name was Trevenen, had an old wife, to whom Sir Arthur thought Lady Laura had sometimes sent some cast-off clothes.

Mr. Trevenen had been baptising a prematurely born child in a high moorland farm. The walk there and back had been steep and long, and his thin lantern-jawed face shone very white through the wintry dusk.

"You must be very tired," Sir Arthur had said, remembering uncomfortably the dinner to which he was himself bent—the chef, the wines, the large house-party.

And Mr. Trevenen had looked up and smiled.

"Not very. I have been unusually cheered as I walked by thoughts of the Divine Love!"

The words had been so simply said; and a minute afterwards the old pale-faced parson had disappeared into the dark.

What did the words mean? Had they really any meaning?

"The Divine Love." Arthur Falloden did not know then, and did not know now. But he had often thought of the incident.

He leaned over, musing, to gather a bunch of harebells growing on the edge of the stream. As he did so, he was conscious again of a sharp pain in the chest. In a few more seconds, he was stretched on the moorland grass, wrestling with a torturing anguish that was crushing his life out. It seemed to last an eternity. Then it relaxed, and he was able to breathe and think again.

"What is it?"

Confused recollections of the death of his old grandfather, when he himself was a child, rose in his mind. "He was out hunting—horrible pain—two hours. Is this the same? If it is—I shall die—here—alone."

He tried to move after a little, but found himself helpless. A brief intermission, and the pain rushed on him again, like a violent and ruthless hand, grinding the very centres of life. When he recovered consciousness, it was with the double sense of blissful relief from agony and of ebbing strength. What had happened to him? How long had he been there?

"Could you drink this?" said a voice behind him. He opened his eyes and saw a young man, with a halo of red-gold hair, and a tremulous, pitying face, quite strange to him, bending over him.

There was some brandy at his lips. He drank with difficulty. What had happened to the light? How dark it was?

"Where am I?" he said, looking up blindly into the face above him.

"I found you here—on the moor—lying on the grass. Are you better? Shall I run down now—and fetch some one?"

"Don't go——"

The agony returned. When Sir Arthur spoke again, it was very feebly.

"I can't live—through—much more of that. I'm dying. Don't leave me. Where's my son? Where's my son—Douglas? Who are you?"

The glazing eyes tried to make out the features of the stranger. They were too dim to notice the sudden shiver that passed through them as he named his son.

"I can't get at any one. I've been calling for a long time. My name is Radowitz. I'm staying at Penfold Rectory. If I could only carry you! I tried to lift you—but I couldn't. I've only one hand." He pointed despairingly to the sling he was wearing.

"Tell my son—tell Douglas——"

But the faint voice ceased abruptly, and the eyes closed. Only there was a slight movement of the lips, which Radowitz, bending his ear to the mouth of the dying man, tried to interpret. He thought it said "pray," but he could not be sure.

Radowitz looked round him in an anguish. No one on the purple side of the moor, no one on the grassy tracks leading downwards to the park; only the wide gold of the evening—the rising of a light wind—the rustling of the fern—and the loud, laboured breathing below him.

He bent again over the helpless form, murmuring words in haste.

Meanwhile after Sir Arthur left the house, Douglas had been urgently summoned by his mother. He found her at tea with Trix in her own sitting-room. Roger was away, staying with a school friend, to the general relief of the household; Nelly, the girl of seventeen, was with relations in Scotland, but Trix had become her mother's little shadow and constant companion. The child was very conscious of the weight on her parents' minds. Her high spirits had all dropped. She had a wistful, shrinking look, which suited ill with her round face and her childishly parted lips over her small white teeth. The little face was made for laughter; but in these days only Douglas could bring back her smiles, because mamma was so unhappy and cried so much; and that mamma should cry seemed to bring her whole world tumbling about the child's ears. Only Douglas, for sheer impatience with the general gloom of the house, would sometimes tease her or chase her; and then the child's laugh would ring out—a ghostly echo from the days before Lady Laura "knew."

Poor Lady Laura! Up to the last moment before the crash, her husband had kept everything from her. She was not a person of profound or sensitive feeling; and yet it is probable that her resentment of her husband's long secrecy, and the implications of it, counted for a great deal in her distress and misery.

The sale of the pictures, as shortly reported by Douglas, had overwhelmed her. As soon as her son appeared in her room, she poured out upon him a stream of lamentation and complaint, while Trix was alternately playing with the kitten on her knee and drying furtive tears on a very grubby pocket-handkerchief.

Douglas was on the whole patient and explanatory, for he was really sorry for his mother; but as soon as he could he escaped from her on the plea of urgent letters and estate accounts.

The August evening wore on, and it was nearing sunset when his mother came hurriedly into the library.

"Douglas, where is your father?"

"He went out for a walk before tea. Hasn't he come in?"

"No. And it's more than two hours. I—I don't like it, Duggy. He hasn't been a bit well lately—and so awfully depressed. Please go and look for him, dear!"

Douglas suddenly perceived the terror in his mother's mind. It seemed to him absurd. He knew his father better than she did; but he took his hat and went out obediently.

He had happened to notice his father going towards the moor, and he took the same path, running simply for exercise, measuring his young strength against the steepness of the hill and filling his lungs with the sweet evening air, in a passionate physical reaction against the family distress.

Five miles away, in this same evening glow, was Constance Bledlow walking or sitting in her aunts' garden? Or was she nearer still—at Penfold Rectory, just beyond the moor he was climbing, the old rectory-house where Sorell and Radowitz were staying? He had taken good care to give that side of the hills a wide berth since his return home. But a great deal of the long ridge was common ground, and in the private and enclosed parts there were several rights of way crossing the moor, besides the one lonely road traversing it from end to end on which he had met Constance Bledlow. If he had not been so tied at home, and so determined not to run any risks of a meeting, he might very well have come across Sorell at least, if not Radowitz, on the high ground dominating the valleys on either side. Sorell was a great walker. But probably they were as anxious to avoid a casual meeting as he was.

The evening was rapidly darkening, and as he climbed he searched the hillside with his quick eyes for any sign of his father. Once or twice he stopped to call:

"Father!"

Th sound died away, echoing among the fields and hollows of the moor. But there was no answer. He climbed further. He was now near the stream which descended through the park, and its loud jubilant voice burst upon him, filling the silence.

Then, above the plashing of the stream and the rising of the wind, he heard suddenly a cry:

"Help!"

It came from a point above his head. A sudden horror came upon him. He dashed on. In another minute a man's figure appeared, higher up, dark against the reddened sky. The man put one hand to his mouth, and shouted through it again—"Help!"

Douglas came up with him. In speechless amazement he saw that it was Otto Radowitz, without a coat, bareheaded, pale and breathless.

"There's a man here, Falloden. I think it's your father. He's awfully ill. I believe he's dying. Come at once! I've been shouting for a long time."

Douglas said nothing. He rushed on, following Radowitz, who took a short cut bounding through the deep ling of the moor. Only a few yards till Douglas perceived a man, with a grey, drawn face, who was lying full length on a stretch of grass beside the stream, his head and shoulders propped against a low rock on which a folded coat had been placed as a pillow.

"Father!"

Sir Arthur opened his eyes. He was drawing deep, gasping breaths, the strong life in him wrestling still. But the helplessness, the ineffable surrender and defeat of man's last hour, was in his face.

Falloden knelt down.

"Father!—don't you know me? We'll soon carry you home. It's Duggy!" No answer. Radowitz had gone a few yards away, and was also kneeling, his face buried in his hands, his back turned to the father and son.

Douglas made another agonised appeal, and the grey face quivered. A whisper passed the lips.

"It's best, Duggy—poor Duggy! Kiss me, old boy. Tell your mother—that young man—prayed for me. She'll like to—know that. My love——"

The last words were spoken with a great effort; and the breaths that followed grew slower and slower as the vital tide withdrew itself. Once more the eyes opened, and Douglas saw in them the old affectionate look. Then the lips shaped themselves again to words that made no sound; a shudder passed through the limbs—their last movement.

Douglas knelt on, looking closely into his father's face, listening for the breath that came no more. He felt rather than saw that Radowitz had moved still further away.

Two or three deep sobs escaped him—involuntary, almost unconscious. Then he pulled himself together. His mother? Who was to tell her?

He went to call Radowitz, who came eagerly.

"My father is dead," said Falloden, deadly pale, but composed. "How long have you been here?"

"About half an hour. When I arrived he was in agonies of pain. I gave him brandy, and he revived a little. Then I wanted to go for help, but he begged me not to leave him alone. So I could only shout and wave my handkerchief. The pains came back and back—and every time he grew weaker. Oh, it was *angina*. I have seen it before—twice. If I had only had some nitrite of amyl! But there was nothing—nothing I could do." He paused, and then added timidly, "I am a Catholic; I said some of our prayers."

He looked gravely into Falloden's face. Falloden's eyes met his, and both men remembered—momentarily—the scene in Marmion Quad.

"We must get him down," said Falloden abruptly. "And there is my mother."

"I would help you to carry him, of course; but—you see—I can't."

His delicate skin flushed deeply. Falloden realized for the first time the sling across his shoulder and the helpless hand lying in it. He turned away, searching with his eyes the shadows of the valley. At the moment, the spot where they stood was garishly illuminated by the rapidly receding light, which had already left the lower ground. The grass at their feet, the rocks, the stream, the stretches of heather were steeped and drenched in the last rays of sun which shot upon them in a fierce concentration from the lower edge of a great cloud. But the landmarks below were hard to make out—for a stranger's eyes.

"You see that cottage—where the smoke is?"

Radowitz assented.

"You will find a keeper there. Send him with three or four men."

"Yes—at once. Shall I take a message to the house?"

Radowitz spoke very gently. The red-gold of his hair, and his blue eyes, were all shining in the strange light. But he was again as pale as Falloden himself. Douglas drew out a pencil, and a letter from his pocket. He wrote some words on the envelope, and handed it to Radowitz.

"That's for my mother's maid. She will know what to do. She is an old servant. I must stay here."

Radowitz rushed away, leaping and running down the steep side of the hill, his white shirt, crossed by the black sling, conspicuous all the way, till he was at last lost to sight in the wood leading to the keeper's cottage.

Falloden went back to the dead man. He straightened his father's limbs and closed his eyes. Then he lay down beside him, throwing his arm tenderly across the body. And the recollection came back to him of that hunting accident years ago—the weight of his father on his shoulders—the bitter cold—the tears which not all his boyish scorn of tears could stop.

His poor mother! She must see Radowitz, for Radowitz alone could tell the story of that last half hour. He must give evidence, too, at the inquest.

Radowitz! Thoughts, ironic and perverse, ran swarming through Falloden's brain, as though driven through it from outside. What a nursery tale!—how simple!—how crude! Could not the gods have devised a subtler retribution?

Then these thoughts vanished again, like a cloud of gnats. The touch of his father's still warm body brought him back to the plain, tragic fact. He raised himself on his elbow to look again at the dead face.

The handsome head with its grizzled hair was resting on Radowitz's coat. Falloden could not bear it. He took off his own, and gently substituted it for the other. And as he laid the head down, he kissed the hair and the brow. He was alone with his father—more alone than he ever would be again. There was not a human step or voice upon the moor. Night was coming rapidly on. The stream rushed beside him. There were a few cries of birds—mostly owls from the woods below. The dead man's face beside him was very solemn and quiet. And overhead, the angry sunset clouds were fading into a dim and star-strewn heaven, above a world sinking to its rest.

The moon was up before Radowitz came back to the little rectory on the other side of the moor. Sorell, from whose mind he was seldom absent, had begun to worry about him, was in fact on the point of setting out in search of him. But about nine o'clock he heard the front gate open and jumping down from the low open window of the rectory drawing-room he went to meet the truant.

Radowitz staggered towards him, and clung to his arm.

"My dear fellow," cried Sorell, aghast at the boy's appearance and manner—"what have you been doing to yourself?"

"I went up the moor for a walk after tea—it was so gorgeous, the clouds and the view. I got drawn on a bit—on the castle side. I wasn't really thinking where I was going. Then I saw the park below me, and the house. And immediately afterwards, I heard a groaning sound, and there was a man lying on the ground. It was Sir Arthur Falloden—and he died—while I was there." The boy's golden head dropped suddenly against Sorell. "I say, can't I have some food, and go to bed?"

Sorell took him in and looked after him like a mother, helped by the kind apple-faced rector, who had heard the castle news from other sources also, and was greatly moved.

When Otto's exhaustion had been fed and he was lying in his bed with drawn brows, and no intention or prospect of going to sleep, Sorell let him tell his tale.

"When the bearers came, I went down with them to the castle, and I saw Lady Laura"—said the boy, turning his head restlessly from side to side. "I say, it's awful—how women cry! Then they told me about the inquest—I shall have to go to-morrow—and on the way home I went to see Lady Connie. I thought she ought to know."

Sorell started.

"And you found her?"

"Oh, yes. She was sitting in the garden."

There was a short silence. Then Otto flung up his left hand, caught a gnat that was buzzing round his head, and laughed—a dreary little sound.

"It's quite true—she's in love with him."

"With Douglas Falloden?"

Otto nodded.

"She was awfully cut up when I told her—just for him. She didn't cry of course. Our generation doesn't seem to cry—like Lady Laura. But you could see what she wanted."

"To go to him?"

"That's it. And of course she can't. My word, it is hard on women! They're hampered such a lot—by all their traditions. Why don't they kick 'em over?"

"I hope she will do nothing of the kind," said Sorell with energy. "The traditions may just save her."

Otto thought over it.

"You mean—save her from doing something for pity that she wouldn't do if she had time to think?"

Sorell assented.

"Why should that fellow be any more likely now to make her happy——"

"Because he's lost his money and his father? I don't know why he should. I dare say he'll begin bullying and slave-driving again—when he's forgotten all this. But——"

"But what?"

"Well—you see—I didn't think he could possibly care about anything but himself. I thought he was as hard as a millstone all through. Well, he isn't. That's so queer!"

The speaker's voice took a dreamy tone.

Sorell glanced in bitterness at the maimed hand lying on the bed. It was still bandaged, but he knew very well what sort of a shapeless, ruined thing it would emerge, when the bandages were thrown aside. It was strange and fascinating—to a student of psychology—that Otto should have been brought, so suddenly, so unforeseeably, into this pathetic and intimate relation with the man to whom, essentially, he owed his disaster. But what difference did it make in the quality of the Marmion outrage, or to any sane judgment of Douglas Falloden?

"Go to sleep, old boy," he said at last. "You'll have a hard time to-morrow."

"What, the inquest? Oh, I don't mind about that. If I could only understand that fellow!"

He threw his head back, staring at the ceiling.

Otto Radowitz, in spite of Sorell's admonitions, slept very little that night. His nights were apt to be feverish and disturbed. But on this occasion imagination and excitement made it impossible to stop the brain process, the ceaseless round of thought; and the hours of darkness were intolerably long. Memory went back behind the meeting with the dying man on the hillside, to an earlier experience—an hour of madness, of "possession." His whole spiritual being was still bruised and martyred from it, like that sufferer of old whom the evil spirit "tore" in departing. What had delivered him? The horror was still on him, still his master, when he became aware of that white face on the grass—

He drowsed off again. But in his half-dream, he seemed to be kneeling again and reciting Latin words, words he had heard last when his mother was approaching her end. He was more than half sceptical, so far as the upper mind was concerned; but the under-consciousness was steeped in ideas derived from his early home and training, ideas of sacrifice, forgiveness, atonement, judgment—the common and immortal stock of Christianity. He had been brought up in a house pervaded by the crucifix, and by a mother who was ardently devout.

But why had God—if there was a God—brought this wonderful thing to pass? Never had his heart been so full of hatred as in that hour of lonely wandering on the moor, before he perceived the huddled figure lying by the stream. And, all in a moment, he had become his enemy's proxy—his representative—in the last and tenderest service that man can render to man. He had played the part of son to Falloden's dying father—had prayed for him from the depths of his heart, tortured with pity. And when Falloden came, with what strange eyes they had looked at each other!—as though all veils had dropped—all barriers had, for the moment, dropped away.

"Shall I hate him again to-morrow?" thought Radowitz. "Or shall I be more sorry for him than for myself? Yes, that's what I felt!—so marvellously!"

So that when he went to Constance with his news, and under the emotion of it, saw the girl's heart unveiled—"I was not jealous," he thought. "I just wanted to give her everything!"

Yet, as the night passed on, and that dreary moment of the first awakening earth arrived, when all the griefs of mankind weigh heaviest, he was shaken anew by gusts of passion and despair; and this time for himself. Suppose—for in spite of all Sorell's evasions and concealments, he knew very well that Sorell was anxious about him, and the doctors had said ugly things—suppose he got really ill?—suppose he died, without having lived?

He thought of Constance in the moonlit garden, her sweetness, her gratefulness to him for coming, her small, white “flower-face,” and the look in her eyes.

If I might—only once—have kissed her—have held her in my arms!” he thought, with anguish. And rolling on his face, he lay prone, fighting his fight alone, till exhaustion conquered, and “he took the gift of sleep.”

XV

Douglas Falloden was sitting alone in his father's library surrounded by paper and documents. He had just concluded a long interview with the family lawyer; and a tray containing the remains of their hasty luncheon was on a side-table. The room had a dusty, dishevelled air. Half of the house-servants had been already dismissed; the rest were disorganised. Lady Laura had left Flood the day before. To her son's infinite relief she had consented to take the younger children and go on a long visit to some Scotch relations. It had been left vague whether she returned to Flood or not; but Douglas hoped that the parting was already over—without her knowing it; and that he should be able to persuade her, after Scotland, to go straight to the London house—which was her own property—for the winter.

Meanwhile he himself had been doing his best to wind up affairs. The elaborate will of twenty years earlier, with its many legacies and bequests, had been cancelled by Sir Arthur only six weeks before his death. A very short document had been substituted for it, making Douglas and a certain Marmaduke Falloden, his uncle and an eminent K.C., joint executors, and appointing Douglas and Lady Laura guardians of the younger children. Whatever property might remain "after the payment of my just debts" was to be divided in certain proportions between Douglas and his brother and sisters.

The estates, with the exception of the lands immediately surrounding the castle, were to be sold to the tenants, and the dates of the auction were already fixed. For the castle itself, negotiations had been opened with an enormously successful soap-boiler from the north, but an American was also in the market, and the Falloden solicitors were skilfully playing the two big fish against each other. The sale of the pictures would come before the court early in October. Meanwhile the beautiful Romney—the lady in black—still looked down upon her stripped and impoverished descendant; and Falloden, whose sole companion she often was through dreary hours, imagined her sometimes as tragic or reproachful, but more commonly as mocking him with a malicious Irish glee.

There would be some few thousand pounds left for himself when all was settled. He was determined to go into Parliament, and his present intention was to stand for a Merton fellowship, and read for the bar. If other men could make three or four thousand a year within three years or so of being called, why not he? His character had steeled under the pressure of disaster. He realised with a clearer intelligence, day by day, all that had gone from him—his father—his inheritance—the careless ease and self-assurance that goes with the chief places at the feast of life. But if he must now drop to the lower rooms, it would not be "with shame" that he would do that, or anything else. He felt within himself a driving and boundless energy, an iron will to succeed. There was even a certain bitter satisfaction in measuring himself against the world without the props and privileges he had hitherto possessed. He was often sore and miserable to his heart's depths; haunted by black regrets and compunction he could not get rid of. All the same it was his fixed resolve to waste no thoughts on mere happiness. His business was to make a place for himself as an able man among able men, to ask of ambition, intelligence, hard work, and the sharpening of brain on brain, the satisfaction he had once hoped to get out of marriage with Constance Bledlow, and the easy, though masterly, use of great wealth.

He turned to look at the clock.

She had asked him for five. He had ordered his horse accordingly, the only beast still left in the Flood stables, and his chief means of escape during a dreary fortnight from his peevish co-executor, who was of little or no service, and had allowed himself already to say unpardonable things about his dead brother, even to that brother's son.

It was too soon to start, but he pushed his papers aside impatiently. The mere prospect of seeing Constance Bledlow provoked in him a dumb and troubled excitement. Under its impulse he left the library, and began to walk aimlessly through the dreary and deserted house, for the mere sake of movement. The pictures were still on the walls, for the sale of them had not yet been formally sanctioned by the court; but all Lady Laura's private and personal possessions had been removed to London, and dust-sheets covered the furniture. Some of it indeed had been already sold, and workmen were busy packing in the great hall, amid a dusty litter of paper and straw. All the signs of normal life, which make the character of a house, had gone; what remained was only the débris of a once animated whole. Houses have their fate no less than books; and in the ears of its last Falloden possessor, the whole of the great many-dated fabric, from its fourteenth century foundations beneath the central tower, to the pseudo-Gothic with which Wyatt had disfigured the garden front, had often, since his father's death, seemed to speak with an almost human voice of lamentation and distress.

But this afternoon Falloden took little notice of his surroundings. Why had she written to him?

Well, after all, death is death, and the merest strangers had written to him—letters that he was now wearily answering. But there had been nothing perfunctory in her letter. As he read it he had seemed to hear her very voice saying the soft, touching things in it—things that women say so easily and men can't hit upon; and to be looking into her changing face, and the eyes that could be so fierce, and then again so childishly sweet and sad—as he had seen them, at their last meeting on the moor, while she was giving him news of Radowitz. Yet there was not a word in the letter that might not have been read on the house-tops—not a trace in it of her old alluring, challenging self. Simplicity—deep feeling—sympathy—in halting words, and unfinished sentences—and yet something conspicuously absent and to all appearance so easily, unconsciously absent, that all the sweetness and pity brought him more smart than soothing. Yes, she had done with him—for all her wish to be kind to him. He saw it plainly; and he turned back thirstily to those past hours in Lathom Woods, when he had felt himself, if only for a moment, triumphant master of her thoughts, if not her heart; rebelled against, scolded, flouted, yet still tormentingly necessary and important. All that delicious friction, those disputes that are the forerunner of passion were gone—forever. She was sorry for him—and very kind. His touchy pride recoiled, reading into her letter what she had never dreamt of putting into it, just because of the absence of that something—that old tremor—those old signs of his influence over her, which, of course, she would never let him see again.

All the same he had replied at once, asking if he might come and say good-bye before she left Scarfedale. And she had sent him a telegram—"Delighted—to-morrow—five o'clock."

And he was going—out of a kind of recklessness—a kind of obstinate recoil against the sorrowful or depressing circumstance of life. He had given up all thoughts of trying to win her back, even if there were any chance of it. His pride would not let him sue as a pauper; and of course the Langmoors to whom she was going—he understood—from Scarfedale, would take good care she did not throw herself away. Quite right too. Very likely the Tamworths would capture her; and Bletchley was quite a nice fellow.

When he did see her, what could they talk about? Radowitz?

He would like to send a message through her to Radowitz—to say something—

What could he say? He had seen Radowitz for a few minutes after the inquest—to thank him for his evidence—and for what he had done for Sir Arthur. Both had hurried through it. Falloden had seemed to himself stricken with aphasia. His mouth was dry, his tongue useless. And Radowitz had been all nerves, a flickering colour—good God, how deathly he looked!

Afterwards he had begun a letter to Radowitz, and had toiled at it, sometimes at dead of night and in a feverish heat of brain. But he had never finished or sent it. What was the use? Nothing was changed.

That black sling and the damaged hand in it stood for one of those hard facts that no wishing, and no sentimentalising, and no remorse could get over.

"I wish to God I had let him alone!"

That now was the frequent and bitter cry of Falloden's inmost being. Trouble and the sight of trouble—sorrow—and death—had been to him, as to other men, sobering and astonishing facts. The most decisive effect of them had been to make him vulnerable, to break through the hard defences of pride and custom, so that he realised what he had done. And this realisation was fast becoming a more acute and haunting thing than anything else. It constantly drove out the poignant recollection of his father's death, or the dull sense of financial loss and catastrophe. Loss and catastrophe might be at some distant time made good. But what could ever give Radowitz back his art—his career—his natural object in life? The hatches of the present had just got to be closed over this ugly, irreparable thing. "I can't undo it—nothing can ever be undone. But I can't spend my life in repenting it; one must just go forward, and not let that, or anything else, hamstring a man who has got his fight to fight, and can't get out of it."

Undo it? No. But were no, even partial, amends possible?—nothing that could be offered, or done, or said?—nothing that would give Constance Bledlow pleasure, or change her opinion?—efface that shrinking in her, of which he hated to think?

He cudgelled his brains, but could think of nothing.

Money, of course, was of no use, even if he still possessed it. Radowitz, in all matters connected with money, was hypersensitive and touchy. It was well known that he had private means; and it was certainly probable that he was now the richer man of the two.

No—there was nothing to be done. He had maimed forever the vital, energising impulse in another human being, and it could never be repaired. "His poor music!—*murdered*"—the words from Constance Bledlow's horror-stricken letter were always in his mind. And the day after the inquest on Sir Arthur, he had had some conversation on the medical points of his father's case, and on the light thrown on them by Radowitz's evidence, with the doctor who was then attending Lady Laura, and had, it appeared, been several times called in by Sorell during the preceding weeks to see Radowitz and report on the progress of the hand. "A bad business!" said the young man, who had intelligence and was fresh from hospital—"and awful hard luck!—he might have hurt his hand in a score of ways and still have recovered the use of it, but with this particular injury"—he shook his head—"nothing to be done! And the worst of it is that a trouble like this, which cuts across a man's career, goes so deep. The thing I should be most afraid of is his general health. You can see that he's delicate—narrow-chested—a bundle of nerves. It might be phthisis—it might be"—he shrugged his shoulders—"well, depression, bad neurasthenia. And the poor lad seems to have no family—no mother or sisters—to look after him. But he'll want a lot of care, if he's to pull round again. An Oxford row, wasn't it? Abominable!"

But here the sudden incursion of Lady Laura's maid to ask a question for her mistress had diverted the doctor's thoughts and spared Falloden reply.

A little later, he was riding slowly up the side of the moor towards Scarfedale, looking down on a landscape which since his childhood had been so intimate and familiar a part of himself that the thought of being wrenched away from it, immediately and for good, seemed merely absurd.

September was nearly gone; and the trees had long passed out of their August monotony, and were already prophetic of the October blaze. The level afternoon light was searching out the different planes of distance, giving to each hedgerow, elm or oak, a separate force and kingship: and the golden or bronze shades, which were day by day stealing through the woods, made gorgeous marriage with the evening purple. The castle, as he gazed back upon it, had sunk into the shadows, a dim magnificent ghost, seen through mist, like the Rhine maidens through the blue water.

And there it would stand, perhaps for generations yet, long after he and his kindred knew it no more. What did the plight of its last owner matter to it, or to the woods and hills? He tried to think of that valley a hundred years hence—a thousand!—and felt himself the merest insect crawling on the face of this old world, which is yet so young. But only for a moment. Rushing back, came the proud, resisting sense of personality—of man's dominance over nature—of the Nietzschean "will to power." To be strong, to be sufficient to one's self; not to yield, but to be forever counterattacking circumstance, so as to be the master of circumstance, whatever blows it might choose to strike—that seemed to be the best, the only creed left to him.

When he reached the Scarfedale house, and a gardener had taken his horse, the maid who opened the door told him he would find Lady Constance on the lawn. The old ladies were out driving.

Very decent of the old ladies, he thought, as he followed the path into the garden.

There she was!—her light form lost, almost, in a deep chair, under a lime-tree. The garden was a tangle of late blooming flowers; everything growing rank and fast, as though to get as much out of the soil and the sun as possible, before the first frost made execution. It was surrounded by old red walls that held the dropping sun, and it was full of droning bees, and wagtails stepping daintily over the lawns.

Connie rose and came towards him. She was in black with pale pink roses in her hat. In spite of her height, she seemed to him the slightest, gracefullest thing, and as she neared him, she lifted her deep brown eyes, and it was as though he had never seen before how beautiful they were.

"It was kind of you to come!" she said shyly.

He made no reply, till she had placed him beside her under the lime. Then he looked round him, a smile twitching his lip.

"Your aunts are not at home?"

"No. They have gone for their drive. Did you wish to see them?"

"I am in terror of your Aunt Winifred. She and I had many ructions when I was small. She thought our keepers used to shoot her cats."

"They probably did!"

"Of course. But a keeper who told the truth about it would have no moral sense."

They both laughed, looking into each other's faces with a sudden sense of relief from tension. After all the tragedy and the pain, there they were, still young, still in the same world together. And the sun was still shining and flowers blooming. Yet, all the same, there was no thought of any renewal of their old relation on either side. Something unexpressed, yet apparently final, seemed to stand between them; differing very much in his mind from the something in hers, yet equally potent. She, who had gone through agonies of far too tender pity for him, felt now a touch of something chill and stern in the circumstance surrounding him that seemed to put her aside. "This is not your business," it seemed to say; so that she saw herself as an inexperienced child playing with that incalculable thing—the male. Attempts at sympathy or advice died away—she rebelled, and submitted.

Still there are things—experiments—that even an inexperienced child, a child "of good will" may venture. All the time that she was talking to Falloden, a secret expectation, a secret excitement ran through her inner mind. There was a garden door to her left, across a lawn. Her eyes were often on it, and her ear listened for the click of the latch.

Meanwhile Falloden talked very frankly of the family circumstances and his own plans. How changed the tone was since they had discussed the same things, riding through the Lathom Woods in June! There was little less self-confidence, perhaps; but the quality of it was not the same. Instead of alienating, it began to touch and thrill her. And her heart could not help its sudden tremor when he spoke of wintering "in or near Oxford." There was apparently a Merton prize fellowship in December on which his hopes were set, and the first part of his bar examination to read for, whether he got a fellowship or no.

"And Parliament?" she asked him.

"Yes—that's my aim," he said quietly. "Of course it's the fashion just now, especially in Oxford, to scoff at politics and the House of Commons. It's like the 'art-for-arters' in town. As if you could solve anything by words—or paints!"

"Your father was in the House for some time? "

She bent towards him, as she mentioned his father, with a lovely unconscious gesture that sent a tremor through him. He seemed to perceive all that shaken feeling in her mind to which she found it so impossible to give expression; on which his own action had placed so strong a curb.

He replied that his father had been in Parliament for some twelve years, and had been a Tory Whip part of the time. Then he paused, his eyes on the grass, till he raised them to say abruptly:

"You heard about it all—from Radowitz?"

She nodded.

"He came here that same night." And then suddenly, in the golden light, he saw her flush vividly. Had she realised that what she had said implied a good deal?—or might be thought to imply it? Why should Radowitz take the trouble, after his long and exhausting experience, to come round by the Scarfedale manor-house?

"It was an awful time for him," he said, his eyes on hers. "It was very strange that he should be there."

She hesitated. Her lips trembled.

"He was very glad to be there. Only he was sorry—for you."

"You mean he was sorry that I wasn't there sooner—with my father?"

"I think that was what he felt—that there was only a stranger."

"I was just in time," said Falloden slowly. "And I wonder—whether anything matters, to the dying?"

There was a pause, after which he added, with sudden energy—

"I thought—at the inquest—he himself looked pretty bad."

"Otto Radowitz?" Constance covered her eyes with her hands a moment—a gesture of pain. "Mr. Sorell doesn't know what to do for him. He has been losing ground lately. The doctors say he ought to live in the open-air. He and Mr. Sorell talk of a cottage near Oxford, where Mr. Sorell can go often and see him. But he can't live alone."

As she spoke Falloden's attention was diverted. He had raised his head and was looking across the lawn towards the garden entrance.

There was the sound of a clicking latch. Constance turned, and saw Radowitz entering.

The young musician paused and wavered, at the sight of the two under the lime. It seemed as though he would have taken to flight. But, instead, he came on with hesitating step. He had taken off his hat, as he often did when walking; and his red-gold hair *en brosse* was as conspicuous as ever. But otherwise what a change from the youth of three months before! Falloden, now that the immediate pressure of his own tragedy was relaxed, perceived the change even more sharply than he had done at the inquest; perceived it, at first with horror, and then with a wild sense of recoil and denial, as though some hovering Erinys advanced with Radowitz over the leaf-strewn grass.

Radowitz grew paler still as he reached Connie. He gave Falloden a short, embarrassed greeting, and then subsided into the chair that Constance offered him. The thought crossed Falloden's mind—"Did she arrange this?"

Her face gave little clue—though she could not restrain one quick, hesitating glance at Falloden. She pressed tea on Radowitz, who accepted it to please her, and then, schooled as she was in all the minor social arts, she had soon succeeded in establishing a sort of small talk among the three. Falloden, self-conscious, and on the rack, could not imagine why he stayed. But this languid boy had ministered to his dying father! And to what, and to whom, were the languor, the tragic physical change due? He stayed—in purgatory—looking out for any chance to escape.

"Did you walk all the way?"

The note in Connie's voice was softly reproachful.

"Why, it's only three miles!" said Radowitz, as though defending himself, but he spoke with an accent of depression. And Connie remembered how, in the early days of his recovery from his injury, he had spent hours rambling over the moors by himself, or with Sorell. Her heart yearned to him. She would have liked to take his poor hands in hers, and talk to him tenderly like a sister. But there was that other dark face, and those other eyes opposite—watching. And to them too, her young sympathy went out—how differently!—how passionately! A kind of rending and widening process seemed to be going on within her own nature. Veils were falling between her and life; and feelings, deeper and stronger than any she had ever known, were fast developing the woman in the girl. How to heal Radowitz!—how to comfort Falloden! Her mind ached under the feelings that filled it—feelings wholly disinterested and pure.

"You really are taking the Boar's Hill cottage?" she asked, addressing Radowitz.

"I think so. It is nearly settled. But I am trying to find some companion. Sorell can only come occasionally."

As he spoke, a wild idea flashed into Falloden's brain. It seemed to have entered without—or against—his will; as though suggested by some imperious agency outside himself. His intelligence laughed at it. Something else in him entertained it—breathlessly.

Radowitz stooped down to try and tempt Lady Marcia's dachshund with a piece of cake.

"I must anyhow have a dog," he said, as the pampered Max accepted the cake, and laid his head gratefully on the donor's knee; "they're always company."

He looked wistfully into the dog's large, friendly eyes.

Connie rose.

"Please don't move!" she said, flushing. "I shall be back directly. But I must put up a letter. I hear the postman!" She ran over the grass, leaving the two men in acute discomfort. Falloden thought again, with rising excitement: "She planned it! She wants me to do something—to take some step—but what?"

An awkward pause followed. Radowitz was still playing with the dog, caressing its beautiful head with his uninjured hand, and talking to it in a half whisper. As Constance departed, a bright and feverish red had rushed into his cheeks; but it had only made his aspect more ghostly, more unreal.

Again the absurd idea emerged in Falloden's consciousness; and this time it seemed to find its own expression, and to be merely making use of his voice, which he heard as though it were some one else's.

He bent over towards Radowitz.

"Would you care to share the cottage with me?" he said abruptly. "I want to find a place to read in—out of Oxford."

Radowitz looked up, amazed—speechless! Falloden's eyes met Otto's steadily. The boy turned away. Suddenly he covered his face with his free hand.

"Why did you hate me so?" he said, breathing quickly. "What had I done to you?"

"I didn't hate you," said Falloden thickly. "I was mad."

"Because you were jealous? What a fool you were! She never cared a brass farthing for me—except as she does now. She would like to nurse me—and give me back my music. But she can't—and you can't."

There was silence again. Otto's chest heaved. As far as he could with his one hand, he hid the tears in his eyes from his companion. And at last he shook off emotion—with a laugh in which there was no mirth.

"Well, at least, I shouldn't make such a row now as I used to do—practising."

Falloden understood his reference to the soda-water bottle fusillade, by which the "bloods," in their first attack upon him, had tried to silence his piano.

"Can't you play at all?" he said at last, choosing the easiest of several remarks that presented themselves.

"I get about somehow on the keys. It's better than nothing. And I'm writing something for my degree. It's rather good. If I could only keep well!" said the boy impatiently. "It's this damned health that gets in the way."

Then he threw himself back in his chair, all the melancholy of his face suddenly breaking up, the eyes sparkling.

"Suppose I set up one of those automatic pianos they're now talking about—could you stand that?"

"I would have a room where I didn't hear it. That would be all right."

"There's a wonderful idea I heard of from Paris a week or two ago," said Otto excitedly—"a marvellous electric invention a man's at work on, where you only turn a handle, or press a button, and you get Rubinstein—or Madame Schumann or my countryman, Paderewski, who's going to beat everybody. It isn't finished yet. But it won't be for the likes of me. It'll cost at least a thousand pounds."

"They'll get cheaper," said Falloden, his chin in his hands, elbows on knees, and eyes fixed on his companion. It seemed to him he was talking in a dream, so strange was this thing he had proposed; which apparently was going to come to pass. At any rate Radowitz had not refused. He sat with the dachshund on his knees, alternately pulling out and folding its long ears. He seemed to be, all in a moment, in high spirits, and when he saw Connie coming back through the garden gate, with a shy, hesitating step, he sprang up eagerly to greet her. But there was another figure behind her. It was Sorell; and at sight of him "something sealed" the boy's lips. He looked round at Falloden, and dropped back into his chair.

Falloden rose from his seat abruptly. A formal and scarcely perceptible greeting passed between him and Sorell. All Falloden's irritable self-consciousness rushed back upon him as he recognised the St. Cyprian tutor. He was not going to stay and cry *peccavi* any more in the presence of a bloodless prig, for whom Oxford was the world. But it was bitter to him all the same to leave him in possession of the garden and Connie Bledlow's company.

"Thank you—I must go," he said brusquely, as Connie tried to detain him. "There is so much to do nowadays. I shall be leaving Flood next week. The agent will be in charge."

"Leaving—for good?" she asked, in her appealing voice, as they stood apart.

"Probably—for good."

"I don't know how to say—how sorry I am!"

"Thank you. But I am glad it's over. When you get back to Oxford—I shall venture to come and call."

"That's a promise," she said, smiling at him. "Where will you be?"

"Ask Otto Radowitz! Good-bye!"

Her start of surprise pleased him. He approached Radowitz. "Shall I hear from you?" he said stiffly.

"Certainly!" The boy looked up. "I will write to-morrow."

The garden door had no sooner closed on Falloden than Radowitz threw himself back, and went into a fit of laughter, curious, hollow laughter.

Sorell looked at him anxiously.

"What's the meaning of that, Otto?"

"You'll laugh, when you hear! Falloden and I are going to set up house together, in the cottage on Boar's Hill. He's going to read—and I'm to be allowed a piano, and a piano-player. Queer, isn't it?"

"My dear Otto!" cried Sorell, in dismay. "What on earth do you mean?"

"Well, he offered it—said he'd come and look after me. I don't know what possessed him—nor me either. I didn't exactly accept, but I shall accept. Why shouldn't I?"

"Because Falloden's the last person in the world to look after anybody—least of all, you!" said Sorell with indignant energy. "But of course it's a joke! You mean it for a joke. If he proposed it, it was like his audacity. Nobody would, who had a shred of delicacy. I suppose he wants to disarm public opinion!"

Radowitz looked oddly at Sorell from under his finely marked eyebrows.

"I don't believe he cares a hang for public opinion," he said slowly. "Nor do I. If you could come, of course that would settle it. And if you won't come to see me, supposing Falloden and I do share diggings, that settles it too. But you will come, old man—you will come!"

And he nodded, smiling, at his quasi-guardian. Neither of them noticed Connie. Yet she had hung absorbed on their conversation, the breath fluttering on her parted lips. And when their talk paused, she bent forward, and laid her hand on Sorell's arm:

"Let him!" she said pleadingly—"let him do it!"

Sorell looked at her in troubled perplexity. "Let Douglas Falloden make some amends to his victim; if he can, and will. Don't be so unkind as to prevent it!" That, he supposed, was what she meant. It seemed to him the mere sentimental unreason of the young girl, who will not believe that there is any irrevocableness in things at all, till life teaches her.

Radowitz too! What folly, what mistaken religiosity could make him dream of consenting to such a house-mate through this winter which might be his last!

Monstrous! What kind of qualities had Falloden to fit him for such a task? All very well, indeed, that he should feel remorse! Sorell hoped he might feel it a good deal more sharply yet. But that he should ease his remorse at Otto's expense, by offering what he could never fulfil, and by taking the place of some one on whom Otto could have really leaned—that seemed to Sorell all of a piece with the man's egotism, his epicurean impatience of anything that permanently made him uncomfortable or unhappy. He put something of this into impetuous words as well as he could. But Otto listened in silence. So did Constance. And Sorell presently felt that there was a secret bond between them.

Before the aunts returned, the rectory pony-carriage came for Radowitz, who was not strong enough to walk both ways. Sorell and Constance were left alone.

Sorell, observing her, was struck anew by the signs of change and development in her. It was as though her mother and her mother's soul showed through the girl's slighter temperament. The old satiric aloofness in Connie's brown eyes, an expression all her own, and not her mother's, seemed to have slipped away; Sorell missed it. Ella Risborough's sympathetic charm had replaced it, but with suggestions of hidden conflict and suffering, of which Lady Risborough's bright sweetness had known nothing. It was borne in upon him that, since her arrival in Oxford, Constance had gone through a great deal, and gone through it alone. For after all what had his efforts amounted to? What can a man friend do for a young girl in the fermenting years of her youth? And when the man friend knows very well that, but for an iron force upon himself, he himself would be among her lovers? Sorell felt himself powerless—in all the greater matters—and was inclined to think that he deserved to be powerless. Yet he had done his best; and through his Greek lessons he humbly knew that he had helped her spiritual growth, just as the Greek immortals had helped and chastened his own youth. They had been reading Homer together—parts both of the "Iliad" and the "Odyssey"; and through "that ageless mouth of all the world," what splendid things had spoken to her!—Hector's courage, and Andromache's tenderness, the bitter sorrow of Priam, the pity of Achilles, mother love and wife love, death and the scorn of death. He had felt her glow and tremble in the grip of that supreme poetry; for himself he had found her the dearest and most responsive of pupils.

But what use was anything, if after all, as Radowitz vowed, she was in love with Douglas Falloden? The antagonism between the man of Sorell's type—disinterested, pure-minded, poetic, and liable, often, in action to the scrupulosity which destroys action; and the men of Falloden's type—strong, claimant, self-centred, arrogant, determined—is perennial. Nor can a man of the one type ever understand the attraction for women of the other.

Sorell sat on impatiently in the darkening garden, hoping always that Connie would explain, would confess; for he was certain that she had somehow schemed for this preposterous reconciliation—if it was a reconciliation. She wanted no doubt to heal Falloden's conscience, and so to comfort her own. And she would sacrifice Otto, if need be, in the process! He vowed to himself that he would prevent it, if he could.

Connie eyed him wistfully. Confidences seemed to be on her very lips; and then stopped there. In the end she neither explained nor confessed. But when he was gone, she walked up and down the lawn under the evening sky, her hands behind her—passionately dreaming.

She had never thought of any such plan as had actually sprung to light. And she understood Sorell's opposition.

All the same, her heart sang over it. When she had asked Radowitz and Douglas to meet, each unbeknown to the other, when she had sent away the kind old aunts and prepared it all, she had reckoned on powers of feeling in Falloden, in which apparently only she and Aunt Marcia believed; and she had counted on the mystical and religious fervour she had long since discovered in Radowitz. That night—after Sir Arthur's death—she had looked tremblingly into the boy's very soul, had perceived his wondering sense of a special message to him through what had happened, from a God who suffered and forgives.

Yes, she had tried to make peace.

And she guessed—the tears blinding her as she walked—at the true meaning of Falloden's sudden impulse, and Otto's consent. Falloden's was an impulse of repentance; and Otto's had been an impulse of pardon, in the Christian sense. "If I am to die, I will die at peace with him." Was that the thought—the tragic and touching thought—in the boy's mind?

As to Falloden, could he do it?—could he rise to the height of what was offered him? She prayed he might; she believed he could.

Her whole being was aflame. Douglas was no longer in love with her; that was clear. What matter, if he made peace with his own soul? As for her, she loved him with her whole heart, and meant to go on loving him, whatever any one might say. And that being so, she would of course never marry.

Could she ever make Nora understand the situation? By letter, it was certainly useless to try!

PART III

XVI

CONSTANCE BLEDLOW stepped out of the Bletchley train into the crowded Oxford station. Annette was behind her. As they made their way towards the luggage van, Connie saw a beckoning hand and face. They belonged to Nora Hooper, and in another minute Connie found herself taken possession of by her cousin. Nora was deeply sunburnt. Her colour was more garishly red and brown, her manner more trenchant than ever. At sight of Connie her face flushed with a sudden smile, as though the owner of the face could not help it. Yet they had only been a few minutes together before Connie had discovered that, beneath the sunburn, there was a look of tension and distress, and that the young brown eyes, usually so bright and bold, were dulled with fatigue. But to notice such things in Nora was only to be scorned. Connie held her tongue.

"Can't you leave Annette to bring the luggage, and let us walk up?" said Nora.

Connie assented, and the two girls were soon in the long and generally crowded street leading to the Cornmarket. Nora gave rapidly a little necessary information. Term had just begun, and Oxford was "dreadfully full." She had got another job of copying work at the Bodleian, for which she was being paid by the University Press, and what with that and the work for her coming exam, she was "pretty driven." But that was what suited her. Alice and her mother were "all right."

"And Uncle Ewen?" said Connie.

Nora paused a moment.

"Well, you won't think he looks any the better for his holiday," she said at last, with an attempt at a laugh. "And of course he's doing ten times too much work. Hang work! I loathe work: I want to 'do nothing forever and ever.' "

"Why don't you set about it then?" laughed Connie.

"Because——" Nora began impetuously; and then shut her lips. She diverged to the subject of Mr. Pryce. They had not seen or heard anything of him for weeks, she said, till he had paid them an evening call, the night before, the first evening of the new term.

Connie interrupted.

"Oh, but that reminds me," she said eagerly, "I've got an awfully nice letter—to-day—from Lord Glaramara. Mr. Pryce is to go up and see him."

Nora whistled.

"You have! Well, that settles it. He'll now graciously allow himself to propose. And then we shall all pretend to be greatly astonished. Alice will cry, and mother will say she 'never expected to lose her daughter so soon.' What a humbug everybody is!" said the child, bitterly, with more emphasis than grammar.

"But suppose he doesn't get anything!" cried Connie, alarmed at such a sudden jump from the possible to the certain.

"Oh, but he will! He's the kind of person that gets things," said Nora contemptuously. "Well, we wanted a bit of good news!"

Connie jumped at the opening.

"Dear Nora!—have things been going wrong? You look awfully tired. Do tell me!"

Nora checked herself at once. "Oh, not much more than usual," she said repellently. "And what about you, Connie? Aren't you very bored to be coming back here, after all your grand times?"

They had emerged into the Corn. Before them was the old Church of St. Mary Magdalen, and the modern pile of Balliol. In the distance stretched the Broad, over which the October evening was darkening fast; the Sheldonian in the far distance, with its statued railing; and the gates of Trinity on the left. The air was full of bells, and the streets of undergraduates; a stream of young men taking fresh possession, as it were, of the grey city, which was their own as soon as they chose to come back to it. The Oxford damp, the Oxford mist, was everywhere, pierced by lamps, and window-lights, and the last red of a stormy sunset.

Connie drew in her breath.

"No, I am not sorry. I am very glad to be back—though my aunts have been great dears to me."

"I'll bet anything Annette isn't glad to be back—after the Langmoors!" said Nora grimly.

Connie laughed.

"She'll soon settle in. What do you think?" She slipped her arm into her cousin's. "I'm coming down to breakfast!"

"You're not! I never heard such nonsense! Why should you?"

Connie sighed.

"I think I must begin to do something."

"Do something! For goodness' sake, don't!" Nora's voice was fierce. "I did think you might be trusted!"

"To carry out your ideals? So kind of you!"

"If you take to muddling about with books and lectures and wearing ugly clothes, I give you up," said Nora firmly.

"Nora, dear, I'm the most shocking ignoramus. Mayn't I learn something?"

"Mr. Sorell may teach you Greek. I don't mind that."

Connie sighed again, and Nora stole a look at the small pale face under the sailor hat. It seemed to her that her cousin had somehow grown beautiful in these months of absence. On her arrival in May, Connie's good looks had been a freakish and variable thing, which could be often and easily disputed. She could always make a certain brilliant or bizarre effect, by virtue of her mere slenderness and delicacy, combined with the startling beauty of her eyes and hair. But the touch of sarcasm, of a half-hostile remoteness, in her look and manner, were often enough to belie the otherwise delightful impression of first youth, to suggest something older and sharper than her twenty years had any right to be. It meant that she had been brought up in a world of elder people, sharing from her teens in its half-amused, half-sceptical judgments of men and things. Nothing was to be seen of it in her roused moments of pleasure or enthusiasm; at other times it jarred, as though one caught a glimpse of autumn in the spring.

But since she and Nora had last met, something had happened. Some heat of feeling or of sympathy had fused in her the elements of being; so that a more human richness and warmth, a deeper and tenderer charm breathed from her whole aspect. Nora, though so much the younger, had hitherto been the comforter and sustainer of Connie; now for the first time, the tired girl felt an impulse—firmly held back—to throw her arms round Connie's neck and tell her own troubles.

She did not betray it, however. There were so many things she wanted to know. First—how was it that Connie had come back so soon? Nora understood there were invitations to the Tamworths and others. Mr. Sorell had reported that the Langmoors wished to carry their niece with them on a round of country-house visits in the autumn, and that Connie had firmly stuck to it that she was due at Oxford for the beginning of term.

"Why didn't you go," said Nora, half scoffing—"with all those frocks wasting in the drawers?"

Connie retorted that, as for parties, Oxford had seemed to her in the summer term the most gay and giddy place she had ever been in, and that she had always understood that in the October and Lent terms people dined out every night.

"But all the same—one can think a little here," she said slowly.

"You didn't care a bit about that when you first came!" cried Nora. "You despised us because we weren't soldiers, or diplomats, or politicians. You thought we were a little priggish, provincial world where nothing mattered. You were sorry for us because we had only books and ideas!"

"I wasn't!" said Connie indignantly. "Only I didn't think Oxford was everything—and it isn't! Nora!"—she looked round the Oxford street with a sudden ardour, her eyes running over the groups of undergraduates hurrying back to hall—"do you think these English boys could ever—well, fight—and die—for what you call ideas—for their country—as Otto Radowitz could die for Poland?"

"Try them!" The reply rang out defiantly. Connie laughed.

"They'll never have the chance. Who'll ever attack England? If we had only something—something splendid, and not too far away!—to look back upon, as the Italians look back on Garibaldi—or to long and to suffer for, as the Poles long and suffer for Poland!"

"We shall some day!" said Nora hopefully. "Mr. Sorell says every nation gets its turn to fight for its life. I suppose Otto Radowitz has been talking Poland to you?"

"He talks it—and he lives it," said Connie, with emphasis. "It's marvellous!—it shames one."

Nora shrugged her shoulders.

"But what can he do—with his poor hand! You know Mr. Sorell has taken a cottage for him at Boar's Hill—above Hinksey?"

Yes, Connie knew. She seemed suddenly on her guard.

"But he can't live alone?" said Nora. "Who on earth's going to look after him?"

Connie hesitated. Down a side street she perceived the stately front of Marmion, and at the same moment a tall man emerging from the dusk crossed the street and entered the Marmion gate. Her heart leapt. No! Absurd! He and Otto had not arrived yet. But already the Oxford dark, and the beautiful Oxford distances were peopled for her with visions and prophecies of hope. The old and famous city, that had seen so much youth bloom and pass, spoke magic things to her with its wise, friendly voice.

Aloud, she said—

"You haven't heard? Mr. Falloden's going to live with him."

Nora stopped in stupefaction.

"What?"

Connie repeated the information—adding—

"I dare say Mr. Sorell didn't speak of it to you, because—he hates it."

"I suppose it's just a theatrical *coup*," said Nora, passionately, as they walked on—"to impress the public."

"It isn't!—it isn't anything of the kind. And Otto had only to say no."

"It's ridiculous!—preposterous! They'll clash all day long."

Connie replied with difficulty, as though she had so pondered and discussed this matter with herself that every opinion about it seemed equally reasonable.

"I don't think so. Otto wishes it."

"But why—but *why*?" insisted Nora. "Oh, Connie!—as if Douglas Falloden could look after anybody but himself!"

Then she repented a little. Connie smiled, rather coldly.

"He looked after his father," she said quietly. "I told you all that in my letters. And you forget how it was—that he and Otto came across each other again."

Nora warmly declared that she had not forgotten it, but that it did not seem to her to have anything to do with the extraordinary proposal that the man more responsible than any one else for the maiming—possibly for the death—of Otto Radowitz, if all one heard about him were true, should be now installed as his companion and guardian during these critical months.

She talked with obvious and rather angry common sense, as one who had not passed her eighteenth birthday for nothing.

But Connie fell silent She would not discuss it, and Nora was obliged to let the subject drop.

Mrs. Hooper, whose pinched face had grown visibly older, received her husband's niece with an evident wish to be kind. Alice, too, was almost affectionate, and Uncle Ewen came hurrying out of his study to greet her. But Connie had not been an hour in the house before she had perceived that everybody in it was preoccupied and unhappy; unless, indeed, it were Alice, who had evidently private thoughts of her own, which, to a certain extent, released her from the family worries.

What was the matter? She was determined to know.

It happened that she and Alice went up to bed together. Nora had been closeted with her father in the little schoolroom on the ground floor, since nine o'clock, and when Connie proposed to look in and wish them good night, Alice said uncomfortably—

"Better not. They're—they're very busy."

Connie ruminated. At the top of the stairs, she turned—

"Look here—do come in to me, and have a talk!"

Alice agreed, after a moment's hesitation. There had never been any beginnings of intimacy between her and Connie, and she took Connie's advance awkwardly.

The two girls were however soon seated in Connie's room, where a blazing fire defied the sudden cold of a raw and bleak October. The light danced on Alice's beady black eyes, and arched brows, on her thin but very red lips, on the bright patch of colour in each cheek. She was more than ever like a Watteau sketch in black chalk, heightened with red, and the dress she wore, cut after the pattern of an eighteenth-century sacque, according to an Oxford fashion of that day, fell in admirably with the natural effect. Connie had very soon taken off her tea-gown, loosened and shaken out her hair, and put on a white garment in which she felt at ease. Alice noticed, as Nora had done, that Connie was fast becoming a beauty; but whether the indisputable fact was to be welcomed or resented had still to be decided.

Connie had no sooner settled herself on the small sofa she had managed to fit into her room than she sprang up again.

"Stupid!—where are those letters!" She rummaged in various drawers and bags, hit upon what she wanted, after an impetuous hunt, and returned to the fire.

"Do you know I think Mr. Pryce has a good chance of that post? I got this to-day."

She held out a letter, smiling. Alice flushed and took it. It was from Lord Glaramara, and it concerned that same post in the Conservative Central Office on which Herbert Pryce had had his eyes for some time. The man holding it had been "going" for months, but was now, at last, gone. The post was vacant, and Connie, who had a pretty natural turn for wire-pulling, fostered by her Italian bringing up, had been trying her hand, both with the Chancellor and her Uncle Langmoor.

"You little intriguer!" wrote Lord Glaramara—"I will do what I can. Your man sounds very suitable. If he isn't, I can tell you plainly he won't get the post. Neither political party can afford to employ fools just now. But if he is what you say—well, we shall see! Send him up to see me, at the House of Lords, almost any evening next week. He'll have to take his chance, of course, of finding me free. If I cotton to him, I'll send him on to somebody else. And—*don't talk about it!* Your letter was just like your mother. She had an art of doing these things!"

Alice read and reread the note. When she looked up from it, it was with a rather flustered face.

"Awfully good of you, Connie! May I show it—to Mr. Pryce?"

"Yes—but get it back. Tell him to write to Lord Glaramara to-morrow. Well, now then"—Connie discovered and lit a cigarette, the sight of which stirred in Alice a kind of fascinated disapproval,—"now then, tell me what's the matter!—why Uncle Ewen looks as if he hadn't had a day's rest since last term, and Nora's so glum—and why he and she go sitting up at night together when they ought to be in their beds?"

Connie's little woman-of-the-world air—very evident in this speech—which had always provoked Alice in their earlier acquaintance, passed now unnoticed. Miss Hooper sat perplexed and hesitating, staring into the fire. But with that note in her pocket, Alice felt herself at once in a new and detached position towards her family.

"It's money, of course," she said at last, her white brow puckering. "It's not only bills—they're dreadfully worrying!—we seem never to get free from them, but it's something else—something quite new—which has only happened lately. There is an old loan from the bank that has been going on for years. Father had almost forgotten it, and now they're pressing him. It's dreadful. They know we're so hard up."

Connie in her turn looked perplexed. It was always difficult for her to realise financial trouble on a small scale. Ruin on the Falloden scale was intelligible to one who had heard much talk of the bankruptcies of some of the great Roman families. But the carking care that may come from lack of a few hundred pounds, this the Risboroughs' daughter had to learn; and she put her mind to it eagerly.

She propped her small chin on her hands, while Alice told her tale. Apparently the improvement in the family finance, caused by Connie's three hundred, had been the merest temporary thing. The Reader's creditors had been held off for a few months; but the rain of tradesmen's letters had been lately incessant. And the situation had been greatly worsened by a blow which had fallen just before the opening of term.

In a former crisis, five years before this date, a compassionate cousin, one of the few well-to-do relations that Mrs. Hooper possessed, had come to the rescue, and had given his name to the Hoopers' bankers as guarantee for a loan of £500. The loan was to have been repaid by yearly instalments. But the instalments had not been paid, and the cousin had most unexpectedly died of apoplexy during September, after three days' illness. His heir would have nothing to say to the guarantee, and the bank was pressing for repayment, in terms made all the harsher by the existence of an overdraft, which the local manager knew in his financial conscience ought not to have been allowed. His letters were now so many sword-thrusts; and post-time was a time of terror.

"Father doesn't know what to do," said Alice despondently. "He and Nora spend all their time trying to think of some way out. Father got his salary the other day, and never put it into the bank at all. We must have something to live on. None"—she hesitated—"none of the tradesmen will give us any credit." She flushed deeply over the confession.

"Goodness!" said Connie, opening her eyes still wider.

"But if Nora knows that I've been telling you"—cried Alice—"she'll never forgive me. She made me promise I wouldn't tell you. But how can you help knowing? If father's made a bankrupt, it wouldn't be very nice for you! How could you go on living with us? Nora thinks she's going to earn money—that father can sell two wretched little books—and we can go and live in a tiny house on the Cowley Road—and—and—all sorts of absurd things!"

"But why is it Nora that has to settle all these things?" asked Connie in bewilderment. "Why doesn't your mother——"

"Oh, because mother doesn't know anything about the bills," interrupted Alice. "She never can do a sum—or add up anything—and I'm no use at it either. Nora took it all over last year, and she won't let even me help her. She makes out the most wonderful statements—she made out a fresh one to-day—that's why she had a headache when she came to meet you. But what's the good of statements? They won't pay the bank."

"But why—why——" repeated Connie, and then stopped, lest she should hurt Alice's feelings.

"Why did we get into debt? I'm sure I don't know!" Alice shook her head helplessly. "We never seemed to have anything extravagant."

These things were beyond Connie's understanding. She gave it up. But her mind impetuously ran forward.

"How much is wanted altogether?"

Alice, reluctantly, named a sum not much short of a thousand pounds.

"Isn't it awful?"

She sighed deeply. Yet already she seemed to be talking of other people's affairs!

"We can't ever do it. It's hopeless. Papa's taken two little school-books to do. They'll kill him with work, and will hardly bring in anything. And he's full up with horrid exams and lectures. He'll break down, and it all makes him so miserable, because he can't really do the work the University pays him to do. And he's never been abroad—even to Rome. And as to Greece! It's dreadful!" she repeated mechanically.

Connie sprang up and began to pace the little room. The firelight played on her mop of brown hair, bringing out its golden shades, and on the charming pensiveness of her face. Alice watched her, thinking "She could do it all, if she chose!" But she didn't dare to say anything, for fear of Nora.

Presently Connie gave a great stretch.

"It's damnable!" she said, with energy.

Alice's instinct recoiled from the strong word. It wasn't the least necessary, she thought, to talk in that way.

Connie made a good many more enquiries—elicited a good many more facts. Then suddenly she brought her pacing to a stop.

"Look here—we must go to bed!—or Nora will be after us."

Alice went obediently. As soon as the door had shut upon her, Connie went to a drawer in her writing table, and took out her bank-book. It had returned that morning and she had not troubled to look at it. There was always enough for what she wanted.

Heavens!—what a balance. She had quite forgotten a wind-fall which had come lately—some complicated transaction relating to a great industrial company in which she had shares and which had lately been giving birth to other subsidiary companies, and somehow the original shareholders, of whom Lord Risborough had been one, or their heirs and representatives, had profited greatly by the business. It had all been managed for her by her father's lawyer, and of course by Uncle Ewen. The money had been paid temporarily in to her own account, till the lawyer could make some enquiries about a fresh investment.

But it was her own money. She was entitled to—under the terms of her father's letter to Uncle Ewen—to do what she liked with it. And even without it, there was enough in the bank. Enough for this—and for another purpose also, which lay even closer to her heart.

"I don't want any more new gowns for six months," she decided peremptorily. "It's disgusting to be so well off. Well, now,—I wonder—I wonder where Nora keeps those statements that Alice talks about?"

In the schoolroom of course. But not under lock and key. Nobody ever locked drawers in that house. It was part of the general happy-go-luckishness of the family.

Connie made up the fire, and sat over it, thinking hard. A new cheque-book, too, had arrived with the bank-book. That was useful.

She waited till she heard the schoolroom door open, and Nora come upstairs, followed soon by the slow and weary step of Uncle Ewen. Connie had already lowered her gas before Nora reached the top landing.

The house was very soon silent. Connie turned her light on again, and waited. By the time Big Ben had struck one o'clock, she thought it would be safe to venture.

She opened her door with trembling, careful fingers, slipped off her shoes, took a candle and stole downstairs. The schoolroom door creaked odiously. But soon she was inside and looking about her.

There was Nora's table, piled high with the books and note-books of her English literature work. Everything else had been put away. But the top drawer of the table was unlocked. There was a key in it, but it would not turn, being out of repair, like so much else in the house.

Connie, full of qualms, slowly opened the drawer. It was horrid—horrid—to do such things!—but what other way was there? Nora must be presented with the *fait accompli*, otherwise she would upset everything—poor old darling!

Some loose sheets lay on the top of the papers in the drawer. The first was covered with figures and calculations that told nothing. Connie lifted it, and there, beneath, lay Nora's latest "statement," at which she and her father had no doubt been working that very night. It was headed "List of Liabilities," and in it every debt, headed by the bank claim which had broken the family back, was accurately and clearly stated in Nora's best hand. The total at the foot evoked a low whistle from Connie. How had it come about? In spite of her luxurious bringing up, there was a shrewd element—an element of competence—in the girl's developing character, which was inclined to suggest that there need be no more difficulty in living on seven hundred a year than seven thousand, if you knew you had to do it. Then she rebuked herself fiercely for a prig—"You just try it!—you Pharisee, you!" And she thought of her own dressmakers' and milliners' bills, and became in the end quite pitiful over Aunt Ellen's moderation. After all it might have been two thousand instead of one! Of course it was all Aunt Ellen's muddling, and Uncle Ewen's absent-mindedness.

She shaded her candle, and in a guilty hurry copied down the total on a slip of paper lying on the table, and took the address of Uncle

Ewen's bank from the outside of the pass-book lying beside the bills. Having done that, she closed the drawer again, and crept upstairs like the criminal she felt herself. Her small feet in their thin stockings seemed to her excited ears to be making the most hideous and unnatural noise on every step. If Nora heard!

At last she was safe in her own room again. The door was locked, and the more agreeable part of the crime began. She drew out the new cheque-book lying in her own drawer, and very slowly and deliberately wrote a cheque. Then she put it up, with a few covering words—anxiously considered—and addressed the envelope to the Oxford branch of a well-known banking firm, her father's bankers, to which her own account had been transferred on her arrival at Oxford. Ewen Hooper had scrupulously refrained from recommending his own bank, lest he should profit indirectly by his niece's wealth.

"Annette shall take it," she thought, "first thing. Oh, what a row there'll be!"

And then, uneasily pleased with her performance, she went to bed.

And she had soon forgotten all about her raid upon Uncle Ewen's affairs. Her thoughts floated to a little cottage on the hills, and its two coming inhabitants. And in her dream she seemed to hear herself say—"I oughtn't to be meddling with other people's lives like this. I don't know enough. I'm too young! I want somebody to show me—I do!"

The following day passed heavily in the Hooper household. Nora and her father were closeted together all the morning; and there was a sense of brooding calamity in the air. Alice and Connie avoided each other, and Connie asked no questions. After luncheon Sorell called. He found Connie in the drawing-room alone, and gave her the news she was pining for. As Nora had reported, a cottage on Boar's Hill had been taken. It belonged to the head of an Oxford college, who had spent the preceding winter there for his health, but had now been ordered abroad. It was very small, pleasantly furnished, and had a glorious view over Oxford in the hollow, the wooded lines of

Garsington and Nuneham, and the distant ridges of the Chilterns. Radowitz was expected the following day, and his old college servant, with a woman to cook and do housework, had been found to look after him. He was working hard, at his symphony, and was on the whole much the same in health—very frail and often extremely irritable; with alternations of cheerfulness and depression.

"And Mr. Falloden?" Connie ventured.

"He's coming soon—I didn't ask," said Sorell shortly. "That arrangement won't last long."

Connie hesitated.

"But don't wish it to fail!" she said piteously.

"I think the sooner it is over the better," said Sorell, with rather stern decision. "Falloden ought never to have made the proposal, and it was mere caprice in Otto to accept it. But you know what I think. I shall watch the whole thing very anxiously; and try to have some one ready to put into Falloden's place—when it breaks down. Mrs. Mulholland and I have it in hand. She'll take Otto up to the cottage to-morrow, and means to mother Radowitz as much as he'll let her. Now then"—he changed the subject with a smile—"are you going to enjoy your winter term?"

His dark eyes, as she met them, were full of an anxious affection.

"I have forgotten all my Greek!"

"Oh no—not in a month. Prepare me a hundred lines of the 'Odyssey,' Book VI.! Next week I shall have some time. This first week is always a drive. Miss Nora says she'll go on again."

"Does she? She seems so—so busy."

"Ah, yes—she's got some work for the University Press. Plucky little thing! But she mustn't overdo it."

Connie dropped the subject. These conferences in the study, which had gone on all day, had nothing to do with Nora's work for the Press—that she was certain of. But she only said—holding out her hands, with the free gesture that was natural to her—

"I wish some one would give me the chance of 'overdoing it'! Do set me to work—hard work! The sun never shines here."

Her eyes wandered petulantly to the rainy sky outside, and the high-walled college opposite.

"Southerner! Wait till you see it shining on the Virginia creeper in our garden quad. Oxford is a dream in October!—just for a week or two, till the leaves fall. November is dreary, I admit. All the same—try and be happy!"

He looked at her gravely and tenderly. She coloured a little as she withdrew her hands.

"Happy? That doesn't matter—does it? But perhaps for a change—one might try——"

"Try what?"

"Well!"—she laughed, but he thought there were tears in her eyes—"to do something—for somebody—occasionally."

"Ask Mrs. Mulholland! She has a genius for that kind of thing. Teach some of her orphans!"

"I couldn't! They'd find me out."

Sorell, rather puzzled, suggested that she might become a Home Student like Nora, and go in for a Literature or Modern History Certificate. Connie, who was now sitting moodily over a grate with no fire in it, with her chin in her hands, only shook her head.

"I don't know anything—I never learnt anything. And everybody here's so appallingly clever!"

Then she declared that she would go and have tea with the Master of Beaumont, and ask his advice. "He told me to learn something"—the tone was one of depression, passing into rebellion—"but I don't want to learn anything!—I want to do something!"

Sorell laughed at her.

"Learning is doing!"

"That's what Oxford people think," she said defiantly. "I don't agree with them."

"What do you mean by 'doing'?"

Connie poked an imaginary fire.

"Making myself happy"—she said slowly, "and—and a few other people!"

Sorell laughed again. Then rising to take his leave, he stooped over her.

"Make me happy by undoing that stroke of yours at Boar's Hill!"

Connie raised herself, and looked at him steadily.

Then gravely and decisively she shook her head.

"Not at all! I shall keep an eye on it!—so must you!"

Then, suddenly, she smiled—the softest, most radiant smile, as though some hope within, far within, looked out. It was gone in a moment, and Sorell went his way; but as one who had been the spectator of an event.

After his departure Connie sat on in the cold room, thinking about Sorell. She was devoted to him—he was the noblest, dearest person. She wished dreadfully to please him. But she wasn't going to let him—well, what?—to let him interfere with that passionate purpose which seemed to be beating in her, and through her, like a living thing, though as yet she had but vaguely defined it even to herself.

After tea, which Mrs. Hooper dispensed with red eyes, and at which neither Nora nor Dr. Hooper appeared, Constance found a novel, and established herself in the deserted schoolroom. She couldn't go out. She was on the watch for a letter that might arrive. The two banks were only a stone's throw apart. The local post should deliver that letter about six.

Once Nora looked in to find a document, and was astonished to see Connie there. But she was evidently too harassed and miserable to talk. Connie listened uneasily to the opening and shutting of a drawer, with which she was already acquainted. Then Nora disappeared again. What were they trying to do, poor dears!—Nora, and Uncle Ewen? What could they do?

The autumn evening darkened slowly. At last!—a ring and a double knock. The study door opened, and Connie heard Nora's step, and the click of the letter-box. The study door closed again.

Connie put down her novel and listened. Her hands trembled. She was full indeed of qualms and compunctions. Would they be angry with her? She had meant it well.

Footsteps approaching—not Nora's.

Uncle Ewen stood in the doorway—looking very pale and strained.

"Connie, would you mind coming into my study? Something rather strange has happened."

Connie got up and slowly followed him across the hall. As she entered the study, she saw Nora, with blazing eyes and cheeks, standing by her father's writing-table, aglow with anger or excitement—or both. She looked at Connie as at an enemy, and Connie flushed a bright pink.

Uncle Ewen shut the door, and addressed his niece. "My dear Connie, I want you, if you can—to throw some light on a letter I have just received. Both Nora and I suspect your hand in it. If so, you have done something I—I can't permit."

He held out a letter, which Connie took like a culprit. It was a communication from his Oxford bankers to Professor Hooper, to the effect that, a sum of £1100 having been paid in to his credit by a person who desired to remain unknown, his debt to them was covered, and his account showed a balance of about six hundred pounds.

"My dear!"—his voice and hand shook—"is that your doing?"

"Of course it is!" interrupted Nora passionately. "Look at her, father! How dared you, Connie, do such a thing without a word to father! It's a shame—a disgrace! We could have found a way out—we could!"

And the poor child, worn out with anxiety and lack of sleep, and in her sensitive pride and misery ready to turn on Connie and rend her for having dared thus to play Lady Bountiful without warning or permission, sank into a chair, covered her face with her hands, and burst out sobbing.

Connie handed back the letter, and hung her head. "Won't you—won't you let the person—who—sent the money remain unknown, Uncle Ewen?—as they wished to be?"

Uncle Ewen sat down before his writing-table, and he also buried his face in his hands. Connie stood between them—as it were a prisoner at the bar—looking now very white and childish.

"Dear Uncle Ewen——"

"How did you guess?" said Nora vehemently, uncovering her face—"I never said a word to you!"

Connie gave a tremulous laugh.

"Do you think I couldn't see that you were all dreadfully unhappy about something? I—I made Alice tell me——"

"Alice is a sieve!" cried Nora. "I knew, father, we could never trust her."

"And then"—Connie went on—"I—I did an awful thing. I'd better tell you. I came and looked at Nora's papers—in the schoolroom drawer. I saw that." She pointed penitentially to a sheet of figures lying on the study table.

Both Nora and her uncle looked up in amazement, staring at her.

"It was at night," she said hurriedly—"last night. Oh, I put it all back!"—she turned, pleading, to Nora—"just as I found it. You shouldn't be angry with me—you shouldn't indeed!"

Then her own voice began to shake. She came and laid her hand on her uncle's shoulder.

"Dear Uncle Ewen—you know, I had that extra money! What did I want with it? Just think—if it had been mamma! Wouldn't you have let her help? You know you would! You couldn't have been so unkind. Well then, I knew it would be no good, if I came and asked you—you wouldn't have let me. So I—well, I just did it!"

Ewen Hooper rose from his table in great distress of mind.

"But, my dear Connie—you are my ward—and I am your guardian! How can I let you give me money?"

"It's my own money," said Connie firmly. "You know it is. Father wrote to you to say I might spend it now, as I liked—all there was, except the capital of my two thousand a year, which I mayn't spend—till I am twenty-five. This has nothing to do with that. I'm quite free—and so are you. Do you think"—she drew herself up indignantly—"that you're going to make me happy—by turning me out, and all—all of you going to rack and ruin—when I've got that silly money lying in the bank? I won't have it! I don't want to go and live in the Cowley Road! I won't go and live in the Cowley Road! You promised father and mother to look after me, Uncle Ewen, and it isn't looking after me——"

"You can't reproach me on that score as much as I do myself!" said Ewen Hooper, with emotion. "There's something in that I admit—there's something in that."

He began to pace the room. Presently, pausing beside Connie, he plunged into an agitated and incoherent account of the situation—of the efforts he had made to get even some temporary help—and of the failure of all of them. It was the confession of a weak and defeated man; and as made by a man of his age to a girl of Connie's, it was extremely painful. Nora hid her eyes again, and Connie got paler and paler.

At last she went up to him, holding out again appealing hands.

"Please don't tell me any more! It's all right. I just love you, Uncle Ewen—and—and Nora! I want to help! It makes me happy. Oh, why won't you let me!"

He wavered.

"You dear child!" There was a silence. Then he resumed—as though feeling his way—

"It occurs to me that I might consult Sorell. If he thought it right—if we could protect you from loss——!"

Connie sprang at him and kissed him in delight.

"Of course!—that'll do splendidly! Mr. Sorell will see, at once, it's the right thing for me, and my happiness. I can't be turned out—I really can't! So it's settled. Yes—it's settled!—or it will be directly—and nobody need bother any more—need they? But—there's one condition."

Ewen Hooper looked at her in silence.

"That you—you and Nora—go to Rome this Christmas time, this very Christmas, Uncle Ewen! I think I put in enough—and I can give you such a lot of letters!"

She laughed joyously, though she was very near crying.

"I have never been able to go to Rome—or Athens—never!" he said, in a low voice, as he sat down again at his table. All the thwarted hopes, all the sordid cares of years were in the quiet words.

"Well, now you're going!" said Connie shyly. "Oh, that would be ripping! You'll promise me that—you must, please!"

Silence again. She approached Nora, timidly.

"Nora!"

Nora rose. Her face was stained with tears.

"It's all wrong," she said heavily—"it's all wrong. But—I give in. What I said was a lie. There is nothing else in the world that we could possibly do."

And she rushed out of the room without another word. Connie looked wistfully after her. Nora's pain in receiving had stirred in her the shame-faced distress in giving that lives in generous souls. "Why should I have more than they?"

She stole out after Nora. Ewen Hooper was left staring at the letter from his bankers, and trying to collect his thoughts. Connie's voice was still in his ears. It had all the sweetness of his dead sister's.

Connie was reading in her room before dinner. She had shut herself up there, feeling rather battered by the emotions of the afternoon, when she heard a knock that she knew was Nora's.

"Come in!"

Nora appeared. She had had her storm of weeping in private and got over it. She was now quite composed, but the depression, the humiliation even, expressed in her whole bearing dismayed Connie afresh.

Nora took a seat on the other side of the fire. Connie eyed her uneasily.

"Are you ever going to forgive me, Nora?" she said, at last.

Nora shrugged her shoulders.

"You couldn't help it. I see that."

"Thank you," said Connie meekly.

"But what I can't forgive is that you never said a word——"

"To you? That you might undo it all? Nora, you really are an absurd person!" Connie sprang up, and came to kneel by the fire, so that she might attack her cousin at close quarters. "We're told it's 'more blessed to give than to receive.' Not when you're on the premises,

Nora! I really don't think you need make me feel such an outcast! I say—how many nights have you been awake lately?"

Nora's lip quivered a little.

"That doesn't matter," she said shortly.

"Yes, but it does matter! You promised to be my friend—and—you have been treating me abominably!" said Connie, with flashing eyes.

Nora feebly defended herself, but was soon reduced to accept a pair of arms thrown round her, and a soft shoulder on which to rest an aching head.

"I'm no good," she said despairingly. "I give up—everything."

"That's all right!" Connie's tone was extremely cheerful. "Which means, I hope, that you'll give up that absurd copying in the Bodleian. You get about twopence halfpenny for it, and it'll cost you your first-class. How are you going to get a First I should like to know, with your head full of bills, and no sleep at nights?"

Nora flushed fiercely.

"I want to earn my living—I mean to earn my living! And how do you know—after all"—she held Connie at arm's length—"that Mr. Sorell's going to approve of what you've done? And father won't accept, unless he does."

Connie laughed.

"Mr. Sorell will do—exactly what pleases me. Mr. Sorell"—she began to search for a cigarette—"Mr. Sorell is an angel."

A silence. Connie looked up, rather surprised.

"Don't you agree?"

"Yes," said Nora in an odd voice.

Connie observed her. A flickering light began to play in the brown eyes.

"H'm. Have you been doing some Greek already?—stealing a march on me?"

"I had a lesson last week."

"Had you? The first I've heard of it!" Connie fluttered up and down the room in her white dressing-gown, occasionally breaking into a dance-step, as though to work off a superfluity of spirits.

Finally she stopped in front of Nora, looking her up and down.

"I dare you to hide anything again from me, Nora!"

Nora sat up.

"There is nothing to hide," she said stiffly.

Connie laughed aloud; and Nora suddenly sprang from her chair, and ran out of the room.

Connie was left panting a little. Life in Medburn House seemed certainly to be running faster than of old!

"I never gave him leave to fall in love with Nora!" she thought, with an unmistakable pang of common, ordinary jealousy. She had been so long accustomed to take her property in Sorell for granted!—and the summer months had brought her into such intimate contact with him. "And he never made love to me for one moment!—nor I to him. I don't believe he's made love to Nora—I'm sure he hasn't—yet. But why didn't he tell me of that Greek lesson?"

She stood before the glass, pulling down her hair, so that it fell all about her.

"I seem to be rather cut out for fairy-godmothering!" she said pensively to the image in the glass. "But there's a good deal to do for the post!—one must admit there's a good deal to do—Nora's got to be fixed up—and all the money business. And then—then!"

She clasped her hands behind her head. Her eyelids fell, and through her slight figure there ran a throb of yearning—of tender yet despairing passion.

"If I could only mend things there, I might be some use. I don't want him to marry me—but just—just——"

Then her hands fell. She shook her head angrily. "You humbug!—you humbug! For whom are you posing now?"

XVII

FALLODEN HAD just finished a solitary luncheon in the little dining-room of the Boar's Hill cottage. There was a garden door in the room, and lighting a cigarette, he passed out through it to the terrace outside. A landscape lay before him, which has often been compared to that of the Val d'Arno seen from Fiesole, and has indeed some common points with that incomparable mingling of man's best with the best of mountain and river. It was the last week of October, and the autumn was still warm and windless, as though there were no shrieking November to come. Oxford, the beautiful city, with its domes and spires, lay in the hollow beneath the spectator, wreathed in thin mists of sunlit amethyst. Behind that ridge in the middle distance ran the river and the Nuneham woods; beyond rose the long blue line of the Chilterns. In front of the cottage the ground sank through copse and field to the river level, the hedge lines all held by sentinel trees, to which the advancing autumn had given that significance the indiscriminate summer green denies. The gravely rounded elms with their golden caps, the scarlet of the beeches, the pale lemon-yellow of the nearly naked limes, the splendid blacks of yew and fir—they were all there, mingled in the autumn cup of misty sunshine like melting jewels. And among them, the enchanted city shone, fair and insubstantial, from the depth below; as it were, the spiritual word and voice of all the scene.

Falloden paced up and down the terrace, smoking and thinking. That was Otto's open window. But Radowitz had not yet appeared that morning, and the ex-scout, who acted butler and valet to the two men, had brought word that he would come down in the afternoon, but was not to be disturbed till then.

"What lunacy made me do it?" thought Falloden, standing still at the end of the terrace which fronted the view.

He and Radowitz had been nearly three weeks together. Had he been of the slightest service or consolation to Radowitz during that time? He doubted it. That incalculable impulse which had made him propose himself as Otto's companion for the winter still persisted indeed. He was haunted still by a sense of being "under command"—directed—by a force which could not be repelled. Ill at ease, unhappy, as he was, and conscious of being quite ineffective, whether as nurse or companion, unless Radowitz proposed to "throw up," he knew that he himself should hold on; though why, he could scarcely have explained.

But the divergences between them were great; the possibilities of friction many. Falloden was astonished to find that he disliked Otto's little fopperies and eccentricities quite as much as he had ever done in college days; his finicky dress, his foreign ways in eating, his tendency to boast about his music, his country, and his forebears, on his good days, balanced by a brooding irritability on his bad days. And he was conscious that his own ways and customs were no less teasing to Radowitz; his Tory habits of thought, his British contempt for vague sentimentalisms and heroics, for all that *panache* means to the Frenchman, or "glory" to the Slav.

"Then why, in the name of common sense, are we living together?"

He could really give no answer but the answer of "necessity"—of a spiritual need—issuing from a strange tangle of circumstance. The helpless form, the upturned face of his dying father, seemed to make the centre of it, and those faint last words, so sharply, and, as it were, dynamically connected with the hateful memory of Otto's fall and cry in the Mannion Quad, and the hateful ever-present fact of his maimed life. Constance too—his scene with her on the river bank—her letter, breaking with him—and then the soft, mysterious change in her—and that passionate, involuntary promise in her eyes and voice, as they stood together in her aunts' garden—all these various elements, bitter and sweet, were mingled in the influence which was shaping his own life. He wanted to forgive himself; and he wanted Constance to forgive him, whether she married him or no. A kind of sublimated egotism, he said to himself, after all!

But Otto? What had really made him consent to take up daily life with the man to whom he owed his disaster? Falloden seemed occasionally to be on the track of an explanation, which would then vanish and evade him. He was conscious, however, that here also, Constance Bledlow was somehow concerned; and, perhaps, the Pole's mystical religion. He asked himself, indeed, as Constance had already done, whether some presentiment of doom, together with the Christian doctrines of forgiveness and vicarious suffering, were not at the root of it? There had been certain symptoms apparent during Otto's last weeks at Penfold known only to the old vicar, to himself and Sorell. The doctors were not convinced yet of the presence of phthisis; but from various signs, Falloden was inclined to think that the boy believed himself sentenced to the same death which had carried off his mother. Was there then a kind of calculated charity in his act also—but aiming in his case at an eternal reward?

"He wants to please God—and comfort Constance—by forgiving me. I want to please her—and relieve myself, by doing something to make up to him. He has the best of it! But we are neither of us disinterested."

The manservant came out with a cup of coffee.

"How is he?" said Falloden, as he took it, glancing up at a still curtained window.

The man hesitated.

"Well, I don't know, sir, I'm sure. He saw the doctor this morning, and told me afterwards not to disturb him till three o'clock. But he rang just now, and said I was to tell you that two ladies were coming to tea."

"Did he mention their names?"

"Not as I'm aware of, sir."

Falloden pondered a moment.

"Tell Mr. Radowitz, when he rings again, that I have gone down to the college ground for some football, and I shan't be back till after six. You're sure he doesn't want to see me?"

"No, sir, I think not. He told me to leave the blind down, and not to come in again till he rang."

Falloden put on flannels, and ran down the field paths towards Oxford and the Mannion ground, which lay on the hither side of the river. Here he took hard exercise for a couple of hours, walking on afterwards to his club in the High Street, where he kept a change of clothes. He found some old Marmion friends there, including Robertson and Meyrick, who asked him eagerly after Radowitz.

"Better come and see," said Falloden. "Give you a bread and cheese luncheon any day."

They got no more out of him. But his reticence made them visibly uneasy, and they both declared their intention of coming up the following day. In both men there was a certain indefinable change which Falloden soon perceived. Both seemed, at times, to be dragging a weight too heavy for their youth. At other times, they were just like other men of their age; but Falloden, who knew them well, realised that they were both hag-ridden by remorse for what had happened in the summer. And indeed the attitude of a large part of the college towards them, and towards Falloden, when at rare intervals he showed himself there, could hardly have been colder or more hostile. The "bloods" were broken up; the dons had set their faces steadily against any form of ragging; and the story of the maimed hand, of the wrecking of Radowitz's career, together with sinister rumours as to his general health, had spread through Oxford, magnifying as they went. Falloden met it all with a haughty silence; and was but seldom seen in his old haunts.

And presently it had become known, to the stupefaction of those who were aware of the earlier facts, that victim and tormentor, the injured and the offender, were living together in the Boar's Hill cottage where Radowitz was finishing the composition required for his second musical examination, and Falloden—having lost his father, his money and his prospects—was reading for a prize fellowship to be given by Merton in December.

It was already moonlight when Falloden began to climb the long hill again, which leads up from Folly Bridge to the height on which stood the cottage. But the autumn sunset was not long over, and in the mingled light all the rich colours of the fading woodland seemed to be suspended in, or fused with, the evening air. Forms and distances, hedges, trees, moving figures, and distant buildings were marvellously though dimly glorified; and above the golds and reds and purples of the misty earth, shone broad and large—an Achilles shield in heaven—the autumn moon, with one bright star beside it.

Suddenly, out of the twilight, Falloden became aware of a pony-carriage descending the hill, and two ladies in it. His blood leapt. He recognised Constance Bledlow, and he supposed the other lady was Mrs. Mulholland.

Constance on her side knew in a moment from the bearing of his head and shoulders who was the tall man approaching them. She spoke hurriedly to Mrs. Mulholland.

"Do you mind if I stop and speak to Mr. Falloden?"

Mrs. Mulholland shrugged her shoulders—

"Do as you like, my dear. Only don't expect me to be very forthcoming!"

Constance stopped the carriage, and bent forward.

"Mr. Falloden!"

He came up to her. Connie introduced him to Mrs. Mulholland, who bowed coldly.

"We have just been to see Otto Radowitz," said Constance. "We found him—very sadly, to-day." Her hesitating voice, with the note of wistful appeal in it, affected him strangely.

"Yes, it has been a bad day. I haven't seen him at all."

"He gave us tea, and talked a great deal. He was rather excited; but he looked wretched. And why has he turned against his doctor?"

"Has he turned against his doctor?" Falloden's tone was one of surprise. "I thought he liked him."

"He said he was a croaker, and he wasn't going to let himself be depressed by anybody—doctor or no."

Falloden was silent. Mrs. Mulholland interposed.

"Perhaps you would like to walk a little way with Mr. Falloden? I can manage the pony."

Constance descended. Falloden turned back with her towards Oxford. The pony-carriage followed at some distance behind.

Then Falloden talked freely. The presence of the light figure beside him, in its dark dress and close-fitting cap, seemed to thaw the chill of life. He began rapidly to pour out his own anxieties, his own sense of failure.

"I am the last man in the world who ought to be looking after him; I know that as well as anybody," he said, with emphasis. "But what's to be done? Sorell can't get away from college. And Radowitz knows very few men intimately. Neither Meyrick nor Robertson would be any better than I."

"Oh, not so good—not nearly so good!" exclaimed Constance eagerly. "You don't know! He counts on you."

Falloden shook his head.

"Then he counts on a broken reed. I irritate and annoy him a hundred times a day."

"Oh, no, no—he does count on you," repeated Connie in her soft, determined voice. "If you give up, he will be much—much worse off!" Then she added after a moment—"Don't give up! I—I ask you!"

"Then I shall stay."

They moved on a few steps in silence, till Connie said eagerly—

"Have you any news from Paris?"

"Yes; we wrote in the nick of time. The whole thing was just being given up for lack of funds. Now I have told him he may spend what he pleases, so long as he does the thing."

"Please—mayn't I help?"

"Thank you. It's my affair."

"It'll be very, very expensive."

"I shall manage it."

"It would be kinder"—her voice shook a little—"if I might help."

He considered it—then said doubtfully:

"Suppose you provide the records?—the things it plays? I don't know anything about music—and I have been racking my brains to think of somebody in Paris who could look after that part of it."

Constance exclaimed. Why, she had several friends in Paris, in the very thick of the musical world there! She had herself had lessons all one winter in Paris at the Conservatoire from a dear old fellow—a Pole—a pupil of Chopin in his youth, and in touch with the whole Polish colony in Paris, which was steeped in music.

"He made love to me a little"—she said, laughing—"I'm sure he'd do anything for us. I'll write at once! And there is somebody at the Embassy—why, of course, I can set all kinds of people to work!"

And her feet began to dance along the road beside him.

"We must get some Polish music"—she went on—"there's that marvellous young pianist they rave about in Paris—Paderewski. I'm sure he'd help! Otto has often talked to me about him. We must have lots of Chopin—and Liszt—though of course he wasn't a Pole!—And Polish national songs!—Otto was only telling me to-day how Chopin loved them—how he and Liszt used to go about the villages and farms and note them down. Oh, we'll have a wonderful collection!"

Her eyes shone in her small, flushed face. They walked on fast, talking and dreaming, till there was Folly Bridge in front of them, and the beginnings of Oxford. Falloden pulled up sharply.

"I must run back to him. Will you come again?"

She held out her hand. The moonlight, shining on his powerful face and curly hair, stirred in her a sudden, acute sense of delight.

"Oh yes—we'll come again. But don't leave him!—don't, please, think of it! He trusts you—he leans on you."

"It is kind of you to believe it. But I am no use!" He put her back into the carriage, bowed formally, and was gone, running up the hill at an athlete's pace.

The two ladies drove silently on, and were soon among the movement and traffic of the Oxford streets. Connie's mind was steeped in passionate feeling. Till now Falloden had touched first her senses, then her pity. Now in these painful and despondent attempts of his, to adjust himself to Otto's weakness and irritability, he was stirring sympathies and enthusiasms in her which belonged to that deepest soul in Connie which was just becoming conscious of itself. And all the more, perhaps, because in Falloden's manner towards her there was nothing left of the lover. For the moment at any rate she preferred it so. Life was all doubt, expectation, thrill—its colour heightened, its meanings underlined. And in her complete uncertainty as to what turn it would take, and how the doubt would end, lay the spell—the potent tormenting charm—of the situation.

She was sorry, bitterly sorry for Radowitz—the victim. But she loved Falloden—the offender! It was the perennial injustice of passion, the eternal injustice of human things.

When Falloden was half-way up the hill, he left the road, and took a short cut through fields, by a path which led him to the back of the cottage, where its sitting-room window opened on the garden and the view. As he approached the house, he saw that the sitting-room blinds had not been drawn, and some of the windows were still open. The whole room was brilliantly lit by fire and lamp. Otto was there alone, sitting at the piano, with his back to the approaching spectator and the moonlit night outside. He was playing something with his left hand; Falloden could see him plainly. Suddenly, he saw the boy's figure collapse. He was still sitting, but his face was buried in his arm which was lying on the piano; and through the open window, Falloden heard a sound which, muffled as it was, produced upon him a strange and horrible impression. It was a low cry, or groan—the voice of despair itself.

Falloden stood motionless. All he knew was that he would have given anything in the world to recall the past; to undo the events of that June evening in the Marmion quadrangle.

Then, before Otto could discover his presence, he went noiselessly round the corner of the house, and entered it by the front door. In the hall, he called loudly to the ex-scout, as he went upstairs, so that Radowitz might know he had come back. When he returned,

Radowitz was sitting over the fire with sheets of scribbled music-paper on a small table before him. His eyes shone, his cheeks were feverishly bright. He turned with forced gaiety at the sight of Falloden—

"Well, did you meet them on the road?"

"Lady Constance, and her friend? Yes. I had a few words with them. How are you now? What did the doctor say to you?"

"What on earth does it matter!" said Radowitz impatiently. "He is just a fool—a young one—the worst sort—I can put up with the old ones. I know my own case a great deal better than he does."

"Does he want you to stop working?" Falloden stood on the hearth, looking down on the huddled figure in the chair; himself broad and tall and curly-haired, like the divine Odysseus, when Athene had breathed ambrosial youth upon him. But he was pale, and his eyes frowned perpetually under his splendid brows.

"Some nonsense of that sort!" said Radowitz. "Don't let's talk about it."

They went into dinner, and Radowitz sent for champagne.

"That's the only sensible thing the idiot said—that I might have that stuff whenever I liked."

His spirits rose with the wine; and presently Falloden could have thought what he had seen from the dark had been a mere illusion. A review in *The Times* of a book of Polish memoirs served to let loose a flood of boastful talk, which jarred abominably on the Englishman. Under the Oxford code, to boast in plain language of your ancestors, or your own performances, meant simply that you were an outsider, not sure of your footing. If a man really had ancestors, or more brains than other people, his neighbours saved him the trouble of talking about them. Only the fools and the *parvenus* trumpeted themselves; a process in any case not worth while, since it defeated its own ends. You might of course be as insolent or arrogant as you pleased; but only an idiot tried to explain why.

In Otto, however, there was the characteristic Slav mingling of quick wits with streaks of childish vanity. He wanted passionately to make this tough Englishman feel what a great country Poland had been and would be again; what great people his ancestors had been; and what a leading part they had played in the national movements. And the more he hit against an answering stubbornness—or coolness—in Falloden, the more he held forth. So that it was an uncomfortable dinner. And again Falloden said to himself—"Why did I do it? I am only in his way. I shall bore and chill him; and I don't seem to be able to help it."

But after dinner, as the night frost grew sharper, and as Otto sat over the fire, piling on the coal, Falloden suddenly went and fetched a warm Scotch plaid of his own. When he offered it, Radowitz received it with surprise, and a little annoyance.

"I am not the least cold—thank you!"

But, presently, he had wrapped it round his knees; and some restraint had broken down in Falloden.

"Isn't there a splendid church in Cracow?" he asked casually, stretching himself, with his pipe, in a long chair on the opposite side of the fire.

"One!—five or six!" cried Otto indignantly. "But I expect you're thinking of Panna Marya. Panna means Lady. I tell you, you English haven't got anything to touch it!"

"What's it like?—what date?" said Falloden, laughing.

"I don't know—I don't know anything about architecture. But it's glorious. It's all colour and stained glass—and magnificent tombs—like the gate of heaven," said the boy with ardour. "It's the church that every Pole loves. Some of my ancestors are buried there. And it's the church where, instead of a clock striking, the hours are given out by a watchman who plays a horn. He plays an old air—ever so old—we call it the 'Heynal,' on the top of one of the towers. The only time I was ever in Cracow I heard a man at a concert—a magnificent player—improvise on it. And it comes into one of Chopin's sonatas."

He began to hum under his breath a sweet wandering melody. And suddenly he sprang up, and ran to the piano. He played the air with his left hand, embroidering it with delicate arabesques and variations, catching a bass here and there with a flying touch, suggesting marvellously what had once been a rich and complete whole. The injured hand, which had that day been very painful, lay helpless in its sling; the other flashed over the piano, while the boy's blue eyes shone beneath his vivid frieze of hair. Falloden, lying back in his chair, noticed the emaciation of the face, the hollow eyes, the contracted shoulders; and as he did so, he thought of the scene in the Magdalen ballroom—the slender girl, wreathed in pearls, and the brilliant foreign youth—dancing, dancing, with all the eyes of the room upon them.

Presently, with a sound of impatience, Radowitz left the piano. He could do nothing that he wanted to do. He stood at the window for some minutes looking out at the autumn moon, with his back to Falloden.

Falloden took up one of the books he was at work on for his fellowship exam. When Radowitz came back to the fire, however, white and shivering, he laid it down again, and once more made conversation. Radowitz was at first unwilling to respond. But he was by nature *bavard*, and Falloden played him with some skill.

Very soon he was talking fast and brilliantly again, about his artistic life in Paris, his friends at the Conservatoire or in the Quartier Latin; and so back to his childish days in Poland, and the uprising in which the family estates near Warsaw had been forfeited. Falloden found it all very strange. The seething, artistic, revolutionary world which had produced Otto was wholly foreign to him; and this patriotic passion for a dead country seemed to his English common sense a waste of force. But in Otto's cycs Poland was not dead; the White Eagle, torn and blood-stained though she was, would mount the heavens again; and in those dark skies the stars were already rising!

At eleven, Falloden got up—

"I must go and swat. It was awfully jolly, what you've been telling me. I know a lot I didn't know before."

A gleam of pleasure showed in the boy's sunken eyes.

"I expect I'm a bore," he said, with a shrug; "and I'd better go to bed."

Falloden helped him carry up his books and papers. In Otto's room, the windows were wide open, but there was a bright fire, and Bateson, the ex-scout, was waiting to help him undress. Falloden asked some questions about the doctor's orders. Various things were wanted from Oxford. He undertook to get them in the morning.

When he came back to the sitting-room, he stood some time in a brown study. He wondered again whether he had any qualifications at all as a nurse. But he was inclined to think now that Radowitz might be worse off without him; what Constance had said seemed less unreal; and his effort of the evening, as he looked back on it, brought him a certain bitter satisfaction.

The following day, Radowitz came downstairs with the course of the second movement of his symphony clear before him. He worked feverishly all day, now writing, now walking up and down, humming and thinking, now getting out of his piano—a beautiful instrument hired for the winter—all that his maimed state allowed him to get; and passing hour after hour, between an ecstasy of happy creation, and a state of impotent rage with his own helplessness. Towards sunset he was worn out, and with tea beside him which he had been greedily drinking, he was sitting huddled over the fire, when he heard some one ride up to the front door.

In another minute the sitting-room door opened, and a girl's figure in a riding habit appeared.

"May I come in?" said Connie, flushing rather pink.

Otto sprang up, and drew her in. His fatigue disappeared as though by magic. He seemed all gaiety and force.

"Come in! Sit down and have some tea! I was so depressed five minutes ago—I was fit to kill myself. And now you make the room shine—you do come in like a goddess!"

He busied himself excitedly in putting a chair for her, in relighting the spirit kettle, in blowing up the fire.

Constance meanwhile stood in some embarrassment with one hand on the back of a chair—a charming vision in her close fitting habit, and the same black *tricorne* that she had worn in the Lathom Woods, at Falloden's side.

"I came to bring you a book, Otto, the book we talked of yesterday." She held out a paper-covered volume. "But I mustn't stay."

"Oh, do stay!" he implored her. "Don't bother about Mrs. Grundy. I'm so tired and so bored. Anybody may visit an invalid. Think this is a nursing home, and you're my daily visitor. Falloden's miles away on a drag-hunt. Ah, that's right!" he cried delightedly, as he saw that she had seated herself. "Now you shall have some tea!"

She let him provide her, watching him the while with slightly frowning brows. How ill he looked—how ill! Her heart sank.

"Dear Otto, how are you? You don't seem so well to-day."

"I've been working myself to death. It won't come right—this beastly *andante*. It's too jerky—it wants *liaison*. And I can't hear it—I can't hear it!—that's the devilish part of it."

And taking his helpless hand out of the sling in which it had been resting, he struck it bitterly against the arm of his chair. The tears came to Connie's eyes.

"Don't!—you'll hurt yourself. It'll be all right—it'll be all right! You'll hear it in your mind." And bending forward under a sudden impulse, she took the maimed hand in her two hands—so small and soft—and lifting it tenderly she put her lips to it.

He looked at her in amazement.

"You do that—for me?"

"Yes. Because you are a great artist—and a brave man!" she said, gulping. "You are not to despair. Your music is in your soul—your brain. Other people shall play it for you."

He calmed down.

"At least I am not deaf, like Beethoven," he said, trying to please her. "That would have been worse. Do you know, last night Falloden and I had a glorious talk? He was awfully decent. He made me tell him all about Poland and my people. He never scoffed once. He makes me do what the doctor says. And last night—when it was freezing cold—he brought a rug and wrapped it round me. Think of that!"—he looked at her—half-shamefaced, half-laughing—*"Falloden!"*

Her eyes shone.

"I'm glad!" she said softly. "I'm glad!"

"Yes, but do you know why he's kind—why he's here at all?" he asked her abruptly.

"What's the good of silly questions?" she said hastily. "Take it as it comes."

He laughed.

"He does it—I'm going to say it!—yes, I am—and you are not to be angry—he does it because—simply—he's in love with you!"

Connie flushed again, more deeply, and he, already alarmed by his own boldness, looked at her nervously.

"You are quite wrong." Her tone was quiet, but decided. "He did it, first of all, because of what you did for his father——"

"I did nothing!" interposed Radowitz.

She took no notice.

"And secondly"—her voice shook a little—"because—he was sorry. Now—now—he is doing it"—suddenly her smile flashed out, with its touch of humour—"just simply because he likes it!"

It was a bold assertion. She knew it. But she straightened her slight shoulders, prepared to stick to it.

Radowitz shook his head.

"And what am I doing it for? Do you remember when I said to you I loathed him?"

"No—not him."

"Well, something in him—the chief thing, it seemed to me then. I felt towards him really—as a man might feel towards his murderer—or the murderer of some one else, some innocent, helpless person who had given no offence. Hatred—loathing—abhorrence!—you couldn't put it too strongly. Well then,"—he began poking at the fire, while he went on thinking aloud—"God brought us together in that strange manner. By the way"—he turned to her—"are you a Christian?"

"I—I don't know. I suppose I am."

"I am," he said firmly. "I am a practising Catholic. Catholicism with us Poles is partly religion, partly patriotism—do you understand? I go to confession—I am a communicant. And for some time I couldn't go to Communion at all. I always felt Falloden's hand on my shoulder, as he was pushing me down the stairs; and I wanted to kill him!—just that! You know our Polish blood runs hotter than yours. I didn't want the college to punish him. Not at all. It was my affair.

After I saw you in town, it grew worse—it was an obsession. When we first got to Yorkshire, Sorell and I, and I knew that Falloden was only a few miles away, I never could get quit of it—of the thought that some day—somewhere—I should kill him. I never, if I could help it, crossed a certain boundary line that I had made for myself, between our side of the moor, and the side which belonged to the Fallodens. I couldn't be sure of myself if I had come upon him unawares. Oh, of course, he would soon have got the better of me—but there would have been a struggle—I should have attacked him—and I might have had a revolver. So for your sake"—he turned to look at her with his hollow blue eyes—"I kept away. Then, one evening, I quite forgot all about it. I was thinking of the theme for the slow movement in my symphony, and I didn't notice where I was going. I walked on and on over the hill—and at last I heard a man groaning—and there was Sir Arthur by the stream. I saw at once that he was dying. There I sat, alone with him. He asked me not to leave him. He said something about Douglas, 'Poor Douglas!' And when the horrible thing came back—the last time—he just whispered, 'Pray!' and I said our Catholic prayers that our priest had said when my mother died. Then Falloden came—just in time—and instead of wanting to kill him, I waited there, a little way off, and prayed hard for myself and him! Queer, wasn't it? And afterwards—you know—I saw his mother. Then the next day, I confessed to a dear old priest, who was very kind to me, and on the Sunday he gave me Communion. He said God had been very gracious to me; and I saw what he meant. That very week I had a hemorrhage, the first I ever had."

Connie gave a sudden, startled cry. He turned again to smile at her.

"Didn't you know? No, I believe no one knew, but Sorell and the doctors. It was nothing. It's quite healed. But the strange thing was how extraordinarily happy I felt that week. I didn't hate Falloden any more. It was as though a sharp thorn had gone from one's mind. It didn't last long of course, the queer ecstatic feeling. There was always my hand—and I got very low again. But something lasted; and when Falloden said that extraordinary thing—I don't believe he meant to say it at all!—suggesting we should settle together for the winter—

I knew that I must do it. It was a kind of miracle—one thing after another—driving us."

His voice dropped. He remained gazing absently into the fire.

"Dear Otto"—said Constance softly—"you have forgiven him?"

He smiled.

"What does that matter? Have you?"

His eager eyes searched her face. She faltered under them.

"He doesn't care whether I have or not."

At that he laughed out.

"Doesn't he? I say, did you ask us both to come—on purpose—that afternoon?—in the garden?"

She was silent.

"It was bold of you!" he said, in the same laughing tone. "But it has answered. Unless, of course, I bore him to death. I talk a lot of nonsense—I can't help it—and he bears it. And he says hard, horrid things, sometimes—and my blood boils—and I bear it. And I expect he wants to break off a hundred times a day—and so do I. Yet here we stay. And it's you"—he raised his head deliberately—"it's you who are really at the bottom of it."

Constance rose trembling from her chair.

"Don't say any more, dear Otto. I didn't mean any harm. I—I was so sorry for you both."

He laughed again softly.

"You've got to marry him!" he said triumphantly. "There!—you may go now. But you'll come again soon. I know you will!"

She seemed to slip, to melt, out of the room. But he had a last vision of flushed cheeks, and half-reproachful eyes.

XVIII

On the day following Constance's visit to the Boar's Hill cottage she wrote to Radowitz:—

"Dear Otto,—I am going to ask you not to raise the subject you spoke of yesterday to me again between us. I am afraid I should find my visits a pain instead of a joy, if you did so. And Mrs. Mulholland and I want to come so much—sometimes alone, and sometimes together. We want to be mother and sister as much as we can, and you will let us! We know very well that we are poor painted things compared with real mothers and sisters. Still we should love to do our best—*I* should—if you'll let me!"

To which Otto replied:—

"Dear Constance,—(That's impudence, but you told me!)—I'll hold my tongue—though I warn you I shall only think the more. But you shan't have any cause to punish me by not coming. Good heavens!—if you didn't come!

"The coast is always clear here between two and four. I get my walk in the morning."

Two or three days a week accordingly, Conistance, or Mrs. Mulholland, or both took their way to the cottage. They did all that women with soft hearts can do for a sick man. Mrs. Mulholland managed the servants, and enquired into the food. Connie brought books and flowers, and all the Oxford gossip she could collect. Their visit was the brightness of the boy's day, and thanks to them, many efforts were made to soften his calamity. The best musical talent that Oxford could furnish was eager to serve him; and a well-known orchestra was only waiting for the completion of his symphony and the result of his examination to produce the symphony in the hall of Marmion.

Meanwhile Connie very rarely saw Falloden—except in connection either with Otto's health, or with the "Orpheus," as to which Falloden was in constant communication with the inventor, one Auguste Chaumart, living in a garret on the heights of Montmartre; while Constance herself was carrying on an eager correspondence with friends of her own or her parents, in Paris, with regard to the "records" which were to make the repertory of the Orpheus. The automatic piano—or piano-player—which some years later became the pianola, was in those days rapidly developing. The difference between it and the Orpheus lay in the fact that the piano-player required hands and feet of flesh and blood for anything more than a purely mechanical rendering of the music provided by the rolls; while in the Orpheus, expression, accent, interpretation, as given by the best pianists of the day, had been already registered in the cylinders.

On the pianola, or what preceded it—then as now—the player provided his own rendering. But the Orpheus, the precursor also of types that have since been greatly perfected, was played by an electrical mechanism, and the audience was intended to listen to Chopin or Beethoven, to Schumann or Brahms, as interpreted by the famous players of the moment, without any intervening personality.

These things are very familiar to our generation. In the eighties, they were only a vision and a possibility, and Falloden's lavish expenditure was in fact stimulating one of the first inventors.

But Connie also was playing an important part. Both Lord and Lady Risborough had possessed devoted friends in Paris, and Connie had made others of her own among the young folk with whom she had danced and flirted and talked during a happy spring with her parents in the Avenue Marceau. She had set these playfellows of hers to work, and with most brilliant success. Otto's story, as told by her vivacious letters, had gone the round. No woman of twice her age could have told it more adroitly. Otto appeared as the victim of an unfortunate accident in a college frolic; Falloden as the guardian friend; herself, as his lieutenant. It touched the romantic sense, the generous heart of musical Paris. There were many who remembered Otto's father and mother and the musical promise of the bright-haired boy. The Polish colony in Paris, a survival from the tragic days of Poland's exodus under the revolutionary skies of the thirties and the sixties, had been appealed to, and both Polish and French musicians were already in communication with Chaumart, and producing records under his direction. The young Polish marvel of the day—Paderewski—had been drawn in, and his renderings of Chopin's finest work were to provide the bulk of the rolls. Connie's dear old Polish teacher, himself a composer, was at work on a grouping of folk-songs from Poland and Lithuania—the most characteristic utterance of a martyred people.

"They are songs, *chère petite*," wrote the old man—"of revolt, of exile, and of death. There is no other folk-song like them in the world, just as there is no history in the world like Poland's. Your poor friend knows them all—has known them all from his childhood. They will speak to him of his torn country. He will hear in them the cry of the White Eagle—the White Eagle of Poland—as she soars wounded and bleeding over the southern plains, or sinks dying into the marshes and forests of Lithuania. It is in these songs that we Poles listen to the very heart-beats of our outraged country. Our songs—our music—our poets—our memories:—as a nation that is all we have—except the faith in us that never dies. *Hinc surrectura*! Yes, she shall rise again, our Poland! Our hope is in God, and in the human heart, the human conscience, that He has made. Comfort your friend. He has lost much, poor boy!—but he has still ears to hear, a brain, an imagination to conceive. Let him work still for music and for Poland—they will some day reward him!"

And as a last contribution, a young French pianist, rising rapidly into fame both as a virtuoso and a composer, was writing specially a series of variations on the lovely theme of the "Heynal"—that traditional horn-song, played every hour in the ears of Cracow, from the tower of Panna Marya—of which Otto had spoken to Falloden.

But all these things were as yet hidden from Otto. Falloden and Constance corresponded about them, in letters that anybody might have read, which had behind them, nevertheless, a secret and growing force of emotion. Even Mrs. Mulholland, who was rapidly endearing herself both to Constance and Radowitz, could only guess at what was going on, and when she did guess, held her tongue. But her relations with Falloden, which at the beginning of his residence in the cottage had been of the coldest, gradually became less strained. To his own astonishment, he found the advice of this brusque elderly woman so important to him that he looked eagerly for her coming, and obeyed her with a docility which amazed himself and her. The advice concerned, of course, merely the small matters of daily life bearing on Otto's health and comfort, and when the business was done, Falloden disappeared.

But strangely amenable, and even humble as he might appear in these affairs to those who remembered his haughty days in college, for both Constance and Mrs. Mulholland quite another fact emerged from their experience of the cottage household during these weeks:—simply this—that whatever other people might do or be, Falloden was steadily, and perhaps unconsciously, becoming master of the situation, the indispensable and protecting power of Otto's life.

How he did it remained obscure. But Mrs. Mulholland at least—out of a rich moral history—guessed that what they saw in the Boar's Hill cottage was simply the working out of the old spiritual paradox—that there is a yielding which is victory, and a surrender which is power. It seemed to her often that Radowitz was living in a constant state of half-subdued excitement, produced by the strange realisation that he and his life had become so important to Falloden that the differences of training and temperament between them, and all the little daily rubs, no longer counted; that he existed, so to speak, that Falloden might—through him—escape the burden of his own remorse. The hard, strong, able man, so much older than himself in character, if not in years, the man who had bullied and despised him, was now becoming his servant, in the sense in which Christ was the "servant" of his brethren. Not with any conscious Christian intention—far from it; but still under a kind of mysterious compulsion. The humblest duties, the most trivial anxieties, where Radowitz was concerned, fell, week by week, increasingly to Falloden's portion. A bad or a good night—appetite or no appetite—a book that Otto liked—a visit that amused him—anything that for the moment contented the starved musical sense in Otto, that brought out his gift, and his joy in it—anything that, for the moment, enabled him to forget and evade his injuries—these became, for Falloden also, the leading events of his own day. He was reading hard for his fellowship, and satisfying various obscure needs by taking as much violent exercise as possible; but there was going on in him, all the time, an intense spiritual ferment, connected with Constance Bledlow on the one side, and Otto Radowitz on the other.

Meanwhile—what was not so evident to this large-hearted observer—Otto was more than willing—he burned—to play his part. All that is mystical and passionate in the soul of a Polish Catholic, had been stirred in him by his accident, his growing premonition of short life, the bitterness of his calamity, the suddenness of his change of heart towards Falloden.

"My future is wrecked. I shall never live to be old. I shall never be a great musician. But I mean to live long enough to make Constance happy! She shall talk of me to her children. And I shall watch over her—perhaps—from another world."

These thoughts, and others like them, floated by day and night through the boy's mind; and he wove them into the symphony he was writing. Tragedy, passion, melody—these have been the Polish heritage in music; they breathe through the Polish peasant songs, as through the genius of a Chopin; they are bound up with the long agony of Polish history, with the melancholy and monotony of the Polish landscape. They spoke again through the beautiful thwarted gift of this boy of twenty, through his foreboding of early death, and through that instinctive exercise of his creative gift, which showed itself not in music alone, but in the shaping of two lives—Falloden's and Connie's.

And Constance too was living and learning, with the intensity that comes of love and pity and compunction. She was dropping all her spoilt-child airs; and the bower-bird adornments, with which she had filled her little room in Medburn House, had been gradually cleared away, to Nora's great annoyance, till it was almost as bare as Nora's own. Amid the misty Oxford streets, and the low-ceiled Oxford rooms, she was played upon by the unseen influences of that "august place," where both the great and the forgotten dead are always at work, shaping the life of the present. In those days Oxford was still praising "famous men and the fathers who begat" her. Their shades still walked her streets. Pusey was not long dead. Newman, the mere ghost of himself, had just preached a tremulous last sermon within her bounds, returning as a kind of spiritual Odysseus for a few passing hours to the place where he had once reigned as the most adored son of Oxford. Thomas Hill Green, with the ragged face, and the deep brown eyes, and the look that made pretence and cowardice ashamed, was dead, leaving a thought and a teaching behind him that his Oxford will not let die. Matthew Arnold had yet some years to live and could occasionally be seen at Balliol or at All Souls; while Christ Church and Balliol still represented the rival centres of that great feud between Liberal and Orthodox which had convulsed the University a generation before.

In Balliol, there sat a chubby-faced, quiet-eyed man, with very white hair, round whom the storms of orthodoxy had once beaten, like the surges on a lighthouse; and at Christ Church and in St. Mary's the beautiful presence and the wonderful gift of Liddon kept the old fires burning in pious hearts.

And now into this old, old place, with its thick soil of dead lives and deeds, there had come a new seed, as to which no one could tell how it would flower. Women students were increasing every term in Oxford. Groups of girl graduates in growing numbers went shyly through the streets, knowing that they had still to justify their presence in this hitherto closed world—made by men for men. There were many hostile eyes upon them, watching for mistakes. But all the generous forces in Oxford were behind them. The ablest men in the University were teaching women how to administer—how to organise. Some lecture-rooms were opening to them; some still entirely declined to admit them. And here and there were persons who had a clear vision of the future to which was trending this new eagerness of women to explore regions hitherto forbidden them in the House of Life.

Connie had no such vision, but she had a boundless curiosity and a thrilling sense of great things stirring in the world. Under Nora's lead she had begun to make friends among the women students, and to find her way into their little bed-sitting-rooms at tea time. They all seemed to her superhumanly clever, and superhumanly modest. She had been brought up indeed by two scholars; but examinations dazzled and appalled her. How they were ever passed, she could not imagine. She looked at the girls who had passed them with awe, quite unconscious the while of the glamour she herself possessed for these untravelled students, as one familiar from her childhood with the sacred places of history—Rome, Athens, Florence, Venice, Sicily. She had seen, she had trodden; and quiet eyes—sometimes spectacled—would flame, while her easy talk ran on.

But all the time there were very critical notions in her, hidden deep down.

"Do they never think about a *man*?" some voice in her seemed to be asking. "As for me, I am always thinking about a man!" And the colour would flush into her cheeks, as she meekly asked for another cup of tea.

Sometimes she would go with Nora to the Bodleian, and sit patiently beside her while Nora copied Middle-English poetry from an early manuscript, worth a king's ransom. Nora got sevenpence a "folio," of seventy-two words, for her work. Connie thought the pay scandalous for so much learning; but Nora laughed at her, and took far more pleasure in the small cheque she received at the end of term from the University Press than Connie in her quarterly dividends.

But Connie knew very well by this time that Nora was not wholly absorbed in Middle English. Often, as they emerged from the Bodleian to go home to lunch, they would come across Sorell hurrying along the Broad, his master's gown floating behind him. And he would turn his fine ascetic face towards them, and wave his hand to them from the other side of the street. And Connie would flash a look at Nora,—soft, quick, malicious—of which Nora was well aware.

But Connie rarely said a word. She was handling the situation indeed with great discretion; though with an impetuous will. She herself had withdrawn from the Greek lessons, on the plea that she was attending some English history lectures; that she must really find out who fought the battle of Hastings; and was too lazy to do anything else. Sometimes she would linger in the schoolroom till Sorell arrived, and then he would look at her wistfully, when she prepared to depart, as though to say—"Was this what I bargained for?"

But she always laughed and went. And presently as she crossed the hall again, and heard animated voices in the schoolroom, her brown eyes would show a merry satisfaction.

Meanwhile Nora was growing thinner and handsomer day by day. She was shedding awkwardness without any loss of that sub-acid sincerity that was her charm. Connie, as much as she dared, took her dressing in hand. She was never allowed to give a thing; but Annette's fingers were quick and clever, and Nora's Spartan garb was sometimes transformed by them under the orders of a coaxing or audacious Constance. The mere lifting of the load of care had let the young plant shoot. So that many persons passing Ewen Hooper's second daughter in the street would turn round now to look at her in surprise. Was that really the stout, podgy schoolgirl, who had already, by virtue of her strong personality, made a certain impression in the university town? People had been vaguely sorry for her; or vaguely thought of her as plain but good. Alice of course was pretty; Nora had the virtues. And now here she was, bursting into good looks more positive than her sister's.

The girl's heart indeed was young at last, for the neighbourhood of Connie was infectious. The fairy-godmothering of that young woman was going finely. It was the secret hope at the centre of her own life which was playing like captured sunshine upon all the persons about her. Her energy was prodigious. Everything to do with money matters had been practically settled between her and Sorell and Uncle Ewen; and settled in Connie's way, expressed no doubt in business form. And now she was insisting firmly on the holiday visit to Rome, in spite of many protests from Uncle Ewen and Nora. It was a promise, she declared. Rome—Rome—was their fate. She wrote endless letters, enquiring for rooms, and announcing their coming to her old friends. Uncle Ewen soon had the startled impression that all Rome was waiting for them, and that they could never live up to it.

Finally, Connie persuaded them to settle on rooms in a well-known small hotel, overlooking the garden-front of the Palazzo Barberini, where she had grown up. She wrote to the innkeeper, Signor B., "a very old friend of mine," who replied that the "*amici*" of the "*distintissima signorina*" should be most tenderly looked after. As for the contessas and marchesas who wrote, eagerly promising their "dearest Constance" that they would be kind to her relations, they were many; and when Ewen Hooper said nervously that it was clear he must take out both a frock-coat and dress clothes, Constance laughed and said, "Not at all!—Signor B. will lend you any thing you want,"—a remark which, in the ears of the travellers to be, threw new and unexpected light on the functions of an Italian innkeeper. Meanwhile she piled up guide books, she gathered maps; and she taught both her uncle and Nora Italian. And so long as she was busied with such matters she seemed the gayest of creatures, and would go singing and laughing about the house.

In another old house in Oxford, too, her coming made delight. She spent many long hours beside the Master of Beaumont's fire, gathering fresh light on the ways of scholarship and scholars. The quarrels of the learned had never hitherto come her way. Her father had never quarrelled with anybody. But the Master—poor great man!—had quarrelled with so many people! He had missed promotions which should have been his; he had made discoveries of which others had got the credit; and he kept a quite amazing stock of hatreds in some pocket of his vast intelligence. Constance would listen at first to the expression of them in an awed silence. Was it possible the world contained such mean and treacherous monsters? And why did it matter so much to a man who knew everything?—who held all the classics and all the Renaissance in the hollow of his hand, to whom "Latin was no more *difficile*, than to a blackbird 'tis to whistle"? Then, gradually, she began to have the courage to laugh; to try a little soft teasing of her new friend and mentor, who was at once so wonderful and so absurd. And the Master bore it well, could indeed never have too much of her company; while his white-haired sister beamed at the sight of her. She became the child of a childless house, and when Lady Langmoor sent her peremptory invitation's to this or that country mansion where she would meet "some charming young men," Connie would reply—"Best thanks, dear Aunt Langmoor—but I am very happy here—and comfortably in love with a gentleman on the sunny side of seventy. Please don't interfere!"

Only with Herbert Pryce was she ever thorny in these days. She could not forgive him that it was not till his appointment at the Conservative Central Office, due to Lord Glaramara's influence, was actually signed and sealed that he proposed to Alice. Till the goods had been delivered, he never finally committed himself. Even Nora had underrated his prudence. But at last one evening he arrived at Medburn House after dinner with the look of one whose mind is magnificently made up. By common consent, the drawing-room was abandoned to him and Alice, and when they emerged, Alice held her head triumphantly, and her lover was all jocosity and self-satisfaction.

"She really is a dear little thing," he said complacently to Connie, when the news had been told and excitement subsided. "We shall do capitally."

"*Enfin*?" said Connie, with the old laugh in her eyes. "You are quite sure?"

He looked at her uneasily.

"It never does to hurry these things," he said, rather pompously. "I wanted to feel I could give her what she had a right to expect. We owe you a great deal, Lady Constance—or—perhaps now—I may call you Constance?"

Constance winced, and pointedly avoided giving him leave. But for Alice's sake, she held her tongue. The wedding was to be hurried on, and Mrs. Hooper, able for once to buy new frocks with a clear conscience, and possessed of the money to pay for them, was made so happy by the bustle of the trousseau that she fell in love with her prospective son-in-law as the cause of it. Ewen Hooper meanwhile watched him with mildly shrewd eyes, deciding once more in his inner mind that mathematicians were an inferior race.

Not even to Nora—only to Mrs. Mulholland, did Constance ever lift the veil, during these months. She was not long in succumbing to the queer charm of that lovable and shapeless person; and in the little drawing-room in St. Giles, the girl of twenty would spend winter evenings, at the feet of her new friend, passing through various stages of confession; till one night, Mrs. Mulholland lifted the small face, with her own large hand, and looked mockingly into the brown eyes:

"Out with it, my dear! You are in love with Douglas Falloden!"

Connie said nothing. Her little chin did not withdraw itself, nor did her eyes drop. But a film of tears rushed into them.

The truth was that in this dark wintry Oxford, and its neighbouring country, there lurked a magic for Connie which in the high summer pomps it had never possessed. Once or twice, in the distance of a winding street—on some football ground in the Parks—in the gallery of St. Mary's on Sunday, Constance caught sight, herself unseen, of the tall figure and the curly head. Such glimpses made the fever of her young life. They meant far more to passion than her occasional meetings with Falloden at the Boar's Hill cottage. And there were other points of contact. At the end of November, for instance, came the Merton Fellowship. Falloden won it, in a brilliant field; and Connie contrived to know all she wanted to know as to his papers, and his rivals. After the announcement of his success, she trod on air. Finally she allowed herself to send him a little note of congratulation—very short and almost formal. He replied in the same tone.

Two days later, Falloden went over to Paris to see for himself the condition of the Orpheus, and to arrange for its transport to England. He was away for nearly a week, and on his return called at once in Holywell, to report his visit. Nora was with Connie in the drawing-room when he was announced; and a peremptory look forbade her to slip away. She sat listening to the conversation.

Was this really Douglas Falloden—this grave, courteous man—without a trace of the "blood" upon him? He seemed to her years older than he had been in May, and related, for the first time, to the practical every-day world. This absorption too in Otto Radowitz and his affairs—incredible! He and Connie first eagerly discussed certain domestic details of the cottage—the cook, the food, the draughts, the arrangements to be made for Otto's open-air treatment which the doctors were now insisting on—with an anxious minuteness! Nora could hardly keep her face straight in the distance—they were so like a pair of crooning housewives. Then he began on his French visit, sitting sideways on his chair, his elbow on the back of it, and his hand thrust into his curly mass of hair—handsomer, thought Nora, than ever. And there was Connie listening spell-bound in a low chair opposite, her delicate pale profile distinct against the dark panelling of the room, her eyes fixed on him. Nora's perplexed eyes travelled from one to the other.

As to the story of the Orpheus and its inventor, both girls hung upon it. Falloden had tracked Auguste Chaumart to his garret in Montmartre, and had found in him one of those marvellous French workmen, inheritors of the finest technical tradition in the world, who are the true sons of the men who built and furnished and carved Versailles, and thereby revolutionised the minor arts of Europe. A small pinched fellow!—with a sickly wife and children sharing his tiny workshop, and a brain teeming with inventions, of which the electric piano, forerunner of the Welte-Mignons of later days, was but the chief among many. He had spent a fortune upon it, could get no capitalist to believe in it, and no firm to take it up. Then Falloden's astonishing letter and offer of funds, based on Radowitz's report—itself the echo of a couple of letters from Paris—had encouraged the starving dreamer to go on.

Falloden reproduced the scene, as described to him by the chief actor in it, when the inventor announced to his family that the thing was accomplished, the mechanism perfect, and how that very night they should hear Chopin's great Fantasia, Op. 49, played by its invisible hands.

The moment came. Wife and children gathered, breathless. Chaumart turned on the current, released the machinery.

"Ecoutez, mes enfants! Ecoutez, Henriette!"

They listened—with ears, with eyes, with every faculty strained to its utmost. And nothing happened!—positively nothing—beyond a few wheezing or creaking sounds. The haggard inventor in despair chased everybody out of the room, and sat looking at the thing, wondering whether to smash it, or kill himself. Then an idea struck him. In feverish haste he took the whole mechanism to pieces again, sitting up all night. And as the morning sun rose, he discovered in the very heart of the creature, to which by now he attributed an uncanny and independent life, the most elementary blunder—a vital connection missed between the power-supplying mechanism and the cylinders containing the records. He set it right; and nearly dead with fatigue and excitement, unlocked his door, and called his family back. Then what triumph! What falling on each other's necks—and what a *déjeuner* in the Palais Royal—children and all—paid for by the inventor's last napoleon!

All this Falloden told, and told well.

Connie could not restrain her pleasure as he came to the end of his tale. She clapped her hands in delight.

"And when—when will it come!"

"I think Christmas will see it here. I've only told you half—and the lesser half. It's you that have done most—far the most."

And he took out a little note-book, running through the list of visits he had paid to her friends and correspondents in Paris, among whom the rolls were being collected, under Chaumart's direction. The Orpheus already had a large musical library of its own—renderings by some of the finest artists of some of the noblest music. Beethoven, Bach, Liszt, Chopin, Brahms, Schumann—all Otto's favourite things, as far as Connie had been able to discover them, were in the catalogue.

Suddenly, her eyes filled with tears. She put down the note-book, and spoke in a low voice, as though her girlish joy in their common secret had suddenly dropped.

"It must give him some pleasure—it must!" she said, slowly, but as though she asked a question.

Falloden did not reply immediately. He rose from his seat. Nora, under a quick impulse, gathered up a letter she had been writing, and slipped out of the room.

"At least"—he looked away from her, straight out of the window—"I suppose it will please him—that we tried to do something."

"How is he—really?"

He shrugged his shoulders. Connie was standing, looking down, one hand on her chair. The afternoon had darkened; he could see only her white brow, and the wealth of her hair which the small head carried so lightly. Her childishness, her nearness, made his heart beat. Suddenly she lifted her eyes.

"Do you know"—it seemed to him her voice choked a little—"how much—you matter to him? Mrs. Mulholland and I couldn't keep him cheerful while you were away."

He laughed.

"Well, I have only just escaped a catastrophe today."

She looked alarmed.

"How?"

"I offended Bateson, and he gave notice!" Connie's "Oh!" was a sound of consternation. Bateson, the ex-scout had become a most efficient and comfortable valet, and Otto depended greatly upon him.

"It's all right," said Falloden quickly. "I grovelled. I ate all the humble-pie I could think of. It was of course impossible to let him go. Otto can't do without him. I seem somehow to have offended his dignity."

"They have so much!" said Connie, laughing, but rather unsteadily.

"One lives and learns." The tone of the words was serious—a little anxious. Then the speaker took up his hat. "But I'm not good at managing touchy people. Good night."

Her hand passed into his. The little fingers were cold; he could not help enclosing them in a warm, clinging grasp. The firelit room, the dark street outside, and the footsteps of the passers-by—they all melted from consciousness. They only saw and heard each other.

In another minute the outer door had closed behind them. Connie was left still in the same attitude, one hand on the chair, her head drooping, her heart in a dream.

Falloden ran through the streets, choosing the byways rather than the thoroughfares. The air was frosty, the December sky clear and starlit, above the blue or purple haze, pierced with lights, that filled the lower air; through which the college fronts, the distant spires and domes showed vaguely—as beautiful "suggestions"—"notes"—from which all detail had disappeared. He was soon on Folly Bridge, and hurrying up the hill he pushed straight on over the brow to the Berkshire side, leaving the cottage to his right. Fold after fold of dim wooded country fell away to the south of the ridge; bare branching trees were all about him; a patch of open common in front where bushes of winter-blossoming gorse defied the dusk. It was the English winter at its loveliest—still, patient, expectant—rich in beauties of its own that summer knows nothing of. But Falloden was blind to it. His pulses were full of riot. She had been so near to him—and yet so far away—so sweet, yet so defensive. His whole nature cried out fiercely for her. "I want her!—*I want her!* And I believe she wants me. She's not afraid of me now—she turns to me. What keeps us apart? Nothing that ought to weigh for a moment against our double happiness!"

He turned and walked stormily homewards. Then as he saw the roof and white walls of the cottage through the trees his mood wavered—and fell. There was a life there which he had injured—a life that now depended on him. He knew that, more intimately than Connie knew it, often as he had denied it to her. And he was more convinced than Otto himself—though never by word or manner had he ever admitted it for a moment—that the boy was doomed—not immediately, but after one of those pitiful struggles which have their lulls and pauses, but tend all the same inevitably to one end.

"And as long as he lives, I shall look after him," he thought, feeling that strange compulsion on him again, and yielding to it with mingled eagerness and despair.

For how could he saddle Connie's life with such a charge—or darken it with such a tragedy?

Impossible! But that was only one of many reasons why he should not take advantage of her through their common pity for Otto. In his own eyes he was a ruined man, and having resolutely refused to live upon his mother, his pride was little more inclined to live upon a wife, common, and generally applauded, though the practice might be. About five thousand pounds had been saved for himself out of the wreck; of which he would certainly spend a thousand, before all was done, on the Orpheus. The rest would just suffice to launch him as a barrister. His mother would provide for the younger children. Her best jewels indeed had been already sold and invested as a dowry for Nelly, who showed signs of engaging herself to a Scotch laird. But Falloden was joint guardian of Trix and Roger, and must keep a watchful eye on them, now that his mother's soft incompetence had been more plainly revealed than ever by her widowhood. He chafed under the duties imposed, and yet fulfilled them—anxiously and well—to the amazement of his relations.

In addition he had his way to make in the world.

But Constance had only to be a little more seen and known in English society to make the most brilliant match that any scheming chaperon could desire. Falloden was aware through every pulse of her fast developing beauty. And although no great heiress, as heiresses now go, she would ultimately inherit a large amount of scattered money, in addition to what she already possessed. The Langmoors would certainly have her out of Oxford at the earliest possible moment—and small blame to them.

In all this he reasoned as a man of his class and antecedents was likely to reason—only with a bias against himself. To capture Connie, through Otto, before she had had any other chances of marriage, seemed to him a mean and dishonorable thing.

If he had only time—time to make his career!

But there would be no time given him. As soon as her Risborough relations got hold of her, Constance would marry directly.

He went back to the cottage in a sombre mood. Then, as Otto proved to be in the same condition, Falloden had to shake off his own depression as quickly as possible, and spend the evening in amusing and distracting the invalid.

But Fortune, which had no doubt enjoyed the nips she had inflicted on so tempting a victim, was as determined as before to take her own capricious way.

By this time it was the last week of term, and a sharp frost had set in over the Thames Valley. The floods were out north and south of the city, and a bright winter sun shone all day over the glistening ice-plains, and the throng of skaters.

At the beginning of the frost came the news of Otto's success in his musical examination; and at a Convocation, held shortly after it, he put on his gown as Bachelor of Music. The Convocation House was crowded to see him admitted to his degree; and the impression produced, as he made his way through the throng towards the Vice-Chancellor, by the frail, boyish figure, the startling red-gold hair, the black sling, and the haunting eyes, was long remembered in Oxford. Then Sorell claimed him, and hurried him up to London for doctors and consultations since the effort of the examination had left him much exhausted.

Meanwhile the frost held, and all Oxford went skating. Constance performed indifferently, and both Nora and Uncle Ewen were bent upon improving her. But there were plenty of cavaliers to attend her, whenever she appeared, either on Port Meadow or the Magdalen flood water; and her sound youth delighted physically in the exercise, in the play of the brisk air about her face, and the alternations of the bright winter day—from the pale blue of its morning skies, hung behind the snow-sprinkled towers and spires of Oxford, down to the red of sunset, and the rise of those twilight mists which drew the fair city gently back into the bosom of the moonlit dark.

But all the time the passionate sense in her watched and waited. The "mere living" was good—"yet was there better than it! "

And on the second afternoon, out of the distance of Magdalen meadow, a man came flying towards her as it seemed on the wings of the wind. Falloden drew up beside her, hovering on his skates, a splendid vision in the dusk, ease and power in every look and movement.

"Let me take you a run with the wind," he said, holding out his hand. "You shan't come to any harm."

Her eyes and her happy flush betrayed her. She put her hand in his, and away they flew, up the course of the Cherwell, through the flooded meadows. It seemed the very motion of gods; the world fell away. Then, coming back, they saw Magdalen Tower, all silver and ebony under the rising moon, and the noble arch of the bridge. The world was all transmuted. Connie's only hold on the kind, common earth seemed to lie in this strong hand to which she clung; and yet in that touch, that hold, lay the magic that was making life anew.

But soon the wind had risen gustily, and was beating in her face, catching at her breath.

"This is too cold for you!" said Falloden abruptly; and wheeling round, he had soon guided her into a more sheltered place, and there, easily gliding up and down, soul and sense fused in one delight, they passed one of those hours for which there is no measure in our dull human time. They would not think of the past; they shrank from imagining the future. There were shadows and ghosts behind them, and ahead of them; but the sheer present mastered them.

Before they parted, Falloden told his companion that the Orpheus would arrive from Paris the following day with a trio of French workmen to set it up. The electric installation was already in place. Everything would be ready by the evening. The instrument was to be placed behind a screen in the built-out room, once a studio, which Falloden had turned into a library. Otto rarely or never went there. The room looked north, and he, whose well-being hung upon sunshine, disliked it. But there was no other place for the Orpheus in the little cottage, and Falloden who had been getting new and thick curtains for the windows, improving the fire-place, and adding some armchairs, was eagerly hopeful that he could turn it into a comfortable music-room for Otto in the winter evenings, while he—if necessary—read his law elsewhere.

"Will you come for a rehearsal to-morrow?" he asked her. "Otto comes back the day after."

"No, no! I won't hear anything, not a note—till he comes! But is he strong enough?" she added wistfully. Strong enough, she meant, to bear agitation and surprise. But Falloden reported that Sorell knew everything that was intended, and approved. Otto had been very listless and depressed in town; a reaction no doubt from his spurt of work before the musical exam. Sorell thought the pleasure of the gift might rouse him, and gild the return to Oxford.

XIX

"HAVE SOME tea, old man, and warm up," said Falloden, on his knees before a fire already magnificent, which he was endeavouring to improve.

"What do you keep such a climate for?" growled Radowitz, as he hung shivering over the grate.

Sorell, who had come with the boy from the station, eyed him anxiously. The bright red patches on the boy's cheeks, and his dry, fevered look, his weakness and his depression, had revived the most sinister fears in the mind of the man who had originally lured him to Oxford, and felt himself horribly responsible for what had happened there. Yet the London doctors on the whole had been reassuring. The slight hemorrhage of the summer had had no successor; there were no further signs of active mischief; and for his general condition it was thought that the nervous shock of his accident, and the obstinate blood-poisoning which had followed it, might sufficiently account. The doctors, however, had pressed hard for sunshine and open-air—the Riviera, Sicily, or Algiers. But the boy had said vehemently that he couldn't and wouldn't go alone, and who could go with him? A question that for the moment stopped the way. Falloden's first bar examination was immediately ahead; Sorell was tied to St. Cyprian's; and every other companion so far proposed had been rejected with irritation.

Unluckily, on this day of his return, the Oxford skies had put on again their characteristic winter gloom. The wonderful fortnight of frost and sun was over; tempests of wind and deluges of rain were drowning it fast in flood and thaw. The wind shrieked round the little cottage, and though it was little more than three o'clock, darkness was coming fast.

Falloden could not keep still. Having made up the fire, he brought in a lamp himself; he drew the curtains, then undrew them again, apparently that he might examine a stretch of the Oxford road just visible through the growing dark; or he wandered in and out of the room, his hands in his pockets whistling. Otto watched him with a vague annoyance. He himself was horribly tired, and Falloden's restlessness got on his nerves.

At last Falloden said abruptly, pausing in front of him—

"You'll have some visitors directly!"

Otto looked up. The gaiety in Falloden's eyes informed him, and at the same time, wounded him.

"Lady Constance?" he said, affecting indifference.

"And Mrs. Mulholland. I believe I see their carriage."

And Falloden, peering into the stormy twilight, opened the garden door and passed out into the rain.

Otto remained motionless, bent over the fire. Sorell was talking with the ex-scout in the dining-room, impressing on him certain medical directions. Radowitz suddenly felt himself singularly forlorn, and deserted. Of course, Falloden and Constance would marry. He always knew it. He would have served to keep them together, and give them opportunities of meeting, when they might have easily drifted entirely apart. He laughed to himself as he thought of Connie's impassioned cry—"I shall never, never, marry him!" Such are the vows of women. She would marry him; and then what would he, Otto, matter to her or to Falloden any longer? He would have been no doubt a useful peg and pretext; but he was not going to intrude on their future bliss. He thought he would go back to Paris. One might as well die there as anywhere.

There were murmurs of talk and laughter in the hall. He sat still, hugging his melancholy. But when the door opened, he rose quickly, instinctively; and, at the sight of the girl coming in so timidly behind Mrs. Mulholland, her eyes searching the half-lit room, and the smile, in them and on her lips, held back till she knew whether her poor friend could bear with smiles, Otto's black hour began to lift. He let himself, at least, be welcomed and petted; and when fresh tea had been brought in, and the room was full of talk, he lay back in his chair, listening, the deep lines in his forehead gradually relaxing. He was better, he declared, a great deal better; in fact there was very little at all the matter with him. His symphony was to be given at the Royal College of Music early in the year. Everybody had been awfully decent about it. And he had begun a nocturne that amused him. As for the doctors, he repeated petulantly that they were all fools—it was only a question of degree. He intended to manage his life as he pleased in spite of them.

Connie sat on a high stool near him while he talked. She seemed to be listening, but he once or twice thought, resentfully, that it was a perfunctory listening. He wondered what else she was thinking about.

The tea was cleared away. And presently the three others had disappeared. Otto and Constance were left alone.

"I have been reading so much about Poland lately," said Constance suddenly. "Oh, Otto, some day you must show me Cracow!"

His face darkened.

"I shall never see Cracow again. I shall never see it with you."

"Why not? Let's dream!"

The smiling tenderness in her eyes angered him. She was treating him like a child; she was so sure he never could—or never would—make love to her!

"I shall never go to Cracow," he said, with energy, "not even with you. I was to have gone—a year from now. It was all arranged. We have relations there—and I have friends there—musicians. The *chef d'orchestre*—at the Opera House—he was one of my teachers in Paris. Before next year, I was to have written a concerto on some of our Polish songs—there are scores of them that Liszt and Chopin never discovered. Not only love-songs, mind you!—songs of revolution—battle-songs."

His eyes lit up and he began to hum an air—to Polish words—that even as given out in his small tenor voice stirred like a trumpet.

"Fine!" said Constance.

"Ah, but you can't judge—you don't know the words. The words are splendid. It's 'Ujejski's Hymn'—the Galician Hymn of '46." And he fell to intoning.

> "Amid the smoke of our homes that burn,
> From the dust where our brothers lie bleeding—
> Our cry goes up to Thee, oh God!

"There!—that's something like it."

And he ran on with a breathless translation of the famous dirge for the Galician rebels of '46, in which a devastated land wails like Rachel for her children.

Suddenly a sound rose—a sound reedy and clear, like a beautiful voice in the distance.

"Constance!"

The lad sprang to his feet. Constance laid hold on him.

"Listen, dear Otto—listen a moment!"

She held him fast, and breathing deep, he listened. The very melody he had just been humming rang out, from the same distant point; now pealing through the little house in a rich plenitude of sound, now delicate and plaintive as the chant of nuns in a quiet church, and finally crashing to a defiant and glorious close.

"What is it?" he said, very pale, looking at her almost threateningly. "What have you been doing?"

"It's our gift—our surprise—dear Otto!"

"Where is it? Let me go."

"No!—sit down, and listen! Let me listen with you. I've not heard it before! Mr. Falloden and I have been preparing it for months. Isn't it wonderful? Oh, dear Otto!—if you only like it!" He sat down trembling, and hand in hand they listened.

The "Fantasia" ran on, dealing with song after song, now simply, now with rich embroidery and caprice.

"Who is it playing?" said Otto, in a whisper.

"It *was* Paderewski!" said Constance between laughing and crying. "Oh, Otto, everybody's been at work for it!—everybody was so marvellously keen!"

"In Paris?"

"Yes—all your old friends—your teachers—and many others."

She ran through the names. Otto choked. He knew them all, and some of them were among the most illustrious in French music.

But while Connie was speaking, the stream of sound in the distance sank into gentleness, and in the silence a small voice arose, naïvely, pastorally sweet, like the Shepherd's Song in "Tristan." Otto buried his face in his hands. It was the "Heynal," the watchman's horn-song from the towers of Panna Marya. Once given, a magician caught it, played with it, pursued it, juggled with it, through a series of variations till, finally, a grave and beautiful modulation led back to the noble dirge of the beginning.

"I know who wrote that!—who must have written it!" said Otto, looking up. He named a French name. "I worked with him at the Conservatoire for a year."

Constance nodded.

"He did it for you," she said, her eyes full of tears. "He said you were the best pupil he ever had."

The door opened, and Mrs. Mulholland's white head appeared, with Falloden and Sorell behind.

"Otto!" said Mrs. Mulholland, softly.

He understood that she called him, and he went with her in bewilderment, along the passage to the studio.

Falloden came into the sitting-room and shut the door.

"Did he like it?" he asked, in a low voice, in which there was neither pleasure nor triumph.

Connie, who was still sitting on the stool by the fire with her face turned away, looked up.

"Oh, yes, yes!" she said in a kind of desperation, wringing her hands; "but why are some pleasures worse than pain—much worse?"

Falloden came up to her, and stood silently, his eyes on hers.

"You see"—she went on, dashing tears away—"it is not his work—his playing! It can't do anything—can it, for his poor starved self?"

Falloden said nothing. But she knew that he felt with her. Their scheme seemed to be lying in ruins; they were almost ashamed of it.

Then from the further room there came to their ears a prelude of Chopin, played surely by more than mortal fingers—like the rustling of summer trees, under a summer wind. And suddenly they heard Otto's laugh—a sound of delight.

Connie sprang up—her face transformed.

"Did you hear that? We have—we have—given him pleasure!"

"Yes—for an hour," said Falloden hoarsely. Then he added—"The doctors say he ought to go south."

"Of course he ought!" Connie was pacing up and down, her hands behind her, her eyes on the ground. "Can't Mr. Sorell take him?"

"He could take him out, but he couldn't stay. The college can't spare him. He feels his first duty is to the college."

"And you?" She raised her eyes timidly.

"What good should I be alone?" he said, with difficulty. "I'm a pretty sort of a nurse!"

There was a pause. Connie trembled and flushed. Then she moved forward, both her little hands outstretched.

"Take me with you!" she murmured under her breath. But her eyes said more—far more.

The next moment she was in Falloden's arms, strained against his breast—everything else lost and forgotten, as their lips met, in the just selfishness of passion.

Then he released her, stepping back from her, his strong face quivering.

"I was a mean wretch to let you do that!" he said, with energy.

She eyed him.

"Why?"

"Because I have no right to let you give yourself to me—throw yourself away on me—just because we have been doing this thing together,—because you are sorry for Otto—and"—his voice dropped—"perhaps for me."

"Oh!" It was a cry of protest. Coming nearer she put her two hands lightly on his shoulders—

"Do you think"—he saw her breath fluttering—"do you think I should let any one—any one—kiss me—like that! just because I was sorry for them—or for some one else?"

He stood motionless beneath her touch.

"You are sorry for me—you angel!—and you're sorry for Otto—and you want to make up to everybody—and make everybody happy—and——"

"And one can't!" said Connie quietly, her eyes bright with tears. "Don't I know that? I repeat"—her colour was very bright—"but perhaps you won't believe, that—that"—then she laughed—"*of my own free will*, I never kissed anybody before?"

"Constance!" He threw his strong arms round her again. But she slipped out of them.

"Am I believed?" The tone was peremptory.

Falloden stooped, lifted her hand and kissed it humbly.

"You know you ought to marry a duke!" he said, trying to laugh, but with a swelling throat.

"Thank you—I never saw a duke yet I wanted to marry."

"That's it. You've seen so little. I am a pauper, and you might marry anybody. It's taking an unfair advantage. Don't you see—what——"

"What my aunts will think?" asked Constance coolly. "Oh, yes, I've considered all that."

She walked away, and came back, a little pale and grave. She sat down on the arm of a chair and looked up at him.

"I see. You are as proud as ever."

That hurt him. His face changed.

"You can't really think that," he said, with difficulty.

"Yes, yes, you are!" she said, wildly, covering her eyes a moment with her hands. "It's just the same as it was in the spring—only different—I told you then——"

"That I was a bully and a cad!"

Her hands dropped sharply.

"I didn't!" she protested. But she coloured brightly as she spoke, remembering certain remarks of Nora's. "I thought—yes I did think—you cared too much about being rich—and a great swell—and all that. But so did I!" She sprang up. "What right had I to talk? When I think how I patronised and looked down upon everybody!"

"You!" his tone was pure scorn. "You couldn't do such a thing if you tried for a week of Sundays."

"Oh, couldn't I? I did. Oxford seemed to me just a dear, stupid old place—out of the world,—a kind of museum—where nobody mattered. Silly, wasn't it?—childish?" She drew back her head fiercely, as though she defied him to excuse her. "I was just amusing myself with it—and with Otto—and with you. And that night, at Magdalen, all the time I was dancing with Otto, I was aiming—abominably—at you! I wanted to provoke you—to pay you back—oh, not for Otto's sake—not at all!—but just because—I had asked you something—and you had refused. That was what stung me so. And do you suppose I should have cared twopence, unless——"

Her voice died away. Her fingers began fidgeting with the arm of the chair, her eyes bent upon them.

He looked at her a moment irresolute, his face working. Then he said huskily—

"In return—for that—I'll tell you—I must tell you the real truth about myself. I don't think you know me yet—and I don't know myself. I've got a great brutal force in me somewhere—that wants to brush everything—that hinders me—or checks me—out of my path. I don't know that I can control it—that I can make a woman happy. It's an awful risk for you. Look at that poor fellow!" He flung out his hand towards that distant room whence came every now and then a fresh wave of music. "I didn't intend to do him any bodily harm——"

"Of course not! It was an accident!" cried Connie passionately.

"Perhaps—strictly. But I did mean somehow to crush him—to make it precious hot for him—just because he'd got in my way. My will was like a steel spring in a machine—that had been let go. Suppose I felt like that again, towards——"

"Towards me?" Connie opened her eyes very wide, puckering her pretty brow.

"Towards some one—or something—you care for. We are certain to disagree about heaps of things."

"Of course we are. Quite certain!"

"I tell you again"—said Falloden, speaking with a strong simplicity and sincerity that was all the time undoing the impression he honestly desired to make—"it's a big risk for you—a temperament like mine—and you ought to think it over seriously. And then"—he paused abruptly in front of her, his hands in his pockets—"why should you—you're so young!—start life with any burden on you? Why should you? It's preposterous! I must look after Otto all his life."

"So must I!" said Connie quickly. "That's the same for both of us."

"And then—you may forget it—but I can't. I repeat—I'm a pauper. I've lost Flood. I've lost everything that I could once have given you. I've got about four thousand pounds left—just enough to start me at the bar—when I've paid for the Orpheus. And I can't take a farthing from my mother or the other children. I should be just living upon you. How do I know that I shall get on at the bar?"

Connie smiled; but her lips trembled.

"Do think it over," he implored; and he walked away from her again, as though to leave her free.

There was a silence. He turned anxiously to look at her.

"I seem"—said Connie, in a low voice that shook—"to have kissed somebody—for nothing."

That was the last stroke. He came back to her, and knelt beside her, murmuring inarticulate things. With a sigh of relief, Connie subsided upon his shoulder, conscious through all her emotion of the dear strangeness of the man's coat against her cheek. But presently, she drew herself away, and looked him in the eyes, while her own swam.

"I love you"—she said deliberately—"because—well, first because I love you!—that's the only good reason, isn't it; and then, because you're so sorry. And I'm sorry too. We've both got to make up—we're going to make up all we can." Her sweet face darkened. "Oh, Douglas, it'll take the two of us—and even then we can't do it! But we'll help each other."

And stooping she kissed him gently, lingeringly, on the brow. It was a kiss of consecration.

A few minutes more, and then, with the Eighth Prelude swaying and dancing round them, they went hand in hand down the long approach to the music-room.

The door was open, and they saw the persons inside. Otto and Sorell were walking up and down smoking cigarettes. The boy was radiant, transformed. All look of weakness had disappeared; he held himself erect; his shock of red-gold hair blazed in the firelight, and his eyes laughed, as he listened silently, playing with his cigarette. Sorell evidently was thinking only of him; but he too wore a look of quiet pleasure.

Only Mrs. Mulholland sat watchful, her face turned towards the open door. It wore an expression which was partly excitement, partly doubt. Her snow-white hair above her very black eyes, and her frowning, intent look, gave her the air of an old Sibyl watching at the cave's mouth.

But when she saw the two—the young man and the girl—coming towards her, hand in hand, she first peered at them intently, and then, as she rose, all the gravity of her face broke up in laughter.

"Hope for the best, you foolish old woman!" she said to herself—"'Male and female made He them!'—world without end—Amen!"

"Well?" She moved towards them, as they entered the room; holding out her hands with a merry, significant gesture.

Otto and Sorell turned. Connie—crimson—threw herself on Mrs. Mulholland's neck and kissed her. Falloden stood behind her, thinking of a number of things to say, and unable to say any of them.

The last soft notes of the Prelude ceased.

It was for Connie to save the situation. With a gentle, gliding step, she went across to Otto, who had gone very white again.

"Dear Otto, you told me I should marry Douglas, and I'm going to. That's one to you. But I won't marry him—and he agrees—unless you'll promise to come to Algiers with us a month from now. You'll lend him to us, won't you?"—she turned pleadingly to Sorell—"we'll take such care of him. Douglas—you may be surprised!—is going to read law at Biskra!"

Otto sank into a chair. The radiance had gone. He looked very frail and ghostly. But he took Connie's outstretched hand.

"I wish you joy," he said, stumbling painfully over the words. "I do wish you joy!—with all my heart."

Falloden approached him. Otto looked up wistfully. Their eyes met, and for a moment the two men were conscious only of each other.

Mrs. Mulholland moved away, smiling, but with a sob in her throat.

"It's like all life," she thought—"love and death, side by side."

And she remembered that comparison by a son of Oxford, of each moment, as it passes, to a watershed "whence equally the seas of life and death are fed."

But Connie was determined to carry things off with a laugh. She sat down beside Otto, looking businesslike.

"Douglas and I"—the name came out quite pat—"have been discussing how long it really takes to get married."

Mrs. Mulholland laughed.

"Mrs. Hooper has been enjoying Alice's trousseau so much, you needn't expect she'll let you get through yours in a hurry."

"It's going to be my trousseau, not Aunt Ellen's," said Connie with decision. "Let me see. It's now nearly Christmas. Didn't we say the 12th of January?" She looked lightly at Falloden.

"Somewhere near it," said Falloden, his smile at last answering hers.

"We shall want a fortnight, I suppose, to get used to each other," said Connie coolly. "Then"—she laid a hand on Mrs. Mulholland's knee—"you bring him to Marseilles to meet us?"

"Certainly—at your orders."

Connie looked at Otto.

"Dear Otto?" The soft tone pleaded. He started painfully.

"You're awfully good to me. But how can I come to be a burden on you?"

"But I shall go too," said Mrs. Mulholland firmly.

Connie exclaimed in triumph.

"We four—to front the desert!—while he"—she nodded towards Sorell—"is showing Nora and Uncle Ewen Rome. You mayn't know it"—she addressed Sorell—"but on Monday, January 24th—I think I've got the date right—you and they go on a picnic to Hadrian's Villa. The weather's arranged for—and the carriage is ordered."

She looked at him askance; but her colour had risen. So had his. He looked down on her while Mrs. Mulholland and Falloden were both talking fast to Otto.

"You little witch!" said Sorell in a low voice—"what are you after now?"

Connie laughed in his face.

"You'll go—you'll see!"

The little dinner which followed was turned into a betrothal feast. Champagne was brought in, and Otto, madly gay, boasted of his forebears and the incomparable greatness of Poland as usual. Nobody minded. After dinner the magic toy in the studio discoursed Brahms and Schumann, in the intervals of discussing plans and chattering over maps. But Connie insisted on an early departure. "My guardian will have to sleep upon it—and there's really no time to lose." Every one took care not to see too much of the parting between her and Falloden. Then she and Mrs. Mulholland were put into their carriage. But Sorell preferred to walk home, and Falloden went back to Otto.

Sorell descended the hill towards Oxford. The storm was dying away, and the now waning moon, which had shone so brilliantly over the frozen floods a day or two before, was venturing out again among the scudding clouds. The lights in Christ Church Hall were out, but the beautiful city shone vaguely luminous under the night.

Sorell's mind was full of mingled emotion—as torn and jagged as the clouds rushing overhead. The talk and laughter in the cottage came back to him. How hollow and vain it sounded in the spiritual ear! What could ever make up to that poor boy, who could have no more, at the most, than a year or two to live, for the spilt wine of his life?—the rifled treasure of his genius? And was it not true to say that his loss had made the profit of the two lovers—of whom one had been the author of it? When Falloden and Constance believed themselves to be absorbed in Otto, were they not really playing the great game of sex like any ordinary pair?

It was the question that Otto himself had asked—that any cynic must have asked. But Sorell's tender humanity passed beyond it. The injury done, indeed, was beyond repair. But the mysterious impulse which had brought Falloden to the help of Otto was as real in its sphere as the anguish and the pain; aye, for the philosophic spirit, more real than they, and fraught with a healing and disciplining power that none could measure. Sorell admitted—half reluctantly—the changes in life and character which had flowed from it. He was even ready to say that the man who had proved capable of feeling it, in spite of all past appearances, was "not far from the Kingdom of God."

Oxford drew nearer and nearer. Tom Tower loomed before him. Its great bell rang out And suddenly, as if he could repress it no longer, there ran through Sorell's mind—his half melancholy mind, unaccustomed to the claims of personal happiness—the vision that Connie had so sharply evoked; of a girl's brown eyes, and honest look—the look of a child to be cherished, of a woman to be loved.

Was it that morning that he had helped Nora to translate a few lines of the "Antigone"?

"Love, all conquering love, that nestles in the fair cheeks of a maiden——"

It is perhaps not surprising that Sorell, on this occasion, after he had entered the High, should have taken the wrong turn to St. Cyprian's, and wakened up to find himself passing through the Turl, when he ought to have been in Radcliffe Square.

THE END.